Praise for

GONDAR

'Exotic, imaginative and gorgeously readable –
exciting enough to take me back to childhood nights
of reading Rider Haggard by torchlight under the
blankets'   *Sunday Times*

'Sex, violence, horror, beauty and love in a well
written and very readable mix'   *Publishers Weekly*

'Authenticity, drama, adventure and excitement . . .
I defy any reader to skip a single page'
Gary Jennings, author of Aztec *and* Spangle

KALA

'Adventure and romance on a lavish scale . . . a fascinating feat of storytelling'
New York Review of Books

THE ORION LINE

'Sensitive, exciting, brilliant'   *Daily Telegraph*

SANCTUARY

'Written in the bestselling spirit of Wilbur Smith,
incorporating love, adventure, violence, intrigue and
tragedy'   *Peterborough Evening Telegraph*

About the author

Nicholas Luard, novelist and explorer, is the author of sixteen books including the international bestseller *Gondar*. A passionate conservationist, he has lived and worked in Africa, and now divides his time between Wales and London. He is married to the writer Elisabeth Luard.

Silverback

Nicholas Luard

CORONET BOOKS
Hodder and Stoughton

First published in Great Britain in 1996 by
Hodder and Stoughton
a division of Hodder Headline PLC
First published in paperback in 1996 by Hodder and Stoughton
A Coronet paperback

10 9 8 7 6 5 4 3 2 1

British Library Cataloguing in Publication Data

Luard, Nicholas, 1937–
Silverback
1. English fiction – 20th century
I. Title
823.9'14 [F]

ISBN 0 340 66674 9

Printed and bound in Great Britain by
Mackays of Chatham PLC, Chatham, Kent

Hodder and Stoughton
A division of Hodder Headline PLC
338 Euston Road
London NW1 3BH

for Jacqueline

1

'We close in thirty minutes, miss,' the attendant at the ticket-desk said. 'We ask people to start moving out ten minutes before that. It doesn't give you long.'

She hesitated.

The man had grey hair and a tired, kindly face. He was worried she was going to waste her money. She glanced back through the glass doors at the Cromwell Road.

Outside the rain was falling in pearl-coloured plumes that the chill December wind was pulling almost sideways to the ground in the lamplit darkness. The last of the waiting taxis drew away, and she could hear the tearful complaints of a fretful child huddled under the museum's arched entrance.

She shivered.

She looked back, shaking her head so that her long hair rippled out in a tawny-golden fan and scattered drops of water across the tiled floor. She gathered her green waxed Barbour round her and reached for her purse.

'I'll go in anyway,' she said.

She gave him the money, took her ticket, and walked through the admission gate.

'If you haven't been in before, have a look at the dinosaur exhibit,' the attendant called after her. 'Very special, it is, everyone loves it.'

She raised her hand in acknowledgement and managed a smile. Then she walked on.

The dinosaur exhibit was on the ground floor on the left. She knew it well. She'd been to the champagne and 'finger-food' reception (what a strange phrase, she'd thought, when the sponsors' PR consultants sent her the invitation) when the display opened. But then of course she'd known the museum – the British Museum of Natural History as it was officially called – for most of her life.

She skirted the dinosaurs and headed on towards the bird collection.

The long vaulted galleries which housed the world's largest collection of stuffed and mounted birds were deserted. It wasn't only almost closing-time but Christmas Eve, and the normal throng of visitors, she guessed, had chosen to go shopping. Her footsteps echoed in the silence and her reflection flickered across the glass-fronted cabinets.

She stopped to look at herself in one of them.

Against a background of Kalahari larks, her face was pale and her eye make-up smudged. Angry at the tears which had caused the damage – with any luck the attendant, who must have noticed the bleared runnels of eye-shadow, would have thought it was the rain – she rummaged for a tissue, wetted it with her tongue, and rubbed her skin clean.

She peered at herself.

Her face wasn't so much pale now as white, white and drawn and ugly. She'd wanted to be proud, defiant, strong. She wasn't. She felt unutterably miserable and lonely. For once the familiar galleries, more like the aisles of some great medieval cathedral, it had often seemed to her, than the exhibition halls of a museum, failed to exert their power to comfort and heal.

From her childhood on the building had been a sanctuary. Now it was as bleak and desolate as the rain-swept December night outside.

Uncontrollably she started to weep again.

The bastard!

It was a trivial, inadequate word, but it was the only one that came to her. He wasn't of course even a bastard, either literally or in what he'd done. He was simply a man, a great joyous bear of a man, a hard-working, hard-drinking journalist who wanted to write books. They'd lived together, sharing the little Chelsea flat, for seven years.

And then that morning he told her he was leaving. He said it over their breakfast coffee which he bought from Luigi's in the Fulham Road and always brewed himself. As she sat listening to him in shock – she was wearing a white cotton jellabah he'd bought her on an assignment in Casablanca – he explained he needed time and space on his own.

His voice was evasive, his eyes were reluctant to meet hers, and she knew it wasn't the full story.

She pressed him.

Slowly, shabbily, the truth came out. She'd introduced him to one of her closest friends, a woman editor of a fashion magazine. The woman owned a house in a village in Provence. She had offered him a job on the magazine and the use of her house as a base to write his books.

'And car rights and bar rights and fucking rights as well?' she stormed.

He didn't answer. He had no need to answer. It was true. She picked up the coffee-pot and hurled it at him. Then she ran out of the house.

When she came back he had gone.

There was no trace of him, not even a forgotten dirty shirt in the laundry basket. He had vacuumed up the entirety of the life he'd lived with her, packed it away in his battered leather suitcases – he modelled his travelling journalist's life-style on Wilfred Thesiger and Robert Byron – and simply departed.

That was less than eight hours ago. Eight hours later she still hated him, she still loved him, she still longed to kill him. Most of all she forlornly wanted peace. What she found instead, in what had always been her sanctuary, were further mindless streaming tears.

'Bastard!' she shouted.

'I'm sorry?'

The voice was startled. She wiped her eyes. A tall bearded young man in a white laboratory coat was standing in the middle of the aisle ten yards away.

Humiliated at being caught sobbing, she glanced around. As embarrassed as she was, the man was standing frozen, blocking the aisle. She would either have to push past him or say something.

'My cat,' she said. 'He was run over by a car today. I was just taking out my anger against the driver.'

She brushed her hair back from her face and forced another smile.

She had no idea how or why the idea of a dead pet had come to her. She had never owned a cat, she didn't even like cats, but the explanation seemed to satisfy the young man.

'Ah.' He relaxed and smiled back sympathetically. 'I quite understand. My girlfriend has two cats. She'd be deeply upset if one of hers died. Did you have yours long?'

She hesitated. 'About seven years. He'd become very special,' she added wildly.

'I know they do. Was yours a species pure-breed or the ordinary

3

domestic strain? My girlfriend's are Siamese. As a zoologist I'm always interested.'

'Just a tabby, black and white. I mean brown and white. I mean—'

She broke off. She looked at the exit again. The young man was still blocking the way. She felt almost as if she were suffocating. She'd launched impetuously into a fantasy. Now the web of its consequences threatened to choke her.

The man turned. He reached into his pocket, pulled out a key, and unlocked one of the cabinets.

'Well, pure-bred or alley-cat they all hunt birds. Although what they'd have made of that old scoundrel Colonel Ruthven's birds, I wonder.'

His movement had at last left the way clear for her to escape. She hesitated. She remained where she was.

'"Riven",' she said.

'I beg your pardon?'

'The name's spelt Ruthven, but it's pronounced "Riven".'

He frowned. 'I've never heard that before.'

'It's Scottish. I read seventeenth-century Scottish history at college. The Ruthvens crop up a lot in the margins as border thieves and cattle rustlers. My tutor taught me how to say their name.'

The young man pulled out a notebook.

'Thank you. It'll make an interesting footnote in the museum's dossier.'

As he wrote she asked, 'Why did you call him a scoundrel?'

'Colonel Ruthven?' He tilted his head. 'The great explorer, the great hunter, the great soldier, and the greatest ornithologist of the twentieth century – the man who gave even more bird-skins to the museum than the whole Rothschild family. A pillar of scholarship and respectable society. Except he wasn't. He was a complete and utter fraud.'

The words were spoken with a chilling sureness and finality.

The young man was smiling, and there was a strangely aggressive, almost triumphant expression on his face. She stood utterly still. She felt cold.

'Why do you say that?' She knew as she spoke that her voice was unsteady.

He reached into the cabinet he'd unlocked and lifted out one of the mounted birds.

'This is what's known as a Ruthven Khama lark. That's how it's

4

recorded in all the books ever since Ruthven found it in the Kalahari seventy years ago. Except it's not. Look—'

He gently raised the wing of the mounted bird and held it out to her. At the base of the wing, at the point where it joined the bird's body, she could just see a neat row of stitches in umber-coloured silk.

'The body belongs to a lark. The wing comes from a weaver. We've proved that by DNA testing of the feathers. The wing and the body belong to different birds. They've been sewn together by a remarkably skilful taxidermist. So have hundreds of others in the Ruthven collection. Bills, claws, legs, they've all been switched around.'

'Why?' She stammered out the question.

'God only knows. A malicious practical joke? Or he wasn't respectable at all, he was mad? Or, and this is my view, he was just a rogue and a liar who wanted to earn himself some cheap fame.'

The young man spoke with a light Scots accent.

'But why's it taken so long to find this out?' She was still struggling for words.

'Simple,' he replied. 'The work's superb. Ruthven had an unblemished reputation for integrity. The areas he collected in were virtually unknown. There was no reason to doubt him, and no one to challenge him. It's only verra recently, with whole species vanishing everywhere, that we began studying the collection to see what's being lost. We use cutting-edge bio-technology methods – they're of course quite new too – and by accident it came to light.'

He paused. 'We'll be publishing the exposé quite shortly. Given the collection's international reputation, it's likely to be reported everywhere. Perhaps someone will come forward with the explanation. It's embarrassing for us but it's the end of Ruthven, I can tell you that.'

She said nothing for several moments. Her chest heaved and she felt as if she was struggling to breathe. The young man looked at her anxiously.

'I'm sorry,' he said, 'I hope I haven't upset you. You're obviously interested in birds. But what with your cat and everything—'

He broke off. She managed to force a smile.

'No, of course not,' she answered. 'It's a fascinating story. I'd like to hear more. Unfortunately I've got to go. Maybe another time.'

Somehow she managed to keep the smile on her face. She walked

5

past him and turned the corner of the aisle. An instant later she burst into tears again and began to run.

She was still running when she crossed the entrance hall and headed down on to the street.

2

'Who is it?'

'It's me, Mum.'

There was a buzz and the latch clicked open. She stepped inside, and walked upstairs.

She had her own set of keys but she preferred not to use them when she arrived unexpectedly. Her mother was waiting for her at the entrance to her flat on the second floor.

'Victoria, darling, how lovely! I didn't think I'd see you until tomorrow.'

They embraced each other and went inside.

'I finished work early,' she said as she took off her dripping Barbour. 'I went to Harrods for some last-minute shopping. There weren't any taxis so I thought I'd walk down here. I'll find one in half an hour when the rush is over.'

It was a plausible explanation. Her mother's flat in Egerton Gardens was only ten minutes' walk from the Knightsbridge store.

'Get yourself a drink, darling. Then come in and get warm. I've just got to make a quick call to Rosalind.'

Her mother disappeared into the sitting-room.

Victoria paused. Then she stepped into the bathroom.

Her mother had grown up in India in the last decades of the raj – she had been almost forty when her daughter, her only child, was born. In India the memsahib's bathroom was a much more important room than in Britain, a richly decorated combination of living space and boudoir as well as a place to wash off the heat and dust of the subcontinent.

Her mother had retained the tradition in her London flat.

There were two tapestry-upholstered armchairs, a glass-fronted bookcase above a dressing-table, a tiered bench of pot plants, several paintings, and above all photographs. Framed in maple or silver, they covered one entire wall, a dense mosaic of a family's life reaching back for more than a century.

7

She went over and studied them.

She'd known the photographs all her life. Her mother and father outside St Margaret's Westminster on their wedding day. Snaps of them at shooting parties and hunts, on their travels, in front of the many houses they'd lived in. More formal and studied portraits of her grandparents and great-grandparents, in uniform, wearing tiaras for balls, standing on the steps of country mansions with armies of servants ranged behind them.

One whole section was devoted entirely to her – in her christening robes, on her first birthday, on holiday in Scotland, with the lacrosse team at school, at the dance her mother gave for her when she was eighteen, at her graduation from university. Her eyes skipped quickly over them. She was looking for one photograph in particular, one she knew was there but hadn't looked at for years.

She finally found it high up on the right-hand side of the collection.

The photograph showed an old man with a hawk-like face, a white moustache and a stiff, erect back, sitting on a verandah with a two-or three-year-old toddler, a little girl, on his knee. Rain must have been falling because there were streaks across the print, but the old man was smiling benignly and the child was gazing up at him in rapture.

She stared at it as intently as the little girl was staring at the old man.

'Darling, where are you?'

Her mother's voice echoed from the sitting-room. She broke away and went through to join her.

'Goodness, how Rosalind does go on,' her mother continued. 'I even had to invoke you to get her off the line. And you haven't even got yourself a drink yet. What on earth have you been doing?'

Victoria poured herself a gin and tonic, and sat down.

'I went into the bathroom to tidy up,' she said. 'Then I started to look at the photographs.'

'Every family should have an archive, and archives need archivists to assemble them. In our case me!'

Her mother smiled.

She was wearing a cashmere tweed skirt and jacket in a cinnabar and charcoal plaid threaded with violet, a ruffled white silk shirt, and she had a double string of Bahrain pearls round her neck. She had beautifully set silver-grey hair, and she looked elegant, confident, and tranquil. But then, her daughter thought, she'd never looked anything else.

'Any particular reason?' her mother went on.

'Reason?'

'Surely, darling, you know them well.'

Victoria sipped her drink and stretched out her legs towards the fire.

'I just wanted to see that one of me and Grandpa again. How old was he when it was taken?'

'The one at Bowley? Well, it was about five years before he died, so he must have been eighty-four. It was such a shame he didn't quite make it to ninety.'

Bowley was her grandfather's house in Hampshire. She could remember the smell of bread being baked by the cook in the kitchen and she thought she could remember the verandah, but the rest of the house was a blur.

'Did I see much of him after that?' she asked.

'Quite a bit at Christmas and in the holidays and so on. But he became terribly lame. He found it very frustrating and we didn't go there as often as before.' Her mother paused. 'Why this sudden interest, darling?'

Victoria hesitated before answering. She glanced at the large round table covered with a floor-length silk quilt beside her mother's chair.

At the table's centre was a vase of copper-coloured chrysanthemums. Every other inch of the surface was covered with more framed photographs. The bathroom pictures were a panorama of an entire family. The table was devoted exclusively to her grandfather. More than once in the past it had occurred to her that the collection wasn't so much a record of his life as a shrine.

She looked back at her mother. When she spoke her voice was studiedly neutral.

'I went into the Natural History Museum the other day. One of the younger curators was rearranging some of the exhibits. I got talking to him. I hadn't realised how important the Ruthven collection was.'

'Of course it's important. The African part is the most important assembled this century. I'm no scientist but it's really the basis for practically all modern studies in ornithology—'

Her mother broke off and laughed. 'Darling, where's all this leading to? You've never been interested in birds before.'

9

Victoria got up and walked to the drinks table to refill her glass. She poured out a small measure of gin, tipped in some tonic, and carefully added a couple of cubes of ice.

She was playing for time.

She had no idea where it was leading to. She didn't even really know what she was doing, except that for reasons she couldn't fathom she was both puzzled and somehow frightened – and she wanted to know why. Suddenly, as she stood there with the ice chinking in the glass, it came to her. Not the answer but the way forward, the way perhaps to find out.

'I had an idea, Mum,' she said as she came back. 'After talking to that young man at the museum, I thought it might be interesting to write something about Grandpa.'

'For you to write something? Good heavens, darling!' Her mother looked astonished. 'What on earth for?'

'I've always wanted to write, you know that.'

It was true.

From her schooldays on Victoria had been determined to become a writer. For a long time her mother, seeing her as a fashionable young novelist, was delighted. Later, after college and the sudden change of direction in her life – Victoria had become a Eurobond dealer in a London merchant bank largely because her boyfriend at the time of her graduation was taking up a career in finance – the ambition faded and her mother stopped encouraging her.

'But there's been a full-scale biography of him already,' her mother went on. 'What can you add to that?'

'I'm a member of the family. There must be papers the author didn't have access to.'

Her mother looked doubtful. 'I think he saw everything. Anyway, I'm not sure it's a particularly good idea to start ferreting through family papers. Read out of context by someone emotionally involved, they can start all sorts of silly hares.'

She looked at her mother sharply.

'Grandpa didn't have anything to hide, did he?'

'Of course not, darling. What an absurd idea! He was the most wonderful man.'

Victoria nodded. 'That's what you've always told me. In which case there's no reason at all for me not to write about him, is there? I loved him too after all.'

'Yes, dear.'

'Good. Then at least I can think about it.'

Victoria finished her drink and took a taxi back to her flat.

The streets were still crowded with last-minute shoppers and every square seemed to have a tree strung with Christmas lights. She caught snatches of carols through the half-open window, and heard the cab-driver amiably talking about the holiday traffic.

Victoria was barely aware of any of it.

All she could think of was that her grandfather, Colonel Jack Ruthven, the only man she had ever really loved – her male role model, she grimaced at the phrase but she knew it was true – and certainly her family's hero, its icon of honour and the provider of its fortune, was about to be exposed as a fraud.

3

'Darling, but this is terrible. Why on earth didn't you tell me earlier?'

'It happened at such short notice,' Victoria answered. 'I knew if I told you, you'd try to alter everything. I just didn't want to mess up your arrangements, Mum.'

Her mother stood in silence for a moment, worried and frowning.

It was Christmas Day. Victoria had arrived at her mother's flat at midday. They'd shared a bottle of champagne and opened their presents to each other – her mother's to her had been a lovely eighteenth-century enamel brooch from S. J. Phillips in Bond Street, while in return Victoria had given her mother a barrel of her favourite Brittany oysters and subscriptions to half a dozen of the glossy magazines she loved reading.

Afterwards they'd had Christmas lunch together, with a pair of grape-stuffed partridges replacing the traditional turkey – 'Just as festive,' her mother, an excellent cook, had said, 'but more delicious and much less fattening.' Now her mother was preparing to leave.

The plan had been the same as for the past seven years ever since Victoria and Charlie set up house together. He had lunch with his parents, she went to her mother, and then the two of them joined up for supper together in the evening. Victoria waited until her mother had put on her coat before she told her it would be different this year.

She didn't tell her the truth, that the day before Charlie had walked out on her. His sudden departure was still too painful and confusing for that. Instead she said he'd been called away on assignment abroad at a few hours' notice. As a journalist it had often happened before.

'What about your skiing trip?' her mother went on.

Victoria had saved up three weeks of her holiday entitlement. The first two weeks were due to be spent skiing with Charlie in Verbier. That had been another casualty of his leaving – she certainly wasn't going to spend two weeks in the resort on her own.

'I'm afraid that's off, too,' Victoria answered.

'Oh dear, oh dear. What on earth are you going to do?' Her mother glanced fretfully at her watch. 'I'm due at Lucy's at four. Then Meg's having a drinks party. Then the Cazenoves are giving dinner. I can't have you going back to that cold flat of yours and spending the rest of Christmas alone—'

She paused and added firmly, 'I'll telephone and say I'm bringing you. Lucy and Meg won't be a problem. Elspeth Cazenove's always fussy about her *placement* but she'll just have to lump it.'

'Mum, please,' Victoria interrupted her. 'I've had a hell of a week and I'm completely bushed. I really don't want to go anywhere. If I can just curl up here in front of the fire and read or watch television, I'll be perfectly happy. I might even stay the night.'

They argued about it for several minutes. In the end Victoria won. Muttering comments about journalists and newspapers, her mother picked up her handbag.

'I'll make sure I get away from Elspeth's early,' she said. 'If you get hungry, have some of the oysters. Just be careful to wrap a cloth round your hand before you open them.'

Victoria smiled. 'Yes, Mother.'

Her mother went out and the hall door slammed.

Victoria waited for five minutes in case as so often she'd forgotten something and returned. The five minutes passed and Victoria stood up. It was almost four o'clock. She had, she guessed, about six hours before her mother came back from her dinner.

She went over to the sitting-room bookcase.

Much larger than the one in the bathroom, it was made from mahogany and glass-fronted. It had belonged to her great-grandfather. One of her earliest childhood memories was staring in fascination at her reflection repeated endlessly in the glass panes when the bookcase had stood in the library of the house they'd lived in in Hampshire.

Then it had been just one of many bookcases containing, it had seemed to her, thousands of books. Struggling to master three-letter words, it was inconceivable to her that anyone could have learnt how to read even a handful of them in an entire lifetime. It was a mystery belonging to the adult world.

Later, when her father died, almost all the books and every bookcase apart from this one was sold. This one had accompanied her mother to London because, her mother said, it had belonged to Great-grandpa and it was such a beautiful object. It had housed then and still did the kernel of Great-grandpa's own collection of books.

Most of them were books on travel, shooting, fishing, big game hunting, exploration, and ornithology. She'd idly opened the glass doors a few times over the years and pulled one or two of the volumes out. They held little interest for her. She liked poetry and fiction. These were solemn and prosaic and filled with Latin names. Their jackets were tattered and the pages browning, and they smelt of mould and dust.

What she had loved were the illustrations.

In the hunting and fishing books there were ink and line drawings, crisp and sharp as frost. In the travel books wonderful dreaming black and white photographs of deserts, marshes, and mountains. In the ornithological works, best of all, even more marvellous plates of exotic birds with feathers glowing in diamond, yellow, lilac, ruby, aquamarine, sapphire, and emerald – colours that might have been ground to pigment from jewels.

Victoria wasn't looking for them now.

She was searching for something else. She found it tucked away on the top shelf. It was the biography of Grandpa her mother had referred to.

Victoria took it back to her chair.

She settled herself down and glanced at the profile of the author on the back of the jacket.

The book had been written fifteen years earlier by a journalist called Roger Jackson. Jackson, she learned. was forty-eight. He apparently had a lifelong interest in Africa, in travel, in wildlife in general, and birds in particular. He had also written books on the Saudi-Arabian royal family, on a billionaire businessman, the collapse of a Spanish bank, and a layman's guide to 'Getting the best out of international airlines'.

His photograph showed a man with a weak face, a wispy beard, and watery eyes.

Victoria thought for a moment.

Nothing about Jackson – from his profile to his list of books – was very convincing. She turned to his foreword and began to read.

Colonel Jack Ruthven [Jackson started] was truly that rare individual, a legend in his own lifetime who became even more of a legend after his death. Soldier, scholar, world traveller, explorer, public servant, distinguished man of letters, there can be few to whom his name is not familiar

– even if they have to pause occasionally before saying why.

When they do it is almost always on recollecting his contribution to the world as ornithologist and naturalist.

It is no exaggeration to say that Ruthven is the founding father, the principal source of all modern studies into birdlife. If birds are, as we now know, the descendants of the dinosaurs, then that means the study of the very origins of human life, if not life itself. On the massive collection of specimens and skins he bequeathed to the British Museum of Natural History the foundations of our current knowledge are built—

Victoria turned the page.

A rich subject for a biography, one might think [Jackson went on], and indeed Ruthven is. Yet a biographer embarking on an account of his career and a study of the man himself faces major problems. For a start much of his life was spent travelling the most remote quarters of the world; the Nepalese Himalayas and the Tibetan plateau, the Kalahari desert, so many other empty quarters and distant landscapes.

He lived it seems off the land and slept in nomad tents or under the stars. No trace or witness of his restless passages remains. It is in the nature of nomadic life that tracks and people vanish once their business at the pass or oasis is done. Ruthven was a nomad and so it was with him.

Then, and the second problem springs straight from the first, almost uniquely for an explorer Ruthven left no journals. In fact he left virtually no private papers at all. All we have are a handful of curt and formal letters, the introductions to his books on natural history, and a few articles he wrote reluctantly, by his own admission, for learned journals. They tell us where at times he was, but offer no insight into what happened while he was there, to his emotions, experiences, and no doubt adventures.

Thirdly, in what ordinarily would have been the best-documented part of his career, his long although interrupted military service, we face an equal blank. With what could seem to his biographer deliberate perversity, although of course it was not, Ruthven elected to work in – or rather was chosen by the authorities for the task – military intelligence. It is in the nature

16

of all such activities that few records are kept, and those few are harder to prise from the archives than a limpet from a rock.

For all of these reasons and no doubt more that derive from Ruthven's own personality, the man will probably always remain an enigma. Yet I believe the fullest picture we are likely to have of him emerges in the following pages. What can never be questioned is his lifelong devotion to the natural world and his total integrity in pursuing his researches for more than sixty years . . .

The foreword continued over the page with fulsome acknowledgements to a large number of people Victoria had never heard of.

She put the book aside and sat thinking for several minutes.

The author, Jackson, was lost. He was out of his depth, flannelling to cover up his evident failure to find out anything at all about Grandpa. That was obvious and none of Jackson's verbosity could conceal it. The book wasn't what Charlie had taught her was called in journalism 'honest'. That didn't mean it was a lie. It meant it was a quick, careless, scissors-and-paste job without any original research or thought.

Jackson or his publisher had decided there was a modest but useful amount of money to be made out of a life of Colonel Jack Ruthven. Jackson had written it as speedily as possible. That was the end of the matter.

Or it would have been if she hadn't met the young curator in the Natural History Museum. If he was right, Grandpa's 'lifelong devotion' to the natural world and his 'total integrity' were a sham. Unless there was some other explanation, he wasn't the most distinguished gentleman naturalist of his generation, he was a cheat.

And very soon he would be exposed. Victoria closed her eyes and shivered. Then she picked up the book again and continued to read.

4

'You're still here, darling, how lovely! I was so hoping you would be.'

It was eleven o'clock and her mother had just come back to the flat. She bent down and kissed Victoria on the forehead.

'All I can say is you missed absolutely nothing at Elspeth's. She had Billy's golfing friends from Sotogrande – dull as ditchwater with their equally dreary wives and all as drunk as owls.'

She bustled around taking her coat off and getting herself a late-night drink.

'A brandy or a Cointreau, darling?'

Victoria shook her head. 'No thanks, Mum.'

Her mother sat down. She wriggled off her shoes and stretched out her long and still, at the age of seventy, extraordinarily elegant legs.

'Bliss to be home!' She smiled. 'And how was your evening, darling, not too forlorn?'

'Not a bit,' Victoria replied. 'I read that man Jackson's book on Grandpa. It was interesting for me, but it's pretty bloodless stuff.'

'I think he did his best,' her mother said vaguely. 'We helped him as much as we could. At least he got most of the facts right.'

The 'facts', Victoria knew after finishing the book, consisted of an unblemished catalogue of success and achievement. The impeccable record started in his childhood and continued through to his old age.

'I also had a look at the photographs,' Victoria went on. 'I've never really looked at them before. Tell me, Mum, about some of them. This one, for instance—'

Victoria stood up and went to the table. She lifted one, which was mounted in a silver frame, and carried it over to her mother's chair.

The photograph showed a group of young men in striped blazers holding oars and standing by a long thin boat, virtually a wooden shell, with a river behind them.

Her mother laughed.

'That's Grandfather in the middle.' Her finger touched the tallest of the young men. 'Cambridge. He was stroke of his college's Eights' Week crew. But of course he could do absolutely anything. Rowing was just one of his sporting hobbies.'

'And this?'

Victoria showed her another photograph.

This one showed him – his imposing presence and aquiline face made him unmistakable – standing in military uniform with a group of soldiers against a background of what appeared to be ruined houses.

Her mother peered through her spectacles.

'It must have been taken in France during the first war,' she said. 'It could be almost anywhere on those terrible battle-fields. As you know, he was awarded the Military Cross twice and a bar to cross them.'

'What about this one?'

Victoria returned with a third photograph.

Mounted in a narrow frame of polished ash, the picture showed four people. Two of them were men. One, unmistakable again, was her grandfather. The second man was much shorter and stouter with a black moustache and strangely intense eyes.

The third person was a woman. She was tall, midway in height between the two men. Cascades of tumbling hair – in the black-and-white photograph it was impossible to tell the colour – surrounded her face and she was looking at the camera with a curious enigmatic smile. She had fine, almost sculpted bones and she looked to Victoria remarkably beautiful. Somehow she seemed to dominate the group.

The fourth person in the photograph was also a woman.

She was smaller than Ruthven and the other woman, a shadowy figure at Ruthven's elbow but with what seemed – it was difficult to tell because of the way the light fell – a bold and resolute face.

'Ah,' her mother said. 'Your grandfather of course. Beside him his friend and business partner, Eric Yeats. Alongside Yeats is his wife Sophia. And then – she's a bit fuzzy, isn't she? – your granny, Granny Lomax.'

'Is this Granny again?'

Victoria had fetched a fourth photograph.

'Yes, darling.' Her mother took only a moment to examine what was clearly the fourth woman in the previous photograph. 'A wonderful woman. She made Grandfather so happy. It was a tragedy when she died so young.'

Victoria frowned. 'Why's she called Granny Lomax? Why not Granny Ruthven? That's what she was.'

'I suppose we just did things like that in those days.' Her mother's voice was as vague as before. 'She was called Lomax when she married Grandpa. We went on calling her that.'

Victoria sat down. 'How did you meet my father, Mum?'

She never referred to him as Dad. She had never known him. In fact, Victoria reflected as she asked the question, it was only the second or third occasion in her life she'd even mentioned him.

Her father simply had never existed – not to her or to anyone else in the family.

'Oh, darling, what a strange thing to ask. I don't know what's got into you—'

Victoria knew her mother well.

She was still smiling, an affectionate and tolerant smile, but her eyes were evasive and the elusiveness in her voice grew by the minute.

'I think I met him in India. Or maybe London. I truly can't remember. We were so unlike you and your generation. We gadded about all over the place. Anyway, it happened. Happily you were the result—'

She leaned forward and touched Victoria on the cheek.

'Darling, it's long ago now, but parts of it are still painful. Let's leave it. It's Christmas. Let's be happy.'

'Yes, Mum—'

Victoria paused.

She didn't want to hurt her mother. The problem was, Victoria was hurt and confused for a whole range of reasons her mother knew nothing about. Charlie, of course – he ranked first and foremost. But even deeper than the wound Charlie's departure had left were the accusations levelled against Grandpa by the young man in the museum.

She could, Victoria knew, setting her mouth tightly as she acknowledged it, live without the bastard. She wasn't sure if she could live with the truth – if it was the truth – about Grandpa. He was the lode-star. She could handle any number of faithless vanishing bastards.

A lode-star was different. You were only given one.

'Whether I write anything about Grandpa or not,' she said, 'I'd still like to know more about him. Who can I go to?'

Her mother thought.

'If you really want to pursue this,' she said, 'I suppose you could

21

have a word with his younger sisters, your great-aunts. But, darling, I'm not at all sure it's sensible.'

Victoria smiled. 'I'm free, white, and over twenty-one.'

'In which case you're sensible enough to stay here tonight.'

'Yes, Mum. And to prove it I'll have a Cointreau now.'

They both laughed and sat together, holding each other's hands.

5

Victoria tried the door but it was locked and bolted.

Instead she rang the bell, tugging down on the heavy rusted iron bell-pull until she heard a rattling chime inside. Then she waited shivering on the doorstep in the dusk.

She had flown to Aberdeen, hired a car at the airport, and driven west. She had been to the house several times as a child, but she'd forgotten how utterly remote and isolated it was. First there were the mountains, the raw sweeping flanks of the northern ramparts of the Cairngorms. As they closed round her, chill and hostile in the weak January light, the road narrowed and began to twist and turn.

She crossed an endless series of humpback bridges over rivers swollen with foaming peat-flecked water, tawny and golden in the occasional shafts of sun that rippled across the dead heather. She climbed higher, the clouds closed in, and it began to rain. She turned on the car's headlamps but for long periods she could barely see the way ahead.

Finally she came to the entrance to the glen.

She pulled into the car park beside the little hotel that stood at the road junction. The hotel was closed – it was only open for the fishing season – but she paused for a few minutes studying the map. She vaguely remembered being taken to the hotel for lunch years before after a long and tiring walk across the hill. The road itself went on to Grantown-on-Spey. The track to the right led up to the Glenmoray lodge.

She took the track and headed on.

Within minutes she'd entered the glen. In the rain and drifting mist its towering walls reared up on either side of her like the dark ramparts of an immense castle. She gritted her teeth and drove on. She crossed another bridge – there was a salmon ladder, she suddenly remembered, which the fish climbed in bounding arcs like shining silver sickles – and at last she saw the lodge in front, perched on a knoll.

'Good evening, miss.'

The bolts had been pulled back and the door opened. Standing in front of her in a pool of light was an old woman with a shawl over her shoulders.

Victoria stood blinking and confused. It was so long since she'd seen her great-aunts that she wasn't sure for a moment if this was one of them. Then she realised they wouldn't have spoken with a Highland accent, and they wouldn't have addressed her as miss.

'I'm Victoria.' She recovered herself and smiled. 'I think my great-aunts are expecting me.'

'Come in, miss.'

The old woman showed her into the hall. She waited while Victoria took off her Barbour and shook out her hair. Then the old woman led her across the echoing flagstones and into the drawing-room.

'It's your visitor, Miss Octavie,' the old woman said.

Great-aunt Octavie was standing before a blazing fire.

As she came forward to greet her, limping slightly and supporting herself on a Highland shepherd's crook with a bone handle, Victoria recognised her instantly. She couldn't think how she could ever have confused her great-aunt with the elderly houseeper.

Octavie was small and grey-haired with a round smiling face and sparkling blue eyes, barely dimmed with age. Great-aunt Maude was struggling to rise from a chair on the other side of the fire. Maude's face was hollower than her sister's but her body was plumper. Both of them were wearing ankle-length tweed skirts in the bold Ruthven tartan – crimson and black threaded with veins of violet. Although Maude was two years younger than Octavie, Victoria remembered, they could well have been twins.

'Dear child, how wonderful to see you!' Octavie embraced her. 'And looking so beautiful. Maude, look at the girl. Isn't she angelic?'

Maude had managed to lift herself to her feet. Limping like her sister, she joined them and peered at Victoria.

'My dear, she's exquisite!'

Maude kissed her too. Victoria pushed back her hair. She had been drenched by rain on her walk between the car and the front door. She felt tired and damp and bedraggled. She blushed.

'I'm a mess,' she said.

'Nonsense!' Octavie replied. 'But have you eaten?'

Victoria nodded.

'You're quite sure?' The question was insistent. 'You young people have to eat. Let's ask Agnes to make you a piece.'

Victoria shook her head emphatically. 'I ate at Heathrow, Great-aunt, then I ate on the plane, then I had another huge sandwich while I was waiting to pick up the car—'

She glanced at the mahogany butler's table in the corner. It was laden with bottles. Gin, she suddenly remembered – so much kept returning to her in waves of memory – was her great-aunts' favoured drink, but she could see bottles of single malt whisky there too.

'I'd love a dram, though.'

'Darling child, you'll have whatever you want.'

A few moments later she was sitting perched on the velvet-upholstered club fender in front of the fire, with Octavie and Maude in chairs on either side of her.

She cupped the glass in her hands. She inhaled the aroma of the malt, she drank and let the warmth of the *usquebaugh* – the 'water of life' as she remembered again it translated from the Gaelic – spread through her.

She glanced at the two old ladies.

Twenty years younger than her grandfather, they were Jack Ruthven's only sisters. How it had happened that Ruthven's mother had waited twenty years after his birth before conceiving again twice in quick succession, Victoria had no idea. Giving birth at almost forty, as their mother must have been, was even more hazardous then than now. Was it simply by chance or was it deliberately planned?

As Victoria sipped the whisky, Great-aunt Octavie spoke.

'Do you keep a diary, Victoria? We do. We looked at ours after you telephoned. Do you know how long it's been since you were here last? Almost eighteen years. How about that? You were nine and we could walk without our damnable sticks!'

She and Maude laughed together.

'It's January, child,' Octavie went on. 'Not the best time of year to visit your decrepit Highland relatives, although we're delighted you did. But with not many years to go, Maude and I have become gossipy, inquisitive old biddies, haven't we Maude—?'

She turned her head to her sister. Maude wrinkled her face and nodded in agreement.

'Why have you come here now, Victoria?' Octavie addressed her again.

Victoria hesitated. Out of the corners of her eyes she was aware that both the old ladies were leaning forward for her answer.

My goodness, she thought, how wrong people can be. Her mother had described the great-aunts as simple, unsophisticated old spinsters. They were not. They hobbled, they lived in an isolated glen, for comfort, she guessed, they daily worked their way through their bottles of gin, but they remained shrewd and perceptive, as sharp as knives.

Victoria lifted her head and looked at the flames.

She could tell them lies or the truth. Lies were out of the question. They would be seen through. The truth, her reason for being there, was equally problematic. She knew nothing about the two sisters' relationship with their older brother. It was, she sensed, vulnerable and protective. The time was too early to embark on that.

As she thought, a memory came to her. At a university lecture she remembered the speaker describing life as God's joke of a compromise to fill the time between birth and death. She would compromise.

She would tell the truth, if not the whole truth.

'You won't approve of this, Great-aunt,' she said, 'but for seven years I've been living with my boyfriend, Charlie. He left me for someone else, someone I'd introduced him to, just before Christmas.'

Her great-aunts were old, they must have been over eighty, spinsters, and certainly old-fashioned in their view of morality and life. Victoria had expected at least small frowns of disapproval. There was nothing.

Only from Maude a murmured 'You poor girl'.

Victoria tilted her head in acknowledgement of the old lady's sympathy.

'Somehow it made me want to look at everything, my whole life, again,' Victoria continued. 'Grandpa was such an important figure in my childhood, I thought I'd start here. Does that make any sense?'

'Of course, my dear.' Octavie nodded. 'Well, he was so important to all of us, wasn't he? You were so small when he died, but how nice you should have realised even then what a great man he was, and come back to Glenmoray—'

She paused. Then, without a change in her tone, she continued. 'Your mother telephoned after you did. She said you were planning to write about Jack.'

Victoria froze. She felt a knot of embarrassment forming in her stomach.

She had no idea that her mother had spoken to the great-aunts – and she cursed her silently. Her story of returning to Glenmoray as part of re-examining her childhood and her life suddenly seemed to have been exposed as a pretence. She felt like a child caught out in a lie. She knew she was blushing and although she tried to fight against the flush on her cheeks, there was nothing she could do.

She took a large swallow of the whisky.

'Mama's got it a little wrong,' she answered. 'I've always wanted to write. Sorting through my own life, trying to make sense of it, seemed a good starting-point. Grandpa was involved, so – if this ever comes to anything – I'll obviously have to include him. But that's all.'

She drank again.

Normally, as she reached down to sip from the glass her head would have been lowered. This time she sat upright and raised the cut-glass tumbler to her lips. She watched the two old ladies.

She was right.

They had been looking at her. Their gaze turned away, they focused on each other, a glance passed between them. The glance was so swift, so fleeting, it might have been a shadow cast by the dancing flames of the fire. Victoria sensed it wasn't.

Grandpa Jack represented something too sensitive to be written about even by an adoring grand-daughter.

'What a splendid idea!' Octavie said. 'Jack would have loved it. I imagine you'll want to record the times when he took you fishing on the lochans up round Ben Buie and Ben More?'

In relief, Victoria nodded enthusiastically.

'Maude, we must surely have some photographs of the girl's visits.'

The two old ladies heaved themselves to their feet and began combing through a pile of leather-bound albums stacked up on one of the room's many tables.

6

Victoria stirred and opened her eyes.

She glanced at her watch.

It was just before 8.00 a.m. She got out of bed and shivered for a moment in the icy chill that filled the large room on the first floor of the lodge. Her great-aunts' bedrooms were along the corridor near the main staircase. She crossed to the window and drew back the curtains. The morning light was thin and washed with rain. Storm clouds were tumbling down the glen and the air smelt metallic and bitter.

Victoria ran back to the bed. She pulled the down quilt up to her chin and lay on her back with her arms crossed behind her head, tucking her hands in behind her hair for warmth.

It was her third day at Glenmoray. The two old ladies had been models of courtesy and affectionate companionship. They were clearly delighted to have her there. They had looked after her, planned excursions for her to make in her car, instructed Agnes, the housekeeper, to take care of her every want.

She might have been their own prodigal grand-daughter returning to a heart-warming welcome at the family hearth. And yet Victoria felt increasingly muddled and lost.

Grandfather Jack.

She was tentative about asking questions but the ones she did put to her great-aunts, they answered easily and fluently. On the surface she learned a considerable amount about her grandfather, about his life, his education and career, and his public service – although, on reflection, she realised it was little more than the hapless Jackson had given in his biography.

What she didn't discover was anything to begin to explain why, if the young man in the museum was right, Ruthven was a forger and a liar. What he'd apparently done was so extraordinary, so calculated and malevolent – he must have wasted the energies of the two generations of scientists who'd trusted him implicitly – it seemed inexplicable.

Perhaps the young man was mistaken. Victoria had considered

that again and again. Somehow she knew he wasn't. She was no ornithologist, but she'd seen the carefully stitched-together wings, the tiny elaborate ribbings of silk that had attached claws to legs, the curious embellishment of feather colourings that transparently owed nothing to nature.

They looked wrong. They smelt wrong. They *were* wrong.

The betrayal wasn't just of the scientific community. Far worse, it was a humiliation and denial of his own family – of her great-aunts, her mother, herself, of all the members of the extended Ruthven clan. To them all, and in his own presentation of himself, Grandpa was a hero.

Instead Jack Ruthven, it seemed, was a crook.

Victoria got out of bed again. She washed in the bowl of water, so cold it burned her cheeks, which Agnes had poured out for her the night before, and dressed hurriedly.

She hesitated.

It still wasn't 9.00. Her aunts, she'd learnt, were late risers. They didn't get up until 11.00. Agnes had her own apartment above the kitchen wing at the rear. She wouldn't come into the main house for at least another hour. Until then Victoria had the place to herself.

'Diaries or letters, my dear?'

It was Octavie the evening before answering one of the few direct questions Victoria had dared put to her.

'Not as far as I know. Jack was a man of action, not words. The only things he wrote – and he did so only as a duty – were a few articles in learned journals. Wasn't that so, Maude?'

Maude nodded. 'Jack hated writing. Give him a gun and a purpose, and he was happy. Give him a blank sheet of paper and he almost sulked.' She chuckled.

'But surely he wrote to the two of you?'

It was the closest Victoria came to being insistent. She regretted what she'd said as soon as she'd spoken. For the second time she sensed rather than saw the old ladies exchange a glance.

'Practically never, my dear,' Octavie replied. 'The occasional postcard, that was all.'

'And I always wish we'd kept them,' Maude agreed. 'But we have a tradition. On Twelfth Night we throw away everything from the past year – holly wreaths, Christmas cards, letters, the lot. It means we can embark on the New Year with a real first footing, a clean slate.'

'We don't throw away the gin, of course.'

The two old ladies laughed happily. Victoria joined in with a smile.

She didn't believe them.

Men of Grandpa's generation were schooled in writing from childhood. Words didn't always come easily to them, but they carried the practice of putting things down on paper, however clumsily, into adult life. It was part of being grown-up, a skill essential to every gentleman.

Jack Ruthven would have written. To his sisters, to his friends, to his daughter. And, almost certainly, he would have kept a diary.

Victoria opened her door quietly and walked downstairs.

The library at Glenmoray was on the ground floor between what her great-aunts called the winter sitting-room, the room with the blazing fire they used in the evenings, and the much larger drawing-room which opened on to the garden and which they only used in summer.

Victoria went into the library. She'd been there once or twice before, always with Octavie or Maude. They'd told her it was where Jack liked to sit and read. From its musty atmosphere, Victoria guessed it had seldom been used since his death.

She stared round at the glass-fronted bookcases. Then she frowned and thought.

'Almost always, you'll find, the answer is the simplest and most obvious one—'

The voice echoing through her head was Charlie's.

It was a year or two ago.

He was sitting before the gas fire on a damp winter night, wiggling his toes happily in front of the flames with his shoes and socks in a sodden little heap beside him. He'd just returned from filing a story he'd been working on for weeks.

Charlie was an investigative reporter. Victoria couldn't remember what the story had involved, only that he had uncovered it, found enough corroboration in his sources to satisfy the paper's lawyers, and written up the copy. It was finished. Tomorrow there'd be another project for him to investigate and pursue. For tonight he was content and relaxed, almost philosophical.

'Don't look for conspiracies, look for cock-ups,' he went on. 'Forget about smudged fingerprints that even the forensic laboratories can't identify. Look for smoking guns and the smell of cordite. That's what ditched Richard Nixon, the most powerful man in the world with the most powerful protective screen round him. His secretary's legs were too short to reach the stop button on the recorder. Machiavelli doesn't bring down empires. People's leg-length does—'

He grinned at her. 'Give us a kiss and a drink, blossom. The story's good. It'll stand.'

Victoria had given him a kiss and a drink that night. She shuddered. Never again. But what hadn't changed, even if everything else had, was what he'd said. If nothing else, she reflected bitterly, the man knew his business.

'Look for what's simplest and most obvious.'

If Ruthven had kept any records of his life, there was only one logical place for him to store them – his library.

Victoria walked slowly round the bookcases, examining the shelves one by one.

The collection, surprisingly, wasn't very large, and her inspection took her less than half an hour. There were, predictably, a whole range of volumes on eighteenth- and nineteenth-century ornithology, alongside works of military history, travel, and exploration. Also, rather more curiously, at the end two shelves devoted entirely to poetry.

There was nothing that could remotely be considered private or personal. No box-files of letters, no journals, not even a diary of engagements.

Victoria went back to the centre of the room.

Puzzled, she chewed on her finger. She stopped. She looked at her hand. In spite of the glass, the bookcases, probably unopened for years, were dusty. Before looking through the last two shelves, the ones that contained the volumes of poetry, she'd wiped off the accumulated grime on her skin – guiltily using one of the window curtains as a cloth.

Her hands were still clean although she'd examined the poetry carefully. She went back to the last two shelves. She glanced to left and right, up and down. Everywhere the dust lay thickly, except where the poetry was housed. There the mahogany surfaces shone bright.

She didn't need to pause, to question why. She knew the reason instantly.

The books of poetry had replaced other books that had been there before. Someone had removed whatever had occupied the space, wiped down the shelves, and filled it up with what stood there now. Judging by the sheen on the rim of the wood, they must also have done it very recently.

'Look for what's simplest and most obvious.'

Victoria heard the door to the kitchen open at the end of the corridor. Agnes had come down to prepare the great-aunts' breakfast. Victoria went through to join her.

'Did ye sleep well, hen?' Agnes asked a few minutes later as Victoria sipped a scalding mug of sweet instant coffee.

'The sleep of the just,' Victoria answered.

Agnes laughed. 'That'll be a new one for Glenmoray.'

She busied herself with preparing the great-aunts' breakfast.

'Great-aunt,' Victoria said an hour afterwards when Octavie had come downstairs and settled herself in the winter sitting-room, 'would you mind if I stayed on today and left tomorrow?'

Frustrated in her search for something revealing about Ruthven, Victoria had told the two old ladies the evening before that she thought she should return south in the morning.

'Dear child,' Octavie laughed, 'stay for as long as you want. Nothing would make us happier.'

'What's that?'

Great-aunt Maude had limped into the room and was peering at the two of them.

'Little Victoria wants to spend another day here,' Octavie said to her sister. 'I've told her she's welcome.'

'Of course she is. How delightful!' Maude sat down too. She stared at Victoria through her half-moon glasses. 'A change of plan, my dear?'

The question was mildly phrased but there was something behind it – something shrewd and searching.

Victoria swallowed.

She glanced at the window and the answer came to her. The clouds had parted and the chill watery light of the early morning had given way to bright sunshine. The air was still wintry, but it was going to be the first dry day since her arrival.

'I haven't really had the chance to get out yet,' Victoria said. 'I thought I'd go up on to the hill. I'd just like to see where Mum and I and Grandpa used to walk—'

Victoria turned from the window and smiled innocently at the old ladies.

33

'I've decided I can't really write anything about Grandpa. It's all been done. I've put that away. But before I go, I'd like to visit the places he loved.'

She let the smile linger on her face.

Octavie nodded. 'It's as you choose, my dear. Of course we'd have helped you in every way but, as you say, it's probably been done. I'll ask Agnes to make you a piece for the hill. Maude and I are out for the day.'

Victoria looked at her guilelessly. 'I didn't know that, Great-aunt.'

'Every second Tuesday Malcolm takes us over to Invercauld for Jean's bridge afternoons. We'll be back for supper. Maude and I will tell you what we've won – or more likely lost – and you can tell us about the hill.'

The car with a fiercely grey-bearded driver at the wheel – Malcolm, Victoria assumed – arrived to collect them at midday.

As soon as they drove away, Victoria went through to the kitchen. Agnes had put her piece, her lunchtime sandwiches, into a frayed shoulder-satchel with leather straps and brass buckles.

'It's the Colonel's,' Agnes said. 'He used to tell me it had carried his pieces in the wildest places in the world, but there was none so wild a place as here in Wester Ross—'

She reached on to the oak dresser, picked up a battered silver flask, and slipped it into the satchel.

'He wouldn't take to the hill without a dram. "Drugs the natives," he said, "before they get me. And drugs me if they get there first"—'

Agnes smiled at Victoria. In her fading grey eyes was a mixture of affection and nostalgia, of long-remembered and important rituals.

'A great man, the Colonel,' she said. 'A young lassie like you won't need his *usquebaugh* unless the mist comes down, but it's here for him.'

Agnes was almost as old as the great-aunts. Victoria put her arms round her. She kissed her and thanked her.

'Have a gay time on the Colonel's hill,' Agnes said over her shoulder as she walked stiffly away for her afternoon rest. 'He loved the tops more than anything.'

'I will,' Victoria called after her.

She waited until the old woman had disappeared. Victoria had slung the satchel over her shoulder. When Agnes' footsteps faded, she took the satchel off and dumped it at her feet. She stood there until she heard the distant sound of a closing door.

Victoria breathed out. She closed her eyes for an instant. Then she started to search.

It wasn't difficult. In fact it was extraordinarily easy.

'Look for what's simplest and most obvious.'

The simplest and most obvious place for old ladies to hide what they didn't want discovered was under their beds. It was the most private place of all, the last refuge of burglars, secrets and nightmares, of all that was most precious and most frightening.

Victoria tried their bedroom doors. Both, for what she guessed was the first time in the lives of Octavie and Maude, were locked. The keys had been removed. The rooms were barricaded against an intruder.

The intruder, the threat, the thief they wanted to wall out, could only be herself.

7

Victoria stood outside the house looking up at her great-aunts' bedrooms.

The house had been built towards the end of the seventeenth century, but the windows were relatively modern. One of the more recent Ruthvens had replaced the original lead-framed glass panels with sliding sash fitments. As she'd guessed, the sashes were raised. However cold the winter, no one of Octavie and Maude's generation would have considered sleeping without the windows half-open.

The problem was, the sills were at least twenty feet above the ground. A drainpipe ran down beside what Victoria thought was Octavie's room. She might be able to use it to get down but it was impossible, she knew, for her to climb it.

She frowned.

She hesitated and thought. Then she headed towards the steadings, the cluster of stone-built barns and outhouses behind the house which had been so vital a part of Glenmoray's life when it was still the centre of a working farm.

Victoria found what she was looking for in the biggest of the steadings. Propped against a wall behind a mound of old newspapers – the old ladies subscribed to *The Scotsman* and evidently never threw a copy away – was a tall wooden ladder. As she tried to pull the ladder round the newspapers, there was a splintering sound and it collapsed.

It hadn't been used for years. Damp and dry rot had eaten the uprights and steps away. All that was left now was a heap of powdery wood.

Victoria swore. She searched the rest of the steadings but there were no other ladders. Then she went inside and stood before the locked bedroom doors again. The more she thought about it, the more certain she was right – and the more her frustration increased.

She clenched her hand and hammered it against the heavy wooden frame. Then she stopped and forced herself to think. She remembered

Charlie, Charlie chuckling in one of his philosophical bouts about his profession.

'We're rogues and bandits, us journalists, robbers if you want a blunter word.' As so often, he was sitting in front of the fire with his shoes off. 'We rob people of the truth they want to hide. We keep company with thieves and we learn thieves' tricks.'

He'd told her many of those tricks. She remembered one now. Cursing him, Victoria returned to the steadings. She found a piece of wire, she picked up an old newspaper, and she went back upstairs.

All the rooms in the house had ancient brass locks with twin sets of keys so they could be opened or bolted from either side. With the passage of time the floors had sunk, leaving a gap between the base of the door and the boards below. Victoria slid the newspaper under Octavie's bedroom door, inserted the wire in the keyhole, and gently jiggled it backwards and forwards.

There was a faint tap as something fell on the other side. She carefully drew the newspaper back. Lying on it was a key. She picked it up, put it in the lock, turned it, and the door opened.

Victoria closed her eyes in relief.

She could feel her heart pounding. Charlie was a bastard but in thieving and treachery he'd been consistent. At least there he'd never let her down.

She went into the room.

Under Octavie's bed were a dozen box-files, crammed with documents so ancient they might have come from the vaults of some lending-house in Victorian London. She opened the first one. On top was a postcard signed J for Jack. Grandpa Jack Ruthven. She shut her eyes again. She was right.

She didn't explore any further. Instead she tried to make a mental calculation of how much space the files had taken up on the library shelves. She guessed it was about six feet. These would only have occupied half that.

Victoria turned.

A door led through to what turned out to be a bathroom. Another door led to a second bathroom, and a third to Maude's bedroom. All were unlocked. Victoria knelt and looked under Great-aunt Maude's bed. A further dozen box-files had been hidden there. The two old ladies had divided up Jack Ruthven's archive between them.

Victoria stood up and glanced at her watch.

It was still barely 2.00 p.m. and at least a couple of hours before

38

Octavie and Maude returned. There was far too much for her to read in the time. She needed days or even weeks, and tomorrow she'd be gone. There was only one answer and it came to her instantly.

She'd take the archive with her. She'd become exactly what the old ladies sensed she might be – a thief.

She ran back downstairs and headed for the steading.

She gathered up a pile of the old copies of *The Scotsman* and returned to Octavie's bedroom. As she passed through the hall she picked up a ball of twine and a pair of scissors, used, she guessed, by the old ladies in the garden. She removed the contents of the first box-file, and repacked it with folded newspaper.

She flipped through the papers she'd taken out until she found a letter from Ruthven's bankers. She scanned it. The letter was of no interest – it simply acknowledged a small credit to his account – but it was what she wanted. Victoria put it on top of the wedge of newspaper and clipped down the rusting spring-arm.

If Octavie or Maude opened the file – and from the dust on the hinges she doubted whether either of them, whatever secrets the file contained, had glanced at it for years – it would look undisturbed.

She put the file carefully back in its place under the bed. She tied up the papers she'd extracted with twine. Then she set about repeating the exercise with the other files – not just those in Octavie's room, but in Maude's too.

She needed to make several trips to the steading and gather up armfuls of the yellowing newspapers before she was through. It took her almost two hours, but finally she finished. She carried the neatly tied bundles of documents down to the front of the house, and loaded them into the boot of her car. She slammed it shut and wearily trudged upstairs again.

Meticulously she checked everything. The boxes were precisely where she'd found them. The bed valances were hanging tidily and level with the floor. The doors between the four rooms – the two bedrooms and the two bathrooms – were closed.

She shut the heavy door that opened from the landing into Great-aunt Octavie's room, put back the key, and turned the lock. Then she went over to the window and swung herself out until she was propped on the sill.

For an instant she felt sick and ashamed.

It wasn't just the distance to the ground, although she felt she was perched on a cliff-top, nor the fragility of the drainpipe. It was the enormity of what she'd done.

Her great-aunts loved her.

They'd taken her into their house and treated her as their own grand-daughter. If they had something to hide about their brother, then that was their affair, not hers. She was remote from Grandpa, two generations remote. They were close to him: blood of his blood, flesh of his flesh. He was real to them, the root-stock. She was an off-shoot, a plant growing up at a distance.

She closed her mind to the thought.

Victoria swung herself round, reached for the iron tube, and began to inch her way down.

'So how was your day, my dear?' Octavie asked as Victoria came into the sitting-room before supper.

'Lovely,' she answered brightly. 'I went out for my walk. I found my way up to Dougal's cairn, where Grandpa used to take me. Then it clouded over and I came back and read in front of the fire.'

She paused and smiled. 'And how about the bridge?'

'As usual.' Great-aunt Octavie waved her hand. 'Tiresome when one loses, rather jolly when one wins. Today was quite jolly, wasn't it, Maude?'

'Only for you, dear,' Maude said crossly from her chair. 'You had that clever Jamie Stuart as a partner. I was stuck with that idiot Murray woman. She took us down four times in a row.'

Victoria was watching both of them closely.

They'd returned several hours earlier. If they'd looked at the box-files or noticed anything unusual in their rooms, she was sure they'd have said something. They were far too blunt and formidable to be inhibited from questioning her. They'd said nothing.

Silently Victoria let out a sigh of relief. They'd no idea what she'd done.

'Next time we'll swap partners,' Octavie answered. 'Let's eat. I'm sure Agnes is ready—'

She took Victoria's arm for support. 'You really have to go in the morning?'

Victoria nodded. 'I must, Great-aunt.'

'How sad, child, how sad. But at least you've found your way back here. You'll return again very soon, won't you?'

Victoria smiled again. 'I promise.'

40

Behind them as they walked towards the dining-room, she could hear the echoing tap of Maude's stick on the slate floor.

Book in London the following evening, Victoria sat down in her flat and started to read through the contents of the first of the box-files.

8

'Dearest Mama: It was quite cold here this week. Matron says I am settling in well. On Sunday we went to church. It was quite warm going to church. I have a new friend. His name is Ewart—'

The next few lines had been vigorously crossed out by a row of Xs in another, evidently adult hand. Whatever the child had said had been censored. Victoria held the letter up to the light. Through the heavy scoring she could just make out what he had written.

'I do not like Ewart much. He is big and fat and kicks me on the knee at the back. Also he gives me Chinese burns after sport when we come out from the bath. Also he gives Chinese burns to Waring. I hate Ewart. So does poor Yeats. I wish Yeats was my friend, but Dr Morgan says Ewart is my friend—'

The letter, now uncensored, continued with a statement that football would start next week, and it was still cold. It ended with a declaration of love for his mother and the hope he would see her soon. In the meantime, he asked, could she please send him one of Mrs Benfield's plum and raisin cakes?

Victoria glanced at the envelope.

The franking date-stamp across the image of a stern and plump Queen-Empress, the monarch who had the same name as herself, was 1 October 1898. Grandpa, Colonel Ruthven, would have been eight. The letter must have been the first he'd sent home after being despatched to boarding school.

She reached into the box and pulled out the next.

An hour later she'd read through the contents of the box. The letters took Ruthven up to the age of thirteen. The last, gleefully written at the end of the summer term in 1903, recorded that he'd just heard he'd been accepted for Eton.

'Wonderful news! I know it's what you wanted and of course it's what I want. I'm sure Dr Morgan will have notified you already. I hope, dear Mama, it makes up for the mistake and you will forgive and forget that now.'

Victoria had already come across the 'mistake'. It had happened a year earlier when Ruthven was twelve, although it wasn't easy to make out exactly what had happened.

From the utter misery in Ruthven's letters at the time and a single letter to his parents from the headmaster, the only one from Dr Morgan in the box, it seemed that Ruthven and Yeats – by now confirmed as his best friend – had been caught trapping pheasants at night by the gamekeeper of a local landowner. The gamekeeper had marched them down to the village police station, where they were identified as pupils at the school and turned over to Dr Morgan.

Dear Lady Ruthven [Dr Morgan's letter read], We have already discussed this sad matter, unparalleled, I may say, in my long experience in education. I have made further investigations. I have concluded your son was woefully misled by the chief instigator of the mischief, the boy Yeats. In confidence I have had deep reservations about Yeats for some time. Tragically they have been proved correct.

I am expelling Yeats from the school forthwith. Your son, in my view, merits and deserves another chance. I feel bound to suspend him for two weeks as an example to his fellow-pupils. I hope you will agree. Afterwards I trust he will return properly chastened, but also able in time to put this behind him and continue in pursuit of the career you, I, and Sir Charles have in mind for him.

Victoria had read the headmaster's letter several times.

She didn't believe a word of it. The wretched Yeats hadn't led the poaching expeditions, it had been Grandpa. In all Grandpa's earlier letters it had been quite clear that Jack Ruthven was the dominant driving force, and Yeats merely a compliant acolyte.

Yeats had been sacrificed, she guessed, on the altar of Dr Morgan's snobbery.

Grandpa was the only son of Sir Charles and Lady Ruthven of Glenmoray. Poor little Yeats was probably the child of some newly rich but still humble shoe or clothing merchant from the Midlands. He had been tossed out and Grandpa obsequiously allowed back into the fold, into the system that would take him on to Eton or Winchester and then to Oxford or Cambridge.

Victoria sat for a moment seething with anger at the injustice of it all. Then she reached for the second box. This contained Ruthven's letters home from Eton.

They covered a period of five years, his life between thirteen and eighteen. Although he was now older and much more fluent on paper than he had been at his first school, there were considerably fewer letters than in the first box. The reason became clear in one of the first he wrote to his mother.

Dearest Mama, well, here I am! Ten days since the carriage dropped off my trunks and old Tom trotted away with you and father inside (inside the carriage, that is, not Tom!) and my head's still above water.

You saw my room. Very fine it is, too. Oh, Mama, you cannot know how good it is to have a place of my own. Not like the Downstill dormitories with the scuffling and snoring, the crowding and shouting and fisticuffs. Just me alone!

M'tutor has called me to his study twice to see how I'm getting on. (Father probably told you at Eton we all call our housemasters m'tutor. The other masters are known as beaks. Just another difference between Eton and other schools!) Mr Waring seems an exceptionally decent sort. I know I'm lucky to be in his house and will learn much from him.

And it's so excellent to be so close to London with the chance to see you most Sundays. I shan't have to write all those letters like from Downstill. I fear I'm still rather hamfisted with pen and paper, as Dr Morgan always said. Now I'll be able to give you my news *face à face*, as you call it – although I promise, Mama, I'll persevere with correspondence.

Victoria worked through the second box. She sat back again and thought.

Written in the stilted language of a child addressing an adored parent – it was clear Ruthven worshipped his mother who had evidently been a formidable character – in many ways the letters made up an unremarkable archive, probably typical, Victoria guessed, of what so many boys of his background and generation might have left behind them.

Lonely and insecure, he had been sent away at eight to boarding school. He had gradually grown in confidence and at thirteen he'd won a place at Eton. There he had blossomed – for some reason

45

'opening like a rose' was a phrase that occurred to her. He was clearly alert, intelligent, and increasingly considered as what he once proudly described as 'one of our dear academy's intellectual elite'.

He was also popular with his fellow-students – he was the youngest boy of his year to be elected to Eton's student governing body, Pop, which among other privileges allowed him to wear embroidered waistcoats – and he developed into a notable athlete. He played cricket and football for Eton and he also – his proudest achievement – boxed for the school. 'Hard pounding, Mama, hard pounding!' was how he described his individual victory in the contest with Eton's great rival, Winchester.

There were only two things that were puzzling. Victoria frowned as she considered them.

Along with the letters there were several mementoes of Ruthven's stay at Eton – some copies of the school magazine, the programme of a play he'd appeared in, sporting fixture lists for the games at which he'd excelled, the school's annual record of the pupils in attendance. The last was simply long lists of names in alphabetical order.

Victoria glanced at them and was about to put them aside when she noticed something.

In the margin of the last page for Ruthven's final year which contained his own name, someone had inked in a large exclamation mark against another name not far below his. Beside the exclamation mark was the comment 'Jumped the last ditch, too!' The handwriting – she knew it well now – was Grandpa's. Her eye travelled to the left.

The name was E. M. Yeats.

There was no means of being absolutely certain it was the same Yeats who'd been expelled after the poaching expedition at Ruthven's first school, but somehow Victoria knew it had to be. She went back to the other annual lists. There was no entry for E. M. Yeats for the first two years. It first occurred in the third year. Ruthven and Yeats must have been the same age, and by then they would have both been sixteen.

From everything Victoria knew about the ancient public schools like Eton and Winchester, a boy invariably entered at thirteen and left for university at eighteen. There was no provision for someone to become a pupil at sixteen midway through the normal scholastic period. Yet that was what Yeats had apparently done.

That was puzzling enough.

Equally puzzling, there was no reference at all to Yeats over the six years from the poaching incident to the enigmatic comment in the final

Eton register. Before his expulsion Yeats had featured in all Ruthven's letters. Afterwards he vanished. It might have been understandable if the two small boys had never met again, but Yeats had turned up at Eton at sixteen.

It seemed inconceivable the two hadn't got together. They had been the closest of friends for four of the most formative years of their childhood. Unintentionally, of course, Ruthven had been the cause of the other boy's disgrace and downfall. Ruthven was the leader and Yeats the follower. Yeats had been made the scapegoat for something that was clearly Grandpa's responsibility.

And Grandpa, bold, noble, and honourable Grandpa, had never referred to it again.

Even stranger was the second puzzle the Eton box of correspondence had revealed. Apart from Ruthven's letters home and the memorabilia of his time at the school, there was just one other letter. It was written by Mr Waring, Ruthven's housemaster or 'm'tutor' as Ruthven called him, and it had been sent to his mother towards the end of Ruthven's final summer term.

My dear Lady Ruthven: I know Jack has told you he has been awarded an entry to Magdalene College at Cambridge. You will of course be delighted. How much I share your pleasure! It is a fitting reward for someone who over the past five years has put down deep roots here, contributed greatly to the community which surrounds him, and by steadfast perseverance forged the makings of a fine young man . . .

The letter went on to dwell fulsomely on Ruthven's academic and sporting achievements, his leadership qualities, and the respect he had engendered in the younger pupils.

I am all the more glad for Jack at this successful outcome [Waring finished], in view of that deeply distressing incident in his third year here. It was a troubling time for all of us; for you and Sir Charles as his parents, for myself, for the Headmaster, and naturally for Jack himself. To his great credit Jack survived it, although I like to think we all played a part in helping him find his feet again.

I am sure he has now put it behind him, and will go on to the future we all envisage for him.

Reading the letter for the first time, Victoria was momentarily confused. She thought Waring was referring to the poaching episode – even the phrase 'put it behind him' was the same as Dr Morgan had used.

Then she realised it couldn't be the same. Whatever had happened, and there was no clue to what it was, years later at a different school something else had taken place which had threatened Grandpa's schoolboy career even more gravely than the escapade with Yeats.

Victoria stared frowning into the darkness.

It had been raining but the pattering of drops had stopped, and she could hear an owl calling somewhere.

It had been in Ruthven's third year at Eton that Yeats had reappeared.

Vaguely and inconsequentially – she had never given it any thought – she'd always assumed Grandpa's life had been one of seamless happiness and achievement. It was what was engrained in her, what she'd been taught for as long as she could remember. Other people made mistakes. They had passages of darkness, loneliness, and confusion.

Not Grandfather.

He was steadfast, an inspiration, a beacon of all the manly virtues against which everyone else should be measured and tested.

'If you ever consider marrying your delightful boyfriend,' her mother once said teasingly, 'before you go down on your knees to propose, think how Grandpa would have viewed him over a second glass of brandy. It's not a bad test, young lady.'

Grandpa Jack had become involved in a poaching scheme with a boy called Yeats. He'd never referred to Yeats again, although Yeats had joined him at Eton. And then Ruthven had been at the centre of another incident which had almost cost him his career.

Victoria reached for the third box.

9

Victoria assumed that the third box would contain whatever Grandpa's mother had kept from his time at Cambridge.

Lady Ruthven – and it could only have been her – had clearly been a meticulous, even obsessive, archivist on behalf of her son. The way she'd arranged everything neatly in chronological order in the first two boxes would have been the envy of any professional cataloguer.

Suddenly the system seemed to change.

The first few documents didn't come from Cambridge and they were postcards, not letters. The franking on them was too blurred to make out the date, but from the black-and-white images of the ports they showed and the different stamps they carried they must have been mailed during a voyage across the Bay of Biscay and down the west coast of Africa.

'Sun, glorious sun!'

The one-line message on the very first, followed by an exuberant drawing of a matchstick figure spread-eagled beneath a huge hand-coloured golden sun, had been sent from Lisbon. The second card came from Gibraltar.

'More!' The even shorter message was followed by an even larger sun.

The third card was also from Gibraltar.

'With wind for pudding!'

It showed the same matchstick figure crouched now with his arms wrapped around his head and thick arrows to indicate the wind.

The fourth and fifth cards, equally exuberant and enigmatic, had been posted in Casablanca on the north African coast and Tenerife in the Canary Islands.

'Little sister Octavie is here in hiding!' was the comment from Casablanca on the reverse of a picture of an Arab lady thickly veiled in a chador. The card from Tenerife showed flying fish and dolphins leaping before a liner's bows. It had been tinted by hand in colour.

'What do you think of my artistic efforts?' Ruthven had written.

'I bought the box, Windsor & Newton's finest portable in black tin, from a derelict old drunk on the waterfront. Said Lear had given it to him in Genoa. Not bad, what? I'm only teasing – at least it's a start.'

And then from Lagos came the first letter which provided part of the explanation.

Dearest Mama: We arrived two days ago and are lying at anchor in the sea-roads outside this old ramshackle port. I have just returned from shore and it is almost midnight. Very close, very humid – happily the sea-winds keep the plaguing insects from us. I wish to sleep but feel I must talk to you first about all that has happened since I left . . .

Ruthven had sailed from London at the end of July on board the P&O liner, *the Southern Star*. His destination was Cape Town in South Africa.

The liner had stopped for a week at Gibraltar, and much of the letter was taken up with the description of a trip he'd made from there on horseback up to the Spanish sierra town of Ronda.

The experience was unforgettable. Eric and I left the Rock at 3.00 a.m. accompanied by a couple of Spanish grooms. We rode for five hours in starlight with only owls for company. Soon after dawn we reached a little pueblo called Jimena. There we breakfasted off coffee and great doorsteps of country bread dipped in olive oil so translucent-green and thick it was like the distillation of a spring meadow. Then we began to climb . . .

I cannot describe what it was like. The austere diamond-like clarity of the air, the tawny colours of the summer-dried countryside, the harsh bull's hide of Spain laid out beneath us, the gathering heat, the sweat on the horses' flanks, the silent companionship of E – no need for us to speak – and the sombre faces of our grooms shadowed by their grey Sevillian hats. Mama, I was in heaven . . .!

In the late afternoon we came to another pueblo, Gaucin, where we stabled our horses at a little travellers' inn. The inn keeps a visitors' book where all who ride up from Gibraltar write their names and comments. I found an entry by your hero, Sir Richard Burton. Beside it was a full page in Arabic in his own hand. Not having an idea what it meant, I signed my own name and somewhat cheekily added I agreed entirely with everything Sir Richard had said. I'm sure you would approve . . .!

The letter continued with a description of the next day's ride, Ruthven's arrival in Ronda, his short stay there, and then his journey back. Afterwards it went on to sketch shipboard life on the *Southern Star* until the liner reached Lagos.

At which point, dearest Mama, for the moment I leave you [he finished]. What lies ahead at the Cape and in Africa is beyond one of those open doors you have so often encouraged me to step through. I value your support and guidance more than anything in the world. I am just so pleased you acceded to my request to accept Eric's offer. Without your backing I might have stepped away from it . . .

I did not and here I am embarked on what I hope will be a noble adventure. Certes, for the moment fortune and a fair wind are at my back. I bless Eric's offer and his father's new-found fortune for that. But most of all I bless you!

Victoria put the letter back into its slot in the box.

She paused.

On instinct she passed over the rest of the box's contents and reached for the documents at the end. They were another group of postcards. She flipped through them, not looking to see what they said but searching for a date-stamp that was legible. She found one.

It was addressed to Lady Ruthven and it had also been sent from Lisbon, like the earlier one with the drawing of the sun. 'Almost back with you!' this one said with the same exuberant exclamation mark after the message.

The date was 21 October 1912. It was almost four years later.

Victoria was baffled.

She hadn't got Jackson's biography of Grandpa with her but she didn't really need to refer to it. Her memory was clear enough. Jackson hadn't made any reference to a stay in South Africa. He'd simply described Ruthven as going from his first private school to Eton, from Eton to Cambridge, and from Cambridge on to service in the First World War.

Victoria's initial reaction was that she'd discovered a minor unknown episode in Ruthven's past – a South African holiday between school and university. That would have been understandable.

Four years weren't a holiday, a minor episode in anyone's life. Particularly between the ages of eighteen and twenty-two, they were a major part of the journey to adulthood. Girls became women, married, and had children. A boy left adolescence behind and became a man.

Jackson must have been an extraordinarily sloppy researcher, or someone had misled him. He'd managed to remove four of the most formative years of Ruthven's life. Ruthven hadn't gone from Eton to Cambridge. He'd sailed to South Africa instead. And whether or not he'd spent the four years there – from the postcards it seemed likely – that raised another question.

Jackson's book spoke of him graduating from Cambridge with a double first. It was impossible. A BA degree course, needed to acquire the two firsts, took three years. Ruthven could only have entered Cambridge in 1913. A year later he was fighting in the war. He couldn't have got his initial first, let alone his second.

In fact he couldn't have got a degree at all.

And then there was Eric whose 'offer' had apparently been the cause of the whole journey, and who'd accompanied Ruthven on the voyage. Who was he? A whole variety of names had been mentioned in Ruthven's letters from Eton, but there hadn't been an Eric among them. It wasn't even clear whether he was a contemporary or an older man.

Victoria ransacked her memory.

The Yeats of the poaching incident who'd later turned up at Eton, if indeed it was the same Yeats, had the initials E. S. Was he Eric? And if he was, what was this offer he'd made to Ruthven? How could an eighteen-year-old boy propose something to a contemporary which would cut short his university career and absorb four years of his life?

Victoria's mind swam.

As she continued to comb through the letters, at least some of the answers began to emerge.

It was indeed the Yeats of Ruthven's first school, and his Christian name was Eric.

That became clear in Ruthven's first letter back to his mother after his arrival in Cape Town.

My goodness, dearest Mama, we are truly romping here if that's the appropriate phrase.

Eric, or his father, or rather his father's connections, must know everyone of interest, wit, fortune (mercantile, mining or otherwise), influence, pedigree, ambition, and no doubt skulduggery in all South Africa. We are meeting them by the boatload. They are wining us, dining us, displaying their daughters for us, and generally treating us like the two finest cocks o'the north the western world has ever sent them . . .

From what followed Victoria managed to work out what had happened.

Eric's father was a friend of the British Governor-General of South Africa. The elder Yeats was a friend and business associate of Cecil Rhodes. He had made a vast and recent fortune through a partnership with Rhodes in various mining enterprises.

Eric Yeats' father had secured a position for his son on the Governor-General's staff. Eric had persuaded his father to find one for Ruthven too, and Ruthven had gone with him to South Africa.

Victoria thought it through.

Nothing of what she'd learnt appeared in Jackson's book, but it was beginning to fall into place. Eric Yeats had indeed probably been the son of some minor merchant. That was why Dr Morgan had dismissed him so summarily from the preparatory school he and Ruthven had attended. Then Yeats' father became immensely rich.

He'd bought his son a place at Eton at the unusual age of sixteen, and the two young men had come together again. Afterwards it was Yeats, with massive financial resources behind him now, who'd made the running.

He'd taken Ruthven with him to Cape Town.

10

Victoria stood up and lit another candle.

There'd been a violent storm at midnight, and the power had failed. Now it was almost 4.00 a.m. and the supply still hadn't been restored.

She paced restlessly round the room. Then she lit a cigarette. She'd virtually never smoked in her life until the past two weeks, until Charlie left. As she talked about his departure with one of her closest friends, Fiona, Fiona had noticed her hands trembling and pressed a cigarette on her to calm her.

Somehow the giddying, soothing sense of the smoke in her lungs had worked. Victoria had relaxed. Since then she'd smoked several cigarettes a day, the rough black Gitanes that Fiona, a painter, had learnt to smoke at her art school in Paris.

Victoria inhaled. Again the tobacco steadied her. She had felt, she still felt, bewildered. Now she could at least begin to concentrate.

She had many bundles of papers to read. So far she'd only been through the first few. They carried Grandpa's career up to his early twenties. In a way the first two bundles were straightforward enough. They took Ruthven through his private school to Eton, and then on to Cambridge.

She looked at the remaining packages piled on the floor beside her chair, and reached for the next group of letters. She began to untie the string. Then she yawned and stopped. She was too tired. She put out her cigarette and went to bed.

Just before she fell asleep she found herself thinking about Ruthven's shadowy boyhood friend, Eric Yeats. For the second time Yeats, whoever he was, seemed to have been involved in a major experience in Ruthven's career.

The telephone rang at 8.30 a.m.

Sleepily Victoria reached out and picked it up.

'Darling! You're back. How lovely. And how was Glenmoray and the old ladies?'

It was her mother. Victoria described her visit and they talked for a few minutes.

Then Victoria said, 'Mum, just remind me about Grandpa. He was a great scholar, wasn't he?'

'Are you still thinking about writing something?' her mother answered. 'Oh, darling, I'm really not sure it makes any sense. I told you before. It's all been done. But since you ask, yes, of course, he was a famous scholar. He was given degrees almost everywhere, even by American universities.'

'I was thinking about Cambridge.'

'Where he started? He was utterly brilliant. He got his double first, of course. Then later they gave him a doctorate. But even as an undergraduate he did much more. He won blues for sports and he was president of all sorts of things—'

Her mother paused. 'Darling, you know all of that. It's in the books. Look it up. Why are you asking me?'

Victoria managed to feign a laugh. 'Just because I got back late and I'm tired, and the great-aunts were talking about him and I'd forgotten.'

'Well, go back to sleep and then come and have lunch. Rosalind's coming round at one without the Sotogrande bores. We'll all go to San Lorenzo.'

'Yes, Mum.'

Victoria put the telephone down.

She thought for a while. Then she dialled directory inquiries. A few minutes afterwards she was speaking to the Bursar of Magdalene College in Cambridge.

She began hesitantly. 'I'm not really sure I've come through to the right place. My name's Victoria Ruthven. I'm the grand-daughter of Colonel Jack Ruthven.'

'Good heavens, Colonel Ruthven!' The voice at the other end of the line was alert and quick and friendly. 'One of our most famous Fellows. How can I help?'

'I'm researching a monograph on him,' Victoria said. 'I wondered if I could come and see what records you've got on his time at Magdalene.'

'Well now.' The Bursar paused in thought. 'I doubt we'll have much, but I'll certainly see what I can unearth. The problem is, I've got to fly out to a conference in Helsinki tomorrow evening. The morning's free, but after that I'm stuck. How much in a hurry are you?'

'I'd like to check this part of his career as soon as I can.'

'Can you make it to Cambridge by, let's say, eleven tomorrow?'

Charlie was a Cambridge graduate. They'd often gone there together. Victoria knew it was barely an hour and a half's drive from London.

'Yes, certainly,' she answered.

'Go to the porters' lodge and get them to direct you to my rooms. I'll see you then.'

The Bursar was younger than she'd imagined a Cambridge college administrator would be, in his early fifties perhaps.

His physical presence was like his voice, as energetic as a leaping salmon. He bounded up to greet her, led her to a chair, and almost thrust her down on to the seat. Then he returned to his desk and picked up a thin sheaf of papers, running his hands through his silver-flecked hair as he looked at them.

'How excellent to have another Ruthven here!' He glanced up. 'Although of course we have women undergraduates now as you must know.'

Victoria shook her head. 'I wasn't aware of it,' she said lamely.

'Oh, yes. It causes all manner of problems from broken hearts to demands for tampon-dispensing machines. But it's probably right. We haven't really moved with the times, but at least we've drifted with them. Although what Colonel Ruthven would have made of it all—'

He broke off and smiled.

'I've done my best, Miss Ruthven, but I fear I haven't come up with much. We've got a new system now, all on computer. We're trying to build archives on our most distinguished graduates and Fellows. The Pepys Librarian runs it. Wonderful chap, a real new-generation boffin. But even he can only get out of his disks what's been put into them. And there's not an awful lot.'

Victoria opened her bag. She pulled out her notebook and glanced at what she'd scrawled down from Jackson's biography.

'My grandfather came up to Magdalene in 1913.'

The Bursar nodded.

'According to family history he graduated with a double first.'

'Ah!' He pressed his fingers together in a thoughtful little steeple.

'Not exactly. In fact technically he didn't graduate at all, but matters were arranged differently in those days.'

'I don't understand.'

'Colonel Ruthven left here after only two terms. He apparently went out to South Africa on a mission for the government. Later he wrote asking to be assessed on his work before leaving. He'd obviously impressed his supervisor considerably. He was graded, as we call it now, as a first.'

Victoria frowned. 'So he was given a first without really getting it at all?'

'That's one way of looking at it. But, as I say, life was different then. There was much more *va-et-vient*, tolerance, academic flexibility.' He chuckled. 'I call it the BPWI era, the golden age before-pigeonholes-were-invented.'

'What about the double first?' The frown was still on Victoria's face.

'I've no idea where that came from, but it's not hard to guess. If you're associated with one first, you tend to get credited with two. It slides into myth.'

Victoria stared at him.

He wasn't only agile and energetic, he was clever and he had no axe to grind. She believed him. What he'd said suggested Grandpa wasn't the obvious fraud she'd begun to imagine from reading the letters and postcards to his mother.

Jack Ruthven hadn't won a first, but he'd been assessed as a first. And it wasn't hard to see how without any manipulation it had been translated into a double first. The rest – the sporting triumphs and the presidencies of clubs and organisations – were probably equally true or at least half-true.

Even in the two brief terms he'd spent at Magdalene, Ruthven had made an impact not just on the college but on the university as well.

'The only other thing I've come up with is this.'

Victoria had been about to ask a question, but the Bursar spoke before her. He pushed a photograph across the desk.

'As I told you, we're building up archives. We appeal in the college newsletter for contributions from the past. Someone sent us this. The Librarian had it scanned and put on disk.'

She looked at the picture.

It showed a group of young men holding tennis racquets. They were wearing striped blazers and ribboned straw hats. They were gazing at the camera with the stiff, uncomfortable expressions of people to whom photography was a new and unsettling experience. One of them was obviously her grandfather.

The others were unknown to her, but their names were printed below. She read through them and checked. The question she'd been about to ask had been answered.

'Colonel Ruthven had a childhood acquaintance,' she said. 'He was called Eric Yeats. I see he's here.'

'Ah, the great Eric Yeats.'

Victoria blinked in astonishment. 'The *great* Eric Yeats?'

'You haven't heard of him?' The Bursar looked at her, equally startled. 'Well, I suppose he was a rather enigmatic figure and certainly before my time, let alone yours. But, yes, he was remarkable. Not only a true double first, if I may say so without disparaging your grandfather, but one of our most generous benefactors this century.'

Victoria's eyes widened again. 'Then he must have been rich?'

'One of the richest men in Britain.'

She shook her head.

It made no sense to her. She'd imagined Yeats as a timid little figure, the son of some dull, socially-aspiring merchant, who'd clung to Grandpa's coat-tails and then, quite wrongly, been made the schoolboy scapegoat for Ruthven's adventures.

Of course, as she'd discovered, Yeats' father had become rich and this had somehow allowed Yeats to take Ruthven to South Africa with him. But she'd no idea quite how wealthy he was, or that he was academically brilliant.

'What was Yeats' degree in?' she asked.

'Anticipating you might ask questions like that, I asked the Librarian for archival printouts of everyone in the photograph.' The Bursar chuckled complacently at his foresight. 'Yeats graduated in the natural sciences, an unusual choice at the time. His particular interest was birds. Here—'

He handed her a slim bundle of papers. 'It's not much, but you can take them away and read them.'

Victoria folded the papers and put them into her bag.

'Where did his money come from?' she asked.

All Victoria was after was confirmation of what she'd deduced from the letters. She got it.

'His father. Mr Yeats senior was one of Cecil Rhodes' partners in the South African gold and diamond mines. Almost overnight they all became, as far as I can tell, multi-millionaires.'

'And of course Eric Yeats died a long time ago?'

'Died?' The Bursar looked at her, puzzled again. 'My dear, Yeats and his wife were murdered in 1939. Their deaths remains one of the great unsolved mysteries of the British colonial presence in Africa, an even greater puzzle for those who concern themselves with such matters than the killing of Lord Erroll.'

Victoria stood up.

She smiled brightly. 'Thank you for all the help you've given me. I'll read the printouts when I get home.'

She drove back to London through the dusk of a bitterly cold January evening.

11

'Danny.' Victoria leaned forward and took his hand. 'How do you start in becoming gay?'

'I beg your pardon?' He stared at her. 'Are you after a lesson in first-step sex techniques? I can certainly provide one, but I'm not sure it'll help much. They kitted us out with rather different plumbing . . .'

He smiled. 'Who's the immensely lucky lady?'

She shook her head and laughed.

Danny was an Ethiopian, tiny, dark-skinned, and exquisitely handsome. Charlie had met him and introduced him to Victoria while he was researching an African story. According to Charlie, he was related to the late Emperor Hailie Selassie through one of the complicated dynastic webs that embraced the Ethiopian royal family.

Danny was certainly rich.

He was nominally an actor, but he seemed to survive in great comfort during the long periods in which in the theatre world's phrase he was 'resting'. He'd been educated at Eton and he spoke English with what Victoria found a delightful mixture of street slang and old-fashioned colloquialisms.

She'd been enchanted by him at their first encounter. Since then he'd become a close and trusted friend. He was flamboyantly homosexual, but one of the rare people she knew she could talk to about it easily and openly.

'It's not me,' she said. 'It's my grandfather.'

'Well, he must have had a whopper, darling. I find it hard enough to get one up the back. If he was navigating through the front too, they should put him on the silver screen. What about Rambo-every-which-way?'

'Please, Danny, don't be vulgar!'

He always had the same effect on her, reducing her to almost helpless laughter.

'I want to know about him. How it might have happened.'

Danny sensed the change in her voice and he responded instantly with his quicksilver sensitivity.

'How what might have happened, darling?'

'He had this friend from his early childhood. Their lives somehow seem to have been linked. I just wonder if they had a homosexual relationship.'

It was the evening after she'd returned from Cambridge.

Victoria had read the printouts the Bursar had given her on the six men in the photograph. The one on Grandpa added little to what she already knew. Four of the others consisted of only a few lines. She didn't know if they had featured in Ruthven's later life. Somehow she didn't think so.

The one on Yeats was the most interesting.

It revealed virtually nothing about the man, but it did chronicle what he and his father had done for the college. The range and amount of their donations were extraordinary. The gifts spanned thirty years and they covered everything from a handsome sum on a head-porter's retirement to financing the building of an entirely new court for fifty undergraduates.

The printout ended with the Librarian's comment: 'Eric Yeats must be counted among the college's most munificent patrons in all its five-hundred-year existence. It seems in retrospect particularly appropriate that one of his closest friends here was Jack Ruthven, later Colonel Ruthven, the war hero, ornithologist and explorer who became one of the college's most distinguished Fellows.'

Victoria hadn't looked at the other bundles of papers she'd removed from Glenmoray.

She wanted to position Grandpa in her mind first, to examine if her guess was right. A homosexual entanglement with Yeats seemed the only way to explain why the two of them had been linked together so often, and at such formative moments of their lives.

Homosexual affairs were common enough at the time, but the world of male homosexuality was utterly unknown to her. That was why she had telephoned Danny. She wasn't sure what she wanted from him or how it might help her. She just wanted to learn something about the way Danny was – and perhaps Ruthven and Yeats had been too.

'It's not like what you think,' Danny answered. 'There isn't just one way of going gay and staying gay, any more than being straight. You can be a Tennessee Williams and go to a dozen cottages and bath-houses every night. Or you can come home and cook dinner for someone every night for fifty years, and never look at anyone else—'

Danny put his elbows on the table and placed his face between his hands.

'You choose your own path. Or rather it chooses you.'

'But how does it begin?' Victoria insisted.

'The same way as it does for you. You look at someone and think, whee, scrummy, I want him!'

'But why?'

'Why a man and not a woman?' Danny gave a graceful little shrug. 'Darling, I don't know. No one does. Mummy didn't love you, she loved you too much. Your father beat you, he didn't. You had too many genes, too few. Your trousers were too tight, or they put you in boxer shorts, or they made you wear dresses because you weren't the daughter they'd longed for. Take your pick.'

Victoria thought. 'Why did my grandfather, if he even did, have a relationship with Eric Yeats?'

'Possibly for the oldest reason in the world. He fell in love. It happens to all of us, even poofs like me. We may go for bums rather than befores, but the principle's the same. We want to have and to hold.'

Danny stretched out and caught her arms.

'Passion, my blossom, passion. It's the curse and miracle of being alive.'

He paused. 'What happened to your grandfather's mysterious friend, this maybe or maybe-not lover, Mr Yeats?'

'He was murdered,' Victoria answered.

'Really? How strange. And in what circumstances? Was Grandpa the mad axeman killer?'

'Of course not.'

The idea of gentle and beloved Grandpa murdering anyone was so ludicrous she'd answered more sharply than she intended.

Danny lowered his head. 'Forgive me for even being born. It was only a simple black man's jest. But such things have happened when lovers fall out.'

'You're impossible, Danny!' Victoria laughed. 'Sorry if I snapped, but it's not very likely. I was thinking more of a mutual boyish infatuation that burned itself out when they grew up. Is that possible?'

'Certainly. All those adolescent pheremones rushing around with no place to go except up the cavity of the likely lad in the next-door bed. And then you grow up and find there's more to life than rear entrances—'

He grinned. 'Unless you're me. I'm so used to back doors, it's the only way I can get in.'

Victoria leaned over the table and kissed him. 'I wish you weren't.'

'No, you don't. We'd have dusky children with ginger hair and quaint Ethiopian noses. An aesthetic nightmare. You're much better off with Charlie.'

'Charlie's gone,' she said flatly.

Danny looked at her, startled. 'You mean he's buggered off, if I can say that without causing offence? Darling, I thought you were a permanent item.'

'Pastures and knickers new,' she answered. 'The bastard!'

'In which case,' Danny said thoughtfully, 'I think we need champagne. Not a bottle but a damn great magnum.'

He beckoned to the waiter.

Victoria took a taxi home from the wine bar in the Fulham Road where she'd met Danny.

The champagne had been exactly what she wanted.

It had made her feel exhilarated, angry, confident, and tired. The long winter drive east to Aberdeen and the flight back had left her exhausted, but the compulsion to stay up until 4.00 a.m. to read the first bundles of the papers she'd brought with her meant she had slept for only a few hours. Now she knew she'd sleep round the clock.

She paid the taxi-driver off and stood for a moment in the chill darkness outside the door to her flat.

Danny had been wonderful.

He hadn't really said anything, he hadn't proved anything, but in a way he'd confirmed the possibility that had occurred to her. He'd put it in a context she could understand. Yes, it was possible Ruthven and Yeats had had a youthful relationship – passion and love were how Danny described what might have been its beginnings.

And if that was so, yes, it was equally possible they'd grown up from it, grown away from it, and gone their separate ways in an adult world, a heterosexual world. Eric Yeats had inherited his father's vast fortune and married. Her grandfather had set out on his extraordinary wandering career and eventually married too.

What she hadn't known until her visit to Cambridge was that Yeats had been murdered. She still had no idea of the circumstances surrounding his death. The printout had merely referred to his 'early and sad demise'. Although his and Ruthven's paths had probably diverged long before, there might be references to it in the papers that remained to be read.

They would have to wait until the morning.

Victoria felt the champagne bubbles in her blood begin to lose their sparkle. An immense weariness overtook her. She thought of Charlie – seeing Danny had reminded her of him – and she swore bitterly and furiously. Then she unlocked the door to her flat.

She went into her bedroom. Without even bothering to undress, she threw herself down on the bed and slept.

12

Victoria didn't quite sleep round the clock, but it was afternoon before she woke.

The dank chill sky outside the windows was already darkening, and she shivered as she got out of bed. She had a bath, she made herself a cup of coffee, then she settled down to read again.

The next five bundles of the Ruthven papers consisted mainly of notebooks. As objects they were remarkably attractive in themselves. They were half-bound in faded scarlet leather, they had vivid marbled endpapers in skeins of emerald and blue, and the pages were thick and a rich creamy-yellow in colour.

The notebooks had been bought either at Harrods or from Green and Stone, the art suppliers who still traded in the King's Road – the names of the two shops were printed on the inside of the card and leather bindings. Victoria remembered buying Charlie his birthday present two years before from Green and Stone.

Charlie had decided he was a painter as well as a journalist. She'd searched for hours and finally found a tiny nineteenth-century iron palette, still in its metal box and filled with the original squares of paint. She doubted whether he had used it much, but she noticed it was one of the objects he'd scooped up and taken with him when he left.

Victoria cursed him again and lit a cigarette. She opened the first notebook.

Sandwiched between its covers and occasionally tucked into its pages were more letters and postcards. It was the same with the other notebooks. Carefully noting where every letter and card came from, she removed them, labelled them with stickers, and put them to one side. Then she turned to what Ruthven had written in the journals themselves. They contained, as she thought, what would interest her most.

She was wrong.

They were Ruthven's ornithological records, check lists of the birds he'd seen and identified on his travels. Each list was dated and the place where it had been compiled named. Glenmoray inevitably featured often, although he'd visited many other sites in Britain from the Norfolk Broads to Wales to the Somerset Levels.

At the start he'd put in occasional comments about the species he'd found. In the Cambrian mountains of Wales he'd written a few lyrical lines about the red kite.

Oh, what glory to see this rarest of Britain's birds! It put me in mind of Gerard Manley Hopkins: 'I saw this morning morning's minion, kingdom of daylight's dauphin . . .' Except it was finer, grander still, a gold and bronze and auburn arrow fired straight from the sun. It planed and wheeled and soared into the broken clouds above me. If angels take material form, then surely they choose this.

The later notebooks spread out geographically to embrace the start of his foreign travels.

There were pages headed 'Camargue, southern France', 'Marshes north-east of Istanbul', 'An area of plain west of Tehran'. The comments became more frequent, and also more detailed and more technical.

'It seems that spoonbills and squacco herons share nesting sites and tolerate without aggression each other's presence,' he wrote on a visit to Spain. 'Tomorrow I shall try to calculate the respective density of their nests in the grove of cork oaks that lie across the lagoon.'

Slowly Victoria turned the pages.

She knew very little about birds, but there seemed to be nothing here except the straightforward observations of a keen and careful eye. Her grandfather had been born towards the end of the Victorian era. He came from a long and honourable tradition of amateur gentlemen naturalists.

All that distinguished him from his contemporaries, what had put him, in the words of his hapless biographer, 'virtually on a level with Darwin', was the breadth of his knowledge and the range of his discoveries. There was certainly nothing to indicate fraud and deceit, let alone on the massive scale the young man at the Natural History Museum had claimed.

Victoria lit another cigarette.

She continued to read through the species lists and the increasingly complicated notes. Then she stiffened.

The year was 1913 and Ruthven had gone back to Spain. He'd based himself somewhere south of Seville – the entry was headed 'Palacio of Dona Ana, Guadalquivir river, Sevilla'. There was the by now familiar check list and ornithological comments. Then he broke off and began to write in a totally different style.

Too hot, too hot, too hot!

Certes, too hot to sleep. And there's no one to talk to and I've drunk the last of the hot-blooded rioja little Juani packed for me, and I'm alive and well and awake.

Have I made my notes on the pratincoles?

Yes, I have. And on the flamingoes, too – although I must remember to try to devise a way to see whether they move between here and the Rhône's delta – and I've also sketched that lynx. I must send the drawing to Mama.

God help me, but it's lovely here. The full moon's reflection on the lake. Owls calling (yes, I've got them all logged). A deer barking. And Dona Ana's rambling delight of a palace, this great hunting lodge, stretching out all round me with its honey-coloured walls of stone.

Did Goya really paint the naked maja here? And was she the Duchess of Alba? And was she his mistress?

I have in front of me one of those colour what-nots they sell at the Prado. I brought it from Madrid. It's not much, murky. But it does show the way her body lies and the folds of it and the way the watcher is drawn inexorably to the place below where she holds the secret. Wouldn't the fieriest of our desires be to learn the secret?

God help me again, but what have you done to me, Eric? Involving me in this whole damn bird game. And then, most of all, finding S.

If there's one place on earth, one place in the entire solar system, I'd like to be now with S, it's here. S naked like the maja. Not doing anything. Just watching her like Goya did with Alba's duchess. That's enough for us mere mortals.

Or maybe Goya did conjoin with her. Can mortals couple with goddesses? Perhaps artists can. Touch them, stroke them with the softness of a flighting owl's wing, hold them for an instant in male human arms – can they?

Oh, dear God, I'm rambling like the palacio's rambling

corridors. I'm probably drunk – too much of Juani's rioja. Good night, sweet prince, and damn you to hell while I'm about it.

Victoria put the notebook down.

She lifted her hands and combed her fingers through her hair. She lit another cigarette.

She was astounded.

Grandpa Jack had always been an island of peace, a pillar of tranquillity. Not just to her but to everyone in the family. None of the turbulent emotions, the tides of love and hate that so tormented everyone else, had ever surged round him. He had simply stood calm and upright, white-bearded and smiling, for ever their patriarch and guardian.

What she'd just read seemed to contradict it all.

It was almost worse than the claim by the young scientist in the museum that Ruthven was a fraud. Ruthven might have been drunk when he wrote it, but the passion, the eroticism, and the confusion could only have been there anyway. He might still be majestic in the way Victoria had always been taught to see him, but he was beginning to appear haunted and blighted too.

The 'Eric' could only be Eric Yeats.

She'd been right about that. Whatever the relationship between the two of them, Yeats had been deeply threaded into Ruthven's life. He'd introduced Ruthven, or so it appeared, to the study of birds. He'd also introduced Ruthven to the mysterious S.

Victoria racked her brains.

There was no one in family history or in the biography or in anything she'd ever read about Grandpa whose name began with S. She was obviously a woman – Ruthven's erotic fantasy about the secret she held between her legs made that clear. The only S Victoria could recall was the Sophia her mother had identified as Yeats's wife.

It was inconceivable that she was the woman who had haunted and tormented the youthful Ruthven. Victoria reached for the next bundle of papers and letters. As she did the telephone rang.

Victoria picked it up.

'Yes?'

'Hello, sunshine, light of my life and consolation of my declining years—'

The laughter was a little uneasy, but the voice was unmistakable. It was Charlie.

'What do you want?' She cut him off.

'Can we possibly meet?'

'Hang on, I'm just going to look in the dictionary for the word I want.' She drummed her fingers on the table for a few seconds. 'I've just found it. It seems to be called no or never or fuck off.'

'Victoria, please—'

'Are you sure you don't mean Angela? She's the one with the embroidered A on her carefully sliding bra-strap.'

'Darling, it's about a story.'

'Oh, lovely. Another fairy-story. You won't need my help with that.'

'Victoria, it's about a man called Yeats,' he pleaded. 'It may involve Jack Ruthven.'

She was already putting the telephone down and she only just caught Charlie's words.

Victoria hesitated, almost in shock. Then she put the receiver back to her ear.

'What do you want to know about Yeats and my grandfather?'

'I'm not sure,' he said. 'It's an assignment from Features. It's strange and interesting. Can I explain it over dinner?'

'If it's going to be dinner, it's going to be very, very expensive. Champagne and quite possibly caviare. And if you're thinking of bringing Angela, forget it. I've just bought a rottweiller. He's been trained from puppyhood to rip bras off sluts. He's coming with me and he's hungry.'

They met at the restaurant Victoria had chosen in Kensington Park Road.

She was deliberately half an hour late. When she got there Charlie was sitting anxiously at the table. He stood up and tried to embrace her, but she pushed him away. She sat down.

'Champagne?' she said.

'On the table.'

She glanced across. She hadn't noticed the bottle, but it was there. He filled her glass.

'Caviare?'

'It comes in every size from a portion up to a kilo. I waited until I knew what you wanted.'

'We'll start with a kilo and work up from there.' Victoria paused. 'And Angela?'

'She's working.'

'I don't know what she charges for half an hour, but hang on to half of it. That's being generous. Serious pimps take eighty per cent.'

'Victoria—'

'Please call me Miss Ruthven, and tell me what you want.'

Charlie closed his eyes. 'Victoria, you're what the Americans call a very feisty lady. You're also being very difficult.'

'I'm neither feisty nor difficult,' she answered. 'I'm just a person, a woman, who got landed with a copper-bottomed silver-plated shit.'

'I think I'd better order caviare.'

'I think you had. Let's start with two kilos rather than one.'

The caviare came. They ate it with chilled vodka. Then they talked.

'Our South Africa desk put me on to it,' Charlie said. 'After the collapse of apartheid all sorts of things happened. Files were opened. Strange stories began to emerge. The creation of the Kimberley diamond and gold mines was one of them—'

He tilted his head to one side in the speculative, frowning gesture Victoria knew so well.

'Kimberley's one story, but there were spin-offs from Kimberley. The original Kimberley investors staked out claims of their own. They created a web of mining interests. Today they underpin the whole South African economy. The tentacles reach out into Botswana, Namibia, Zambia, Zimbabwe, and Angola. Each time you track them back to their beginnings, the same names come up. Among them is a family called Yeats.'

'What's *your* story?' Victoria asked.

'I don't have one yet,' Charlie said. 'But the scenario's fascinating. There were two Yeats, father and son. The son, Eric, inherited his father's fortune. Eric was murdered in Bechuanaland, what's now Botswana. No one seems to know where the money was passed on. It's all tied up in blind trusts registered in the Cayman Islands. The lawyers won't say a damn thing. It's untraceable.'

'Then it doesn't matter. It's just private money.'

'Not quite. It's land and rivers too. The Yeats Foundation – it must have secured charitable status for tax-efficiency reasons – owns a lot of the Okavango delta. In effect it controls the water supply to the Orapa diamond mines. And because of that –' Charlie windmilled his hands expressively '– it dominates Botswana's economy. And then, as the pyramid builds up, because Botswana's become so rich and is actually a lender of money to South Africa, it plays a significant role in determining South Africa's fate.'

Victoria sat in silence. 'What on earth has this got to do with me?' she asked after a while.

'Our people in Johannesburg checked the records. The only other identifiable investor in the Yeats companies was Colonel Ruthven. I thought you might know something about it, might have access to some family papers, might be able to give me a lead to who owns the Foundation now.'

She stared at him.

'So I'm a source, Charlie, am I now?'

'No, darling, of course not. Just a friendly helping hand.'

'I'm not friendly, I'm not a helping hand, and I'm not a source—!'

She got to her feet, shouting. Everywhere in the restaurant heads were turning towards their table.

'I'm a person who loved you and a stupid cunt, a one-time repository for where you put your thingy! Now darling beloved Angela can spread her legs out until you debonairly move on again. Good luck to both of you. Meanwhile, fuck off!'

She paused. She was panting. All round them there was silence. Even the waiters were standing frozen.

'You can keep this!' She hurled what was left of the vodka over him. 'I'm taking the fish eggs with me.'

Victoria picked up the remains of the caviare and stormed out.

13

Victoria sat and wept.

Over and over again she cursed herself.

Not for what she'd done at the end of dinner. That had been the one truly satisfying part of the evening. She'd unhesitatingly do the same again and next time probably break the vodka bottle over Charlie's head. No, it was the realisation of her reason for agreeing to meet him at all.

It wasn't the story about the Yeats companies and Ruthven's apparent involvement in them.

It was, she knew, simply because she wanted to see Charlie again. She'd barely even listened to what he'd said. He'd come on the line and like a fool, an idiot, a swooning lovesick adolescent, she'd agreed.

She thought she'd kept her dignity, a proper professional coldness, but inside her her heart had turned over as soon as she saw him. It had always been like that from the moment they met. Tonight she'd sat and looked at him, at his sleepy heavy-lidded eyes, at his smile, at the powerful but immensely sensitive hands which had so often combed through her hair or run over her body, and it had been too much.

Still enraged but not crying now, Victoria leaped to her feet.

She prowled through the flat searching cupboards and drawers for something he might have overlooked, something she could throw out on to the street.

There was nothing. For a lumbering bear of a man he was extraordinarily neat and methodical. He'd taken everything. There wasn't even a handkerchief, a tube of toothpaste left. He'd removed his entire presence.

And yet the bastard still wanted to use her as a source, a gateway into one of his stories. Victoria opened her mouth and screamed.

A moment later there was a tap on her door. She opened it. Old Mr Foster, her neighbour downstairs, was standing in his dressing-gown on the landing. He looked concerned.

'Are you all right, Victoria?' he asked.

'Yes, of course.'

'I just heard a noise. You can't be too careful nowadays. Those bloody blacks, they break in everywhere. I thought they might have gone for you.'

Victoria smiled brightly. 'I'm afraid it was me shouting. I'm trying something called primal therapy. I won't do it again this late.'

'Well, I'm here if you want me, dear.'

Mr Foster shuffled away down the stairs. Victoria closed the door and sat down again.

Somehow the old man's appearance had broken the spell of misery and resentment that seeing Charlie had cast over her. Victoria began to think rationally again.

She had the remaining bundles of papers and notebooks to go through. She also had questions to consider.

She sat frowning in thought.

Eric Yeats had indeed been a major figure in Ruthven's life. She'd suspected as much and Charlie had confirmed it. Ruthven had been an investor in the Yeats' companies. It almost certainly explained why Ruthven had been able to buy Bowley and left such a large fortune, a fortune that could never have been generated by the large but barren lands of Glenmoray.

The Yeats' mining and commercial interests – or, rather, the Foundation into which they'd been incorporated – were now a significant influence on southern Africa. According to Charlie, their tentacles reached out beyond South Africa itself into Namibia, Zimbabwe, Angola, and Botswana.

Victoria knew nothing about Yeats' death but, again according to Charlie, he'd been murdered in Botswana.

Those aspects of Grandpa's past – the Yeats' empire and Eric Yeats' killing – were complicated enough. Even they didn't begin to exhaust the rest of what in a few weeks Victoria had already begun to learn must have been a remarkably tangled life.

Apart from the completely unexplained twining of Ruthven's and Yeats' lives – and the misadventures that must have changed the career of one and affected the other's – there was S.

Who on earth was she?

Victoria wasn't convinced S was a woman, in spite of her mother's identification of a Sophia as Yeats' wife in the photograph on her table. The references to Goya's *Naked Maja* in Ruthven's notebooks suggested she was female – always assuming the references related to her – but Victoria knew well enough that in the climate of the times sexual transpositions were often made.

Even today the more camp of her own gay friends still referred to an attractive young man as 'she', and Victoria was increasingly sure there had been a homosexual relationship between Yeats and her grandfather.

S was an object of desire, of passionate desire. He, if it was a male, might well have been, in Ruthven's erotic fantasies, a man portrayed as Goya's duchess. Whoever he or she was, Victoria was also fairly sure that both Ruthven and Yeats had carried a fiery torch for the person.

Victoria picked up the letters and postcards she'd carefully extracted from the journals. She started to sift through them.

S was a woman.

It took hours to unravel.

Most of the letters and postcards that interleaved the notebooks had been sent by Jack Ruthven to his mother. They had clearly developed a private language to communicate with each other – Victoria had noticed it before – and the messages were almost written in code.

Strange words or phrases kept cropping up. 'She's weaverity-beaverity towards the hearthstone, but her little "gel's" lame as an autumn lamp-post. Don't worry, darling M. Letters will be left at the glen's mouth.'

Victoria puzzled over the meaning.

Eventually, using references in other letters, she worked it out. Some ambitious mother had been pressing the charms of her daughter on Ruthven. He'd found the girl unattractive, and he was saying he would back away from any further approaches.

The first clue as to how S had entered Ruthven's life, although Victoria had to read further before she confirmed it, was in a letter of thanks from Ruthven to his mother for a present on his twenty-second birthday.

Oh darling Mama, totally and always and unfailingly reliable, the one unchanging point, the beacon star in my life! Of course, it arrived early but so much better that than late. Trust you to be so careful with the steamer sailings!

And what a cornucopia it was! The Fortnum's hamper contained everything I like best and miss most. The books, so superbly chosen, are another feast waiting to be relished. The hat will never leave my head on my travels in the bush. Best of all, far and away best of all, were your water-colour painting of Glenmoray and your poem to me.

How it made my heart ache to be back with you at that place of enchantment. How both you and the noble hills throng my dreams. Well, it won't be long. Meanwhile, I have my anniversary day itself to pass.

Eric took charge of the celebrations for that months ago. I am not allowed to know the plans – they are a fiercely guarded secret – except we go down to Cape Town to stay at the 'Nellie'. (I think I told you that is how the Mount Nelson Hotel is known.)

There I assume we will carouse.

I happened to see a P&O liner is due in the day before we arrive, so I anticipate company. More than that I cannot imagine, although Eric has been positively salivating in triumph these weeks past. What devilish entertainment he has devised only time will reveal.

You naturally will be the first after me to know.

A letter dated two weeks later told what had happened.

Even as Victoria read through the first few lines she was aware something had changed. Ruthven's florid emotional style had for once been replaced by something more studied and restrained.

Well, Eric did his best and I have to thank him for it. Yet it wasn't what I'd expected and certainly not what I wanted.

We arrived at the Nellie two days before my birthday. We settled in. On the day itself Eric had organised a large dinner. As I had guessed the guests were mainly passengers from the P&O ship. Most interesting company they proved, too – I was most struck with a conversation I had with a young man of about my age who will also be joining the Governor-General's staff.

Eric's particular 'surprise' was to have booked passage on the ship for a young woman, a *chanteuse* and dancer from London, named, I think, Sophia. To my considerable embarrassment he had seated her at table next to me. What a fearful tease he can be!

While personable in a way, she was not my type at all and we found little to talk about. However she did prove an excellent entertainer. After dinner she amused us all with ballads and music-hall songs from both London and Paris. Apparently she has quite a reputation.

So that was the celebration and, to be fair to Eric, a very fine and generous one it was, although the guests he'd assembled probably enjoyed it rather more than I did. Five days later he and I headed back north leaving his 'present', the young woman, or so I assume – we didn't see her after the dinner – to take the next sailing home.

Enough of that. Let me tell you of activities since my return . . .

Victoria went on.

She finished the letter and read the first part again. She glanced back at what Grandfather had written about S at the palace of Dona Ana. S and Sophia had to be the same.

Victoria drew in her breath. For the first time that evening she forgot her own misery and smiled.

Lies. All lies.

What Jack Ruthven had elaborately written to his mother was utter rubbish. He betrayed himself with every transparently contrived and disdainful word. She wondered if Lady Ruthven had been taken in by it. It was quite possible. Besotted mothers were capable of believing anything they were told by an adoring only son.

Ruthven didn't want his mother to know the truth. That he'd been beguiled, captivated, overwhelmed by Sophia. Sophia, whoever she was, had spun singing and dancing into the life of a passionate but naive and innocent young man like a hurricane.

And she hadn't just been brought out to Cape Town to sing and dance. Yeats, as Victoria was starting to see, was manipulative and mischievous. Sophia had been bought passage, Victoria was certain, to remove Grandfather of his virginity and even to give him the experience of falling in love.

Ruthven might not have lost his virginity then – all Victoria's instincts told her he hadn't – but that, not the songs, was the devious Yeats' real intended birthday present.

Victoria lit another cigarette and stared into the night.

14

'I'm afraid I haven't got much to go on,' Victoria said apologetically.

'You haven't got much!' the man burst out. 'I've got bugger-all, love. Not even a bloody fiver against the telephone bill. Up whatnot creek without a paddle and the crocs biting holes in the boat, that's me.'

'No, I mean—'

'It's all right, love,' he chuckled. 'I know what you mean. We'll see what we can do.'

He bustled away. Victoria waited.

The man's name was Mr Gable. 'As in Clark Gable', he'd told her. 'For an aspiring spear-carrier to the knights of the theatre, soon to be fabled myself, it seemed a good idea at the time. Better than Ray Smithers, anyway. Not that it ever did much bloody good even with Peregrine in front of it.'

Mr Peregrine Gable was about seventy.

He was short and fat with a bulbous nose, bloodshot eyes, and long white hair that cascaded dandruff over the shoulders of his frayed velvet jacket. Victoria had got his name from a friend who worked as a theatre-set designer. The former Ray Smithers had been an actor who'd developed an obsession with the old-fashioned music-hall.

When his career, even with the new name of Peregrine Gable, had foundered, he'd decided to devote his life to creating a museum and library of the music-hall. Somehow, begging, cajoling, and importuning for funds, he'd secured enough money over the years from theatrical charities to build up his collection.

It had the magnificent title of 'The Thespian's Heritage: All the World's a Stage and Here is the Players' Lifeblood Preserved'. The words were inscribed on a pottery plaque beside the door of his pebble-dash-fronted house in a suburb of Croydon.

Victoria had telephoned, made an appointment, and driven down to meet him.

'How about a steadier to get us on our way?'

He was removing the cork from a flask of what Victoria could see was cooking brandy. It was 10.00 a.m.

She smiled and shook her head. 'Too early for me.'

'Never too early, darling. Because one of these days, particularly at my age, it'll be too late.' He poured himself a glass and swallowed it. He wiped his mouth. 'Sophia? Apart from the date, that's all?'

'Well, it seems she could sing in French and she visited Capetown.'

'My dear, there were hundreds like her at the time. You're young, you've an enchantingly sensitive face, vulgarity is foreign to my nature—'

He waved his hands vaguely. 'How can I put it? They tended to have more than one talent.'

'You mean she could well have been a courtesan?'

'How bold and modern! But what a charming word to use. In other circumstances I might have chosen something earthier. Yes, it's possible. The stage-door Johnnies of the time were beguiled by their beauty. Johnny's money beguiled them. They came to mutually agreeable arrangements.'

'I've heard of it,' Victoria said bluntly. 'It's called prostitution.'

Mr Gable looked profoundly shocked. 'My dear, that's positively audacious.'

'I do live at the end of the twentieth century.' Victoria smiled sweetly. 'Whether she was a courtesan, a prostitute, a *chanteuse*, or all three, could we try to find her?'

'It calls for a further steadier,' he poured himself another drink, 'and we'll try.'

He set off across the floor. Victoria would have followed him. It was impossible.

They were on the first floor of the house. The three rooms it had contained had been knocked into a single space – 'my den, my glory-hole, my library of Alexandria', Mr Gable called it when they entered. The walls were lined with bookshelves, paintings, and hanging racks of posters. The entire floor was covered with mounds of further books, yellowing programmes, music sheets, and crates.

They formed a waist- and sometimes shoulder-high archipelago of dusty islands threaded through with almost impassibly narrow channels. Swaying and pirouetting like a ballet dancer, Mr Gable somehow navigated his way between them.

'No high expectations, love,' he said. 'The task is daunting. There were music-halls all over Britain. Thousands of artistes worked them.

Unless they became famous like Marie Lloyd, and had Sophia been famous I would have recognised her, they frequently changed their names. It made it easier to get bookings.'

He began to burrow through a pile of papers.

'Your quarry might have performed in Leeds as Louise, the capital's nightingale. In London as Matilda, the northern songbird, and only opted for Sophia when she went to Cape Town. On her return she could have gone for Alice, the sweet-throated belle of the colonies. But we'll start here in the smoke with the name you have.'

Victoria sat down on the only available seat, a lopsided, stuffing-spilling leather stool by the door.

It took at least two hours – in the dim January light it was difficult to see her watch.

Mr Gable burrowed away like a badger constructing a sett. Dust rose up in plumes, papers were tossed up and scattered spiralling through the room, sometimes he'd disappear from view altogether and all she could hear was the snuffling, grunting sound of his efforts. Occasionally his head would pop up as if for oxygen.

'Sure you don't want that steadier?'

Victoria said no until midday. Then she gave in. Mr Gable was sweating, she was chilled to the bone.

'Good girl, warms the cockles. Take a swig and spin me over the flask. It's plastic, wonderful invention, so it won't break.'

She took a drink and threw him the bottle. As Mr Gable disappeared again, she sat letting the brandy course through her.

Less than five minutes later she heard a shout of triumph.

'I think we've got it, by God I think we've got it!'

There were a few further moments of frantic scuffling. Then he emerged and danced his way back towards her, singing lines she recognised as Professor Higgins' in *My Fair Lady*.

'Look at this, my own fair lady!'

He was holding a frayed music-hall programme. It was dated 1910. It was from the Finsbury Empire theatre in London and the programme's garish colours were still unfaded.

Second on the bill of attractions was 'The new sensation the capital has been clamouring to see. Straight from her triumph in Paris she brings you the romantic ballads of the naughty boulevards with naturally all your rollicking favourites from home. For the first time we give you – Sophia!'

'And wait, fair lady, wait!'

Mr Gable's voice was hoarse with excitement.

He vanished again to return with a mahogany wooden box. He opened the lid, inserted what looked to Victoria like a complicated cylinder, and turned a brass handle on the box's side.

'Once is coincidence, twice is serendipity,' he said. 'Kevin.'

'I beg your pardon?' Victoria replied.

'Kevin wears gold earrings and a pony-tail. He's what's known as a computer buff. He's also rightly fascinated by the old-time music-hall. He's cataloguing everything I've assembled on what's called disk.'

Victoria looked blank. 'I don't understand.'

'He's starting with the most valuable stuff, the early recordings. They often made them then. Marie Lloyd, of course, but many others as well. I've bought them up from junk-shops for years. I simply don't know what I've got. Kevin showed me his first printout last week—'

Mr Gable paused. 'How I didn't remember I just don't know. It only came back to me when I found the programme. Sophia's on the list. If she's the one and the same as yours, here she is.'

He pressed a little lever. There was a whirring, rattling sound. Then a voice began to sing.

Victoria listened.

At first because the voice was so thin and reedy it was nothing more than a curiosity from the early years of music-recording technology. The sound, the words the woman was singing, conveyed nothing to her. Then the sound grew in depth and resonance, almost certainly, Victoria guessed, because the machine functioned at its best at the centre of the cylinder.

Victoria leaned forward.

The woman was singing in French. It was a Parisian ballad about the Seine and the young lovers who as they walked by the river, followed in their minds its course to the sea. Even if the woman wasn't French, she spoke the language fluently. There wasn't a misplaced stress, an awkwardly pronounced vowel.

She sang with perfect pitch. She sang with passion and regret. She sang as Victoria's own two favourite singers had done, the little sparrow, Edith Piaf, and the equally doomed black American, Billie Holiday, without sentimentality but with buoyancy and hope. The singer, young as she must have been, had looked life in the face. She'd seen it was hard pounding, but she'd decided to go on.

And then the cylinder revolved towards its other side and the voice lost everything it had held moments before. It became once more tinny and flat, a fading curiosity again.

Victoria sat for several moments, almost stunned.

Eighty years later she'd listened to the voice, assuming it was the same voice, and now she didn't doubt it, which had cast its siren song round her grandfather. She looked up for Mr Gable. He'd vanished. Before she could call out for him, he reappeared.

'You think I'm a genius, don't you?' He beamed. 'Of course I am, darling. The problem is, I know what you're going to ask next and I'm not a super-genius. I can't answer it. I may have found Sophia, but that's all I've got. Every time Kevin logs a recording of mine he inputs – isn't that a fashionable word? – every other reference I have too. There's nothing more on Sophia.'

'Nothing?'

He shook his head, spilling more dandruff over his shoulders.

'Kev, brilliant boy, has shown me how to cross-reference. Nothing. She's there in the programme and the recording. Then she vanishes. Finito.'

Victoria stood up.

'You've been wonderful. If you do come across anything else, please telephone me.' She paused. 'Is there anything I can do for you?'

'Absolutely, love. Pay the bloody telephone bill.' He rummaged around and produced it. 'Can't telephone you if I'm cut off, can I?'

Victoria looked at the bill. It was for almost £200. She closed her eyes. Then she reached for her cheque-book and wrote out a cheque for the amount.

'Bless you, fair lady!'

Mr Gable embraced her. She smelt the brandy fumes swirling across her face.

She went downstairs and drove home.

There were still several bundles of the Ruthven archive to go through, but she sensed there were other matters to be dealt with first. She needed to position herself. Before tackling the landscape ahead, she wanted to understand the landscape behind.

As she rounded Marble Arch and headed down the Bayswater Road, she wasn't thinking of any of that.

She was remembering the haunting voice that had sung to her – and to Grandfather – the ballad of the Seine and the lovers who strolled its banks gazing at the river's waters on their way to the sea.

85

15

Victoria hadn't regarded the £200 payment of Mr Gable's telephone bill as an investment.

It was just, she'd thought wearily if gratefully, a thank-you – although an expensive thank-you – for the two or more hours he'd spent searching through his files and coming up with the information about Sophia, and the recording of her voice. He was an engaging eccentric and at least she could afford it.

Mr Gable was on the telephone at 8.30 the next morning. What he said made the payment an investment after all.

'Fair lady, I'm indebted to you. I'm not cut off by the majestic telephone service. They haven't taken me to the Tower and cut off my head. I've told them a cheque's in the post, and I'm speaking to you.'

'So I can hear.'

Mr Gable chuckled. 'Kevin came round last night. You were generous. I always try to reciprocate. There is a little method in my madness. I stack my papers by the year they're dated. I put the young gladiator – can you be a gladiator with a pony-tail and earrings? – on to the stack for the year of Sophia's recording. Our Kev came up with something.'

Mr Gable went on.

If Victoria hadn't already discovered it, she'd have realised then. Mr Gable was a magpie, a collecting vacuum-cleaner who indiscriminately sucked in anything that remotely touched on his obsession. Kevin had been given the name Sophia as a trace. Combing through the pile of documents under the year of the recording, he'd found a booking agent's ledger.

Mr Gable had bought it as part of a job lot that included posters and promotional material, from the liquidator of a long-since bankrupt and defunct theatrical agency. The ledger recorded the artistes the agent handled, their engagements, and the payments made to them – less of course his large commission. Alongside some of the entries were notes, a few of them quite copious.

One entry read: 'Christina (now Sophia) back yesterday from Cape Town. Payment in full received. Will return to Paris to complete agreed autumn season. Says wants to think things over. Will not commit after Paris. NB Invoice Folies November for agreed handling fee.'

'So it really is your Sophia,' Mr Gable finished triumphantly. 'Formerly Christina – Kevin couldn't find anything under that name – she came back from South Africa and went off to the Folies-Bergère in Paris. And that's not all. There's a second ledger, one for the Christmas season—'

He read out the entry. It said simply: 'Notification from Sophia, Paris. Has retired. No further engagements. Final commission payment from FB received. Account closed.'

'How about that then?' Mr Gable chortled. 'We've traced her. She came home. She went to Paris. She left the business.'

Victoria thought. 'What's the date of the first entry?'

'Her return? September 3rd.'

'Thank you, Mr Gable, thank you very much. If you or Kevin turn up anything else, please let me know.'

'Fair lady, for the telephone alone you have my heart and body. Anything more comes with my soul and without charge.'

Victoria rang off.

She didn't need confirmation. If she had, it was there. Grandfather's birthday was in March. Sophia – there was no point in calling her Christina, whatever her real name was she was now firmly fixed in Victoria's mind as Sophia – returned to London in early September. The trip to Britain by liner took three weeks.

She hadn't left only days after Ruthven's birthday, as Ruthven told his mother. She'd stayed on in South Africa for at least four months.

What had happened during those four months? And what had happened afterwards – because Ruthven's passionate and enigmatic reference to her was dated much later?

Victoria glanced at the remaining bundles of the archive.

The answer might lie there, although she doubted it. She would have to read what the bundles contained, but for the moment she was wary and reluctant. Ruthven was reticent. As his letter to his mother showed, he was well capable of concealing himself, of lying. At best, she guessed, the bundles would reveal only a fragment of the truth.

She was better off taking a straight path, her own path, to try to unravel the puzzle. There were several ways forward, but one stood out as the most obvious. It was her starting-point – the birds.

Victoria looked up the number of the Natural History Museum and dialled.

'This is extremely pleasant. I've never been here before.' He glanced round the restaurant. 'To be honest I haven't been to many London restaurants. My salary scale tends to rule them out.'

He smiled.

His name was Watson, Dr Rory Watson. He was the ornithologist she'd encountered in the bird gallery on Christmas Eve. It had taken her several calls and a number of frustrating delays to trace him. When he eventually came on the line she half-remembered his voice but had forgotten he spoke with a Scottish burr.

She'd invited him out to dinner. Now he was sitting opposite her. She'd chosen the restaurant because it was only a few hundred yards away from the museum.

She smiled back. 'So does mine,' she replied. 'But this time Grandpa's paying.'

In the anguish and confusion of the day – Charlie's departure and Watson's claim about Grandpa's forgeries – Victoria had also forgotten what he looked like. He was taller than she remembered. In place of his white laboratory coat, he was wearing a worn tweed suit, leather-elbowed and patterned with grey and rowan. He had dark hair, acute Celtic-blue eyes, and a finely sculpted, rather hollow-cheeked face.

In the luxurious surroundings of the restaurant he looked both vulnerable and strong. He was, she decided to her surprise, extraordinarily attractive.

'Miss Ruthven—'

'I told you it was pronounced Riven,' she cut him off. 'Also, I'm Victoria.'

He blushed. 'Victoria, if I'd known you were his grand-daughter, I'd never have spoken like that, believe me.'

'I'm glad you did. It opened a window. It set me off on a quest.'

'What can I do now?'

'Order first. Then talk.'

The waiter came. They chose from the menu. The food arrived and they began to talk.

'How did you discover about these forgeries, if that's what they are?' Victoria asked.

Watson frowned. He was silent for several moments.

Then he said, 'I suppose like so many things it started as a boy. I grew up in Perth. Then we moved south. My father's an engineer and Ford, who employ him, sent him to Basildon. Before we left we went every year to Edinburgh zoo. I became fascinated by birds. I kept seeing Colonel Ruthven's name in the references on the exhibit labels—'

He lifted his shoulders in a light, almost puzzled shrug.

'When I graduated in zoology and got my post here, I found Colonel Ruthven's specimens were the cornerstone of the museum's collection. I went to my director and got permission to catalogue them properly.'

Watson looked at her intently.

'I never set out to do a hatchet job, I promise you. He was my hero. I wanted to see he was truly recognised. And then bit by bit I found—'

He stopped.

Victoria completed the sentence for him. 'That he was a fraud and most of the specimens were complicated forgeries?'

Watson looked at her unhappily. He said nothing.

'Why would anyone want to do what you say he must have done?' Victoria went on.

He shook his head. 'You asked me that before. I've racked my brains. A massive joke on Darwinism and the scientific community? That's the best I can come up with, but I doubt it. The reason may have been something very intimate, something private and personal. I just don't know. Maybe no one ever will.'

Victoria raised her hand and called for the bill.

'I have his birding checklists at home,' she said. 'Could you come back and have a quick look at them? They might suggest something.'

'Of course, if it doesn't inconvenience you.' He gave her another of his occasional shy smiles. 'The conundrum's almost as much mine as yours, Miss Ruthven.'

'Victoria,' she corrected him again as she signed the credit-card form.

*   *   *

90

'I don't understand—'

Watson shook his head.

It was 10.30 p.m. and they were sitting opposite each other in Victoria's flat. They'd been there for half an hour. Rory Watson had spent the time carefully reading through Ruthven's ornithological notebooks. Victoria sat opposite him in silence.

'They're exemplary,' he went on. 'For the time, of course, but even by today's practices they're remarkable. A modern ornithologist would perhaps have put in more habitat notes, the food sources locally available and so on. But Colonel Ruthven even has quite a number of them.'

'And nothing to indicate the forgeries?'

'Absolutely not. The reverse. Look at this.'

He held out a page to her and pointed at an entry. It read: 'Hoopoe. Spotted on a Kentish farm. Wonderful – that's one for the tally! I'm going to sketch it.'

'Hoopoes almost never range as far as Britain,' he went on. 'They're almost entirely a Mediterranean bird. A few years ago to claim to have seen one here would have branded you as a fantasist. But as more and more records emerge, country diaries and so on, we've discovered reliable sightings over the past two centuries. 1912, the year of the entry, was very dry. In drought years occasional hoopoes migrate north—'

He looked up. 'Your grandfather's observation has been confirmed by others. He must have been a remarkable ornithologist.'

Victoria stared at the page.

Below the note was a small quick painting of a vivid black-and-white bird with the flare of a chestnut-coloured crest of feathers on its head. It had been sketched with energy, passion, and the clear shrewd eyes of a committed observer. It had nothing to do with forgeries.

Victoria gnawed at her knuckles.

'Then why?' she asked. 'Why?'

'I'm sorry,' he said helplessly. 'I just don't know.'

They finished the cups of coffee Victoria had made for them. Then Watson glanced at his watch and stood up.

'You must be ready for your bed,' he said, 'and I should be going.'

'Yes, of course.'

Victoria walked with him into the little hall. She waited while he put on his coat, a heavy, fleece-lined oilskin. She began to open the door. She stopped. She reached out and fingered the worn and faded cloth.

'Do you wear this on the hill?' she asked.

'Yes.' He looked down embarrassed at the patches where the wind and rain had scoured the protective oil away. 'It could maybe do with a service.'

'It certainly could.'

She gave him her quick bright smile, her professional smile that had served her so well so often. Then her expression changed. Her eyes went dark and opaque – she knew that it was what happened to her at moments of stress because Charlie and others from her childhood on had told her so. She did something she had never done in her life before.

'I don't want you to go, Rory. I want you to stay here tonight.'

He didn't answer. He looked at her, open-mouthed and astonished.

'You can sleep on the floor or you can sleep with me,' she went on. 'If you've got a wife, a girlfriend, a boyfriend, whatever, you can telephone and tell them you've got trapped in a mine-shaft disaster—'

It was all that came to her, a line from a Woody Allen movie.

All she knew, furiously, unchallengeably, unstoppably, was she wasn't going to let him go. Not because he was desirable, not out of revenge on Charlie, not even because she was lonely.

Rory Watson hadn't given her what she wanted. He was holding something back, something he almost certainly didn't know he was holding back. She had to prise it out of him.

'Sally,' he stammered, 'my partner, the girl I live with. She's gone back to Edinburgh for the week to see her family. I promised I'd telephone her at eleven.'

'Then you've got five minutes and I've got a telephone,' Victoria said. 'After that it's the floor or my bed—'

The fear, the agony almost, that had coursed over her when she asked him to stay had gone from her. Something had been rinsed away. The past had to be resolved, but the resolution was going to be her own.

'Also,' she added, the smile back on her face, 'I've got a can of oilskin waterproofing and I'm a dab hand at putting it on. I'm not Jack Ruthven's grand-daughter for nothing. We'll deal with your jacket in the morning.'

16

Victoria opened her eyes and glanced at the luminous alarm-clock on her bedside table.

It was 3.00 a.m.

In the gap between the curtains she could see that the sky had cleared and a full moon had risen. A shaft of silver light fell across the bare waxed floorboards and touched the brass knobs of the bed, making them glitter in the darkness. The air was bitterly cold.

Victoria rolled quietly on to her back. She crossed her arms behind her head. Dr Watson – it seemed a much more appropriate name for him than Rory – was lying curled in a warm ball beside her.

She smiled.

In spite of his shyness, his Scottish reserve, it hadn't been difficult to persuade him to sleep with her. In fact, she'd simply told him that was where she wanted him to be. He'd made his telephone call and they'd undressed and then they'd got into bed alongside each other.

After that it was easy.

He wasn't a particularly good lover, not compared with Charlie who had spent a lifetime acquiring endearments and tricks everywhere from the bars of Saigon to the mixed private saunas of California. But he had a strong and bony body, he'd kissed and held her, he'd risen with passion, and then, spent, he'd fallen away and touched her tenderly afterwards.

He was confused – and he'd be even more confused in the morning at the memory of what had happened – but he'd been gentle. That was enough. Compared to the fierce and grubby sexual fumbles of her adolescence, it was more than enough.

And there was far more to it than that.

A shiver rippled through her.

For the first time in her life she felt liberated. It was an extraordinary sensation. She hadn't had many lovers, perhaps four or five, but it was always them, the men, who'd chosen her and made the approach which had led her to bed. She hadn't been a victim, she'd been a willing accomplice. But she'd never taken the initiative.

Until now.

Now she had, and the effect was giddying, intoxicating. She was astonished at her boldness. She'd looked at a man and said: 'You. Now. Here.' And he'd done exactly what she'd told him to do.

In fact she hadn't even really intended to take Rory Watson into her bed. She'd have been quite happy for him to have slept on the floor. She was on the point of pulling out her spare inflatable mattress, when she'd looked at him after he'd telephoned his girlfriend in Edinburgh. He was standing by the telephone, still confused, still remarkably attractive, and in a strange way vulnerable.

'We'd better sleep together,' she said firmly.

And that was it.

She glanced at him. The beam of moonlight had moved. The play of the light caught his naked shoulder. Victoria could see her breath rising in little puffs of steam in the cold. She pulled the coverlet over him to keep him warm. Then she slept again.

'Can I make you a coffee?'

She opened her eyes and yawned. She glanced at the clock again. It was 7.45. He was standing fully dressed at the foot of her bed.

'Lovely!' she answered. 'Everything's in the kitchen out on the table. Black with a spoonful of honey.'

He came back a few minutes later with a steaming mug.

'I hope I've got it right.'

Victoria propped herself up, drew the sheet up over her breasts, and sipped.

'Perfect!'

He'd made a mug for himself. He sat down on the bed and drank it.

'I didn't want to wake you, but I've been up for a while,' he said. 'I've been reflecting on our talk about your grandfather. I've been trying to piece things together. I remembered something. Colonel Ruthven's collection was much the biggest ever given the museum. But other collections were donated at about the same time—'

Victoria sipped the coffee as she listened to him. His Scottish burr was even more pronounced now than last night.

'A few of the skins from another donation have a joint accreditation: Colonel Ruthven and, as I recall, someone called Yeats. Does that name mean anything to you?'

Victoria tensed.

She put the coffee mug down and sat up. The sheet slipped from her chest but she didn't even bother to pick it up again. For a moment she stared at him in silence.

'Yes. He was a friend of my grandfather.'

'In which case I'll look into it further, although I doubt I'll find much more.' He glanced at his watch. 'I'm due at the museum at nine. I should be going—'

He paused. His face was strained and anguished. 'Sally comes back tonight. I shouldn't have done this, but I dearly want to see you again. You were—'

He stopped. He couldn't complete whatever it was he wanted to say.

'Lovely is the word I think you want,' Victoria answered. 'You were too. I think you'd better go and get on with the job.'

He stood up. At the door he turned.

'This has never happened to me before.' He hesitated. 'I mean never ever. Is it what happens to you often?'

'Only on cold Thursdays in January.' She smiled. 'Go away, Dr Watson, and love your Sally. I want some more sleep.'

The door closed. She tucked herself down into the blankets. Victoria didn't sleep.

She thought about the donations Eric Yeats had made in the joint names of himself and Grandfather to the Natural History Museum.

17

'M'selle Ruthwone—'

He fumbled over the impossible name twice and gave up.

'Please call me Victoria,' she said in French. 'It's much simpler.'

'Of course, m'selle.' He paused. 'You obviously speak French well.'

'*Je me défends*, I can look after myself,' she replied. 'I've been in the *quartier* before. I studied at the Sorbonne when I was young.'

He laughed. 'That must have been last year. No wonder you are still so fluent.'

'A little longer ago, but thank you.' She smiled in acknowledgement of the compliment.

'And I am Jean-Luc as in Godard, except my last name is Chagall, as in the painter.'

They shook hands formally.

They were standing in the forecourt of a little house in an alleyway off the Boulevard St Michel. London had been icily cold when she flew out, with sleet sweeping across the runways of Heathrow. Although the afternoon light was beginning to fade, here in Paris the air was benign, almost balmy.

Victoria glanced round.

Iron gates opened on to the Boul Mich. She couldn't see the Seine but she knew it was less than fifty yards away. Somewhere up the Mich in the opposite direction and no further away was the Café Fleur de Lys.

A rush of remembrance came over her.

She'd spent hours there, the Caffle as the students used to call it, arguing, talking over cups of coffee, hoping the handsome young philosophy lecturer who gave the anchor addresses on her French civilisation course might come in for an *anis*.

If he did, she'd had it all planned.

She'd say her father had sent her a birthday cheque to be spent only on food. She'd take him out for a meal. Then they'd go back to her room on the Ile St Louis where she wanted, she would tell him, to unravel some things she didn't understand in the letters between Sartre and Simone de Beauvoir.

They'd discuss the letters over glasses of an excellent armagnac she had waiting. They'd play a game of chess, she had the board ready. And then . . .

It never happened.

The handsome lecturer with his dark tossing hair never came. He probably had a wife in St Cloud and a vegetable patch the scold had told him to dig. Instead Victoria lost her virginity one night when she was despairingly drunk to a Bavarian opera student from Munich. In the morning there was blood on her sheets and the German was gone. So was her jewellery, the money in her handbag, and virtually everything of value she had.

It emerged he wasn't a student at all, let alone of opera. He was a wandering thief who preyed on real students attending foreign universities. The Parisian *flics* were sympathetic but could do nothing. He'd probably moved on to Stockholm, they suggested.

Out of embarrassment, Victoria washed her sheets herself. Then she gritted her teeth and went back to the Sorbonne lectures.

'M'selle—?'

'I'm sorry.' She shook her head and turned back to him. 'I was thinking about what the *rive gauche* was like when I was here ten years ago. Can we go in?'

'Of course.'

Victoria followed M. Jean-Luc Chagall into the house.

She had got his name and address from Mr Gable. There was, she discovered, an almost world-wide network of museums and archives devoted to what was generally called the music-hall. Mr Gable's little collection was, as he told her, 'puny' compared to those of France, Germany, and America. He had put it all together himself. The others were supported by public money.

'I don't approve of foreigners,' he'd said. 'Nasty habits, most of them. Just look at Hitler. But they did invent civilisation and we have to thank them for that. From his letters, Chagall's not a bad cove.'

Jean-Luc Chagall was the curator of the Musée de l'Art Populaire du Chant, Danse, et Théâtre de la Belle Epoque. As he told Victoria, it meant that he was, in effect, France's custodian of the popular culture of the country's golden age from the late nineteenth century to the

First World War, although with the growing nostalgic interest in the music-hall his concerns now ran through to the present day.

'To me it is not the same.' He waved his hands expressively. 'Of course, there have been fine singers and performers in my own time – Trenet and Aznavour and Mireille Matthieu. But a La Goulue? A Josephine Baker? An Edith Piaf? No, m'selle. We deal now with mortals, not with legends.'

He shrugged. 'We keep records on them all. I have done my best with the Sophia who interests you.'

They climbed the stairs.

The room they entered wasn't much bigger than the space Mr Gable had created on the first floor of his pebble-dash house in Croydon, but in every other way it was completely different. Instead of the dust and cobwebs and chaos, there were architect-designed book-stacks, gleaming steel cabinets housing tapes and enhanced CD disk recordings, neat racks for printed memorabilia, and two secretaries seated behind computer screens.

The French, Victoria reflected, took their culture very seriously – and that clearly included the popular art of the music-hall.

'Here, m'selle—'

Chagall led her over to his own desk and sat her down in front of it on a Mies van der Rohe chair, upholstered in black leather.

'We transfer as many as possible of our archives to disk. We keep one copy here and store another for safety in the Bibliothèque Nationale. We constantly update them as further information comes in. I did a search on your Sophia. It yielded, I'm afraid, rather little but I have printed a hard-copy for you.'

He handed her two stapled sheets of paper.

Victoria read through them.

Apart from being in French and headed the Folies-Bergère, they were remarkably like the entries in the ledgers of Sophia's London agency which Mr Gable had shown her. They recorded the dates of her appearances – she had performed there three times – the amounts paid to her, and the commission sent to Britain.

There were also the same notes. The last one said: 'Not available until further notice. Christina leaving for South Africa. Will advise if/when on return.'

Victoria thought.

It squared with everything Mr Gable had told her. Sophia, or Christina as she was still calling herself, had returned from Cape

Town. She'd completed her engagement at the Folies-Bergère. But then – and this was new and intriguing – she'd gone back to South Africa again.

There were only three likely explanations. A professional booking. Eric Yeats. Or Grandfather.

'Have you ever been to the Folies-Bergère?' Chagall asked as Victoria put the papers down.

She shook her head. 'I couldn't afford it, nor could my boy-friends.'

'Will you permit me to take you there this evening? We can get in free – it is one of the few perks of being a folklorique historian.' He laughed. 'And you will see the stage where Sophia sang.'

They dined at a bistro on the Boulevard Montparnasse.

Charlie was a passionate and knowledgeable gourmet. He'd taught her to taste with care and remember everything she'd eaten, and everywhere she'd eaten – 'above all', he'd said, 'in France'. It had become a habit. To her chagrin and irritation she couldn't shake it off.

They had sliced country *saucissons* and salad, a Provençale *bouil-labaisse*, and a salty blue roquefort cheese to finish.

Then they'd gone to the Folies-Bergère. Chagall must have telephoned beforehand because they were welcomed by a smiling doorman and ushered inside to seats in the front row.

Victoria watched the show almost dazed.

The girls were beautiful. They had strong, taut figures, legs that seemed to go on for ever, and breasts that strained with a wonderful expectancy against their glittering sequined halters. They danced, they swirled, they shone. And then they ripped their tops away and surged into the can-can.

As their legs kicked and their skirts rose, they were like ostriches displaying – wild and sensual and exotic. And then suddenly they were gone. The lights dimmed. There was silence as the tumult of applause faded. A woman in a black dress walked slowly out on to the stage.

Her face was pale – she didn't even seem to be wearing any make-up – and she appeared to ignore the audience. She reached for the microphone and began to sing.

'She is Martine,' Chagall whispered to Victoria. 'The reason I wanted you to come here. She is perhaps like Sophia.'

The woman, Martine, was tall.

She had bold blue eyes, a cascade of dark rippling hair, and a face that at first struck Victoria as arrogant and contemptuous in its expression. Then Victoria realized it wasn't so at all. Martine wasn't unaware of her audience, but they didn't really interest her. All she wanted to do was sing and explore her songs as she sang them.

She started with something in German from the Berlin cabaret of the thirties. She changed to English, or rather American, and sang a medley of Cole Porter, Jule Stein, and Rodgers and Hart – *Camelot* seemed to be a particular favourite. Then she switched to her own language.

Victoria sat transfixed.

Martine sang the lyrics of Trenet, Aznavour, and maybe a dozen others. Sometimes she would break off, halt the orchestra, snap her fingers in irritation, and then signal the musicians to start again as she searched for a new way of phrasing the words, of balancing and conveying what they meant to her.

Her voice was bleak and wistful.

Although clear and piercing, for most of the time it was so remote she might have been singing from a waterfall's edge in some distant valley. And then she'd prowl forward to the front of the stage. She'd smile. Her eyes would range over what to her could only have been the impenetrable darkness of the theatre, defying anyone to challenge her.

And she'd sing again. And this time, Victoria felt, it was not just as if she and Martine were alone together in the same room. It was as if they were standing face to face, their lips only inches away, and she could feel the heat of Martine's breath and the sound of her voice washing over her.

Suddenly it was over.

Martine finished with a tribute to Edith Piaf, a rendering of 'La Vie en Rose' delivered as harshly and sadly as the little sparrow used to sing the song herself. She gave a quick single clap of her hands. She smiled. She tossed her head, sending her hair swirling round her upraised neck.

Then, as the audience rose to cheer, she vanished.

'There was something I forgot,' Chagall said. 'I didn't explain the way we code our files.'

He had taken her back from the Folies-Bergère, and they were sitting in the taxi outside her hotel.

103

Victoria had thanked him but she'd said little else. She hadn't needed to. She knew he'd seen the expression of delight on her face as they walked out, and she'd seen the return look of pleasure and gratification on his.

'You have the printout?'

'Yes.' It was still in her handbag.

'At the end you'll find a P reference. It means we know of a painting or a photograph of the person in the file. We're starting to get these scanned and stored – we still have to go to California for the technology. There's a painting of Sophia.'

'A painting?'

He nodded. 'I can't call it up because it's not on disk yet, but I checked where it is. It belongs to a woman called Madame Villedieu. She's very old, the widow of one our richest aeronautical industrialists. She lives in Paris. If you would like to see it, I think I can arrange it.'

'That would be wonderful. Do you know who painted it?'

'Yes. One of our greatest artists of the Impressionist movement. Renoir.'

18

'So what do you think, m'selle?'

The old lady tilted her head and tapped her stick.

There was something angry and challenging about the way she presented herself. There was also something brave. Victoria had noticed it before in the very old. They were close to death, impatient, deeply selfish, and also in a strange way generous. They wanted to share what was left of their time.

Madame Villedieu was prepared to share her Renoir.

Chagall had telephoned her at 7.30 a.m. Madame Villedieu, he said, rose early. He had just spoken to her, through the good offices of an intermediary. She was leaving at midday to visit her grand-daughter in Brittany. But if they could be at her apartment on the Boulevard Haussman by 10.00, she would be glad to receive them.

Victoria stared at the painting.

She drew in her breath. Renoir must have been very old when he painted it, but it was one of the finest things of his she had ever seen.

Encased in a simple gold frame, the painting showed a young woman standing in a garden. Behind her was a lake filled with water-lilies and a blue-green bridge overhung with white roses. From the strange, vivid colour of the bridge, Victoria guessed it had been painted at Giverny, the house of Renoir's friend, Monet. Or if not, that Renoir had transposed the setting of Giverny as the background for the portrait.

The woman was wearing a black velvet dress with a frill of white lace that reached up and encircled her neck.

Hanging down over her breast was a single strand of pearls. Her eyes were blue, her hair, falling in tangled curls, a dense golden maple, her figure strong and curved. Her body had all of Renoir's famed voluptuousness without the over-ripeness that, Victoria thought, too often characterised his view of the women he slept with and painted.

More than anything it was the girl's face, Sophia's face, which caught and held Victoria's attention.

It was bold and strong-jawed and beautiful with fine, nervous nostrils. Her head was tilted slightly to one side. She was looking at the painter, at Renoir, with a questioning, almost quizzical gaze. Here I am, she seemed to be saying, what do you make of me? The lake and the water-lilies have nothing to do with it.

What about me?

'And so, m'selle?'

Victoria shook her head.

She'd been trying to visualise the two of them together, the old Renoir and Sophia in what she was sure must have been the Giverny garden. Renoir drawing on the last of his dwindling energies to paint someone who was clearly a fabled beauty. And Sophia teasing, taunting, challenging him to make sense of her.

She had been seductive and beguiling. Renoir had called on the remnants of his genius. The result was magnificent.

Victoria turned to the old lady. 'It's beautiful,' she said quietly.

'My husband gave it to me,' Madame Villedieu said. 'He was a philanderer. When he'd behaved badly, he gave me jewels. When he'd behaved terribly, he gave me paintings. Once, when he should have been guillotined, he gave me this.'

She peered up at the painting. 'It's among Renoir's best. The old wine, if it's well bottled, lasts. Renoir bottled this well. Monsieur Chagall told me she was a relative of yours.'

'I think she was my grandfather's first girlfriend.'

'Girlfriend?'

She frowned. She glanced at Chagall and waved her hand imperiously. 'We ladies have matters to discuss. Would you kindly leave us for a moment?'

Chagall gave a graceful little Gallic bow and went out.

Madame Villedieu looked at Victoria again. 'Sex obsessed my husband and he thought I was indifferent. He wasn't altogether right—'

She gave Victoria a rogueish, almost wolfish smile.

'That's long ago, long past me, let alone him, poor Lothario in his Breton grave. But the matter, the physical engagement, fascinates me still. Did your grandfather lose his virginity to this girl?'

'I don't know.' Victoria stared at the painting again.

'Your hair's the wrong colour, but what are they called –

genes? – could explain that. Otherwise you are very similar. Did he marry her?'

Victoria shook her head. 'He married late in his life. She was a Scottish girl called Lomax. She certainly wasn't Sophia.'

'And you're Miss Lomax's granddaughter?'

'Yes.'

'*Ma fille . . .*'

The old lady hammered her stick on the floor again. The stick was ebony with an ivory handle carved in the shape of a parrot and mounted in silver at its head.

'I am by birth a Montmorency. I was presented at court to your Queen Mary. Oh, the excitement of choosing the frock, the dressing and the powder and my mother's indecision over the fragance. And then the Daimler at the door and the Palace and the footmen in gold and scarlet . . .'

She paused.

For a moment she was lost in a past of more than sixty years ago. Then her gaze returned to Victoria.

'Before I went to the Palace I had to learn a few phrases in English. "Good evening". "Your Majesty". "Thank you for your invitation to dance". And other trivialities I've forgotten now. My tutor was a sharp young Scotswoman. She was something of a *farceuse*, a tease. Among the other phrases she taught me was this. "It's a wise child who knows its father."'

Like a lizard's, Madame Villedieu's eyes closed.

'It's an even wiser child who knows her grandmother.'

She came to life again and stumped away across the floor.

Chagall was waiting outside the door. So were Madame Villedieu's maid and the chauffeur who was driving her to Brittany. She gave the two employees quick, incisive instructions.

'When I return from Brittany I would like you to come and see me again.'

She was looking at Chagall, she was speaking to him, but although Victoria had no idea what was going through the old Lady's mind, she sensed it was not focused on the Frenchman, it was directed at her.

'You, too, young lady.'

She smiled and held out her hand.

'You will be welcome here always. As a reminder of my husband's romantic wanderings, the dear scoundrel, and for your beautiful

107

ancêtre. For ancestor I am sure she is – with the eyes you share she could be nothing else.'

Victoria hesitated.

Impulsively she did something she had never done before in her life. She didn't know what prompted it. The talk of the presentation at Buckingham Palace, the regality of the old woman, her sheer awesome presence – at once forbidding and embracing.

She too was a queen.

Victoria dropped a quick, light curtsy, half-bending to her knees. She stood up. She reached out and kissed the old lady on both cheeks.

'Thank you, child. And you, Monsieur Chagall, remember I wish you to come back.'

She shook her finger at him.

'Yes, madame.'

She walked away, the ivory-topped stick tapping resolutely again on the floor.

'*Mon Dieu*, you made if I may say so, m'selle, a formidable impression.'

They were driving in a taxi to Charles de Gaulle airport for Victoria's flight back to London.

'Please call me Victoria.'

'Yes.'

Chagall brushed his forehead. He was still bewildered by the encounter between Victoria and the old lady.

'I had not envisaged it that way, but I am grateful. Madame Villedieu is a great benefactress, but she can be immensely difficult. You have broken a lot of ice-floes for me. If you will forgive me I will use you as what the marketing world calls a loss-leader when I approach her in future.'

Victoria laughed. 'Be my guest. I thought she was lovely.'

The taxi drew up at the airport.

Chagall insisted on carrying her bag inside and checking on the flight. It was running thirty minutes late. He took her through to the restaurant and bought them both a coffee.

'May I ask . . .?' He hesitated briefly over her name and then came out with it. 'May I ask, Victoria, what this is all about?'

'What do you mean?'

'You came to Paris. You said you were searching for someone who might once have had an *amitié amoureuse* with your grandfather. Is that all?'

Victoria sipped the coffee.

It was strong and black and thickened with grains that had escaped through the filter. Steam and the aroma of the milled beans rose from the cup. She glanced round the hall. Lines of patient Japanese tourists were waiting for their flights back to Tokyo.

'I was looking for her and for him.' She paused. 'Perhaps I am also looking for myself.'

She didn't know why she said it.

The answer came out unplanned and unconsidered, almost as if someone had plucked a jumble of words from the recesses of her mind, placed them in order, and put them in her mouth to speak. As soon as she'd uttered them, Victoria knew they were true.

Jack Ruthven, Eric Yeats, Sophia, the unexplained mystery of the ornithological forgeries, they were her. Her birthright and her past. They had coloured and shaped her family and herself down the years. They were, literally or not, what the old lady had called her genes.

Chagall delicately touched her hand as it lay on the table.

'I hope you find all the three people,' he said. 'Most of all the youngest and loveliest. Given that one was the great beauty Renoir painted, I trust you will take that as a true compliment.'

He smiled.

At that moment her flight was called. Victoria laughed. She stood up and kissed him. She slung her small overnight bag over her shoulder and headed for the departure gate.

'M'selle—'

Chagall was hurrying after her. 'I don't think Madame Villedieu wishes to talk about the museum. I think she is interested in you. I will keep in touch.'

19

Victoria sat down at the table in her living-room.

She glanced at the winking red light of her telephone answering machine. Nine messages had been left for her while she was away in Paris. She pressed the replay button and listened to them.

The first four were from friends about casual social engagements. The next two were from her mother. Then there was one from Great-aunt Maude. Victoria had left, Maude said, a bag of toiletries in the bathroom at Glenmoray.

Would she like it sent back to her and if so where – Angus, the postie, would arrange for its delivery.

There was no reference to the papers Victoria had taken. The two old ladies, Victoria guessed, hadn't even looked in the box-files under their beds. The files were probably back untouched on the library shelves.

The eighth message was from Mr Gable.

'Good evening, my dear. I gather you are away. Kevin sits opposite me as I speak. Brilliant Kev has a friend, the unusually named Jonah, who is an expert in what I'm told is called enhanced re-recording. Jonah will put your Sophia's song on to – what the hell's it called?'

There was a muttered background conversation.

'Digital-registered high resolution.' Mr Gable returned to the mouthpiece. 'Whatever on earth that means. Anyway, Kevin and Jonah say it will sound *fantastic*, as if you were there when she sang it. I will be sending you the result. The costs, and, my dear, they are steep, can just be absorbed in your generous help towards the payment for this infernal instrument. But if you could see your way to a small further contribution, it would be deeply appreciated.'

Victoria smiled.

She had been making notes as she ran through the tape. She wrote down a note to send a further cheque to Mr Gable. Then she listened to the last of the messages. It came from someone she didn't know and had never heard of.

'I apologise for troubling you, Miss Ruthven. My name is David Evans. I am the son of the late Detective Chief-Superintendent Wynne Evans. I am compiling a private memoir of my father's career—'

The voice was very formal and stilted with a slight Welsh ring to its inflexions. He was evidently reading out from something he'd written before he telephoned.

Victoria listened.

'In the late thirties my father and two colleagues were sent out by Scotland Yard to investigate the murders in the Bechuanaland Protectorate of a wealthy Englishman, Eric Yeats, and his wife. No conclusion was ever reached, but I have my father's private papers on the matter. Recently I was approached by a friend of yours, a Mr Charles Mortimer, who was researching Mr Yeats' career. He told me in passing that you were assessing the life of your grandfather, apparently a close friend and colleague of Mr Yeats, and might have family information on the sad incident—'

There was a pause and the sound of a rustle as if he was turning a page.

'I am normally resident in Dyfed in the Principality. However in view of my father's reputation, the Metropolitan Police have kindly put the Scotland Yard files on his cases at my disposal, and I am spending three weeks in London to go through them. If you feel it would be mutually helpful for us to meet, I would greatly appreciate it.'

He ended by leaving the telephone number of the Joint Services Warrant Officers Club where he was staying.

Victoria thought for a moment.

If Charlie had traced the son of the policeman who'd investigated Eric Yeats' murder, he was obviously not only still pursuing the story but taking it, as the bastard always did, very seriously. Bloody Charlie. Except for once he might have done her a favour.

She still knew nothing about Yeats' death. Nor until then had Victoria any idea that his wife, Sophia, had been murdered too. For some reason, perhaps the closeness she'd come to feel for Sophia after reading the enigmatic fragments in Ruthven's diaries, hearing her sing on Mr Gable's ancient cylinder, and seeing Renoir's portrait of her, Victoria felt profoundly shocked and distressed.

Evans presumably had the full story – or at least as far as anyone knew it.

She picked up the telephone and dialled the number he'd given her.

*   *   *

'Mr Evans? I'm Victoria Ruthven. I'm delighted to meet you.'

He was tall and grey-haired with an angular bespectacled face, worn and earnest and worried.

He was wearing a blue blazer with brass buttons and the insignia of the Royal Navy embroidered on the breast-pocket. He'd been watching the door anxiously for her – they'd arranged to meet at his club – and he stood up instantly when she came in. He looked to be in his mid-sixties, but he could well have been older.

'You're most kind to come here.' He ushered her to a chair. 'Can I offer you a cup of tea or coffee?'

She glanced at her watch. It was 6.30 in the evening, they were in the bar, and she was tired.

Victoria smiled at him. 'I've had a very busy day. Would you mind if I had a whisky, a large one?'

'Of course.'

He looked slightly startled – young women in Dyfed clearly didn't drink whisky, they probably didn't drink at all – but he beckoned to the barman. The whisky came and they started to talk.

'I may be here under false pretences,' Victoria said. 'My grandfather was certainly a close friend of Eric Yeats. Their lives indeed seem to have been bound up together. But I've simply no idea how or where or why Yeats died.'

She paused. 'I'm afraid you may have much more to tell me than I've got for you.'

'You don't know the circumstances of Mr Yeats' death?'

Victoria shook her head.

'Ah.'

There was a ring-bound file on the table. He pulled it towards him and opened it.

'It is a strange story, the strangest and most puzzling, in my father's view, that he encountered.'

Evans told her.

It was certainly an extraordinary story. Yeats and his wife had been living in Cape Town. According to the records they'd travelled to Mafeking in the north of South Africa, and from there further north still to the then tiny frontier town of Maun in Bechuanaland on the edge of the Okavango delta.

'Are you familiar with the geography of the area?' Evans asked.

'No.'

113

'Nor am I. But I understand the delta, then as now, holds one of the greatest wildlife concentrations in Africa. Mr Yeats went there to hunt and collect birds.'

It seemed they had camped close to Maun. Colonel Ruthven, an old friend of Yeats and a fellow ornithologist, had arrived there with his wife and set up a separate camp a week earlier. The two men made several trips into the delta looking for new species, while the women remained behind.

At the end of their safaris – the word, Victoria learned, was simply an African term for a journey – Yeats and Ruthven returned to their respective camps. Apparently the plan was that the two couples should independently head back for South Africa the following day.

In the early hours of the morning before their departure Yeats and his wife died of gunshot wounds.

'Both their bodies were found in the Boteti river,' Evans said. 'The river runs slowly but by morning it had carried the bodies a hundred yards downstream from their camp. By then the bodies had also been ravaged by crocodiles.'

That night the couple had apparently dined with Ruthven and his wife at Maun's one little hotel. According to the Tswana head-waiter, who'd made a deposition to Evans' father, Yeats had stormed away from the dining-table shouting, 'I'm going to sleep in camp. If you want to come back with me in the morning, I'm gentleman enough to make space. If you don't, you can make your own bloody way home.'

'There are several other statements,' Evans went on. 'One person recalls hearing shouts later in the night, another talks of shots being fired. They're very vague and unsatisfactory, but they were all my father had to go on.'

Victoria frowned. 'What did he make of it?'

'He didn't really reach a conclusion,' Evans answered. 'It could have been an African thief, except the Tswana hate killing, most of all white people. It could have been some European bandit who'd seen them at the hotel. In those days I gather Maun was a wild place. Yeats was known to be rich. He and his wife might have been the victims of a bungled attempted theft. Or it might have been what the coroner decided.'

Evans paused. 'He concluded it was a domestic quarrel. Yeats shot his wife and then turned his gun on himself. Officially, for the record, my father agreed with that. Privately, he didn't.'

Victoria stared at him. 'Why not?'

'My father was what would now be called an "expert" on ballistics. He wasn't an expert at all, just a man who'd used guns all his life and knew about them. He read the records and studied the coroner's photographs. In his journal he says Mrs Yeats was killed by a hand-gun, and the wound that killed her husband was caused by a high-velocity rifle bullet. Logically Yeats couldn't have been responsible for both their deaths.'

Evans put down his file.

'What's your opinion?' Victoria asked.

'I don't have one,' Evans answered. 'My father interviewed Colonel Ruthven later in London. Colonel Ruthven, according to the notes, was remarkably cooperative and anxious to help but could contribute nothing. He expressed only "shock and dismay", in my father's words, at Mr Yeats' death.'

Victoria was silent for several minutes.

'May I have another whisky, Mr Evans, another large one?' she said eventually.

'Of course. This time I think I'll join you.'

The drinks came. Victoria looked at the insignia on the crest on Evans' jacket pocket.

'What branch of the navy were you in, Mr Evans?' she asked.

'For my sins the most unpopular of all.' For the first time he smiled, a thin and weary smile. 'Naval Intelligence. I left the navy to follow my father into the police. Of course, I've been retired for a number of years now.'

'Silly me for even asking,' Victoria said. 'I should have known.'

She finished the whisky faster than she had ever finished a drink before.

'Are we both thinking the same?' she demanded as she put the glass down.

'Perhaps we are, Miss Ruthven.'

He wasn't looking at her now. His gaze was scanning the room, deliberately avoiding her eyes.

'Why this memoir about your father?'

'The American novelist, William Faulkner, once wrote: "The past is all we've got." It may be true. I'd like to find out.'

Victoria stood up.

For a second she hesitated. Then she bent down and kissed him on the forehead.

'Thank you for my drinks. If I find out anything about the past, I'll send a postcard.'

She walked rapidly out of the room.

As she hailed a taxi on the street she reflected she'd suddenly started to kiss quite a number of rather strange people. It was, she decided, a pleasant and interesting experience.

20

Although Victoria had only been out of her flat for a couple of hours, there were another nine messages on her answering machine.

The time between 6.00 and 8.00 p.m., the period she'd been away, was of course the time when most people did their telephoning. She played the messages through. The first was from her mother, anxious once again to know how she'd got on with the great-aunts at Glenmoray.

The next four were casual calls from friends. The sixth was from Charlie.

'Hello, angel,' he said. 'It's me. Listen—'

She didn't even bother to listen. She ran the machine forward. If Charlie had anything to say to her, the bastard could put it in a letter.

The seventh message was from Jean-Luc Chagall in Paris.

'Good evening, m'selle, Victoria if I may still call you that. Madame Villedieu has just telephoned me. I go to see her next week on her return from Brittany. She has something to discuss with me. Meanwhile, she thought it would amuse you to have a photograph of Renoir's Sophia. She has asked me to arrange the photography, which I will do.

'I have your telephone number but not your address. May I have it to send on the print?'

The eighth message was from Rory Watson.

'Hello, Victoria, it's me, Rory. I'm calling from a pay-phone in the museum. I've spent the day in the rooms where we store our ornithological skins. I thought there were just a few with a joint Ruthven-Yeats attribution. I'm wrong. On a quick count almost half of them are credited to them both, far more than I'd thought—'

He must have run out of money then as the line went dead. The ninth message – he'd clearly dug into his pockets – was from him too.

'I'll go on looking.' He paused. 'Sally, my girlfriend, has come back from Edinburgh. I think she knows something's happened, although I haven't said anything. I really feel a wee bit confused. I would love to see you again, but if you don't wish it, I will understand. Perhaps you could let me know here.'

Victoria turned the machine off.

She sighed.

Long ago she'd learnt the best way to tackle problems was to deal with them swiftly and head-on. She rummaged in the drawer where she kept the postcards she bought when she visited art collections. She found one, appropriately a study of two swans by Dürer.

'Rory,' she wrote on it. 'You were and are lovely. Anything you find out about my grandfather, Eric Yeats, or anyone else connected with them, please let me know. But that's it. For the rest it's over and out. *Finito*, as the Poles or Bulgarians say. My love to Sally at a suitable moment. Have a happy day and a happy life. V.'

She read through it.

The words were somewhat brutal. In her experience uncompromising directness was the best way to convey messages like that. She put the postcard in an envelope, sealed and stamped it.

Victoria rocked back in her chair. She ran her hands through her hair and tried to gather her thoughts together.

They were a tangle, a web of unresolved complications.

Three weeks earlier she'd been living safely and tranquilly with Charlie as she'd done for years. On Christmas Eve Charlie had simply upped and walked out. It had been the worst betrayal she'd ever known, made all the more wounding because he'd left her for Angela.

In search of at least momentary relief from the misery, she'd gone to the one place of safety she knew, the Natural History Museum – and there the rest of her world had started to disintegrate.

Since then she'd become a thief. Stealing the papers from the great-aunts was certainly theft, and from time to time she felt haunted by guilt. Ruthven might have been her grandfather but he, their adored elder brother, was so much closer to them, and the letters and journals must have been infinitely precious.

Afterwards her life seemed to have spun almost out of control.

She'd taken Rory Watson to her bed and made love to him. It wasn't just that she hadn't slept with anyone apart from Charlie for years. It was the first time she'd ever taken a sexual initiative, her first-ever one-night stand of her own choosing.

Victoria smiled.

It was against all her instincts, all the lessons of her upbringing. It

118

was probably unnecessary, almost certainly unwise, and her mother would have been appalled. But she'd done it and she didn't regret it. Apart from anything else it had given her an almost reckless sense of confidence. Charlie had 'chosen' her. She'd been the utterly passive partner in the relationship. Now she was making her own choices.

She glanced at the envelope containing the card to Rory. Not only could she make choices, she could unmake them too. It was an exhilarating discovery.

And of course the encounter had yielded the information about Eric Yeats.

She had begun with her grandfather. She had learnt of Yeats' presence in his life, a presence that reached back into Ruthven's childhood, with dimensions to it – the incidents at school and Cambridge – which were still enigmas. Charlie, bloody Charlie, had told her about the Yeats' African empire.

She'd discovered the existence of Sophia or Christina or whatever she was really called.

Victoria still didn't have a last name for her, but she'd heard her sing all those years ago and she'd seen Renoir's portrait of her. She'd been told by the dry, gaunt-faced Mr Evans of Yeats' and Sophia's murder, and the presence of Grandfather in a hunting camp close to where they were killed on the night of their deaths.

Thinking of Mr Evans, Victoria laughed out loud.

The pained expression on his face when she asked for a whisky had been wonderful. But it wasn't that. It was remembering again her pleasure, after kissing him on the forehead, what a relief it was to discover she could kiss people who were virtual strangers – like Monsieur Chagall and Madame Villedieu and the wily, importuning Mr Gable.

It was all part of selecting a man and taking him to bed. It was part, perhaps, of unshackling the past, of at last growing up – part of freedom.

Except that so far it hadn't helped her at all on the quest she hadn't so much embarked on but been inexorably drawn into.

Why, if Dr Watson was right, had Ruthven littered the greatest collection of ornithological specimens ever donated to the Natural History Museum with forgeries that could only have been devised by a tormented and perverted mind?

Victoria steeled herself and reached for the next bundle of diaries and letters.

21

This is brutal stuff.

I remember reading that the Duke of Wellington described Waterloo as hard pounding. God knows how he would have found words for this. Hard pounding doesn't begin to describe it. If the world's end is near, then surely this must be its brink.

It was quite unlike anything Victoria had read by him before.

It was a diary entry written by Ruthven in the trenches of the First World War. The date was 1915 and the place somewhere near Arras in northern France. Everything else Victoria had read had been addressed to someone, most often his mother. Even when it hadn't been specifically addressed in this way, Victoria always sensed it had been written to be read.

Not this. This was private. This was for Ruthven alone. This was the torment and agony he'd had to deal with on the battle-field.

In their wisdom my superiors in Intelligence have decided we embrace control of snipers. They have made me commanding officer in our sector. I lead a life that's at once privileged and perilous – if there can be any degrees of peril in such a murderous engagement. The privilege comes from the need to take the riflemen – I choose them myself by instinct and eye – back from the front line to test and train and instruct them.

The Hun is a fearsome, well-disciplined foe.

His own snipers are his best weapon in this close-combat form of warfare. We have to match them. I weed out seven from every ten I pick. Fine men, the losers, but simply not up to scratch for what's in front. It takes boldness, aggression, hatred (I fear that's true), most of all an eye for the land.

They have to be like foxes, badgers. They must want to live and want to kill. The other three, the ones I keep, I kick, curse, cajole, encourage, and tutor, until I get what

I want. I take them back to the lines – and then the peril starts.

Bad enough for me, far worse for them.

I position them out in front of the trenches in trees, on mounds and hummocks, occasionally where the land fits in ditches. I take them there myself. I am vulnerable while I'm doing it, but, God help them, God bless them, they are under threat all the time until I pull them back. They see the flash of a Jerry sniper's rifle when he fires, but, my goodness, he sees theirs as they answer. And he retaliates.

I go back to the dugout. They lie out naked in front.

Lovely to be an officer! Irony – does anyone know what the word means any more? There's nothing lovely about this for anyone anywhere. I may miss the snipers' bullets, but the shells still crash down round the dugout. Sooner or later one's going to score a hit.

I'm luckier than most. I know better how to look after myself. I learned the skills in Africa. I know how to keep myself dry. I know how to stack duckboards in shelves when the rain pours in. In spite of the gunfire I still sleep well. I try to pass on the ideas to the Tommies, but English soldiers are English urban men. The concept of adaptability is difficult for them.

The Scots are different. We've got a battalion of Argylls on our left. They wrap themselves in their plaids, play their pipes, and eat their oatmeal bannocks. The Jocks have half the rate of sickness and nutritional problems – and they scare the wits out of Jerry.

The ladies from hell, Jerry calls them when he hears the skirl and realises they're coming forward. He tends to run like a rabbit. I don't blame him.

Oh, God, to be back at Glenmoray!

Victoria read on.

The war seemed to drift aimlessly backwards and forwards. At one moment Ruthven was advancing, at another retreating. From time to time he was away from the front line, instructing a new group of snipers at some village several miles behind. Always he returned to the trenches.

He chronicled the days monotonously and desolately. There was the endless stench, the endless damp, the endless acres of mud and devastated trees on every side. Occasionally he recorded some particularly vivid incident. It was invariably tragic.

I have given up smoking. Not much in that one might think except there's an excellent reason.

I suppose all wars from Troy onwards accumulate myths and legends. This one certainly has. Almost everyone smokes – John Player cigarettes with that splendid bearded sailor on the packet are the favourites. Bless the good ladies at home who collect the money, buy them, and send them out to us. They are a real comfort to so many.

And yet . . .

There's a story, I've heard it often in the trenches, that one shouldn't use a match to light more than two cigarettes. Use it thrice and a Jerry sniper's got just enough time to pinpoint you. Ridiculous! Except for what happened tonight.

Sergeant Boscombe, who supplies my own team of snipers with ammunition and must be the bravest man I've ever known, went out with me tonight. We climbed Fontroi ridge and did the usual routine, flashing a quick red beam to all the places we'd positioned the men. We got the right signals back, an equally quick flash from them. For once they were all fine.

We went back to the trench.

Boscombe's corporal, Wickham, was with us. It was a bright moonlit night and the three of us stood looking out over the terrain ahead. Boscombe pulled out a packet of Player's. He gave us each a cigarette. He lit mine, then Wickham's, then his own with the same match.

He was still bending over his when a Jerry fired. All of us were head and shoulders above the parapet. With the moon behind us we thought we were safe. I ducked for the floor, pulling Wickham down with me. It was too late for Boscombe. The shot took him straight through the throat. He was thrown back and fell and that was it.

Whether Jerry had seen the match or whether we'd got the moon's angle wrong or whether it was just one of those random shots – we fire them on both sides to remind the other we're here and close and dangerous – I will never know.

Poor Boscombe. Such a decent and loyal man, such a fine soldier. God knows where I'll find a replacement for him. I must write to his wife, widow as she now is. I won't mention the cigarettes but as sure as there's a God in heaven, I won't ever touch one again.

I will, Victoria thought defiantly.

The only shots people are going to fire at me are emotional ones like Charlie did. If it wasn't over-dramatic to feel so, and she didn't think it was, in a sense they also killed in a different way. They took purpose and trust away from your life, they made you numb. It might only be a small death, but it was still a death of something.

She lit a cigarette. She held the match until it had burnt down and was scorching her fingers, challenging some sniper in her mind to fire at her. Then she read on again.

Ruthven's last entry had been in the early autumn.

Autumn turned to winter. It was a particularly wet and chill winter with rain almost every day. Water rose waist-high in the trenches, and conditions, even for someone as versatile and experienced in the techniques of survival as Jack Ruthven must have been devastating.

With December the frosts began. The cold, savage as it was, came as a relief to him.

'At least the mud is hardening,' he wrote.

You can walk across its surface, rather than wade through it. I just wish I had omnipotent powers of tuition over the men. Poor souls, they come from the streets. They're as brave as lions but they just don't know where they are. Sun, rain, cold, everything is a devilish unknown experience. They have lost contact with the living landscape. How have we as a society let this happen?

Winter drew on and then Christmas came.

'I wonder whether it will be possible for anyone years ahead to believe what happened three days ago,' Ruthven wrote on 28 December. It was of course Christmas Day.

On Christmas Eve I couldn't make my usual tour of the observation points from which we signal my snipers. I'd slipped and ricked my ankle. Sergeant Jamieson – Boscombe's replacement and a fine one he's proving, although no Boscombe – did it on his own.

He came back to the trench and said, 'It's all gone quiet,

sir. No one's firing, not on either side, not even when there's discernible movement. I asked Agnew, that good new lad, why not, and he said he'd had a chat with his mates and they'd just decided to let it be. Jerry seems to have done the same.'

Then Christmas Day and silence. No small-arms fire, no guns, nothing.

I was up early. At dawn it was icy. We had cirrus cloud overnight but when daybreak came the sky cleared. I looked out over the ground as the sun rose. It was wrecked and mutilated, of course, the same drear panorama of trampled and shell-furrowed earth I've been guarding, waging war over now for eighteen months.

There were crisps of frost shining on some of the furrows and for the first time I can remember a few birds calling – God knows why in late December.

And then that utter fool Balding, the little gunner who's been attached to us as a runner and so well named because even at nineteen most of his hair's gone, Balding jumped up. He took the football the lads play with, God knows how, but the Geordies even manage to boot it around in the trenches, and he booted it out in front.

He ran after it. I shouted at him to stop. But, no, he went on running. He caught up with it in the mud, he seemed to play with it, dance with it. Then he kicked it against a stump. It was a mighty blow and he stood there laughing as it bounced back towards Jerry's lines.

I was still shouting, 'Get down, you idiot, get down!'

Jerry didn't fire. The ball skidded into one of their digs. It disappeared and then it was tossed out. And then three or four of them appeared. They looked as fearful as us, all muddied and grey. And so young, God help me, so young. But they were laughing and they started to kick the ball about, and Balding – I'll see he's court-martialled of course (my joke) – damned Balding joined them.

Others from our side joined them. I kept on shouting warnings, but they all mixed in. I don't know how long it lasted. Maybe an hour or so. Then there were clouds and dusk and rain, and the two sides backed away.

We're in the trenches again.

I don't know about Balding. I'll either try to have him shot by firing squad, or put him forward for one of the Queen Empress's Crosses. Military discipline suggests the first. Natural justice, and the inspiration he gave to all of us that day – Jerry and Tommy alike – points to a VC.

I'll probably just kick him in the what-nots and punt him home to Bow or Battersea or Lambeth, or wherever the wretch comes from.

What a splendid man! If I was Jerry and I'd seen him coming, football at feet or Lee Enfield in hand, I'd have chucked the whole show. There's no arguing with the likes of a Balding.

The diary entry finished with a heavily scored line. Underneath the line was a looping arrow pointing to the next page.
Victoria turned the page. It was the last one in the notebook.
'Eric, dear Eric,' the entry read.

My wretched recalcitrant Balding was a threat to all the good order our armed forces hold dear. Should I have called him to account, and had the man shot – fraternising with the enemy and all that? Or what? Tell me, old companion, and consult our Sophia too. Oh God, I need guidance.

There were more words, smudged and then crossed out. Victoria tried to read them, but it was impossible. She closed the book and put it away.
In the worst of all possible conditions – there couldn't have been any worse than the Flanders trenches midway through the First World War, Ruthven was still in his mind turning to Yeats for advice – to Yeats and to Sophia.

22

'Victoria! Great to see you,' he said, smiling. 'How was the break?'

'Fine,' she answered. 'Scotland and Paris, although maybe January's not the best month to see either of them. Still, it was lovely.'

His name was Stein, Jacob Stein.

He was half-American, half-British, and her line manager at the brokerage house. He was a cheerful, ambitious man, married and, sadly, with a Down's syndrome child who was his constant preoccupation. He and Victoria had had an excellent working relationship from the day she joined the firm. Occasionally on Friday evenings he'd invite her out for a drink and talk distraughtly about his child.

'Splendid to have you back,' he went on. 'Just at the right moment, too. There's bundles happening in the Eurobond market, lots for you to get your teeth into.'

'Jake.' She paused. 'I'm not coming back.'

'What?' He looked at her, astounded. 'You're here. What do you mean?'

'I've come to hand in my notice, to say goodbye.'

Stein thought for a moment. 'Are you, dare I ask, pregnant? If so, you know well enough about our time-off scheme.'

She laughed. 'No, I'm not pregnant.'

'Have you been headhunted?' He looked at her much more sharply now.

'No. They've tried in the past. I've always turned them down. I've been happy here. But they haven't come after me this time.'

'Then what the hell is it?'

'Something private.' She shrugged. 'Something I've got to track down and discover.'

'Like travel? A round-the-world trip? A sabbatical? A soul-search?'

'It could involve all of those,' she replied. 'But it's different, more personal. Not self-indulgence, I hope, just something I have to do.'

Stein had been sitting behind his desk with his feet propped up casually on top. He swung his legs off, stood up, and came over to her.

'Listen to me, Victoria,' he said. 'I'm going to make a speech – you're valuable to us. But you're valuable to yourself too. The world out there's steel-bottomed bastard-hard. The market's shrinking. If you drop off into what looks like a lifeboat, it's difficult to climb back on board, here or anywhere else. Nature, they say, abhors a vacuum. People take your place. They're tough to elbow aside—'

He stopped. He drew in his breath. 'End of homily. But it's true. Are you sure you know what you're bloody doing?'

'Yes. Entirely. Absolutely. End of story.'

Stein went back to his desk and sat down again. He was silent for several moments.

'You're good, Victoria. I want to keep you. I'm going to do something I've never done before. As of this moment you're on one month's unpaid phantom pregnancy leave. At the end of it you can hand in your resignation or not as you choose.'

'But I'm really going—'

'For Christ's sake,' he shouted. 'I'm the boss. Shut up and get out of here.'

'Yes, Jake.'

She stood up. As she left she saw him plucking angrily at the red braces which held up his trousers.

'Furthermore,' he called after her, 'if you can't save your soul in a month, then you haven't got one dime's-worth of saving!'

Victoria smiled and headed for the lift.

She was committed now.

Perhaps she had been from the moment she entered the museum and Rory Watson spoke to her. She was grateful to Jake Stein for keeping the job open for her for a month. More than grateful, she was touched and flattered. She'd always liked working there, and particularly working for him. It was clearly reciprocated.

Stein was kindly but hard-headed. He wouldn't have said what he had if he didn't mean it and didn't value her. Victoria had no idea if a month would be enough, or even if she'd want to go back. But it was a lovely generous gesture and it warmed her.

She opened the file under her desk and looked up her last bank statements.

She kept two accounts. In one she banked her salary, and drew on it to pay her living expenses. The other was really a savings account. Grandfather – it was ironical or appropriate that it should have been him – had set up a trust fund for her when she was born.

Each quarter the trust paid her a dividend. Over the years the trust's capital had grown and the dividends were now considerable. She salted them away on deposit as what she laughingly called her 'run money' – money to be used at a moment of crisis.

This wasn't a crisis. Or perhaps in a way it was. In any event, there was more than enough in the run-money account for what she needed. It would last a month, it would last as long as she required.

How strange, Victoria thought, that it was Ruthven himself who was financing her search for him. Victoria considered her mother. Her mother was also the beneficiary of one of the trusts Ruthven had created. Her trust was much larger than Victoria's – she had lived her life extremely comfortably without ever working.

The great-aunts, Ruthven's sisters, lived well too. They also presumably had been provided for. Glenmoray couldn't produce their income. It was just another remote and costly Scottish estate which demanded far more than it ever gave back.

Where on earth had the money come from?

It was yet another unexplained strand in the puzzle. It would almost certainly lead, she guessed, back to Yeats and South Africa. Meanwhile there was India and then Nepal.

Ruthven had been withdrawn from the trenches in France and sent to train Gurkha riflemen in Nepal. The continuation of his wartime journal had told her that. Inevitably at the time he'd gone to Nepal by way of India with Delhi as his main staging-post. Either in Delhi or when he reached the Nepalese Himalayas, something had happened which changed the course of Ruthven's life.

Tucked into the pocket of the end board of the leather-bound journal was a postcard. It was addressed to Eric Yeats but apparently for some reason it had never been sent. The sepia photograph on the front of the card showed an imposing Victorian building named the Raj Hotel. On the back alongside Yeats' name and address were a few scrawled sentences.

I leave tomorrow for Kathmandu. Back here in a few months, maybe October. S has been here to sing. Oh my God, Eric, the world has turned widdershins on its axis. The crown of the earth doth melt and the soldier's pole is fallen. Nothing will ever be the same. My life is changed beyond recall, and I must talk here, here, here, where it has happened, where I am leaving my turbulent heart. Can you not come when I return, for S, I understand, returns to Delhi too? Be with me if energy and soul can make the journey.

I need you, I need you. The hotel holds letters and telegraphs for me. Bless you. JR.

Victoria picked up the telephone and dialled the travel agent that Charlie, who travelled constantly, had told her to use when they first started to live together.

'Mary?' she said. 'It's Victoria, Victoria Ruthven. I'd like to go to Delhi, stay perhaps two or three days, and then fly on to Kathmandu. As soon as possible. In Delhi I'd particularly like to stay at a hotel called the Raj. How does it look for flights?'

There was a seat available on the Delhi flight the next day. Victoria went out and collected her ticket. She returned to her flat, tidied it up, and packed for the journey. She was having dinner with her oldest and closest girlfriend, Fiona, who lived very close. Before she left she glanced round.

The boxes of her grandfather's papers were piled up by the table. She stared at them. They looked vulnerable and somehow tempting, as if they held valuables as well as secrets. Victoria had stolen them for her own reasons. If a thief broke in while she was away, it suddenly occurred to her, he might steal them too – or at least plunder them and hurl the carefully-arranged contents at random across the room.

On impulse she decided to take them with her.

Fiona, she knew, would be happy to look after the boxes until she got back. Victoria carried them downstairs, loaded them into her car, and drove off.

She felt slightly irrational, but also unaccountably safer.

23

As the taxi drove Victoria in from Delhi airport to the centre of the city, she sat forward transfixed, gazing through the window.

She'd been to Tangier and Marrakesh, to Rome, Paris, and Athens in high summer when all five cities were thronged and pulsing with life.

She had never seen anything like this.

There was the heat first, a sultry, humid, clinging heat that after the first ten minutes had left her blouse and cotton slacks stained with patches of sweat. Then there was the light, silvery and harsh and grained with dust. After that the smells, the raw stench of open drains, diesel fumes, cinnamon and nutmeg and a dozen other roasting burning herbs from the street-sellers' food-stalls, the scents of raw red earth and occasionally bleach-scoured stone.

Most of all it was the people, the noise they made, the colours they flaunted that dazed her.

Stream after stream of humanity flowed along every street like shoals of fish frantically fleeing the pursuit of dolphins. They talked, they shouted, they screamed, they cursed. They were dressed in every colour of the rainbow, from the brilliant saris of the women to the gaudy dresses of the children to the white *dhotis* of the men to the filthy ochre and umber rags of the beggars.

Butting their way through them were exotically decorated, overloaded buses with passangers hanging from the roof and perched on the bumpers. Ancient taxis, like the one she was in, their horns constantly blaring. Rickshaws and rusting bicycles, carts and ox-drawn waggons, and the occasional majestic Rolls-Royce, coasting along the street like some disdainful shark.

All Victoria could think of was that it was like a great canvas by Brueghel at his most crowded, tumultuous best, suddenly brought to life and transposed from Holland to capture instead the surging rhythms of the urban East.

Then the taxi swung in through the towering iron gates of the Imperial Raj Hotel, and the clamour and the smells faded. Victoria got out beneath the broad roofed portico built to admit the carriages of the Raj.

'Miss Ruthven?'

There were three of them. The first, a smiling young man in a dark suit, looked like one of the hotel's under-managers. The other two were turbaned servants.

'Truly, you must forgive us,' the young man went on. 'Normally we would have sent the limousine to collect you. There was a misunderstanding about your flight number and arrival time. Our deepest and most sincere apologies—'

He spread out his hands. 'However, all that matters is you are here. Let us now make you truly welcome.'

Victoria thanked him.

She glanced round. A garden and stretches of green lawn swept away on both sides of the hotel drive. There were tall trees and dark, inviting pools of shade and the sound of water falling from fountains. Peacocks strolled the grass and a dozen other servants were tending broad beds of flowers.

The hotel belonged to a different world from the rank and deafening squalor of the city. It must have remained virtually unchanged since Jack Ruthven was there.

She went inside.

Victoria's room on the first floor was cool and high-ceilinged, with a large antique fan to move the air and a verandah overlooking a small lake. By the time she was shown up to it, a young sari-clad girl – the hotel had its own distinctive saris – had almost finished unpacking her case.

'Would the memsahib like a shower or a bath?' the girl asked.

'A bath, I think.'

The girl ran it for her. Then she bowed gracefully and left.

Victoria soaked herself in the water, dissolving the cramped tiredness that the long flight had worked into her muscles. She got out, dressed, and then just as she finished putting her clothes on, the telephone rang on her bedside table.

'Miss Ruthven?'

It was another of the fluting Indian voices – older than the one which had greeted her at the hotel entrance – she was already beginning to adjust to.

'This is Mr Swami. I am general manager of the Raj Hotel. I trust you are settling in with comfort?'

'Very much so, Mr Swami.'

'We had a fax from your booking agent in London, UK. She advised us you were researching a literary work on your grandfather, Colonel Ruthven. The hotel has always kept, if I may say so, excellent records. My staff have examined them. May I invite you to look at what they have found over a glass of what I promise you, if you have not tasted it before, is our truly excellent Indian champagne?'

'Thank you. I'd be delighted.'

Victoria met him an hour later in a reception room that led off his office.

Thirty years older, with greying hair, Mr Swami might have been – perhaps he was – the father of the under-manager who had met her at the door. He was the same height, he had the same beaming, olive-skinned face, he was wearing the same dark suit and fresh white silk shirt.

'What a true delight!' He held her hand briefly between both of his. 'Also a great privilege. Naturally I never knew Colonel Ruthven but in many quarters, important quarters, his name remains one of deep honour. However, first the champagne.'

He poured out a glass from a frosted dark-green bottle. Victoria tasted it. Mr Swami was right. It was excellent, light and dry and fragrant.

'It's lovely,' she said.

'Aha.' He laughed with pleasure. 'It's my little jest for European visitors. No one from UK, Europe, believes India can make champagne, but we do. Modestly, I say it's not too damn bad. However, you are not here to drink the fizz. Instead for Colonel Ruthven—'

He turned and picked up a couple of sheets of printed paper from the table behind him.

'You are of course welcome to go through our visitors' books yourself,' he said, 'but I thought your researches would be made easier if my staff did it for you. It is a tradition for everyone who stays at the Raj to sign. There are thousands of names. Colonel Ruthven visited us several times. These are the dates—'

Victoria glanced at the sheets.

Grandfather had been at the hotel on half a dozen occasions over a period of four years from 1917 to 1921. There was then a long gap.

133

He'd returned for a further three visits in 1924. After that there was nothing.

It was the earlier visits that interested her most. Before Victoria could put the question she was about to ask, Mr Swami answered it for her.

'Your agent also said you were interested in a cabaret artiste by name Sophia,' he said. 'The Raj had a great reputation for its entertainments. We booked many performers from foreign climes to tickle the fancies of our guests. We have misfortunately no such detailed records of them. However I remembered we hold a store of old cabaret programmes from the time. We found these.'

Mr Swami handed her two pieces of yellowing card printed in fading colour.

The first announced that 'Sophia' – no other name was given for her – would be singing in the ballroom every night after dinner for two weeks. Sophia was, the card said, 'A songstress of international renown who comes naturally to the Raj, on her first visit to the sub-continent after her triumphs in Paris, London, and Capetown'.

The second announced her return for a second engagement three months later. 'By demand and acclaim, now needing no introduction, the nightingale Sophia again!' The engagement this time was for four weeks, double the length of her first booking.

Victoria glanced back at the sheets which listed Ruthven's visits. The dates of the two of them being there coincided almost to the day.

'There is one matter more,' Mr Swami went on. 'The staff of the Raj is very, very loyal. We are loyal to them. In the days of Colonel Ruthven we had a polo field. The head groom was Jankarit Singh. He is ninety but we still pay him a modest stipend for a couple of hours every day to observe the horses. They are used only for guests' riding requirements now.'

He paused. 'I spoke to Jankarit. He remembers Colonel Ruthven well. Would you like to speak to him?'

'Very much,' Victoria replied.

'Then tomorrow I arrange it. Now,' Mr Swami gave his fluting laugh, 'another glass of our Indian champagne, for you must surely write of it too!'

For a ninety-year-old Jankarit Singh was extraordinarily clear-eyed and agile.

He was squatting in the shade of the stable roof when Victoria arrived next morning. He rose easily to his feet at her approach, bowed, and templed his hands in greeting.

'Memsahib.'

Barefoot and dressed only in a loin-cloth, he sank respectfully to his haunches again. Almost a century of service to the raj had taught him this was how you faced them, they on their feet, you on the ground. His greeting had been so dignified, Victoria felt momentarily uncomfortable.

She sat down on a bench half-covered with lovingly polished saddles and bridles to bring herself closer to him. Behind them the ponies in the stalls neighed and whinnied.

'Mr Swami tells me you knew my grandfather.'

'Well, memsahib, well. He was great sahib.'

His voice was clear and his English, though heavily accented, fluent.

'And you remember him after all this time?'

'I remember all who come to Raj.' He smiled and tapped his head lightly. 'I go soon, this too. But until then I remember, the Colonel sahib among best. He was a great sahib,' he repeated.

'How did you meet him?'

'Come here to ride,' Jankarit answered. 'Not for polo. After, he play that too very strong. My goodness, strong, he was six-handicap fellow. No, first time just to ride with his memsahib. Many times I saddle up and take them out—'

He waved his hand, gesturing at the crowding buildings beyond the hotel park's walls.

'Long time past, memsahib. Different then. We ride all where we wish.'

'And his memsahib,' Victoria hesitated. 'They were good friends?'

'Oh, my goodness!' Jankarit laughed. 'Sometimes Colonel sahib say: "Leave us, Jankarit, go away." They unmount, I take horses by reins, then I go. But I see them, cannot help it, close together, oh, so close—'

For an instant he looked perturbed. 'I trust this does not matter now, memsahib?'

'Of course not, Jankarit. What happened at the end?'

'They both go away. Then they come back and it is same again. Then another friend of the Colonel sahib comes, another sahib. For a time I take out three. Then they all go. After that whenever the Colonel sahib comes back, it is alone, just for polo.'

135

Victoria thought. 'When the Colonel sahib left first, do you know where he went?'

'Of course.' Jankarit glanced up at her, puzzled she didn't know herself. 'He goes to Kathmandu. He wishes to climb in the snows. I give him name of my cousin as possible sirdar.'

He paused.

His fingers traced a thoughtful pattern in the dust at his feet. When he spoke again there was an almost wistful edge in his voice.

'I am not from Delhi, memsahib. I am here since fifteen years of age. I learn about horses here, I love them, I marry Delhi girl. But I come from mountain you name Everest. That is why I can give the Colonel sahib my cousin's name. He from same village on Everest.'

'Is your cousin still alive?'

Jankarit rocked back on his heels chuckling.

'No, memsahib. Few men living as old as yours very truly. My cousin, he became famous sirdar. Then he fell off rock-face on K2. But his grandson, he went to college in Bombay. Now he back in Kathmandu as guide in mountaineering museum.'

They talked for a while longer. Then Victoria thanked him, inclining her head with her hands clasped in response to his graceful bow. She left the old man with the ponies stirring restlessly in the heat behind him, and went back to the hotel.

She had another favour to ask of Mr Swami.

He came down to the tall and dusky reception hall within moments of her calling his office from the front desk.

'Yes, Miss Ruthven?'

'Would you be immensely kind,' Victoria gave him her most winning smile, 'could your admirable helpers check the visitors' book again? I'd really like to know if at the time of my grandfather's second visit here, there was someone else staying in the hotel, a man called Mr Eric Yeats.'

Mr Swami beamed. 'No problem, dear lady, no problem in the world.'

She went up to her room and waited.

24

It was midday and immensely hot in her bedroom in spite of the overhead fan.

Victoria had a cold shower. She let the water rinse over her. It wasn't in fact cold but lukewarm like her bath the night before. She came out of the huge marble-floored bathroom and thought briefly of trying to sleep. She was still tired from the flight from London and the dizzying, tumultuous impact of Delhi, which had hit her like a physical assault.

She abandoned the idea.

She knew she wouldn't sleep. Instead she put on fresh clothes – every change of clothing she made was dusty and damp with sweat within an hour – and sat at the window. She looked down over the little lake. Its utterly still surface shone like beaten polished steel in the sun.

Victoria thought she knew what had happened.

Sixty years ago Jack Ruthven had been here. By coincidence at the same time so had Sophia. It wasn't really a great coincidence. At the time the Raj was one of the great hotels of the world, just the sort of place a cabaret singer and entertainer like Sophia, a *chanteuse* as Mr Gable had called her, and Victoria loved the word, would have been booked into.

On his way to Nepal, it was also the obvious place Ruthven would have chosen to stay. They had met again. And—

They had made love.

'Please, please, please!' Charlie had implored her once. 'Don't call it that, that appalling euphemism of the British middle classes. Give it its true Anglo-Saxon name – fucking.'

Something about what he said irritated her. 'Then why doesn't your bold, up-to-the-minute, dynamic, investigative newspaper call it that?'

'We have to cater to the whole spectrum of the A-B-C market.' He waved his hands vaguely. 'Take in their sensitivities at either end. The

137

advertising and marketing folk demand it. We'll get there. If I had my way, we'd be there right now.'

He rambled on.

Well, Charlie, the swine, the cunt – another old but unusable newspaper word – had had his own way. He'd got there with Angela.

Victoria almost trembled with anger.

With a deliberate act of will she dismissed the memory of him. Apart from anything else, it was making her hotter and sweatier. She concentrated on Grandfather again.

In the Raj Hotel, perhaps on this floor, perhaps in this very room, Jack Ruthven had made love to Sophia. And, Victoria guessed, he'd lost his sexual virginity as he did it.

Ruthven had entered the hotel as an innocent. He'd left it as a sexually initiated man.

She had no way of proving it. She doubted she ever would. It was only an intuition, but an intuition backed by his diary entry, the conjunction of the dates he and Sophia had been here, and the smiling reminiscences of old Jankarit.

So close, memsahib, so close.

Victoria thought of how she'd lost her own virginity. The only legacy of what was supposed to be a momentous life-changing experience was a hangover and some bloodstains on her sheets. For Ruthven, she sensed, it had been very different.

He came from a different world. A world before the contraceptive pill, before sexual liberation, a world of utterly different values. From all Victoria had read and been told, sex was dark then, a mystery, virtually forbidden outside marriage. Some men went to prostitutes to be initiated. Not passionate and idealistic young men like Ruthven.

He'd had, if Victoria was right, a homosexual relationship with Yeats. That was relatively normal, whatever its physical expression had been. Then suddenly he'd changed tracks. Ruthven had taken another sexual path. He'd swung away from men and he'd had his first physical encounter with a woman, his first climax, in the Raj.

For him, if it had happened like that, the experience must have been truly momentous. It wasn't just a rite of passage. Allied to the passion he seemed to have felt for Sophia, it must have been devastating, something which had changed his life.

And then when he'd returned to stay at the hotel for Sophia's second engagement there, the two had been joined by a third companion who'd accompanied them out riding with Jankarit.

'Miss Ruthven?'

The telephone rang and Victoria had picked it up. It wasn't Mr Swami, it was one of his assistants.

'Yes,' Victoria replied.

'The general manager has asked us to send you up some information,' a young female voice said. 'We have it printed. A staff member will bring it to your room if that is convenient.'

'Thank you.'

A few moments later there was a knock at her door. Outside was a turbaned waiter holding a silver salver. On it was another printed sheet.

Victoria took the sheet back into the room and studied it.

It was almost academic. She'd known what the hotel's records would show even before she'd asked Mr Swami to check them.

Eric Yeats had been a guest at the Raj throughout her grandfather's and Sophia's second stay there.

25

Victoria looked out of the plane's porthole window.

When she checked in at Delhi airport for the flight to Kathmandu, a helpful clerk had advised her to choose a seat on the left.

'They are much favoured,' he said. 'You will see the whole range of the Himalayas, Everest, Annapurna, and the rest. A wonderful sight, miss.'

She glimpsed them now.

At first there had been cloud as they flew north. Then suddenly the mountains emerged out of the thickly coiling greyness which cloaked the land below.

Victoria drew in her breath.

Great ramparts of ice and snow-covered rock stretched away before her, rearing so tall that although she knew the plane must be flying tens of thousands of feet high, they rose above it. They swept the clouds away and soared over them. Light glittered off their flanks of whiteness and poured like water in cascades of constantly changing colours, violet, turquoise, emerald and gold, into the deep-cut valleys below.

They were, she knew, among the oldest landscapes on the earth's surface. They looked fierce and infinitely dangerous – she could imagine the Himalayan winds and storms, the mountains' sons and daughters, raging round them like defiant children trying to provoke implacable, immovable parents. They also looked noble and serene.

Grandfather had headed for them after leaving the Raj in Delhi. There was nothing strange in the direction he'd taken. He'd been assigned to instruct Gurkha snipers, and the Gurkhas came from Nepal. Except their training camps were in the foothills and he'd pressed on upwards.

Why?

Ruthven loved hills. They'd surrounded Glenmoray. But the Scottish tops were quite unlike these massive, daunting peaks. Harsh as they could be in winter, they were tiny and almost benign in comparison to the Himalayas. What could have driven him up into the hostile snows?

The plane's abrupt descent into the Kathmandu valley cut short her wonderings.

Victoria clipped tight her seat-belt, and braced herself for landing at what she'd been told was one of the world's most hazardous airports. The flight landed safely. Half an hour later she was on her way into the city.

Kathmandu was a city of birds.

Victoria discovered that even before the taxi brought her to its heart. It was early evening. There were birds everywhere. They thronged the sky in clamouring flocks. They dipped and dived and swirled round the car. They clustered in perches on roof gutters and telephone cables, making them sag almost to breaking-point.

Some of the species she recognised, the scavenging kites and crows, the starlings and swallows. Others were unknown to her. All of them twined in skeins of intermingling flight that enveloped Kathmandu in a canopy of beating wings, and an orchestra of cries and song.

The sun fell behind the mountains within minutes. The moon lifted. And still the birds called and turned in precisely measured waves. And then suddenly as she reached her hotel, they were gone. Kathmandu was silent in the darkness.

She went inside.

There was a message waiting for her. Mr Swami, at Victoria's request, had spoken to Jankarit and obtained the number of Jankarit's great-nephew. He'd telephoned the Himalayan Mountaineering Foundation, and asked the young man to meet Miss Ruthven.

The message said he would be glad to receive her at 10.00 the following morning.

The young man's name was Rhoshan Shivar.

In the morning Victoria went down to the reception desk.

'How do I get to the Himalayan Mountaineering Foundation?' she asked.

She pushed the piece of paper with the message and address on it across the counter. The clerk studied it. He went away and consulted a colleague.

'This not the place of the Foundation,' he said when he returned. 'This is the monastery of Ghatma Buddha.'

Victoria pulled back the message and studied it again.

He was right. The message didn't mention the Foundation, but it did give the Ghatma Buddha monastery as the meeting-place. In her tiredness the night before – she still hadn't fully recovered from the exhaustion of the long-haul flight from London – she hadn't noticed it.

'How do I get there?' she asked.

'Very easy, miss. A taxi if you like, but is simple walking distance. I show you.'

He pulled out a street map and marked it with a red pencil. Victoria set off on foot.

There were still birds all round, but the great swarming flocks of the evening before had gone. Instead under the humid sky of the Kathmandu valley there was what she was rapidly becoming used in the subcontinent.

Open sewers and the stench of what they carried or held clogged and rotting at their clay barriers. Beggars clouded in flies and pleading for alms. A press of people with cripples on trolleys shouting for space as they wheeled their way among them. Men arguing ferociously or walking hand-in-hand in silence. Beautiful women and girls, who both belonged to the throng and somehow stood apart from it, weaving their way through in their cool, billowing saris.

And overhead vultures, always circling and observing.

Brought up in an urban environment, Victoria had been taught vultures were birds of death. Then she'd read somewhere that they were in fact indicators of life. They could only flourish where life flourished.

She smiled at the memory of the book, a description of expeditions across the Kalahari desert, she recollected, and turned into the gateway that fronted the Ghatma Buddha monastery.

'Miss Ruthven?'

Rhoshan Shivar was waiting for her just inside the gate.

Victoria had imagined him as a young man. Startled, she saw that he was about fifty. Then she remembered that Jankarit was ninety, and almost two generations separated him from his great-nephew. It made sense that Rhoshan was middle-aged.

He was wearing leather sandals and a simple saffron-coloured robe. His head was shaven and he had a kindly, wrinkled face with dark and smiling eyes. He led her through into a little courtyard and offered her a seat on a stone bench under the shade of a fig-tree.

A fountain spilled out water at the courtyard's centre, its spray

143

cascading tiny rainbows under the play of the fierce sunlight. Other monks in the same saffron robes padded silently in the background.

'As you know, Mr Swami telephoned me,' he said. 'He told me you were researching the life of your grandfather. How can I help?'

His English was fluent, although he spoke it with an American accent.

Victoria wasn't sure how to answer. What she was confronted with was totally unexpected. She opened her mouth and closed it again without speaking. Rhoshan noticed her confusion.

He laughed gently.

'Let me explain. I administer the Himalayan Mountaineering Foundation in my spare time. It's an obligation I owe to my father and grandfather. Their work as sirdars to climbing expeditions earned me my education first here in Kathmandu and then at Columbia University in the United States. But first and foremost I am as you see me now: a monk in the service of Buddha.'

He had sat down at her feet, his robe spread out like a cascade of yellow water-lilies over his crossed legs.

'My grandfather came here from Delhi,' Victoria said. 'He was meant to be training Gurkhas, but in his diaries he says he wanted to climb.'

Rhoshan nodded. 'I looked up the Foundation's records. For recent years they are very extensive and detailed. For Colonel Ruthven's period they are skimpy. However I extracted some dates and destinations.'

He opened a little leather pouch on the belt round his waist and handed her a sheet of paper. It was yet another computer printout. Victoria read through it.

She frowned. 'He tried to climb Everest twice, and Annapurna once?'

'So the records show.'

'And he failed?'

Rhoshan paused for an instant before answering. 'He didn't reach the peaks. That is not the same as failing.'

'But wasn't it strange he even tried?' Victoria insisted. 'I mean, at the time?'

She knew almost nothing about mountaineering, although she was well aware that Everest was the highest peak on earth and Annapurna not far short of it. She also knew that in Ruthven's day Nepal was a tightly closed kingdom which admitted only a few Europeans, restricting them almost entirely to approved British officers dealing with Gurkha recruitment.

It seemed extraordinary that Grandfather would have been allowed to roam the country, let alone that with no history of climbing in his background he would have wanted to tackle two of the world's greatest mountains.

'With respect, Miss Ruthven, nothing about mountains and men is strange. They are there to challenge and complement each other. I was born in the village of Tengatsu at ten thousand feet on the Everest slopes. I learned as a child that if a man wishes to climb, nothing will stop him.'

'But why climb, anyway?'

'Ah—'

Rhoshan stopped. He smiled again.

'I think I understand now. I sense you are not pursuing facts and figures and dates. You are looking for explanations and reasons. Please do not answer if you wish not, but am I perhaps right?'

Victoria didn't reply for several moments.

She thought.

Rhoshan was of course right. His dark, smiling eyes had somehow seen through to what she was after. She didn't feel threatened by the realisation, but she still felt vulnerable enough about the madcap, impetuous nature of the quest she'd embarked on, that when she tilted her head in agreement it was almost reluctantly.

'Although I've no real evidence for it,' she said, 'I think my grandfather had a passionate life-changing experience in Delhi. For some reason, he seems to have run away from it. He came here to climb. Why?'

As she spoke, Victoria realised that unaccountably she was blushing. If Rhoshan noticed it, he gave no sign.

'People come to mountains to search, to escape, or to do both,' he said. 'Most come to search. Truths are to be found in the high snows, anxieties resolved, love and direction defined. Perhaps that was what Colonel Ruthven was after.'

'But he came back several times.'

'Maybe the search was uncompleted. No search is easy and escape impossible.'

Victoria sat motionless.

Rhoshan's voice was calm and quiet.

Although completely different in its intonations, it reminded her for the first time in twenty years of her childhood nanny's voice, the soft Scots tones that had so often stilled her in the night when she'd had nightmares and couldn't sleep.

'He left Nepal,' she said. 'He left India. He went back to Africa. Could he still have been searching then?'

'Of course,' Rhoshan replied. 'It is a journey without end. Yet even if never reaching it, one can travel the paths of the jungles and deserts in truth's pursuit just as well as the mountain snows.'

Victoria stood up.

The sunlight, far stronger now than when she'd come into the monastery, was still rippling and shining through the fountain's waters, and the other saffron-clad monks were still padding silently backwards and forwards along the shadowy cloister that surrounded the courtyard.

Rhoshan accompanied her back to the gateway. He took her hand between his and pressed it. He gazed at her and gave her the same warm smile with which he'd welcomed her arrival.

'Miss Ruthven, may I say this? You say you are looking for Colonel Ruthven. I suggest you are really looking for yourself. You are looking for home. I believe the journey towards it is itself home.'

He bowed and turned away.

Dazed and wondering, her mind thronged with images from what he'd said, Victoria stepped out on to the street. It was one of the strangest and most memorable encounters she'd ever had. Most of all she remembered Rhoshan's words towards the end.

Jungles and deserts were just as valuable paths towards the truth as the Himalayan snows.

Grandfather had gone back from India to the jungles and deserts of Africa.

26

'Miss Ruthven?'

Victoria looked at her, surprised.

'Yes,' she answered.

The woman who'd addressed her was a smartly dressed young policewoman.

They were both standing on the doorstep of the entrance to the house which contained her flat. It was 8.00 a.m. and Victoria had just returned home from London airport after taking the overnight flight from Delhi. The Heathrow taxi was pulling away and her suitcase was still in her hand.

'I'm very sorry, miss,' the woman PC said, 'your flat seems to have been broken into. It was reported to us an hour ago by your neighbour, a Mr Foster. Two of our rapid-response officers are upstairs.'

Victoria followed her inside.

As she went through the hall door she saw it had been jemmied open and was hanging by one hinge. She climbed to the first floor. The same had happened to her own door. Mr Foster, an early riser, must have noticed the damage to both doors when he went out to collect his milk and newspaper.

'Hello there.' The young uniformed policeman who greeted Victoria was balding and smiling. 'Sorry about this, very sorry. Glad you were away – on holiday, I believe? – when it happened. We've got some real sods on the manor. Much better be out of their path if they get boozed up and decide to go nicking.'

Victoria went through to her bedroom.

The second policeman, equally bald but older than the first and clearly his superior, turned round from where he was standing by her bedside table.

'Good morning, miss,' he said. 'You'll be the tenant. I'm Detective Conway. I'm from Forensic.'

He was wearing a white laboratory coat over his uniform and from the fine-haired brush and pot of powder in his hand, he'd obviously been recording fingerprints.

'Could you have a check round for what's missing?' he went on. 'Have a look at your jewellery box. A drawer maybe where you keep credit cards and cheque-books. Silver if you've got any, and so on.'

He was polite and helpful. Victoria went round the flat doing as he'd asked.

She'd never been burgled before.

The flat had obviously been systematically ransacked. It was in a certain amount of disarray, with drawers pulled out and cupboard doors open, but there was none of the wanton damage she'd always been told accompanied a break-in – the smashed ornaments and excreta on the floor. Also, although she had little in the way of jewellery and silver, none of it had been taken as far as she could tell.

Victoria returned to the bedroom, puzzled.

'I'll need to check again,' she said, 'but it doesn't look as if anything's gone.'

The policeman slipped a camera he'd been using into the pocket of the laboratory coat.

'I've logged a selection of prints,' he said. 'If you could come down to the station, say tomorrow – arrange a convenient time with the WPC – and give us your own prints, then we can chuck them out and see if we're left with anything useful.'

He was wearing plastic gloves. He peeled them off and walked with her back into the living-room. He studied the door again.

'People talk about professional criminals,' he said. 'It's nonsense. All criminals are professional. A kid of fifteen does his first few jobs, and he's a professional. He needs to be to stay ahead of the game. Except look at this—'

He bent down and pointed at the broken door jamb.

'You had a double tumbling mortice and a London bar to back it up. Just what our crime prevention officers recommend. To open this, chummy needed bolt-action cutters and a selection of angled levers. Now, that's *really* professional stuff. And then he gets in and he doesn't take anything—'

He stood up. 'What you do, miss?'

Victoria looked blankly at him. 'I'm just a dealer in the Eurobond market.'

'Ever bring any files home?' He smiled. 'I'm not a money man myself, but I read the columns. All that skulduggery with takeovers and insider dealings. I mean, the people in the fast lane can make millions out of it. Nothing that might apply there?'

Victoria shook her head. 'I've never brought anything home. It wouldn't help anyone even if I had. And anyway I gave up my job a month ago.'

'Just an idea.' He rubbed his chin reflectively. 'A right puzzle, this one. We'll check the prints, but I'd guess they'll be yours. Chummies who use bolt-cutters and angled levers wear gloves too.'

She accompanied him down the stairs to the front door.

The WPC and the young policeman were talking together by the police car a few yards away. On the doorstep the older man turned and shook her hand.

'I'll give you a tip, miss,' he said. 'I shouldn't but I will. Most break-ins today are by druggies after something they can steal and trade for a fix. A good fix costs forty pounds. Put that out on the table in cash, they'll take it, and they'll bugger off and leave you alone.'

'Thanks.' Victoria smiled at him. 'I'll follow the advice.'

'Best I can do. It doesn't solve chummy here. Whoever he was, he wasn't your run-of-the-mill druggie.'

He frowned, perplexed. Then he lifted his hand and walked away to join his colleagues.

Victoria tidied up.

It took her less time than she'd expected. As she'd realised in her first quick assessment of the break-in, there'd been no vindictive damage. It was more as if a clever and determined child, wilfully searching for something they wanted, had scattered all her possessions across the floor. Victoria gathered up everything and stored it away again.

Within two hours the flat was looking almost as she'd left it when she flew out to Delhi.

She poured out a large whisky.

Then she sat down and reached for her address book. She telephoned her insurance company, her landlord, her builder, her local locksmith. Half an hour later everything was in train. Her insurance claim would be met, new doors and new locks would be installed before the day was out, everyone was sympathetic.

Victoria poured another whisky.

She glanced at her telephone answering machine. It was giving out a sequence of red signals, indicating the messages left on it, and she realised she hadn't played them back. She drank and pressed the play-button.

'Sunshine, it's me. Where on earth are you? I have truly been looking for you everywhere. Mary says she thinks you be abroad. If you are now back, please call me. *Please*. Listen. I think I may have made a little mistake—'

It was Charlie's voice.

Victoria cut the message off and ran the tape forward. A little mistake. Charlie had made the biggest bloody mistake of his life, and the bastard could live with it – and the bitch Angela too.

'Darling.' It was her mother now. 'I'm a little worried. You seem to have gone off the air, as they say. Please ring as soon as you can. Various, well, problems appear to be cropping up. Octavie and Maude have been on to me after your visit. Darling, we really must talk. This is something quite serious for all of us.'

The third message was from Rory Watson. The message rambled on for several anguished minutes.

'Hello, Victoria? I'm calling again from the box in the passageway here at the museum. Victoria, this is difficult, verra difficult, but I must get it off my chest.

'Sally knew something had happened. She asked me and I told her. Maybe I shouldna have but I did. She has moved out and gone to stay with her friend Catriona. She says she would like to meet you and see. She is very angry. Can you do that, see her, I mean?

'Also, I am discovering more about your grandfather and his friend, Mr Yeats. They seem to have been yoked together in their ornithological expeditions. Please telephone me at the office. I will call you back from this damnable box.'

Victoria thought for several moments. Then she ran the tape on again.

Interspersed between several casual messages from friends were two from Carter, Kenright. They were the firm of solicitors who had handled her family's legal affairs for years. Victoria had barely ever had any contact with them, there'd been no need, but she knew their name well enough.

The first call was from a secretary asking her to get in touch with Mr Carter as soon as possible. The second a few days later was from Mr Carter himself. Carter, she vaguely remembered, was the firm's senior partner.

'This is James Carter,' the voice said. 'I understand from your mother you may be abroad. If you pick up this message while you're away, or if not as soon as you get back, I would urge you to contact me immediately. There are matters I feel we should discuss immediately. I do hope to speak to you very soon.'

Victoria had never known what the word 'mellifluous' meant as a description of someone's voice. She did now. It meant it was quiet, charming, resonant, and in this case filled with menace.

There were other messages but she didn't want to listen to them. She switched off the machine and poured herself a third whisky. She folded her arms over the table, lowered her head into them, and wept.

Her life was being invaded and pillaged. She didn't know who the intruders were, but she knew who'd built the Trojan horse which had let them in.

It was herself.

Victoria hadn't the slightest idea who'd broken into the flat, but she knew what they were after. The boxes, files, and papers she'd taken from the great-aunts at Glenmoray. It hadn't even needed the nice balding policeman to plant the idea in her mind. She'd realised that almost as soon as she came in, certainly after she'd walked round and seen nothing of her own was missing.

'Very professional,' he'd said, puzzled.

Someone not only professional but almost certainly violent – you had to be equipped for violence to carry bolt-cutters and angled levers – had cut his way into what Victoria always regarded as her sanctuary. Then there was Charlie. Both pleading – she'd never imagined him doing that – and still defiantly buoyant – no doubt on his way back home, the swine, to screw Angela.

And her mother with her curious, carefully phrased insinuations. And Rory Watson, another whiner, Victoria had decided, with his worries about his girlfriend Sally and his new information, whatever that might be, about Grandfather's collection. And finally the soft-voiced, sinister-sounding James Carter.

And because Victoria was free, white, and over twenty-one, because she'd embarked on a course and she'd never walked away from anything she'd started until it was finished, she'd have to deal with them all.

She laughed with what she knew was an edge of hysteria. Then, exhausted and dizzy from the three whiskies, she threw herself on her bed.

She fell asleep. She didn't even notice the hammering when the men arrived to replace the door.

'Sally?' Victoria smiled brightly at the young woman in front of her. 'I'm Victoria Ruthven.'

Victoria pulled up a chair and sat down opposite her.

They were in a wine bar in Chelsea.

Victoria had compiled a list in her mind of what needed to be dealt with. For no particular reason she'd put Sally, Rory Watson's girlfriend, at the head of the list. Rory had left her telephone number at the end of his message. She'd telephoned Sally and asked her out for a drink.

'Where's Rory?' Victoria went on.

'Still at the museum, I guess.' Sally shrugged. 'We're meant to be meeting later for supper.'

Victoria looked at her.

She wasn't beautiful but in a strange, almost pre-Raphaelite way she was remarkably attractive, with long and dark tumbling curls of hair, a pale face, and dark eyes. She looked sulky and resentful, but also curious. She kept eyeing Victoria watchfully.

'What do you do?' Victoria asked.

'Didn't he tell you?'

Victoria shook her head.

'Much the same as him except it's up in the Museum of Childhood in Bethnal Green. I'm an assistant curator—'

She spoke about her work. As she did her expression changed. Her face lost its chill, hostile gaze and became more alive, almost eager and bright. She finished, and the dark suspicious reserve returned.

'All right, that's me,' she said. 'What about you?'

'I'm just a banker, or I was,' Victoria shrugged. 'I'm not anything any more.'

'Why did you pick on him?'

'Accident. I wanted to learn about my grandfather. We had dinner and it happened. No plan, no grand design, nothing. Just that. It's over, finished, gone. He's your man, not mine.'

Sally stared at her.

Victoria knew that even in the small and short space of time and experience they were sharing, a turning-point had come. The young woman could either accept what she'd said, or reject it.

Sally accepted it. She nodded. A swift smile crossed her face which until then had been bleak and unforgiving.

'Men are bastards, aren't they?'

Victoria leaned back and laughed. 'Don't tell me! I'm one of the world's experts on that – and I'm not talking about Rory!'

Sally wrinkled her forehead.

The mood, the atmosphere between them, had totally changed. They'd met as combatants. Now they were almost companions.

'Rory's really got it in for your grandpa,' she said. 'I don't quite know why except Rory's a real radical. He hates money and privilege and the upper classes, and everything they stand for. He can rage on for hours about it. The politics of envy, some people call it.'

Victoria thought of the anger she'd seen in his eyes the first time she'd met him in the museum.

She nodded.

'He wants to trash Colonel Ruthven,' Sally went on. 'He'll do it, too. Impossible to stop him when his science and his politics fit together. They become a crusade. Ideally he'd like to see your grandfather burnt at the stake with him putting in the torch.'

'I rather guessed it,' Victoria said, 'but thanks for the warning.'

She bought Sally another glass of wine.

27

Victoria looked round the room in astonishment.

For a moment she was so surprised, so caught off-balance, she almost gasped. She had difficulty in keeping control of her expression. She managed to steady herself and sit down in the chair that had been offered her.

Her hands were trembling but she tucked them away out of sight between her knees.

'I think everyone's very glad you're able to be here, Miss Ruthven, or would you allow me the informality sometimes permitted the old and let me call you Victoria?'

He peered at her over the top of his gold-rimmed half-glasses. She gave him a quick glazed smile and nodded.

He was Mr James Carter, senior partner in the family's firm of solicitors. She'd telephoned in reply to the messages left first by his secretary and then by him, and arranged to come into the firm's offices. She had no idea what he wanted to talk to her about, although she guessed that in some way it might involve her grandfather.

She'd been prepared for almost anything – except this. As well as Mr Carter, seated round the table were his secretary, a young man Victoria assumed was his assistant, and then – and this was what had astounded her – her mother and the two great-aunts, Octavie and Maude.

Her mother, impeccably dressed in one of her most elegant two-piece suits in heavy cotton-silk from Worth, was carefully avoiding looking at her. Octavie and Maude were gazing at her with hard, fixed expressions on their faces that were close to hatred. In Scotland, in spite of the occasional bickering between themselves, they'd been benign and gentle. They'd been like that, as far as Victoria could remember, on all her visits to Glenmoray from her earliest childhood.

Everything had suddenly changed.

They sat on either side of Mr Carter with a terrible intense glare in their eyes. Immensely ancient but still powerful, they looked to Victoria like falcons pitilessly examining what might be their last prey.

The change was so odd, so shocking, so frightening, it made her feel physically sick. She controlled herself again and listened to Mr Carter.

'A good solicitor, and I would like to think I'm at least a competent one, serves many functions,' he said. 'We do conveyancing, we prepare wills, we handle litigation. Sometimes, perhaps our most important role, we can act as umpires. We can halt quite unnecessary divisions within a family. We can if you like make peace.'

Victoria stared at him. 'What do you mean?'

'You recently visited your great-aunts.' He indicated Octavie and Maude with a small graceful wave of his hand. 'They subsequently discovered a whole collection of papers entrusted to them by their late brother had disappeared. If you can help secure their return, I'm sure this whole matter can be put to rest.'

There was a moment's silence.

Victoria thought.

Her hands, clasped in her lap, were shivering again. She remembered what Charlie had taught her. Never complain, never explain. If you're caught out, either go on to the attack or apologize with roses. It was no time for roses – rose-time was over.

'Are you accusing me of stealing the papers?' she demanded.

'Of course not, my dear.'

Mr Carter made a bland, deprecatory gesture. Victoria's mother was still gazing out of the window. The two great-aunts were still watching her fiercely and angrily.

'We'd just like your assistance in returning them to the place where they rightfully belong.'

'Why? Do they reveal something shameful or dishonest about my grandfather?'

'Naturally not.' He gave her a patronising smile. 'Colonel Ruthven was one of the most honourable men my firm has ever dealt with. No, it's a question of sentimental value and, under law, property rights. The papers belong to your great-aunts.'

'They belong much more to me,' Victoria snapped in reply. 'My great-aunts were his sisters. I'm his only blood descendant.'

She no longer cared about Mr Carter, about the two predatory old ladies, even for the moment about her mother. They were all childhood authority figures and they had suddenly lost their authority.

She was in the wrong, Victoria knew that. But she was also being manipulated and abused, and it enraged her.

They had something to hide and they were trying to coerce her into submission, into giving the papers back with whatever secrets they contained. That bewildered her too because from all she'd read so far, Grandfather's files contained nothing except the rough-and-tumble antics of a passionate young man with, perhaps, the hint of a homosexual relationship.

It was hardly a reason for all this. The rising tide of anger in her must have come out in her voice. Mr Carter drew his hands thoughtfully across his face, and abruptly changed tack.

'Victoria, you're the beneficiary of a discretionary trust created for you by your grandfather. Your mother is a trustee, so am I, so are your two great-aunts.'

'I know that,' Victoria said. She frowned. 'What do you mean?'

'The trustees have discretionary powers to withhold income distribution if they feel the beneficiary is using the funds unwisely.'

It was a moment before Victoria took in the pedantic legal phraseology. Then she realised what he meant. They were going to cut off her allowance from the trust.

She felt stunned. She could barely believe it. She turned towards her mother.

'Mum, do you know about this?'

'Darling.' For the first time her mother turned to face her. 'All this is so, so unnecessary. I do think Mr Carter is right. I do think you owe Octavie and Maude an apology. Those papers really are private, there's nothing remotely interesting in them but they should go back to Glenmoray. Please be sensible.'

Victoria bristled. 'And if I'm not, not "sensible"?'

Her mother's face was acutely unhappy. 'Darling, it just won't do. I must be guided by family considerations and advice.'

Victoria sat for an instant, stiff and frozen.

The faces of all the other four were turned towards her. Her mother's looked anxious, Mr Carter's grave and inscrutable, the two great-aunts' no longer angry but fearful, almost pleading. Victoria's gaze ranged round them. She pushed back her chair and got to her feet.

She didn't give a damn for any of their personal or professional considerations. They had, she knew, formed a conspiracy against her. If it wasn't so bitter and humiliating it would almost have been laughable – two old Scottish ladies, her own mother, and a respected lawyer forming a concert party to blackmail and virtually to threaten her.

They could and would cut off her money, Victoria had no doubt of that. But they couldn't kneecap her, they couldn't stop her. They had something to conceal and they thought it belonged only to them. It didn't. It was hers too, just as much and maybe even more.

'Someone broke into my flat yesterday,' she said. 'I think I can find out who he was, what he was after, and who sent him. I shall let you know. I'm sure it will interest you all.'

Victoria turned and walked from the room. Behind her there was silence.

The offices of Carter, Kenright were just off the Strand.

Less than fifty yards away and in the Strand itself was a pub, a favourite haunt of Charlie's, where she'd often met him after both their working days finished. She didn't mind about its associations with him now. Victoria wasn't sure she minded about anything.

She was trembling in a mixture of fury, confusion, and fear.

Before she could even begin to think ahead, she needed to 'steady' herself, as Mr Gable would have put it. She needed a large and very strong drink. She went into the pub. She ordered a double vodka and tonic, and sat down at a table beside the bow-fronted window that looked over the street.

She'd hardly taken a sip when the swing doors with their engraved glass panels opened and clanged shut. She glanced up incuriously. The pub was almost empty, it was still too early for the evening business, but someone else had come in.

It was Charlie.

He glanced round the bar. He spotted her and checked. Then he came over to the table.

'Victoria—'

'You've got one thing right,' she answered. 'At least that's my name.'

'Can I sit down?'

'If I were you I'd buy a drink first. Sure as hell I won't be buying one for you. And, no,' she added, 'don't offer me one. These days I buy my own.'

He went back to the bar and returned with a tankard of beer. He looked awkward and embarrassed.

'Victoria, this is serendipity. Did you get my message? I really do want to talk to you.'

Serendipity was a word Charlie had taught her. It meant, as far as Victoria could remember, happiness by coincidence.

'Nothing serendip about this,' she said. 'Just chance and me wanting a drink. How's beloved Angela?'

'Poor Angela has problems—'

His forehead furrowed and he hunched his shoulders sadly as if he was contemplating one of the world's tragedies.

'She's gone back to Magnus to try and resolve them.'

Magnus, a temperamental set-designer, was Angela's husband.

'Meaning his cock may be longer and harder than yours?'

Charlie stared at her with an expression of genuine shock.

'That's vulgar and abusive. I said in my message I'd made a mistake. But Angela has her sensitivities, so do I, so probably does Magnus.'

'But not me? I'm the Teflon lady, fireproof, right?'

'If you're going to behave like this, I don't think I do want to talk to you.'

Charlie started to rise. Victoria shook her head.

'Sit down, Charlie,' she said. 'You've got something to say to me. I've got something to say to you.'

He slowly returned to his seat.

Victoria knew he would. Not because he loved her, even if he ever had loved her. Not because of any lingering pocket of affection from their seven-year relationship – she regarded the term with derision now. Not out of guilt for abandoning her for Angela.

No. For none of that. Charlie was a journalist. He was after a story. That was why he'd telephoned and asked her out to dinner. Why he'd telephoned again and left the message she hadn't even listened to. Why he'd come over to her table a few minutes ago. And why he wouldn't go now.

'Who starts?' he said.

'You,' Victoria answered.

'Does the word Silverback mean anything?'

She thought. 'No, nothing at all.'

'It didn't to me either until I looked it up,' Charlie said. 'It's a term used for the patriarch of a gorilla clan. The clan leaders are almost always old, they have grey hair down their spines, zoologists call them silverbacks.'

'And so?'

Victoria didn't understand him. She couldn't see what, in one of her old Scottish nanny's favourite expressions, it had to do with the price of fish on Friday.

'I told you about the Yeats Foundation,' Charlie went on. 'Normally vehicles like that are watertight. They're set up and exist on their own. Not this one. It seems it's a spin-off from something called Silverback Corporation, a private South African company.'

Victoria still couldn't grasp where he was leading. 'What's that got to do with me?'

'Silverback covenants eighty per cent of its profits to the Foundation. They're tax-exempt. But it keeps twenty per cent and although its slice of the revenue is taxed, the net income now must be vast. The Johannesburg registry shows Silverback had only two founding shareholders. They were Eric Yeats and Colonel Ruthven—'

Charlie broke off. 'Someone or some people somewhere, or their heirs and assigns, are not only seriously rich – they're becoming richer by the day.'

Victoria tried to absorb what he'd said.

At that moment she couldn't. She knew it concerned her, she knew she'd have to deal with it. But for now there were far more important, more pragmatic, matters on her mind.

She looked at Charlie. She swallowed her pride, her humiliation, even the loathing she'd begun to feel for him – and she hated herself for the waves of fury that still surged over her. They were sterile and destructive, but fight against them as she would, they still battered her mind.

And yet she needed him. He was the only way out she could see ahead of her. She finished her drink and licked her lips, tasting the last tangy fragments of juniper in the gin.

'I'm nearly out of money, Charlie, and I want a job,' she said.

'You're *what*?' Charlie gazed back at her, astounded. 'You've got a job, and much better paid than mine. And you've got your trust fund. God knows, what else do you want?'

'It's not like that any longer.'

Victoria told him.

It took an enormous effort of will. At least to begin with. And then she found herself becoming liberated, bold, even reckless. The walls of reserve and respectability which had fortified her life started to crumble. She found she didn't care any longer about dignity and self-respect.

'I've always done things for you,' she finished. 'What can you do for me?'

It took Charlie several moments to absorb what she'd told him. He sat frowning.

'I could go to Features,' he said eventually. 'Depending on what turns up, the Yeats–Silverback story could be a significant one. It might run across two pages. They'd probably allow me to buy in research services for a few weeks.'

'Do it, Charlie,' Victoria said. 'You've got yourself a researcher.'

'Is this a step towards peace?'

She shook her head violently. 'On a personal level it's a step towards bugger-all. Make your peace with Angela when she trots back. This is just professional because you owe me one.'

Victoria stood up and left before he could say anything else.

28

'Victoria—'

She turned.

She'd just got back from her encounter with Charlie and she was standing on the landing about to open her newly replaced door. It was her neighbour on the floor below, Mr Foster. She hadn't seen him since her return from India and Nepal.

'I'm so sorry about the break-in,' he went on. 'I hope you didn't lose too much. It was me who called the police. I felt I had to because of the front door being smashed open too. I do hope that was all right with you.'

'You did absolutely the right thing, Mr Foster, and thank you. The police told me you'd telephoned. Happily I don't seem to have lost anything – perhaps because I haven't got anything a self-respecting burglar would want.'

She smiled at him.

Mr Foster scratched his head. He was a quiet, nervous man, but he looked even more worried than usual.

'There was something else while you were away,' he said awkwardly. 'I didn't tell the police this, because I didn't think it was relevant. In fact I thought it might be an intrusion. A man was here looking for you the morning after you left. He rang my bell in mistake for yours.'

'A man?' Victoria tensed. 'What sort of man?'

It might just conceivably have been one of her friends, but that was unlikely. She hadn't told anyone she was going abroad, and they'd have assumed she was following the normal pattern of her life, out all day at work. The only other remote possibilities were Charlie and Rory Watson.

From Mr Foster's description it was obvious it wasn't either of them.

'Tall and thin, as I remember,' Mr Foster said, 'with a somewhat balding head. Very polite he was and well-dressed too. A bit like a retired bank manager, if I can put it like that. The only thing I noticed was his accent. A little sing-song, rather like the Welsh.'

'Did he leave his name?'

'No. He said he'd return when you got back.'

'Thank you, Mr Foster. You're the eyes and ears of the street, our very own neighbourhood watch,' Victoria laughed. 'He was probably an insurance salesman, but please try to get his name if you see him again.'

'I will, Victoria. I just thought I ought to mention it. I try to keep an eye on things.'

He peered up at her, rather proud of himself. Then he shuffled away.

Victoria went into her flat. She went straight over to the table on which the telephone sat. She flipped through her address book, lifted the receiver, and dialled.

'Mr Evans?' she asked after the voice answered.

'Yes.'

'This is Victoria Ruthven,' she said. 'I've been abroad as you know. While I was away my flat was broken into. The local police tell me it was a very professional entry. It was either done by an experienced criminal or someone with long experience of criminal methods—'

She paused.

There was silence at the other end of the line.

'I have a neighbour with sharp ears and eyes. He sits at his window, twitching his white gauze curtain and watching the street. He's given me an excellent description of the would-be thief. I haven't passed it on to the police yet because nothing seems to have been taken—'

Victoria stopped again. There was still utter silence at the other end.

'But I will, believe me, if necessary I will,' she continued. 'Meanwhile, if you still have contacts in the criminal community as even retired policemen are reported to do, you can tell them there is nothing here they may be looking for. Nothing!'

Without giving him a chance to say anything, Victoria slammed the receiver down so hard that a fragment of the plastic mouthpiece broke off and spiralled away across the floor.

She was seething with anger.

The threat she'd made in the conference room at Carter, Kenright, that she could find out who'd burgled her, had been an entirely empty one then. It was simply a defiant response to the pressure they were putting her under. She hadn't the slightest idea who'd broken into the flat.

She did now.

It was retired Detective-Inspector Evans. It could only have been him. And Victoria had little doubt why he'd done it. He'd contacted the great-aunts or her mother or even Mr Carter, and they'd pointed him in the right direction. They'd also probably and discreetly paid him.

It suited all of their interests, not least Mr Evans'. If he'd been caught or challenged he could reasonably say he was only trying to recover stolen property. He was a longstanding member of the police fraternity, he could tap into the professional freemasonry of his former colleagues, he could hold his position and get away with it.

The bastard. Except he hadn't succeeded.

Victoria took a quick bath. She called Fiona. Then she dressed and went down to the street. Before setting off, she looked to left and right to check whether anyone was sitting in a parked car or lingering in the spaces of shadow between the street-lamps. It was something she'd never done before, something she thought only paranoiacs did.

Not any longer.

As far as she could tell there was no one. She headed for Fiona's flat. It was only a few streets away, but as she walked Victoria found she was constantly looking over her shoulder. She got to the flat, rang the bell, and Fiona let her in.

'V!' Fiona stared at her, shocked. 'You look a wreck. What on earth's happened?'

'Too much,' Victoria answered wearily, 'and none of it fun.'

'I told you I was going out, but I can cancel Tom.'

Victoria shook her head. 'I'll be fine in a while. I'd just like to stay here and read. Nothing's happened to those boxes I left, has it?'

Victoria glanced across the room to where she'd deposited Ruthven's archives. They looked untouched.

'Of course not,' Fiona said. 'What is all this?'

'Just a messy family tangle which seems to involve a lot of other people, a lot of money, and a whole load of other problems too.'

'Is Charlie involved?'

Fiona had known Charlie throughout Victoria's relationship with him. When he walked out, Fiona was the first person Victoria had told.

'In a way, but not directly.'

Fiona frowned. 'V, why don't I stay and you tell me all about it?'

Victoria put out her arms and kissed her.

'You go,' she said. 'I probably just want to be on my own and go through all this damn stuff. You may well find me asleep on the floor when you get back.'

Fiona hesitated.

'All right,' she said, 'but you sleep on my perfectly good Z-bed and you sleep there for as long as you want. I'm not talking one night, I'm talking weeks if you choose.'

She turned and unfolded the bed which already had its linen tucked into the mattress. She smoothed down the pillow.

'Are you sure you don't want me to stay?'

Victoria shook her head again. She smiled. 'I'll settle for a cup of coffee in the morning.'

Fiona smiled back. Five minutes later she'd gone. Victoria went over to the boxes of papers.

She'd been through the childhood letters.

She'd read the postcards and letters from South Africa, the journals describing his life in the trenches in the First World War, the strange entries for India and Nepal afterwards. There were gaps between them all and the gaps grew longer.

Ruthven might have been trained and expected to write, but fluency with the written word either hadn't come easily to him or much of what he'd written had been lost. The remaining notebooks were in a way a puzzle to Victoria and she had to tease her way through them.

They were not so much journals as ledgers, detailing investments and accounts, profits and, very occasionally, losses. It was a jigsaw of entries and figures which eventually she pieced together.

Ruthven was recording the growth of Silverback, the company he and Eric Yeats had founded and which now lay, according to Charlie, behind the Yeats Foundation. They had bought ranches and cattle. They had invested in mines, hotels, railways, and vineyards. They were one of the founding members of the consortium which had set up South Africa's electrical power supply industry, and of another group which had pioneered telephone communications.

Silverback's interests seemed to range everywhere throughout the southern half of the continent. There was no indication of where the capital for the company's investments had come from, but it wasn't hard to guess. Ruthven would have had nothing from the barren uplands of Glenmoray, and wouldn't have been able to borrow against them.

The money could only have come from Eric Yeats, or rather from the fortune his father had made from his association with Cecil Rhodes. And yet somehow, if Victoria read the accounts rightly, the two of them, grandfather and Yeats, had been joint partners. Yeats had put up all the money and Ruthven had taken half the profits.

Except as an extraordinarily quixotic and generous gesture by Yeats, it made no sense. Not even taking into account, if Victoria was right, a long and deep homosexual relationship between them. Not even the arrival of Sophia in their lives.

Something was missing.

Victoria went back to the ledgers. She combed through them again forlornly. There seemed to be nothing there except the columns of figures she'd studied before. And then right at the end, in the last of the leather-bound volumes, she found something that had escaped her attention.

Tucked into a small wallet inside the back board of the last journal, a wallet presumably intended to store bills and receipts, was a tiny day-by-day diary. It was a five-year diary bound in thin but fine red Moroccan leather. Five-year diaries, she remembered reading somewhere, were all the vogue at the time. This one was filled in with entries in what to Victoria was by now Ruthven's unmistakable hand – angular and sloping and containing the occasional misspelling.

The entries weren't anything like as full as in the earlier journals. They were more in the way of notes and jottings. Perhaps he was constricted by the brief space the diary panels gave him. Perhaps his own style of communication had changed. Whatever the reason, they were still intermittently filled with passion.

Victoria had to leaf through the pages carefully to find those moments – most of the pages recorded the weather, social engagements, and developments in the Silverback enterprise – but now and then she found something else, something entirely different. It was as if late at night after recording the day's catalogue of events, Ruthven had been impelled to set down something far more personal and important to him.

On 4 October 1922 he wrote:

The Scharnlust farm is a good purchase, I'm sure of that.
     It took us the whole damn day to agree the deal with those

gimlet-eyed voortrekkers' sons, but we won in the end. Why did Eric spoil it afterwards? We should have been celebrating together. Instead he was at his worst, teasing, mocking, jeering. Of course we need the Yeats' funds. But without me, without what I can put into the pot, the money might as well be tossed into the currents off the Cape.

For God's sake, I know these people. Eric doesn't, he just doesn't understand them. What the hell is he playing at?

Two weeks later there was an entry saying: 'The Scharnlust deeds signed today. Eric contrite and peace reigns. We had a proper celebration.'

A month afterwards there was another and much more intriguing entry.

Sophia is on her way here. She has news. She gave this, without saying what it was, in a letter to E although not to me. Is E more radiant, more brilliant and interesting than I? simply don't believe it. Oh, vanity, vanity! Tomorrow I shall look with more than my usual scrupulous care in my shaving-mirror.

A month later still, apparently in a much darker and more sombre mood and in a vein much closer to the unfettered writing in his earlier journals, he wrote an entry that spilled over several pages.

We have her again. We dined at the Nellie. This time it was her treat, her surprise, though I bet the account was slipped into E's pocket at the evening's end. I asked E this morning. He wouldn't say. Just laughed.

Anyway, it was the best table and she'd chosen the flowers and the wine (she's conceived a passion for Meerlust) and the food. Very simple. She goes for harbour-caught fish. It was a silvery-skinned pink-fleshed bass. She'd bought it herself off some angler on the front. What the Nellie's chef made of it when she strode into the kitchen and dumped it on his table, I just don't know. I can't imagine it's ever happened before.

We ate and then she told us. She said: 'What are you going to do about it?' E just laughed. 'We are in cabinet,' he said. 'Sensible cabinet decisions are only arrived after long and quiet reflection.' He reached out and took not her hand, but mine.

Christ (if he'll forgive me for invoking his name), I sometimes think E's mad!

Victoria turned the diary's pages.

There were three months of mundane entries about the progress of Silverback. Then another quick flash of personal writing from Ruthven.

Well, we've always done it like that. We did it in that jape at school. E's idea, but most are. The coin tossed and the decision made. So it's fallen once again. Why S accepted it so blandly and so smiling – aren't Moors meant to smile (or was that Iago?) – I don't know.

Women are hell. Beautiful and desirable, but hell. And I, God help me, because of that wretched coin, the losing fall, am going to be left with the leavings, what I think the Latin scholars call the detritus.

Why can't matters be simpler? Why can't they be as they were before? Why can't we go back to the bush, sleep out under clean stars, bathe naked in fresh rivers, search for our birds, talk over fires?

Why the hell has S with her baggage and luggage, her freight and consignments and all her damn impedimenta, invaded our lives again?

And yet, oh God, on that mistaken coin's toss, I shall miss you, my dear heart, for ever.

Victoria sat very still. Then she turned the pages again. The next entry, after further ranks of figures, was a hurried note.

I have heard from the girls. They are sending me a certain Margaret Lomax. They say she is bonny and of their age. She's the stalker's daughter on the Sandwood beat of Kilearn which marches with Glenmoray to the north. They say I should remember her as a child from the winter *ceilidhs*.

Well, I don't, but I trust the sisters' judgement.

I can't be doing with what's on offer here, these sour-faced trekkers' daughters with their belief in the whips their fathers laid across them. Harry needs something gentler. Firm, maybe, but with a bit of wisdom and kind words in it. Also a voice to learn from that doesn't speak in the grating accent of the Afrikaans.

A West Highland nurse could well be the answer. I hope in picking this little Maggie Lomax the sisters have chosen well.

29

Harry.

It was the first time he'd been mentioned. No one ever talked about Harry. He was, in the phrase of the time, a bounder – a gambler, a wastrel, a drunk. He'd kept a stable of mistresses, or they'd kept him. He bought beautiful racehorses, which consistently failed to win, and elegant cars, Mercedes, Daimlers, and Ferraris, which he wrecked in crashes within days of purchasing them.

He plundered and fornicated and charmed his way through life. And then at the age of fifty he died. The coroner decided after the inquest it was an accident, Harry had tripped over his gun while out shooting duck. The coroner was a kind and sensitive man, keen to give the benefit of doubt, keen to protect the feelings of the family.

Harry hadn't died in a misadventure with his shotgun.

The man, drunk as he might have been, was far too experienced with weapons for that. He'd run out of possibilities and hope and maybe ladies to look after him. He was in despair and he'd killed himself with as much dignity as he could summon.

None of which might have mattered except as a tragic example of the perils of being born. Apart from one fact.

Harry, Victoria realized with a sense of shock – registering the fact for the first time – shameful, dismissed, hidden, and buried Harry, was her father.

Victoria spent the night with Fiona. Then when Fiona went off to work in the morning, she returned to her own flat.

There was as usual a whole collection of messages on her answering machine. Victoria played through them quickly. There was only one she was interested in, from Charlie. As she approached the end she was beginning to think he hadn't telephoned.

In fact his was the last message of all.

'Victoria, I'm not going into the office today, I'm working from home. However I got the features editor before he left his place.

Good news, but it's important we meet to talk it through. Give me a call just as soon as you get back. I'll come straight into town and we'll get together.'

Over the past month Charlie had had three different homes. The first with her, the second with the bitch Angela, now this third one, for which he'd left the number, with a male journalist friend of his who lived in Ealing. The bastard was cavalierly moving on like a vagrant hopping freight trains.

Victoria cursed him again and dialled.

They met in a wine bar off the King's Road. Victoria got there first with Charlie typically arriving almost an hour after he'd promised.

'Sorry for being a couple of minutes late.' He dropped into the chair opposite hers. 'Something I had to check out.'

He was wearing a rumpled velvet jacket, an open-necked white silk shirt with frayed cuffs, and a scuffed pair of suede shoes so badly worn they were like the tyres on a cowboy truck. His hair was tousled, he'd cut himself twice while shaving, and his eyes were deeply shadowed.

Victoria could guess what he'd been doing.

Charlie had been drinking and playing poker until the early hours with what he called 'the school'. Victoria didn't believe he even really enjoyed poker. It was something he had to do as part of his presentation of himself. Charlie had missed out on all the glamorous icon conflicts of the post-war years, even Vietnam because he was just too young, but he gave a superb impression of a war correspondent who'd covered every one.

The late-night drinking and poker-playing were part of the hard-bitten, cynical image.

She'd seen through it almost from the start. Until now she'd never minded. Now she did. She felt all the more humiliated because she'd taken care to dress smartly and carefully herself. The matter was so important it hadn't occurred to her to do anything else.

Charlie had just shambled in, playing his usual role and expecting her to be taken in by it. It was pathetic and insulting. Victora could barely restrain herself from telling him so, but she fought down her anger and instead looked at him with utter distaste.

'I've wasted an hour,' she said icily. 'What's the "good" news?'

'Three weeks as my research assistant at the paper's so-called generous rates, which are in fact quite generous. Also reasonable

172

expenses.' Charlie paused. 'Those include your ticket to Cape Town with me tomorrow evening.'

'My *what*?' Victoria said.

'Our stringer out there's been digging into the whole Yeats–Ruthven axis,' Charlie answered. 'Both got married in Cape Town. Cape Town keeps civil marriage records, but it didn't then record births. The odds are one or other marriage, probably both, resulted in what the lawyers call issue. If they did, Silverback is likely to have been handed on to the next generation. Who the hell else do people give private corporations to except their children?'

Victoria blinked. 'And you expect me to fly out there with you to try to find out?'

'Blossom, you asked me to get you a job,' Charlie replied. 'I've done better. I've got you free to Cape Town and beyond if we need it. Isn't that what you wanted?'

Victoria stared round the bar.

Try as she would, her thoughts wouldn't fall into any coherent pattern. They tumbled at random like fragments of coloured flakes in a constantly shaken kaleidoscope. Yes, she wanted a job. Yes, she'd asked Charlie to find her one – or Christ's sake, he owed her that at least.

But, no, she hadn't envisaged working for him except in a purely token sense. It was just a matter of him settling his dues to her, and, my God, after living for seven years rent-free in her flat he'd only be paying a fraction. And no, she hadn't thought of going to Africa. Except now after what she'd learnt, after what he'd told her, it made a circular sort of sense.

She was looking for an answer to a question.

Why had Jack Ruthven apparently forged so many specimens in the world-famous collection of bird-skins he'd given to the British Museum?

At least that had been the starting-point. Since then the past had thrown up a whole raft of other questions. All the still-hidden answers seemed tied together in a web that spread almost everywhere from the bleak enclosed private schools of England, where boys like Grandfather and Yeats were taught Christian ideals and almost encouraged to form homosexual relationships, to the British raj in India and Africa.

Then there was Sophia, Silverback, and the extraordinary action taken by Victoria's family and its lawyers over her trust fund. There was Eric Yeats' murder and now Charlie's revelation that Yeats and Grandfather were both married in Cape Town.

Even before she met Charlie this time, Victoria had begun to sense that the explanation lay in Africa, and that sooner or later she'd have to go there.

Charlie was offering her a way to do it.

'Of course when I say research, I do mean research,' Charlie added.

Victoria frowned. 'What do you mean?'

'I wasn't going to be given just any researcher, even if I could screw one out of Features at all. I had to argue the case, which meant fighting your corner. I said you were Colonel Ruthven's granddaughter. I said you had access to family information which could materially flesh out and complete the story.'

'Are you saying you sold me not as a researcher, but for my name and what I know?'

Charlie shrugged. 'I got you the job.'

'You bastard!'

He grinned. 'Are you coming?'

Victoria didn't answer. She gazed at him bitterly through narrowed eyes. The distaste on her face before had been replaced by an expression of what she knew could only signal hatred. Charlie must have registered it. She didn't care, in fact she was glad.

Except it didn't matter. She was stuck.

The flight from Heathrow to Cape Town landed in the South African dawn.

Luckily the plane was half-empty which meant Victoria didn't have to sit next to him. While Charlie dozed across the aisle, she sat for most of the night looking through the window at the starlit sky.

The paper's freelance Cape Town representative, their stringer as he was known in the world of the press, was waiting to meet them. Franjie Viljoen was a small, balding man with a tanned face and a thick moustache. He took them out to his car and drove them into the city.

'I've checked you into the Belvedere,' he said. 'Nice little place down on the harbour and close to the Nellie. Didn't know the arrangements, so went for separate rooms. You can change that if I've got it wrong.'

He barked out a sound that was something between a chuckle and a leer.

'Separate hotels would have been better,' Victoria snapped.

Charlie laughed. 'It's been a long flight, Franjie. That sounds fine.'

'Whatever you say, man. I've put the whole day aside. What's the score?'

'We'll dump our stuff at the hotel, shower, and breakfast,' Charlie answered. 'Then the registry first.'

'Let's go for it, man.'

They reached the hotel, and Viljoen waited while they bathed and had breakfast. Then the three of them climbed back into his car, and headed for the city's land registry. It was housed in an elegant red-brick colonial building, dwarfed now by the steel and concrete towers of Cape Town's modern commercial district that surrounded it on every side.

'Always been known as the land registry,' Viljoen said as they climbed the stairs to the second floor, 'because land claims and transactions were the most important they recorded. But in colonial times they kept other records too.'

They went into a vaulted gallery.

Victoria glanced a round. The walls were lined with shelves filled with leather-bound books. Running down the gallery's centre was a row of old and dark wooden tables with sloped reading stands on top of them. Spread open across the stands and held in place by brass clips were a number of huge ledgers.

Viljoen led them across to one of the ledgers. He pointed at an entry in neat but slightly faded copperplate writing at the centre of the page.

'Here it is,' he said. 'The librarian said I could leave it out ready for you.'

With Charlie at her side, Victoria peered down.

The entry recorded the marriage on 20 November 1921 of Eric Mortimer Yeats to Sophia Smith. The religious ceremony had taken place at the Anglican church of St Anthony's. Three days later, as required under Cape Colony law which was modelled on British law, it had been registered here.

'And this is the other one.' Viljoen took them over to another open ledger, 'I got the librarian to leave it out too.'

The entry in the second ledger showed that three years later John Charles James Ruthven had married Margaret Lomax at the same church.

Charlie lifted his head. He looked at the almost endless ranks of books on the shelves. He wrinkled his face.

'How the hell did you trace these two, Franjie?'

Viljoen gave his snorting bark of laughter, this time with pleasure.

'Pure genius, man! No, to be honest it's all been transferred to computer. The city keeps this for heritage. I keyed in the names. Only one Ruthven ever got married here, and among the Yeats – not many of them either – only one Eric. I just thought you'd like to see the original.'

Viljoen was carrying a briefcase. He opened it and pulled out some papers.

'Here's a complete printout for each of you of what you've been looking at.'

As Charlie and Victoria scanned the printouts, Viljoen added, 'So where now, man?'

Charlie glanced up. He thought.

'I want to see the city, Franjie,' he said. 'I want to get inside its skin. As it is now, but mostly then.'

They'd been inside the gallery for less than fifteen minutes.

As they went out Victoria's mind was trying to take in two things. Yeats had married Sophia, Sophia Smith as she gave her last name, although equally that could be one of the many aliases she used. And her grandfather had married the Scots nanny, Maggie Lomax, his sisters, Victoria's great-aunts, had sent out to look after Harry.

Victoria had always been told that her father, Harry, was Grandfather and Granny's son. Or rather she hadn't been told so. There was no need. It was just as much a fact of life as the daily rising of the sun.

Except it wasn't true.

Harry was the son of Grandfather and Sophia. Sophia and not Granny Lomax was Victoria's grandmother.

30

The tour lasted the rest of the day, with Charlie sitting alongside Viljoen in the front of the car and Victoria behind them.

They went everywhere.

They drove slowly along the clamorous front of the deep-water working harbour, and then into the formerly derelict area of it which had been transformed into a gleaming pedestrian complex with blue-painted railings, wooden walkways, and bustling cafés. They took the cable car to the top of Table Mountain and gazed out over Robben Island, the prison where among so many others Nelson Mandela had been incarcerated.

They visited a shantytown on the city's outskirts, and saw and smelt the squalor and stench in which the ever-growing tide of migrant blacks lived. They went out to Sandown and watched the pods of whales, barely a hundred yards away, diving and blowing in the lilac-blue waters of the Indian Ocean with sharks and dolphins thronging round them.

They lunched at a vineyard in one of Cape Town's suburbs.

They visited the Kirstenbosch Botanical Gardens, Cecil Rhodes' gift to the city, and strolled among beds of the strangest, most brilliantly coloured flowers Victoria had ever seen. They had an old-fashioned afternoon tea at the Mount Nelson Hotel, walking slowly through the high-ceilinged halls on their way to eat cucumber sandwiches and drink 'infusions made to Earl Grey's receipt' under canopies on the lawn, just as the colonial administrators arriving from England had done for generations.

And then in the dusk they headed back to their own hotel.

'Thanks, Franjie,' Charlie said as they got out. 'That was good.'

'My pleasure, man,' Viljoen replied. 'I've put tomorrow on hold. Anything special you want?'

Charlie thought for a moment.

'This is a real long shot,' he said. 'I'm getting the feel but the colour's

177

not quite there yet. Any chance of talking to someone around at the time who could give it to me first-hand?'

'Hell, that's not easy. You're talking seventy years ago.' Viljoen rubbed his chin. 'I'll see what I can do. No promises, but I'm not a genius for nothing, man!'

He laughed and drove away.

Upstairs ten minutes later Victoria lay back in her second bath of the day.

She'd poured almost half a flask of Floris oil into the bath, and she closed her eyes, letting the scented water ripple soothingly round her. Her body felt utterly limp and drained after the almost sleepless flight and the long day in the car, but strangely her mind was clear and alert.

In her misery and anger at Charlie's betrayal of her, she'd forgotten one thing about him.

He was wonderful at his job.

No one, she reflected, falls in love without reasons. One of the reasons she'd been attracted to him, perhaps the main reason, was the quality of his mind. In spite of all his posturing and pretence, he was a superb journalist. She'd been reminded of that today when for hour after hour she'd seen his mind and his professional dedication at work.

Charlie had sat with his notebook on his knee, filling page after page with Viljoen's answers to his incisive questions, or his notes on what they'd seen.

Politics, the geographical and historical positioning of a harbour city like Cape Town, the taste of the Cape's wines, the smells of the shantytown, the distant resonances of the Robben Island prison, the shapes of the buildings, the images of a black child playing in the dust or a white chauffeur-driven businessman passing them in a Mercedes, the meaning of unfamiliar phrases like line-caught fish.

Charlie absorbed it all.

He could do more than absorb it. He could distil it, flush away the dross, and then bottle the essence in writing that wasn't just lean and economical, but at its best evocative, almost magical. Charlie could create stories.

Victoria smiled.

That was one of Charlie's problems, maybe the major one. Writing. Like almost every journalist she knew, and she'd come to know many during the seven years they'd spent together, Charlie wanted to be a writer. Not a reporter who turned in articles, however good and strong and perceptive. But a real author, someone who wrote books.

Books were different from journalism. Books lasted. Books, Charlie and his friends believed, gave you immortality.

Like almost all of them, Charlie had never managed to do it. No doubt he'd told Angela he was really a proper writer, and his work on the paper was just a way to fill in time and pay the rent. For an instant Victoria almost felt a surge of sympathy for him. Then she remembered who had paid the rent over their years together – not Charlie, but her.

Before she could get angry again, there was a knock at her bedroom door.

'Who is it?' she called out.

'It's me, Charlie.'

She got out of the bath, wrapped a towel round her, and went to the door. Charlie was standing outside holding a bottle of what looked like champagne.

'South African sparkling,' he said, 'but dry and very good. Can I come in?'

'When I'm dressed.'

She closed the door in his face.

Victoria dried herself and dressed slowly. When she opened the door again, Charlie was still there. She beckoned him in. Charlie uncorked the bottle and filled the two glasses on the bedroom cabinet.

'What do you want?' she demanded as he handed her one of the glasses.

'Victoria, you haven't got any reason to trust me. The reverse. But try for the last time. Drink first and I'll tell you.'

Her body was aching. She wanted him out of the room. She drained the glass in a few quick gulps.

'I've done it,' she said. 'So?'

'Tell me about your grandfather.'

Afterwards Victoria wasn't sure what happened then.

Charlie was right about the wine.

It was straw-coloured, crisp, and tasted of grapes and warmth and sunlight. Perhaps because of her exhaustion it was extraordinarily invigorating – from the first swallow she felt the bubbles break in her mouth and the alcohol enter her bloodstream.

It wasn't just the champagne. Loneliness. Desolation. The alienation from her family. The gestures she'd made like taking Rory Watson to her bed, a bold gesture of freedom it had seemed then which now appeared futile. The multiplying threats from people like Evans and the break-in at her flat. They all came together and they were all too much.

Most of all it was not having someone to talk to. Charlie was a devious and manipulating bastard. He was also an ear and he was there.

Dizzy and confused on one level but with her mind still functioning on another, Victoria talked to him.

She told him everything from the beginning. Her visit to the museum and Watson's claim about the forgeries. Her stay with the great-aunts at Glenmoray and her removal of the diaries. And then everything that had happened since.

Charlie listened intently. When she finished he was silent for a while.

'Do you want something to eat?' he asked eventually.

Victoria shook her head. She was much too tired to eat.

'Fine, I understand. But I've had an idea. I'm going to go away and work on it. If I can sort it out, I'll bring it to you in the morning.'

Charlie did something then that he'd never done before. He bent down, took her hand, and kissed it. Then he left.

Victoria fell on to the bed and wept briefly for reasons she had no idea about. Within minutes and still fully dressed she was asleep.

She was still asleep when Charlie knocked on the door again in the morning. In his hand was a bundle of papers. He held them out to her.

'I wrote it during the night,' he said.

Victoria glanced drowsily at the first page.

At the top was the date and then a heading: 'Copy from Charlie – slug it The Silverback Story'. She looked up at him, puzzled, pointing at the heading.

'What does this mean?'

'Slug it? All these years together and you still don't know?' He chuckled. 'Journalistic shorthand. A slug's a metal bar the old-fashioned typesetters used to put in between a story's title and the copy – the words – that followed, to tell the story. We still use it if we telephone in from some godforsaken place that hasn't got computer linkup.'

'And what is the story?'

'What I think happened,' Charlie answered. 'Guesses and speculation mostly, but at least it's honest and I think it could be true—'

He opened the door again.

'Read it under its header.' He grinned. 'Forget about me. Think of it as the product of a poor but fairly honest hack's best efforts to re-create the past. I believe this is what happened.'

Charlie went out.

Victoria propped herself up in bed and began to read.

31

Sophia leaned over the rail and gazed forward.

She was standing on the open platform outside the observation lounge of the *Southern Star*'s top deck. She shivered slightly and drew her cloak round her shoulders. The day would be hot – each day had been hotter and more humid since the liner left Southampton three weeks ago – but it was very early morning, not quite yet dawn, and the air was still cool.

The captain had announced they would reach Cape Town soon after sunrise. He'd advised any passengers who wanted to get a first glimpse of Table Mountain in the dawn light to be up early. Surprisingly few had chosen to do so. There were two or three on the other side of the platform, but apart from them Sophia was alone. The others, she guessed, were sleeping off the celebrations of the night before to mark the end of the voyage.

Mist swirled round her.

From time to time as it parted she could see silvery skimming flashes of flying fish and the graceful arcs of leaping dolphins in the sea below. The mist cleared, the sun rose, and suddenly she saw the mountain – a great tower of dark rock with its flat table-like top, and a huddle of white buildings round the harbour at its foot.

An hour later the *Southern Star* nudged its way carefully into its berth. Sophia went down to her cabin to check her luggage was ready to be taken ashore. A smartly uniformed black porter came to collect it. As she followed him down the gangplank, Sophia checked for an instant.

For perhaps the hundredth time since she left England she wondered what she was doing there, what she'd let herself in for.

'A gentleman at table seventeen would be very glad if you would join him for a glass of champagne,' Klaus said.

Sophia glanced at him sharply. 'What sort?'

Klaus spread out his hands. 'Young and undoubtedly a gentleman. Also sober. I think proper, Miss Sophia.'

Klaus was Swiss-German and one of the brigade of deputy head-waiters at the Victoria music-hall.

Sophia, the second-but-last-act, had come off-stage fifteen minutes earlier, and the show had just ended. The audience in the cheap seats in the lower and upper sections of the auditorium would be thronging the public bars. At the much more expensive tables on the balcony, the gentry would be lingering and talking as they finished their drinks.

Sophia hesitated.

Klaus had obviously been paid to bring the invitation. However in her two weeks at the Victoria she'd come to trust him. She knew he'd filtered out any number of the usual approaches from the rich drunks and aristocratic lechers who used the balcony as their peep-show and playground.

Sophia was intrigued.

'I trust you're right, Klaus, she said. 'I need five minutes to tidy up, but you can say I'll accept – although I can't stay long.'

She wiped off the last of her heavy stage make-up, highlighted her face gently with the much softer and lighter colours she used outside the theatre, and gave her hair a quick vigorous brushing so the long auburn, almost copper-coloured curls spun out and cascaded round her neck and shoulders.

Sophia glanced quickly in the mirror. Then she set off for the balcony.

'Miss Sophia, what a pleasure! My name's Eric Yeats. Do sit down.'

Klaus had described him as young, but he was even younger than she'd expected, perhaps twenty-two to her own eighteen years. At first glance he wasn't very impressive. In fact, he was almost ugly. He was short and pudgy with a fat, sallow-skinned face that was already developing jowls, a thick moustache, and black pomaded hair slicked back against his head.

Sophia registered all of that but what she noticed even more vividly, what saved him, were his eyes.

They were extraordinary. Large and dark, they seemed to shine with laughter, mischief, and most of all intelligence. They were commanding eyes, the eyes of a much older man. Bold and penetrating, they seemed to look deeply into her and somehow invite her to join in the delight he felt in what he found there.

Unsettled, but for an instant almost mesmerised, Sophia sat down.

There was a bottle of champagne on the table. He poured her a glass and they talked. Yeats spoke with an easy, graceful fluency, with the confidence again of a much older man, in a voice that was as much at odds with his awkward body as his eyes – a voice that was warm and strong and resonant.

'This isn't the first time I've listened to you, my goodness, no,' he said. 'It's my sixth visit. Your voice is pure delight, so too, if I may say so, is your physical presence on the stage. So much so it's taken all those visits to pluck up enough courage to ask to meet you.'

'Thank you.'

'Dare I ask where you come from?'

'You may dare and I may dare not answer.' Sophia smiled. 'Let us say anywhere and everywhere.'

Yeats laughed. 'An elegant riposte! But surely I can ask where your next engagement is?'

'I go to sing in Paris in a few weeks.'

'Do you sing in French?'

'Yes.'

'You have given me a clue, but I shall not pursue it.' He I laughed again. 'And after Paris?'

Sophia tilted her head. 'It depends on the engagements I am offered.'

'I would like to offer you an engagement—'

Yeats leaned forward.

It was an extraordinary proposal.

His closest friend, Yeats said, had his birthday in three months' time. Yeats was so enchanted by her voice he wanted Sophia to sing at the dinner he was giving to mark the occasion. The dinner was being held in Cape Town where they were both living – Yeats was returning to South Africa in a couple of days.

It would mean a three-week voyage out on a P&O liner, a week in Cape Town, and then the return trip – or, if she wanted, she could stay on for a while, enjoy the winter sunshine, and perhaps sing in the Cape. Yeats would pay her handsomely for the engagement, compensate her for any work she'd have to turn down, and of course take care of all her expenses.

'Should it sound a little strange, a little extravagant on my part,' he finished, 'I can only say the friend is very dear to me. And fortunately I'm in a position to indulge my whims. Also think of it. A dank, drear winter here. Golden health-giving sunlight there. Do you have a choice?'

Yeats' seductive laughter echoed out again.

Sophia had listened almost in disbelief. She was still dazed but her composure had returned to her. Suddenly she was wary.

'I am a singer and that's all I am,' she said bluntly.

'My dear, you are much more than a singer,' Yeats answered. 'You are a great artiste but above all a lady. You will be treated as such.'

They talked for a while longer.

185

Then Yeats left. Before he went he gave her the address where he was staying in London, with a request Sophia give him her answer in the morning. If she accepted, it would just give him time to make the arrangements before his ship sailed for the Cape.

Sophia lay awake in her lodgings for most of that night. In the morning she sent a message to him by cab saying she would come. Yeats visited her that evening and they went through all the details of her trip.

As he was leaving, Sophia asked, 'What is your friend's name?'

'He's called Jack,' Yeats answered. 'I am sure you will like him. Indeed, if it is not too bold a word, I think you will love him.'

Now, three months later, she was stepping ashore at Capetown.

From the moment Eric brought her in, Ruthven was barely able to take his eyes off her.

Eric of course staged her entrance with his usual flamboyant theatricality. He waited until the hundred guests he'd invited for the birthday dinner were seated, and only two chairs were empty – those on either side of Jack whom he'd placed in the seat of honour at the main table. Then he came forward with Sophia on his arm.

As Yeats came in, the private dining-room of the Mount Nelson was filled with talk and laughter and the bustle of the waiters moving behind the chairs. The clamour faded and the movement stilled. Eric walked the length of the room and stopped beside Ruthven.

'Jack, may I give you your birthday present?' he said.

He and Sophia had walked through the room arm-in-arm. Yeats let go of her arm then and Sophia held out her hand.

'Sophia,' she said, smiling. 'Happy birthday, Jack.'

For an instant as he took her hand Ruthven noticed the expression on Yeats' face. He was laughing, laughing with exuberant delight at the surprise he'd caused, but his eyes were bright with the manipulative devilry Ruthven had seen so often before.

Then the three of them sat down and afterwards Ruthven forgot everything apart from Sophia.

She was wearing a floor-length gown cut deep from her neck in a V that ran down to the division between her breasts. It was made of oyster-coloured satin but so pale it looked almost bridal-white in the candlelight. Unlike the other women in the room she wore no jewellery apart from a tiny silver snake pinned to her shoulder.

Her arms were bare and her skin had a faint golden sheen, supple and silky. Her face, framed by the great ramparts of her tumbling hair, was pale and fine-boned with delicate nostrils and a full mouth that occasionally parted in an enchanting smile.

It was her eyes that caught Ruthven most.

They were grey–green and flecked with fragments of peat-brown, like the waters of one of the rushing Glenmoray burns after an autumn rainfall. Thoughtful and distant, they gave nothing away. They examined and absorbed, but they were impenetrable. Whatever they saw, whatever secrets they uncovered, they kept to themselves.

Ruthven had never met a woman like her. It wasn't just that she was beautiful and desirable. It was far more than that. She was powerful. She was dream-like. She was magical.

They talked.

Afterwards Ruthven couldn't remember what they'd talked about. On his side the conversation was stiff and stilted. On hers quiet and considered, but more graceful and eloquent. She didn't say much but Ruthven was astonished, thinking about it again afterwards, at how assured and mature she was – and she was clearly even younger than him.

And then after dinner she stood up and walked on to the little stage Eric had prepared for her. The room fell silent, the waiters backed into the shadows by the walls, and she began to sing.

She sang for almost an hour. She sang everything from the ballads of the Victorian music-hall to the marching songs of the Boer wars to a medley of plaintive lyrics from Paris. Everyone listened spellbound, not even the waiters moved.

And then abruptly she finished. She bowed and returned to the table amid ringing waves of applause.

'Happy birthday, Jack,' she said, smiling.

She kissed him lightly on the cheek. An instant later, with Yeats escorting her, she was gone.

Ruthven sat stunned.

The guests began to get up and leave, pausing by his chair to congratulate him on his birthday on their way out. He thanked them and gave them mechanical smiles, but he was barely aware of them. Finally when the room was almost empty, Eric came back.

'So, do we approve of the present?' Yeats asked. 'Or do we send it back? It comes from a very high-quality emporium, and merchandise can always be exchanged.'

Ruthven ignored him. He didn't even take in what Eric was saying.

'How long is she here for?' he asked. 'She said something about a week before she sails home again.'

'That's what she agreed. She turns round when the ship turns round.'

'For God's sake, Eric.' Ruthven seized his arm. 'She can't go. She's got to stay.'

'Well now—'

The familiar mischievous smile was back on Yeats' face. This time there was an element of triumph in it.

'How do you propose to achieve that?'

'Help me, my old friend, help me.'

32

'What do you think?' Charlie asked.

For the first time since Victoria had known him there was an edge of anxiety in his voice.

She didn't answer him directly. 'When did you do it?' she said.

'Last night after I left you.'

'But how? I mean, how do you know what Yeats and Sophia looked like?'

'Our picture library goes back into the twenties,' Charlie answered. 'We've got several photographs of them together at various Silverback mine openings. I went through them when I was handed the story. The pix are black-and-white, of course. Obviously I'm guessing. With Yeats it wasn't too difficult. He looks black-and-white. With Sophia I just used my imagination.'

'And the rest, the birthday party and the singing?'

'Dream-world again, but from what you told me.' Charlie grinned. He was still hesitant. 'How does it stack up?'

'I think it's amazing, Charlie,' Victoria said. 'I think it could even be true.'

She read through the pages again.

They were astonishingly vivid, even down to the detail of the waiters ceasing to move when Sophia began to sing. She had no idea if it had really happened like that, but it fitted in with everything she'd read in Ruthven's diaries and it was utterly convincing.

Victoria looked up at him.

Charlie had, she knew, a remarkable memory. Yesterday he'd used a notebook, but he didn't really need that. When she'd described the contents of the Ruthven archives he hadn't even taken notes. He'd simply remembered everything she said.

He was also, she realised with something of a shock, an even better writer than she'd thought. Not just as a reportage journalist – she'd known that for years. But as what he'd always wanted and never quite dared to be, an imaginative story-teller.

She was about to tell him so when the telephone rang. It was Franjie Viljoen. He was waiting for them in the lobby. They went down to join him.

'Seventy years no problem,' the tanned little South African chuckled. 'Eighty years a little problem. Ninety years, well, now we're moving into thicker bush. But that's where I grew up, man, where I know how to track the stock—'

Viljoen paused.

'She's called Mama Angelina N'duma. She's ninety-seven, for Christ's sake, would you believe it? Her mother was a Nellie kitchen-maid. Mama Angelina helped her with the dishes from the turn of the century to the start of the war. And, so she says, she heard your Miss Sophia sing.'

Viljoen beamed at them triumphantly.

'Don't just stand there, you evil little voortrekker,' Charlie said. 'Let's go see the lady before she pops her clogs.'

They got into Viljoen's car and drove out to the Helensburg suburb of Capetown.

On the way Charlie asked him, 'How the hell did you find the old biddy?'

'I could say genius, man, which would be true, or I could say common sense, equally true,' Viljoen answered. 'Here in South Africa, man, we have a tribal system, what you maybe call clans. Xhosa tribes, Zulu tribes, Tswana tribes, coloured tribes, white tribes. We keep the land and jobs in the tribe. They get passed on—'

He turned the car into a wide tree-lined avenue and started searching for the address.

'I went to the Nellie, I asked round among the staff. I said anyone here with family from long back at the hotel? One of the under-managers say yes. He's Mama Angelina's great-grandson. Like all of his family he works there, except now he's front of house in a suit while she was a piccaninny helping her ma in the kitchen.'

Viljoen gave another thick chuckle. 'We're tight, man, tight, all of us. From Zulu to Boer we stick together. Simple if you know the system. Otherwise you're up the creek without a donkey's dork to steer by.'

He found the address and parked the car. They climbed the stairs of a small modern apartment building and rang the bell on the second floor. Mama Angelina let them in.

Victoria had never met anyone that old before.

She was wizened, a little hunched, a little lame, but her eyes were bright and alert and her mind clear. Victoria tried to imagine what her life had been like. She'd been born before the turn of the century and would have grown up, according to Viljoen, as a virtual slave in a little mud-walled rondavel on one of the meadows which then encircled the heart of the city.

Since then she'd lived through two world wars, South Africa's long years as an isolated fortress republic run by the white masters of apartheid, now she was a citizen of an independent nation, equal under law to all her fellow-citizens, black or white. And she was proud of it.

'Never thought the day would come, but it did. And I voted, oh my goodness me, Mama Angelina voted!'

She shook with laughter.

They were sitting in her living-room. The tiny apartment, she'd told them proudly, had been bought for her by her grandson, the father of the young man who still worked at the Mount Nelson.

'Not for Nelson Mandela and his damn Xhosas, oh no, sir, not for him ever. Mama Angelina voted for Mr Verwoerd. He's a good man. Nothing against white folk. They keep peace and make jobs. Always did.'

'Mama Angelina—'

Viljoen leaned forward. He'd suggested he put the questions to her. Charlie had agreed and told him what they wanted to know.

'Can you tell us what it was like at the Nellie, back when you were very small and your mama worked there in the kitchens?'

She thought. Then she started to talk.

Like many of the very old her memory was like a funnel which grew broader and let in more and more light the further back it went. The recent past, in her case this meant at least the last seventy years, was muddled and hazy. The vote she said she'd cast for the Afrikaans leader Verwoerd must have been for de Klerk – Verwoerd had been assassinated a generation earlier.

But when she spoke of her childhood, her recall was total. She seemed to remember everything and she never hesitated for an instant as she spoke about it.

'Eleven months we spend at the Nellie,' she said, 'then one month we go back to the kraal. Oh, it was lovely at the Nellie. Two dorms, like we called them, they had, one for women, one for men. Mama and me, naturally, we sleep with the women. Then sometimes Saturdays, them men try to come in. Oh, my dear!'

Mama Angelina slapped her face and giggled.

'Never did you see such things! But the rest it was work, work, work, from sunrise to late. Mama and the other women in the kitchen washing pans and scrubbing, us children carrying water-pails and doing whatever and then sometimes sitting out back and playing. Not when the ships come in, oh, my dear, not then. Nellie fills up and we all, women and children, on the racket day-round, night-round. Never did stop.'

'Mama,' Viljoen said, 'your great-grandson, he said you heard Miss Sophia sing. How was that?'

When he spoke to her, Viljoen's voice lost its harsh and flat Afrikaans accent, and somehow took on the lilting rhythms of African speech.

'Never forget it.' Mama Angelina shook her head for emphasis. 'Never, never forget it. Ship comes in. Mama tells me there's big, big party and I got to look sharp. I look sharp all evening. Kitchen, well, those days, it was across from the private dining-room. We do dinner, we listen while they having their fun and noise, then they go silent. Lady starts to sing—'

She paused.

She was thinking back. Not because she needed to remember, but because the memory was still so powerful and immediate she needed an instant to adjust to the impact the occasion had had on her.

'Mama, she takes my hand. "Come on, child," she says, "we done our work. We go listen to the lady." We slip in by the waiters' door, swing both ways, it did. Inside, the manager, Mr Meegeren. Strong man, but good man. My mother strong too. They like each other. He smile but don't say nothing. So we listen—'

Mama Angelina drummed her fingers on the arm of her chair.

She was unaware of them now, Victoria thought. Her mind was focused on a far-distant past that was much more real than the presence of the three of them in the room now.

'Miss Sophia!' She smiled. 'Such a lady, such a great lady! And sing? Oh, my dear, she sings like all the bush doves together. No one, none of those great people, so much as moves. I hold my mama's hand and my mama's still, still as the great people. So am I. We all hear the doves. And then she finishes and, my dear, there is such cheering and clapping of the hands as you will never hear.'

She stopped. There was silence in the room for several moments. Then Viljoen gently prompted her.

'What happened then, Mama?'

'Then?'

She had taken in the question but her mind still wasn't with them.

'Mama, she says, "Maybe if we stay here, the lady comes by and we thank her." The lady doesn't come by. The people go and still we stay, Mama still hoping she passes. Then when the room is almost empty, Mr Meegeren comes up. He says to my mama, "You are Xhosa, Mama, you come from the kraal. You know the bush. The lady and the two gentlemen go safari in the bush shooting and a-hunting for birds. Far, far away for many days in the big bush. They will need baking and cooking, Mama. They will need you."'

The old woman's eyes were bright, and her head was held high.

'The white folk need my people in the bush. They can kill things, but they cannot eat.'

The old woman laughed and shook her head. 'There, my dear, I tell you the truth.'

'So what did your mama say, Mama Angelina?'

'My mama not scared of the bush. I know that, and that is not why she does not agree at once. I am scared, but not of the bush, only that she will leave me behind. I hold her hand tight. She looks at Mr Meegeren one long time. Then she say, "Yes, sir. I will go with the white folk. But my Angelina, she must come too."'

She burst into laughter again.

'Oh, my dear, I am so happy, so deep with relief. So that is how my mama and I go to the bush with Miss Sophia and the two great gentlemen. Many oxen and three great waggons and all the horses and cattle a man could need. Such preparations, such provisions, and my mama and I with a big cook-waggon all to ourselves, all a rattle and a bumping through the bush—'

Mama Angelina shook her head reflectively.

'Far, far north we go. Many days across the yellow lands and the brown lands and the green lands where the pink birds fly. Oh, my Lord, my dear, how those gentleman did shoot and how Miss Sophia did laugh at night. And then we came to the hills and, my dear, there we found such things as you will never dream.'

Mama Angelina's head suddenly dropped.

Viljoen tried to coax more out of her but it was useless. The excitement of visitors, the vivid recollections she'd summoned from the past, had exhausted her. She continued to smile at them, but she could give nothing more.

They stood up. Victoria embraced the old lady. Then they left and drove back into Capetown.

On the way Charlie said, 'Thanks, Franjie. You did fine. No, we didn't get everything. Hell, at ninety-seven we were lucky to get anything at all. But we got enough to take us forward. Miss Sophia didn't take the next week's liner back to Britain. She stayed and went on safari north with Yeats and Ruthven—'

Charlie paused and looked back at Victoria. 'I'm going to have another crack at a reconstruction. Slug it again: "Copy from Charlie – The Silverback Story".'

Viljoen glanced round from the wheel, puzzled. 'What's all this, man?'

'I'm the Venerable Bede,' Charlie said. 'Writing the history that never got written.'

Viljoen frowned. 'I'm not with you, man.'

Charlie grinned. 'Don't lose any sleep over it. I'm the one who stays up late. Unlike you, you little kaffir-basher, I've got work to do.'

Copy from Charlie – The Silverback Story

'Are you warm enough, Sophia?'

As usual, it was Eric who saw to her comfort, Jack who reaped the reward of her smile.

The air was cold in the mountains, and Sophia was glad of the thick blanket Eric had strapped to her saddlebags before they began the ascent. Gentleman Jack and Eager Eric, she called them. Or sometimes, to herself, Beauty and Beast.

They were now in the high hills, close to their destination, Sophia sensed – although it was part of their agreement that she did not yet know where exactly that was.

The journey across the Kalahari had been the most extraordinary and enthralling experience of Sophia's life. Quite apart from the attentions of the two young men who paid court to her, she loved the clear bright air, the scent and beauty of the veldt and the ever-present delight of the animals and birds.

When Eric had first suggested the trip, spreading out the maps with their tiny pictures of zebra and wildebeest, the lions and leopards which filled the great blank spaces of unchartered territory, her heart had leapt.

'It should take three months in all,' he said. 'The rains are due round Christmas, but we'll have you back by then.'

'Where are we going?'

'North,' Jack Ruthven answered, his blue eyes sparkling. 'Eric has the charts and surveys of his father's engineers. He has concocted a plan to delve into the seams they didn't follow. God willing, they'll yield crocks of gold.'

'For me as well?' Sophia laughed. 'Why me?'

'Because there have to be three musketeers and without you we're only two,' Eric answered. He gripped her arm and his dark eyes held hers. 'Trust us. You're a full partner in the enterprise, as long as you ask no questions until we gain Eldorado. Then you share it.'

'Partners? In all things?'

'In all things!'

'Even you?'

Her eyes danced as they flickered between one and the other. She was still girl enough to be wooed – and girl enough to find the thrill of adventure irresistible.

'We too.'

'In that case – agreed. But I shall need it in writing.'

'Signed in blood! Jack, fetch pen and paper!'

They pricked their fingers, dipped the pen in the scarlet liquid, and signed.

Sophia laughed.

It was absurd. A wild adolescent prank, a romantic schoolboy adventure, and they were like schoolboys, she thought. Although she was three years younger there were moments when she felt a thousand years older than either of them.

And yet they weren't schoolboys. Eric, young as he was, was cunning, ruthless, and ambitious. He had his father's fortune behind him, but he wanted to make something significant of his own. And Jack, for all his good nature, his blue eyes and commanding presence, wasn't just a brave and handsome presence. He had steel in his soul.

Human affairs, human relationships, humanity itself, it occurred to Sophia, were much more subtle and complicated than she'd ever imagined.

Jack and Eric had recklessly and boyishly signed in blood. It wasn't either boyish or reckless. It was a fearsome commitment. They'd pursue the matter through to the end. It was in the nature of the two of them. And they'd honour the obligation they'd made to her.

Sophia refused to travel in the waggons, choosing a handsome bay gelding as her mount.

Although she had ridden side-saddle in London's Rotten Row, and gone on morning gallops in the Bois de Boulogne in Paris, this kind of riding was quite different.

She was glad she had allowed Eric to take her down to the Indian outfitter in Cape Town to be measured for the full safari wardrobe. A pair of divided skirts, one thick, one thin; a fitted jacket, snug to the waist and buttoned with deer-horn buttons; a riding cloak made of oiled cotton, and a dozen soft cotton shirts in a becoming shade of beige.

She was glad she had chosen to ride astride.

She loved the feel of the horse between her thighs almost as much as she loved the brilliance of the stars which glittered in the velvet dome of the

196

night sky as they pitched camp. The two young men kept the party supplied with fresh meat. They were some twenty strong with the drovers and the ox-boys and the cook and her little daughter, and the three strong hunters who did the tracking and the skinning.

And in the evening Sophia sang – not for the golden sovereigns her admirers threw on the stage, or the bills tucked in her bodice in the hope of further favours – but for the sheer joy of being young and strong and healthy in the most beautiful place on earth.

'Eric?'

'Miss Sophia, nightingale of the desert, what is your pleasure?'

'Just thank you, Eric.'

'Not I. Thank Jack.'

'Why not you?'

His dark eyes were unfathomable.

'Me too, if you wish. But I only brought you here. It was Jack who kept you.'

It took a month to cross the desert to the shores of the great inland delta the Tswana called the Kingdom of Beyond, but which the map described as the Okavango swampland.

It was scarcely a swamp at all, but broad channels of clear water which flowed between rafts of matted vegetation. Herds of splayed-toed antelope scattered light-footed as birds among the reeds.

'David Livingstone named this paradise on earth, the Garden of Eden,' Jack told Sophia, slipping his arm through hers as she stood on the bank to watch the lilytrotters spreading their spidery feet.

'Beware of the snake,' said Eric, joining them.

Sophia laughed, turning her extraordinary eyes on her two admirers.

'If I am to play Eve, which of you shall be my Adam?'

Eric's dark eyes caressed her, causing her to shiver a little as his gaze touched her lips, moved down to her slender throat, the swell of her breasts beneath the thin cotton, the curve of the waist, the fullness of the hips, the length of the legs.

If she had been beautiful in her oyster satin gown on the stage in Cape Town, she was a thousand times more beautiful now, with her tanned face and rosy cheeks, her hair bleached paler still by the desert, her elegant figure newly muscled from the day's riding.

Jack Ruthven's wooing wasn't as subtle. He took every opportunity to slip an arm under hers, to help her on and off her restless mount, to touch her hand as he handed her a horn beaker of wine. She shivered, too, at his touch, feeling the current which flowed between them.

Nevertheless, throughout the journey, Eric and Jack had treated her as they had promised, with perfect propriety. They were gallant and attentive, certainly, but each kept a watchful eye on the other, and there was never a moment when one of them was out of earshot of the other.

If Eric paid her a compliment, Jack immediately followed suit. They were like two impala rams circling a favoured doe, neither trusting the other. If Eric brought her a genet-skin rug he had bartered for with the little yellow-skinned bushmen, Jack would soon appear with an ivory figurine, a honeycomb, a necklace made of porcupine quills, anything to divert attention from his rival's gift.

'Jack, Eric – which of you am I to choose?' laughed Sophia. 'Bring me a rose in winter and I am yours!'

After the marshes of the delta, they followed the course of a broad, slow-moving river into wilder country. Groves of mopane scrub and thick papyrus fringed the shores, and the waggons lumbered heavily in the wake of the straining oxen. This was tsetse fly territory, and several of the beasts succumbed to the swamp fevers.

For a week they turned inland and due north, cutting their way through scrub and bush towards a range of mountains which had been visible in the distance since they left the banks of the river.

The air was heavy now, and a dense mist lay low to the ground each morning. Huge eagles patrolled the skies, plummetting down on unseen prey only to rise again immediately with a snake or a lizard dangling helpless from the fierce claws. Among the fever trees pale as cream, the great grey shapes of elephants moved with slow grandeur. In the sudden clearings they came upon families of graceful giraffe and lumbering wildebeest, heavy-antlered tsessaby, waterbuck flashing the half-moon markings on their rumps.

By the time they reached the forests which cloaked the lower slopes of the hills, it was clear to Sophia from the mounting excitement of the two young men that they were nearing their destination.

That same morning they happened upon a village, a cluster of odd little makeshift huts set in a clearing. The natives were friendly and curious, evidently fascinated by their strange pale-skinned visitors. The women were astonished by Sophia's auburn hair and the softness of her peach-pale skin, touching and stroking her whenever they had a chance. The men bartered, providing the travellers with roots and greens in exchange for the deer-meat the two hunters had taken with their rifles.

After some discussion with the headman through one of the boys who spoke a little of their dialect, Eric engaged a pair of native guides, Mtumbi and Ngali, hill-men, small and dark-skinned. On their advice, Eric and Jack decided to leave the waggons and the teams of oxen in the care of the drivers to await their return from the mountains.

'We travel light – you will have to make do with what we carry in our saddlebags, Miss Sophia.'

The little group with their two guides repacked the horses and set off through the densely wooded slopes towards the distant peaks.

The air was colder now, and the morning mists swirled until long after the sun was high in the midday sky, its brilliant beams slanting down through the overhead canopy, scattering the grass with golden light.

There were glimpses of dappled antelope and strange monkeys, all black and white, and brilliantly coloured parrots. The trees had pale trunks hung about with vines and great clusters of grey moss like ostrich-feather boas.

At night they slept on the ground, huddled together for warmth by the embers of the fire, with the two young men on either side of Sophia, their guns ready to hand, two sentries posted to keep watch. And each evening Sophia sang, her beautiful voice rising to the velvet sky, clear and sweet as a bird.

It was Sophia's singing which drew the gorillas.

The small company had pitched camp beneath an overhanging crag in the mouth of a shallow cave. They lit a fire to cook the evening stew, and afterwards let the embers die down to a pale glow. The moon was full and the mountains were bathed in a silvery light. Even the usually nervous Africans saw no need to pile more logs on the fire to keep up a protective blaze.

The two young men, their bellies full, were leaning with their backs against the wall of rock, smoking their evening pipeful of scented Turkish tobacco, and they had opened a bottle of brandy, the last of the Cape Town stores, when the great apes appeared.

The creatures came silently, making no sound as they moved to form an outer ring around the circle of flames listening to Sophia's song.

They were like ghosts – one moment they were not there, and the next moment there were dozens of them, a whole tribe of mothers and babies, aunts and uncles and grandmothers, and towering above them, the patriarch, the silverback, his great brows lowered over glittering eyes, the white mane pale as snow in the moonlight.

Sophia didn't falter in her singing. Her voice was pure and true, as innocent as Eve in the Garden. All around her in the soft pale light the great grey beasts swayed and surged.

199

Jack was the first to break the spell – perhaps because the silverback came too close and he feared for Sophia's safety. Eric was the first to reach for his gun, but by then Jack already had his pistol in his hand. Afterwards, no one knew who had fired the first shot. The detonations came as fast as drumbeats, the echoes bowling across the ravines, funnelled by the rocks, splinters flying everywhere. And then the silence, the blood and the bodies.

Eric picked up and examined one of the bloodstained splinters of rock. 'Jack! Look at this!'

Jack peered down at the glistening shard in Eric's outstretched hand.

'Good Lord—'

Eric was shaking with excitement. 'What did I tell you! I knew it was there!'

A warning growl, guttural and full of menace, made the two young men swing round. The patriarch, the silverback, had returned to gather up his dead.

Eric moved towards where Sophia stood in the mouth of the cave, motioning her to get behind him.

'Don't move – whatever happens!' he whispered. He raised his gun.

Gently, with infinite care, the old gorilla began to lay his vast hand first on one and then on another of the still-twitching bodies. As he did so, he made little grunts of distress, punctuated with warning rumbles in the direction of his human enemy.

If Sophia hadn't known perfectly well that he was only a dumb creature, she would have thought that he understood, that he was bewildered by the savagery of these creatures who looked so like himself.

For an instant too, Sophia thought she could see tears in his eyes.

Then the shot rang out. The huge animal stumbled, recovered for an instant, and crashed to the ground. Agonisingly he lifted his great head, the silvery halo gleaming, the eyes dark glistening pools. With one great heave he was upright again, moving towards them, his gaze fixed on Sophia as if in supplication.

'No!' Sophia's scream arced through the air.

She ran forward. At that moment Eric raised the gun again to take aim for a second time. With a sweeping blow of her arm she knocked the weapon upwards. From somewhere to her left a shot rang out.

This time it was Jack who had fired, and at point-blank range. The great beast stood for an instant, his voice rumbling in his chest, his eyes piercing under lowered brows, and then he turned, the silvery mane like a cloak, streaked now with blood.

200

It was not hard to follow his trail – the silverback was king of the forest and even unhurt had no reason to conceal his tracks.

Afterwards Sophia had no notion of how long they climbed in pursuit of the wounded gorilla, she only knew that the two men were like creatures possessed. She hated them then – both of them equally – for the blood lust which was on them. The blood and the greed, for the creature's refuge yielded the treasure they had been seeking.

Although none of them knew it yet, the narrow valley into which the wounded gorilla led them was the one identified by the geologists employed by Yeats' father as containing a seam of potentially diamond-bearing rock.

It was Yeats who confirmed the discovery when they explored it the next day. He found a tiny surface-cast pebble. He abraded its surface with his knife and saw the glint of steely-white light. It was a diamond. He searched and found more.

They were all equally small.

They didn't have the purity and quality of gemstones, they could only be used industrially – or grinding and polishing and carving. But they were still diamonds, and their worth was vast. And undoubtedly somewhere among them were real jewels, the jewels that had been traded in the markets of antiquity and found their way into the collections of every queen from Cleopatra to the Queen Empress herself.

When the three young people returned from the hills, their pockets were laden with the stuff of what Mama Angelina had rightly called dreams.

It was this treasure, this glittering life-blood trapped in the black heart of the volcanic rock, now bathed in the blood of the rarest creatures on earth, from which the mighty conglomerate known as Silverback was later to be born.

That was for the future. For now, there was a price to be paid for earthly treasures – a price which no one of the three could escape. On the last night of the return journey, Eric put his proposal to the other two.

'There will be surveys to be done, machinery to be installed, a workforce to be engaged. It's a risk of course, but my father's company is in the business. It would be better if I handled the practical side – that is if we all agree. Jack?'

Jack nodded immediately.

'Sophia?'

Sophia turned her eyes on Eric, and then on Jack. She was beautiful then, more beautiful than ever, the most desirable woman in the world. Her eyes were mysterious – but in the depths of them was anger.

She drew herself up. 'I want none of it.'

Jack recoiled as if he had been slapped. It was inconceivable that she should reject the proffered riches – inconceivable that she should turn her back on such an offer.

Eric, knowing what was in her mind, put out his hand and stroked her cheek.

'You cannot escape your fate, my songbird. No more than those magnificent creatures in the forest could escape theirs. We belong together.'

Sophia's gaze held his. Steady, candid, filled with rage and despair at the two men's butchery.

'You and Jack, perhaps. Not I.'

'You're wrong, Sophia. We are three together for always.'

Eric's own eyes glittered, small and bright – reptilian, thought Sophia, suddenly aware of the danger she was in, had always been in – for as long as she had kept company with them.

He stepped forward and kissed her.

The kiss took her completely by surprise. He kissed her on her lips, then he turned and kissed Jack too. A snake's embrace, stolen, swift, without compromise or pity. A warning, or a keepsake, or an expression of love – it was many years before she decided which it was for either of them.

Then the war came – that terrible war of mud and trenches – and changed everything.

34

'Could it really have been like that? I mean, Yeats kissing them both?' Victoria asked.

Charlie tossed back his head and laughed.

'I think that's the greatest compliment I've ever been paid,' he said. 'At least you're suggesting it's possible.'

It was the following day.

Victoria didn't know how late he'd stayed up, but she guessed it was deep into the early hours of the morning. He'd arrived at her room fifteen minutes ago and given her what he'd written during the night.

'But I mean, how do you *know*? How can you be so sure?'

'I'm not, but I'm a journalist, blossom,' Charlie answered. 'One gets a feeling for stories, for what's true and what's not even when you don't have it all. Eye-witness accounts always have seeds of truth – even when they're from someone as old as Mama Angelina. Mama Angelina comes from a long line of storytellers. It's the African tradition, and oral history is remarkably reliable when it's all there is.'

'And you think they found diamonds?'

'Someone found diamonds,' he said. 'It's the first trading item detailed in Silverback's accounts. Franjie Viljoen turned that up.'

'And Yeats and Ruthven called it Silverback because of the gorillas?'

'People choose names for reasons, for relevance. If there were gorillas there, it makes sense.'

'It's a bit of a long shot.'

'Aim the long shot right, and it still hits the target. According to Mama Angelina's geography, they were certainly in gorilla territory.'

'Why do you think they had equal shares?'

'Guesses,' Charlie said, 'it's almost all guesses. I think they used Yeats' father's fortune for both seed corn and development money. But Yeats wanted to do something on his own. He broke free of Dad's

203

riches once the building blocks were in place. And because he was a manipulator, he locked your grandfather into the business. Nothing like money for securing control over a person's life.'

'Preserving their relationship?'

'That'd be a key element. I have a feeling this is more complicated. There's an odd flavour to it.'

'Sophia? Why did she refuse her share?'

'I don't know she did.' Charlie shrugged. 'It's just another guess, but she doesn't figure on any of the shareholders' registers. I think Yeats and Ruthven may have made a pact to look after her. It would be in the spirit of the time. Or perhaps she felt responsible for the massacre of the gorillas.'

'For God's sake, Charlie, you don't know there were any gorillas, let alone that they were massacred. This is fantasy.'

'Helen of Troy and Paris and Agamemnon were fantasy for three thousand years,' Charlie said. 'Then a tubby little German called Schliemann dug some holes in the ground in Turkey. Now it seems they weren't fantasy after all.'

'It's not the same.'

'It's exactly the same, except much more likely,' Charlie said. 'Love and hate, they're different sides of the same coin.'

'I thought good journalists never used clichés.'

'Good journalists use good clichés,' He grinned at her. 'But that's about as far as Mama Angelina can take us, bless her old bones.'

Victoria picked up his pages again. 'And now?'

'I've been trying to figure it out. Eric Yeats' original fortune came from his father. Yeats senior – this from the ferreting Franjie Viljoen again – was the son of a Cheshire farmer. He, Yeats' father, enlisted with the second battalion of the twenty-four regiment. He came to South Africa where he met Rhodes, and the whole financial bandwaggon started to roll. The reason he came across Rhodes was simple: he and his regiment were the heroes of Rorke's Drift.'

Victoria stared at him.

'I'm not much of a historian, but one of our teachers was what used to be called a colonial – she didn't approve of what she termed our coloured cousins. She was always going on about "further Zulu atrocities".'

'Top of the class, Miss Ruthven. What else?'

'Seven VCs before breakfast?'

Charlie nodded. 'More after dinner. One of them was Yeats' father.'

Victoria frowned. 'What's it got to do with Sophia – or Grandfather Jack, or even young Eric?'

'Yeats and Ruthven and Sophia, if I'm right, found a seam of industrial diamonds,' Charlie said. 'They created Silverback to work the seam. Then the First World War started. It should have scattered them, broken up whatever tangled relationships they had. Apparently not. One of the ropes that may have kept them together, at least Yeats and Ruthven, could have been their service in the army—'

Charlie paused.

'The original records of the Second/Twenty-Fourth's exploits at Rorke's Drift are kept in London. There are copies at Rorke's Drift itself, together with the regiment's subsequent history. Eric Yeats served in the war. I'm fairly damn sure he'd have done so in his father's old regiment. In which case we may learn what he did and where he went.'

'You're a devious bastard, Charlie,' Victoria said.

'As a description of a journalist, that's tautology, darling.'

Charlie grinned at her again.

'It'll be the twenty-fourth ye'll be wanting, if I'm not mistaken?'

The little old man peered up at them out of the dim recesses of a dusty glory-hole tacked on to the back of the museum at Rorke's Drift – a reconstruction of the original mission house, complete with wax dummies and son-et-lumière effects.

In spite of the crudity of the display, Victoria found the place moving, with its graphic visual account of the defence of the undefendable, the bravery and heroism of men determined to survive against all the odds. Unselfishness too, as the soliders retreated further and further into the heart of the building, dragging their wounded with them.

Sergeant Scott, as the man was called, in spite of his name and accent was a Cape Coloured, a member of that mixed-blooded race of descendants of the Malay tied-labourers who had been brought into the Cape two centuries earlier to serve their Dutch colonial masters as house-servants.

In Sergeant Scott's case, he proudly explained, his great-grandmother was a freed-woman. She had bought her liberty and taken service in the kitchen of a missionary family from the Borders. As was not unusual at the time, she adopted the family's surname, having none of her own. Her descendants inherited the Scots accent and continued in the family tradition – the girls taking employment as domestic servants, their brothers enlisting in the British Army's Catering Corps.

Sergeant Scott, the last of his line, had seen service as a young man in Burma, and again in India as the subcontinent threw off the colonial yoke.

After serving His Majesty faithfully, the regimental cook, on his return to the land of his birth, fell victim to a most unglamorous accident. A young squaddie on spud-bashing duty managed to tip a cauldron of boiling soup over him. Six months and several yards of skin-graft later, he was invalided out of the army and given the job of archivist to the regiment at Rorke's Drift.

'As you see for yourselves, I'm nae bonnie enough for public consumption,' said the old man ruefully, rubbing the patchwork of scarlet down one side of his face. 'So the job suits me well enough. Folks like ye dinnae care one way or another who gives them the information, as long as it's correct. Now what more can ye tell me about your grandfather?'

'Not mine – my wife's.'

Charlie glanced at Victoria.

'She's a little shy about it.' He leaned across the counter and lowered his voice conspiratorially. 'Her grandparents never actually married. But there *is* the legacy from Great-aunt Millicent – and we'd like to see it gets into the right hands.'

'Nae bother to me, sir,' Sergeant Scott grunted. 'I'll need to fax off to headquarters for clearance – they're terrible sticklers for the paperwork. But it'll only take a couple of hours, and there'll be nae need to mention the details. In the meanwhile I'll need a wee while to find the right box. Can I have the name again?'

They walked outside and waited. Charlie looked around.

'My God,' he said happily. 'I've wanted to see this all my life.'

Apart from the Visitor Centre, Rorke's Drift was indistinguishable from any other little cluster of colonial houses all over British imperial Africa. The walls of the houses were white, the roofs red-tiled. Pastel-painted verandahs looked out over neatly mani-cured lawns. A regiment of roses stood stiffly to attention in their well-weeded beds.

Had it not been for the pink bougainvillaea scrambling round every porch, Victoria thought, it could have been a surburb of Cneltenham or Guildford.

'Doesn't look as if butter's ever melted in its mouth,' she said.

'That's the point,' Charlie replied. 'What you see is the domestic expression of what made us so successful. Discipline and a tidy mind. That and the Gatling gun. Except—'

He glanced at the hill behind them. 'It isn't just roses. This was the scene of some of the greatest acts of heroism in history. This was where we flowered and probably where we fell.'

Charlie went back inside.

Sergeant Scott was still trying to get his faxes through to Johannesburg. Charlie re-emerged into the sunlight.

'We've certainly got an hour and probably more,' he said. 'We'll go to Isandhlwana. It's only a few miles over the rise. That's where we were good and truly buried.'

'Who's the famous "we"?' Victoria asked as they headed for the car.

'You and I, Ruthven, Yeats, and Sophia, every single damn one of us,' Charlie replied. 'The Greek empire ended at Thermopylae, Rome's at the city's gates, France's in a valley called Dien Bien Phu. Ours ended here—'

He opened the door and started the car's engine.

'We beat back the Zulu Impis and we won. Except we didn't. We lost. The collapse of the Liverpool docks, the erosion of Manchester as the world's greatest manufacturing city, the winding-down of London, Edinburgh, and Cardiff, it all starts here—'

Charlie looked at her.

'Eighty-nine men held out against ten thousand Zulu warriors. The warriors retreated. The day before the Zulus were victorious. Failing to take Rorke's farm afterwards was just a little mistake. They'd already killed the Empire,, severed its jugular, and buried it at Isandhlwana.'

He set off. 'We're going to see the imperial grave where Yeats' father won his Victoria Cross.'

35

In spite of her conviction that all wars were nothing more than deadly men's games, Victoria found the romance of the story irresistible.

Isandhlwana, twelve miles across the veldt and reached by a muddy unmarked track, wasn't so much a township as an informal encampment pitched on beaten earth.

Sprawled across the plain beneath the rock which marked the battleground were clusters of makeshift dwellings made of old car tyres, cardboard and plastic punctuated with the occasional clutch of rondavels – the round thatched huts of rural Africa. There seemed to be no real heart to the place, only a square mansion, crumbling and in need of repair, with a small notice saying it housed mementoes of the battle.

Charlie parked the car behind the museum. A young Zulu woman, plump and swathed in a brightly coloured cotton kanga, appeared to accept their money, carefully stamping tiny scraps of paper clipped together with paperclips. The place had an air of faded gentility – as if it commemorated not a bloody conflict, but the centenary celebration of some seaside town which had seen better days.

One side of the tall airy hall was hung with banners – regimental colours lost in the battle. Captured British Army uniforms and weaponry were displayed on shop-window dummies, their painted faces incongruously innocent. The other side of the hall was banked with glass cases containing Zulu finery – intricate ostrich-shell beadwork adorning the shields and spears, feather-fringed armbands and anklets, carved assegais and painted war-drums.

Charlie wandered around.

'The Zulus are Shaka's creation,' he said. 'A murdering bastard, but also genius. He organised his warriors into Impi regiments, and trained the daylights out of them. European troops congratulated themselves when they covered fifteen miles in a day, the Zulus could manage fifty.'

The centrepiece of the display was a large tablescape of the battleground. Charlie leaned over it.

'Fifty years after Shaka, his nephew Cetshwayo came to power. He was trouble too and we decided to teach him a lesson. We brought the might of the Empire here to give him a bloody nose and send him packing. It didn't work out like that.'

The tablescape was strung with little illuminations showing the battle-lines. Charlie switched them on.

'Cetshwayo wasn't really a general, he didn't even have a battle plan. Just twenty thousand warriors after blood. They were out to wash their spears and they did. We had almost a thousand troops here. At the end of the day only fifty-five of them were still alive.'

'And Rorke's Drift?' Victoria said.

'That's the strangest part of all. A drift's a name for a ford on a river. There was a small mission, a farmhouse, and a tiny hospital there. The few Isandhlwana surivors broke and ran for it. They joined the little garrison. The Zulu Impis followed and attacked again. They fought for hours, through the afternoon and into the night. A handful of Europeans against thousands of chanting, assegai-wielding black warriors. And this time we won, or rather we held out. We battled for every inch, we retreated to a few burning rooms, but the Zulus couldn't breach them. At dawn they gave up and tramped away.'

'What about Eric Yeats' father?'

'He was awarded a VC, but the story's odd.' Charlie rubbed his chin. 'He survived Isandhlwana, he brought the news of the massacre to Rorke's Drift, he took part in its defence. Or so he claimed, but his name doesn't figure in lists of the garrison. Four weeks later, he pops up at regimental headquarters with tales of rescuing women and children. It's a convincing tale, and he gets his gong. Except—'

Charlie switched off the display and walked outside. He stood looking up at Isandhlwana hill.

'The story then starts to come apart. Rumours of bribery and payoffs begin to circulate in the officers' mess. It emerges young Lieutenant Yeats isn't an officer at all, in fact he's not even an enlisted man but a navy powder-monkey who jumped ship in Durban and was posted as a deserter. A court martial is set up in a hurry, and just as quickly abandoned. The man's a hero. The last thing anyone wants is a scandal. Yeats keeps his medal and a back-dated commission on condition he retires gracefully. He does just that, he meets Cecil Rhodes, who knows nothing except he's a VC, and Rhodes was always a pushover for imperial heroes, and the rest is history – or rather money.'

Charlie looked at her wryly.

'If his son, Eric, really was a deceitful bounder, then he's got an excellent pedigree – it's all in the breeding.'

He glanced at his watch.

'Four o'clock. Time to get back and find out what Sergeant Scott has unearthed.'

Sergeant Scott was waiting for them at the door of the Rorke's Drift museum.

The 'Closed' sign was firmly in place, and there was an unhappy frown on the old man's face.

'I dinna ken how to tell ye this, but headquarters have refused their permission. I didna give them any indication as to who was making the inquiry, but wee Jock – he's my second cousin in charge of the office – told me the order came from the highest authority. Seems that some journalist has been queering the pitch for ye. The authorities are terrible nervous of journalists. I said ye were no journalists but a bonnie wee lassie and her husband, looking to hand over a legacy to a cousin. But they wouldna be having it. I'm verra sorry.'

He looked genuinely upset.

Victoria opened her mouth to protest, but Charlie squeezed her arm warningly.

'Never mind, Sergeant. I'm sure we'll get the information some other way.' Charlie smiled reassuringly.

He turned to Victoria. 'We'll have to find ourselves somewhere for the night.'

The sergeant beamed. 'Now there I can help ye. Second bungalow on the left, and tell Mrs MacIntyre Tommy sent ye. She takes in paying guests and ye'll find it clean and cheap.'

A couple of hours later, after a sturdy meat-tea with Mrs MacIntyre, Victoria found herself glaring at Charlie over a romantically draped double bed in the best guestroom.

'Looks fine for me. Where are *you* sleeping, Charlie?'

'I'm not. There's work to do.'

'What do you mean?'

'The good sergeant left a box on the desk, and I've no doubt it's the one we're after. The padlock on the door's flimsy enough – nothing a coil of wire won't fix.'

'I'll come with you.'

'You won't. You'll stay right here.'

'Why? You'll need someone to keep watch. Thieves always do.'

'I'm not a thief. I'm an investigative journalist about my legitimate business.'

He chuckled. 'Anyway, you can bail me out if I get caught.'

Victoria stared at him. 'You're not just a bastard, Charlie,' she said, 'you're a real crook too.'

'Modestly, I have a reputation for delivering my stories.'

He went out. As the door closed, Victoria picked up a pillow and hurled it against it.

It was approaching dawn when Charlie came back into the room. Victoria sat up sleepily and glanced at her watch. It was almost 5.00 a.m. She realised he couldn't have spent all the intervening time trying to extract the papers from the museum. He must have been doing something else.

She was right.

'Something else for you. I think it works.' His voice was jubilant. 'Now budge over and let me sleep.'

Charlie stripped off. He always slept naked, and his muscular body was achingly familiar to her.

He rolled into the warm hollow she had just vacated, and was asleep instantly. Victoria had forgotten he could do that – just switch off and drop into oblivion like a cat. It was one of the things – the only thing, apart from his infidelity – which had irritated her about his lovemaking. He was a good lover. No one who loved women as much as he did could be anything but that. But then, when the lovemaking was over and she was feeling happy and ready for a little tenderness, he distanced himself. He went into a private, separate world.

Victoria shook her head.

The bastard, the selfish philandering bastard. For two pins she would— do what? She stopped herself. Charlie's sex-life was no business of hers any more. She had made up her mind on that, and she wasn't going to change it just because they had ended up sharing a room.

On the table beside her was a new bundle of pages he'd written. Curiosity got the better of her irritation.

Victoria began to read.

36

Copy from Charlie – The Silverback Story

Major Eric Yeats raised his head gingerly over the parapet of the bridge and peered through the darkness.

The night was dark and moonless, but the last of the evening light showed the faint and familiar outline of the cathedral at the centre of Rheims.

Because he was nervous, his left hand rested on the handle of an ornately scrolled pistol tucked into his belt. With the other he motioned to his companion, a slender figure in an ill-fitting German uniform, to keep out of the line of sight.

After a moment, Yeats nodded.

The two figures scurried forward, moving from bush to bush through the churned vineyards only recently abaondoned as no-man's-land. They moved swiftly and silently towards their objective, an oak door set into the embankment beneath the bridge. The door marked the entrance to a tunnel, one of many bored through the chalky substrata to form a network of underground cellars which in peaceful times were used to store the precious wines of Champagne, but now, in wartime, served as an armoury, a secure depot for thousands of tons of ammunition and guns.

Rheims was the city of champagne – although it had been four long years since the wines had been made.

For four years now the vineyards had been a battleground, the precious vines churned and crushed. The red earth could yield no more than these tangles of wire and spars of splintered wood, spent shells and protruding lumps of metal which identified the grape-producing fields round France's coronation city for what they had now become – a battle-field.

It was in Rheims that the Maid of Orleans had crowned her reluctant prince. In Rheims too that the old vintner monk Dom Perignon discovered the alchemy which turned sharp white wine into nectar fit for the gods.

Rheims was all things to all men, a romantic city, a city of dreams.

Sophia had found herself there at the outbreak of war, the last stop on a tour of the cities of Belgium and northern France. The August Bank Holiday of 1914 was a bad time for an Englishwoman to be caught behind German lines, but Sophia's French was good enough to pass muster in the night-clubs which now catered to the Kaiser's officers.

If anyone questioned her, she claimed Irish nationality and a more than passing acquaintance with Sir Roger Casement, then engaged in drumming up support in Germany for Sinn Fein. Her beauty as much as her singing made her much sought after by the young army blades hungry for the Mädchen of the Rhine.

Sophia was sparing with her favours. She was after better fish to fry than young officers looking for a good-time girl. When the Graf Otto von Meitner walked into the cellar where Sophia was topping the bill, she knew she had found her protector.

On the face of it at least, Otto von Meitner was everything to make a woman's heart beat faster.

Tall and fair, with aquiline features, brilliant blue eyes and full, almost girlish lips, he had an air of assurance which gave him an easy authority. The Graf – a courtesy title denoting the rank of Count – was the second son of an ancient family, a warrior clan who had amassed vast wealth and lands since they first bore arms in the days of the Crusaders. He had followed family tradition and enlisted in the Kaiser's bodyguard, an elite corps of officers of good family like himself.

As a professional soldier, charming and well-born, he had risen rapidly to become the youngest general in the Imperial Army. With the German advance into France and the capture of Rheims, he had been given overall responsibility for the occupied territories of the province of Champagne.

As soon as he saw Sophia he wanted her for his own.

He had always collected beautiful things – and Sophia was undoubtedly the loveliest thing he had ever seen. He installed her in his apartment in one of the great houses the champagne-makers had built, and made her his hostess – but that was all. To Sophia's surprise the Graf didn't ask anything more of her than to preside over his all-male supper-parties, sing when required – particularly Goethe's love-songs – and, on very rare occasions, to be 'kind' to one of his guests.

'Ja, mein general,' Sophia would say.

It seemed that 'mein general' favoured his own sex, although the proprieties had to be observed with the maintenance of an official mistress. The arrangement suited Sophia well, and she settled down in comfort to await the outcome of the war. The Graf was generous with clothes and jewellery – and she had a maid for her personal needs.

Insulated from the horrors taking place only a few miles to the south, Sophia had never been so pampered.

In July of 1918, things began to change fast.

The streets of Rheims filled up with wounded. The news from the front was increasingly grim. The French, reinforced by American troops, were beginning to advance under Marshal Foch. For the first time it seemed possible Germany might lose the war. The supper-parties ceased, and Otto – on the rare occasions he returned to the apartment – was usually drunk.

One evening in late August, as Sophia listened to the noise of no-longer distant gunfire, Otto brought seven of his young officers home and requested that Sophia be 'kind' to them all.

Three of them were too drunk to take advantage of her, and one, a shy young boy, tried to protect her. But the other three prevailed and Sophia had no choice but to submit. Her body was bruised and battered, and she had made up her mind it would never happen again.

Sophia didn't sleep that night.

She waited until her violators had fallen into a drunken stupor, dressed herself in one of the discarded uniforms, and made her way through the silent house to the secret door which led down into cellars beneath. In recent weeks, it seemed the battle-lines were closer. By day the gunfire was deafening, the noise shaking the elegant houses, banging and rattling the windows, shattering glass and setting the mangy dogs who roamed the streets to a perpetual howling. At night the noise abated. It was almost completely muffled in the underground chambers which honeycombed the city.

She moved quietly through the darkened vaults past the massed ranks of dusty bottles stored necks downward in their wooden *pupitres*.

The Kaiser's officers liked good wine, and had declared the cellars off limits to their troops, leaving the bottles in their racks, with the exception of the arched bottling-cellars nearest the entrance, where the armaments were stored behind iron grilles under armed guard.

Otto would often send her to fetch a particular vintage when he had important guests, and Sophia knew the vast cellars by heart, by touch, and even in the dark. One of these passages ran through to the outskirts of the city, emerging in the vineyards.

A crack of moonlight under an oak door told her she had found it. Cautiously, her heart thumping, she pushed the door open. She stumbled forwards until she had reached the shelter of a small copse. Then she collapsed.

*   *   *

'Here, Bert. Take a butcher's at this.'

The voice belonged unmistakably to the south London slums. A rough hand tugged at her uniform jacket. One of the buttons burst, revealing the outline of a breast.

'Christ, it's a woman.'

A second pair of boots appeared beside the first. The second voice also came from south London but it was deeper, more threatening.

'Must be one of Jerry's female spies the sarge warned us about.'

'What'll we do with her?'

'Put one in her head, mate. That's what we've been told. Orders is orders. And the bitch probably done for a lot of good blokes.'

Sophia heard the snap of a hand-gun being cocked.

She struggled to her feet, drawing herself up to her full height. Her cheeks flamed and her eyes flashed.

'I'm English,' she shouted. 'Same as bloody you! You kill me and they'll put you in front of a firing-squad, both of you!'

The first man, the one who'd drawn his gun, recoiled. He stared at her.

'Then what the hell are you doing rigged up in Kraut stuff?' he demanded suspiciously.

'Field Intelligence,' Sophia improvised wildly. 'Behind the lines. Take me to your commanding officer. If he isn't satisfied, he can shoot me. But of course he won't, he'll know exactly who I am. For God's sake, do I sound like Jerry?'

The two muttered together uncertainly.

Then the second soldier, the taller and more authoritative one, said, 'You got a gun?'

'No.'

'Search her, Jack, just to be sure.'

Hands patted her body and scoured the earth round where she'd been lying.

'All right, we'll take you in.' The voice was grudging. 'We'll have the pistols on you. Try to make a break and that'll be it.'

They marched her away.

'Sophia, such a surprise!'

In spite of the military haircut and the uniform, the young officer into whose presence she had finally been taken was strangely familiar. For an instant she couldn't place him — he had grown a moustache and his face was in shadow.

Even when she knew, she still couldn't convince herself it was true.

'Eric, is it really you?'

Sophia broke down in tears. Yeats came into the tent's lamplight, moved round the campaign desk at its centre, and took her hands.

'Yes, it's me,' he said. 'Calm yourself, dear girl. You're safe now.'

Sophia wept uncontrollably for several minutes. Then she shook away the tears and peered at him.

'Oh, God, Eric, you can't imagine what I've been through.'

'Sit down and tell me.'

Sophia might have been amazed to see him, but Yeats had known all along she was in Rheims – although it was many years before he told her how and why.

At the time she thought his presence was a miracle. What she did not know was that he had been tracking her throughout the war.

When war broke out he'd enlisted in his father's old regiment. The British High Command was inept, but not so inept they didn't recognise the value of a young officer whose upbringing among the South African Boers meant he spoke excellent German.

'We have an interesting and important job for you, Yeats,' a staff colonel told him when he reached London. 'You're being seconded to Military Intelligence on special duties.'

Yeats was slipped into Germany through neutral Switzerland, and joined the Kaiser's army as a Boer who hated the British. His fluent command of English secured him his next secondment, this time to German Intelligence. Throughout the three years of the trench war, he came and went between the lines with impunity, each side considering him a valuable agent.

In the course of his work Eric learned all about Sophia's war, and the arrangements she had made for her survival. There had even been an evening in Rheims when Otto had invited him to one of his famous soirées. Yeats had had to plead a temporary indisposition to avoid confronting Sophia face to face.

Now he let her tell him the story in her own words.

He reflected as he listened that even exhausted, white-faced, and tear-streaked, Sophia was still the most beautiful woman he had ever met. Brave too. She was also, he thought with amused admiration, cunning enough to have prepared her story, and a good enough actress to tell it with complete conviction.

Yeats knew better than to believe a word of it.

Sophia's tale was that she had spent the war as a prisoner in a forced labour camp stitching uniforms for German soldiers.

'It was truly appalling, you can't imagine what we all suffered. We were constantly hungry, it was bitterly cold, and the guards used to beat us if the commandant decided we weren't working hard enough.'

'But in the end when the Allies advanced and the German war-machine began to break down, you stole a uniform and managed to escape?' Yeats suggested gently.

She looked at him, her eyes steady. 'That was it exactly.'

'And was this labour camp the infamous one in the centre of Rheims? The one the Boche set up in the wine-cellars?'

She hesitated for a fraction of a second. 'How did you know?'

Yeats smiled. 'You sing lovely songs, Sophia, and you tell wonderfully imaginative stories. Now you're going to tell me another story, a true one this time, and you're going to sing for your supper — well, you always did that, didn't you?'

The Allies had no desire to destroy Rheims. It had to be taken, but with the least damage possible.

The French were deeply sensitive about the city's great cathedral. The powerful feelings the great edifice aroused were well known to the German High Command, who had decided to install Big Bertha, the gigantic howitzer named for the wife of Gustav Krupp, at Rheims' heart.

Throughout the summer of 1918 the huge gun, crudely targeted but deadly in its enormous capacity to deliver explosives, had been pounding the suburbs of Paris. The gun's range was sixty-five miles — not quite enough to allow it to bombard the capital itself, but more than enough to cause devastation and panic all round.

Moved around at night on railway tracks the gun was, too, almost invulnerable to being traced for Allied counter-attacks.

It wasn't so much the casualties Big Bertha caused — they stood at 800 the night Sophia was brought before Yeats — but the psychological damage inflicted on the civilian population that made it a matter of such urgency for the Allies to find the gun.

Big Bertha was savaging the heart of France. The gun had to be neutralised. The only way to do that was to find it in its daytime bunker.

The task had been given to Yeats. It was a virtually impossible assignment — until Sophia's arrival. She changed everything. Not only did she know the underground caverns like the back of her hand, but if challenged, she had a perfectly plausible reason to be there.

She knew everyone, and her friend and protector, Otto, remained in command of the German forces which still nominally controlled Rheims.

'I fear you're going to have to go back into the city,' Yeats said.

Sophia looked at him, terror-struck and distraught.

'I can't,' she pleaded. 'What they did to me, you'll never know. But I know, I know!'

She began to scream.

The screams went on and on, high-pitched and frantic and desperate. Yeats listened to the sound imperturbably. Eventually she was silent. She stood in front of him heaving and trembling.

'An hour,' he said. 'A bowl of stew, a glass of wine, and you'll be fine. The best guide, I'd hazard, that I and the team of sappers I'll have with me will ever have had.'

Yeats smiled.

'It's what you pay, Sophia, for sleeping with the enemy. With any luck the price will be small and we can rub the slate clean. I know Jack would want you to be there. Remember the three musketeers?'

Sophia looked at him with hatred but with far more than hatred – with sickening fear.

An hour later they set off.

The Germans were still clinging to the city, but Sophia took them – Yeats and half-a-dozen explosives engineers – to the entrance to the champagne caverns. They made their way through the vaults and came out into a little courtyard she knew well.

She directed them to the railway sidings where, she knew, Big Bertha was usually lodged for the night. Then she left them to it. Sophia waited. An hour afterwards there was an explosion, the biggest she'd ever heard, and a plume of fire and smoke rose over the roof.

Sophia went on waiting.

An hour later still Yeats returned. His face was blackened and of the six men who'd gone out with him, only two were there now. He looked grim and desolate, and the two remaining sappers were bloodied.

'Let's get out,' Yeats said. 'It's done, it's over.' Sophia led them back through the vaults.

It was over, the war was over. They returned to camp towards dawn. Yeats showed her to a small single tent. He lit a candle for her but Sophia blew it out almost instantly. She threw herself down on the truckle-bed and sobbed.

Yes, the war had ended.

Life should have ended with it. The trouble was it hadn't. Life was too messy, too strange, too stubborn. It was like water. It filled pools and spilled over and went on flowing.

Life, she thought bitterly, would start again tomorrow.

37

At 10 a.m. Mrs MacIntyre gave up.

She couldn't imagine what was keeping her guests in bed so late – unless, as she'd guessed, they were a honeymoon couple and couldn't bear to tear themselves away from their love-making. She left a note on the stairs saying where they could find breakfast, and went round for her morning cup of coffee with her old friend and neighbour, Mrs van der Moeve.

Mrs van der Moeve, also a policeman's widow who still lived in police accommodation as the housekeeper, had had overnight guests too. They were two officers from headquarters in Pretoria, no less. One of them, it turned out, had served with her Ted. It had been quite like old times.

When Mrs MacIntyre returned home at eleven there was still no sign of movement from the guest bedroom. She knocked on the door.

'Will you not be wanting breakfast before you go?' she called.

'Good heavens, Mrs MacIntyre, we'll be down straight away,' Victoria answered.

Victoria had finished reading what Charlie had written hours before. She'd thought about it for a long time, then she'd gone to sleep again. Now she dressed.

She went back to the sleeping form curled in the bed. She put out a hand to stroke his cheek, her way for so long of waking him, then she stopped herself. She turned the gesture into an impersonal shake of his shoulder.

'Wake up, Charlie.'

Charlie's tousled head rose from the pillow, his sleepy face breaking into a smile at seeing her.

'Victoria—'

He said her name with such tenderness, there at the edge of sleep, that her heart turned over. For an instant she forgot. For an instant she thought he was going to reach up and pull her to him, and that she would, as she had so often in the past, lower herself happily into his arms.

She checked herself. She held back. She said with what she knew was a forced curtness, 'It's late. We should have been up long ago.'

He rubbed his stubbled face. 'What's the time?'

In the old days, the reply would have been easy. Unspoken, it would have been: *time to make love*. That moment was gone – gone for good.

She said, 'Time to be on our way.'

Victoria stilled the turmoil she'd momentarily felt. She went out and walked downstairs.

As she sat over her coffee in Mrs MacIntyre's kitchen, she thought again about the story Charlie had conjured up.

Eric Yeats was a very strange man. Charlie clearly had that right. Charlie was probably right that Yeats was a dangerous one too. As for her grandfather, Jack, his letters to his mother from the trenches painted a more familiar picture of the terrible warfare in which so many young men suffered and died.

Ruthven had survived, but at what cost? Did the loss of so many of his friends mean that he was left with no choice? Was that why he had coupled his life with Yeats'? And what of Sophia, if she was indeed now in Eric's power?

Had Sophia also felt those yearnings – or was she too hurt, too betrayed, ever to trust a man again?

So far Victoria had held back the notes she had made on her trip to India – they somehow seemed too dangerous, too revealing. After all, Ruthven was her grandfather, blood of her blood, flesh of her flesh, bone of her bone. What Victoria couldn't understand or explain was the affinity she felt with Sophia – her admiration for Sophia's stubbornness and bravery, her pain at the indignities Sophia had been made to suffer. In that at least, Victoria knew Charlie was right.

But then again, was it all in Charlie's head, was he manipulating the feelings she had for her grandfather and Sophia?

Charlie was a remarkably perceptive and skilful writer.

Victoria had always known that, although this – the re-creation of a distant past peopled by distant and complicated figures – was a wholly new dimension to his talent. Was it a trick, a game which she was equally guilty of playing because she was so desperate to understand and find answers to what had happened?

It could of course equally involve Charlie too. He'd always

wanted to write, rather than be just a hack, as in his darker and bleaker moments he sometimes referred to his profession – those few occasions when he wasn't posturing as his generation's Hemingway or its verbal Capa.

Perhaps this was his chance, his story. Or perhaps it didn't matter.

Victoria shook her head.

It was in the end her own quest. She was locked into it. Her need for a resolution had a life of its own. She didn't mind being woven into a web of Charlie's weaving. Occasionally, as when she'd woken him that morning and seen his laughing eyes, so familiar, so tender, and so enragingly faithless, she had no wish to break free.

Sophia and Eric, Jack and Eric, Sophia and Jack.

Sophia and Jack? Was that the secret? Cold waves rippled across her stomach. Was it possible that was where the story was leading? Maybe Charlie's late-night conjectures, his spinning out of an imagined narrative over his endless glasses of whisky, could tease out a plausible truth – or even a real truth.

What was a real truth?

Victoria had no idea, but she made up her mind. She would give Charlie the last of what she'd gathered – her notes and her garnerings from the archive she'd stolen.

She needed to know what he would construct from the scraps.

They ate their late breakfast, paid their small account, and Mrs MacIntyre saw them out to their car.

The road curved past the little museum, where a busload of tourists were making their way up the slope towards the entrance. Through the open door they glimpsed Sergeant Scott bustling about in the hallway.

'Looks like business as usual,' Charlie said. 'I doubt anyone's noticed anything.'

At the crossroads on the outskirts of Rorke's Drift, he pulled up on the verge.

'Where to now?'

Victoria had been shuffling through a bundle of brochures she had picked up in the museum. She pulled out the map and began to plot a route.

'Left at the T-junction. Back to the main road. Then we pick up the autoroute to Durban – the Umfolozi game reserve's off on the left.'

'Grandfather's territory?'

Victoria nodded. 'He helped set it up, but he wouldn't recognise it now. There's a new luxury camp there in the hills. I've reserved a bungalow. Two bedrooms. One each.'

'Just what I want,' Charlie said. 'Nice and peaceful.'

Victoria glanced at him.

She wasn't sure what reaction she wanted, but what she'd got was instantly familiar. A little smile – rueful, charming, and boyish. She knew the expression that accompanied it only too well. The facial equivalent of an apologetic shrug of the shoulders, a visual excuse that the damage he'd caused to their years together had nothing to do with him.

It meant nothing to Charlie – unless to convey that boys would always be boys.

Anger rose in Victoria's throat.

Seven years. Seven long years of believing, of forgiving, of being persuaded to overlook what he assured her were no more than mild flirtations. Until Angela. Victoria had been astonished at how hard it was to forgive that final betrayal. Seducing Rory Watson and taking him to her bed – and she *had* seduced the young scientist, there was no doubt about that – had been a pointless, meaningless response.

She knew, in retrospect, that quite apart from the shock of Rory's claims about her grandfather, it had been an act of boldness, of defiance, a hair-of-the-dog to cure a hangover. Or even an inoculation – a little dose of the virus so you didn't catch the disease itself. Love was a disease. Easy to catch and hard to cure. And the convalescence was hell.

Her encounter with Rory had simply, achingly, reminded her of what she had lost – of how much she missed Charlie. Worse, she had behaved as badly towards the poor innocent Rory and his delightful girlfriend Sally as Charlie had behaved towards her.

Vengeance, she remembered reading in a Spanish proverb, was a dish best eaten cold. It wasn't. The Spaniards, like the French, like so many foreigners, were so often wrong.

Vengeance wasn't a dish worth eating at all.

Yet the bitterness was still there. Victoria had forgotten how much she hated Charlie – how much reason he had given her to hate him. Suddenly, unprompted, it came out of her uncontrollably.

'Bastard,' she said. 'Weak, two-timing, fucking bastard! What the hell am I doing here with you?'

The ferocity of her sudden outburst rocked Charlie. The car swerved for an instant as her rage hit him. He corrected the wheel and righted the steering again.

'If you're thinking about what I guess you're thinking about,' he said lamely, 'then I'm sorry, truly sorry.'

'So that's what I need to hear? You're sorry? Sorry? Wonderful!'

Charlie didn't answer.

He drove on. He changed gear and passed a line of trucks. The car joined the highway and moved into the stream of traffic heading for Durban. Victoria stared at him. For once, perhaps for the first time she'd known him, his face was taut and pale.

She turned back to the map.

After an hour she said, 'Take the next turning on the left.'

Victoria looked at him again as they swung off the highway, then on to a minor road, and then on to the dirt-track that led to the reserve.

He was insufferable. Insufferably arrogant. He deserved to be taught a lesson.

By the time they reached the hilltop with its snowy cap of little bungalows, even the extraordinary beauty of the place – the drive through the bush with its herds of startled zebra, ungainly wildebeest, the family of browsing giraffe, the majestic rhino who momentarily blocked their path – had lost its power to soothe her.

As far as Victoria was concerned, Africa could go hang.

She hadn't meant it to happen like this. It was a mistake. She had hoped that in finding out the truth she might understand who and what she was, what she could be in the future. It had been on impulse that she'd trusted Charlie to find it for her, to breathe life into what was no more than an urnful of bones. She hadn't thought the bones would come to life, put on flesh and blood. Her flesh and blood. Still less that the flesh would bruise and the blood would flow.

Charlie was a writer. His armoury was words. He was a teller of tales, a spinner of dreams, a weaver of fables.

A liar.

That was how, seven years ago, he had caught her – with poetry and deceit. And he had held her too. For seven years he had held her. But seven years ago she had been no more than a young girl, secure in her innocence. She'd been trapped by her own arrogance too, that particular arrogance of youth which believes itself invincible.

Seven years ago.

Victoria had been the same age as Sophia when she accepted Yeats' invitation to visit Cape Town. She hadn't suffered as Sophia had suffered, but Victoria knew she too had changed. The innocence was gone – and with it the certainty.

And yet, and yet – it seemed Charlie could still spin his tales, still hold her with his lies, if lies was what they were. Victoria knew she would give him the notes she had made in India, that she'd wait anxiously for the story he'd fashion from the threads of that half-remembered time.

What was it he had done to her?

How had he somehow managed to make her see herself in Sophia? And which of the two men did he see himself as – because he must have identified with one of them? The heroic Jack, the devious Eric? Both?

Or neither?

The bungalows in the Umfolozi reserve were, Victoria thought, delightful – simply furnished but comfortable, each with its tiny patch of garden.

In high summer, the gardens were brilliant with colour. Bougainvillaea rambled across reed-thatch in drifts of pink and white blossom. Blue-bloomed plumbago and tiny clusters of white jasmine dripped from the eaves. Along the pathways, clumps of spike-flowered sugarbush were starred with nectar-sipping sunbirds, bright as butterflies.

The place was both beautiful and strange. It was strangely familiar, too.

As a small girl, Victoria had been fascinated by the botanical watercolours of the South African bush which hung in her grandfather's library. To a child, the enchantment lay not so much in the images themselves, exquisite though they were, as in the crazy appropriateness of their names. She remembered the toad tree with its warty-skinned fruits, the sausage tree all hung about with pendulous seed-pods, the fever tree with its ghostly branches.

Snuff-box, curry-bush, bottle-brush, dog-plum, baboon's breakfast – all were fuel for the fairy-tales she remembered Ruthven telling her as she sat on his knee listening spellbound.

She was glad of the whitewashed bathroom and the plentiful hot water, and sank into it gratefully.

She dressed carefully for the evening meal – the lodge was

226

apparently known for its restaurant – choosing the only formal dress she'd brought with her, in deep violet silk with a short skirt and revealing neckline. She examined herself critically before leaving the room.

She wasn't sure why she was going to so much trouble – unless, at the back of her mind, there was the certainty that dressing for dinner was what, under similar circumstances, Miss Sophia would have done.

Ex-lovers were always a challenge, and Sophia must have had many of them. It wasn't that Victoria wanted Charlie back. It was just that she wanted him to regret her loss. She wanted to hold him for just long enough to be sure she still had the power to hurt him.

It was a rueful realisation. In fact it was spiteful and unpleasant. It was also sadly, Victoria acknowledged, as true as any of the other tangled emotions she felt about Charlie.

She walked along the paved pathway to the restaurant.

The open-sided bar at the entrance was full of excited tourists on their first visit to Africa. The group there that night were keen bird-watchers. They were exchanging sightings of species they hadn't seen before, and ticking off names on their life-lists. Charlie was sitting with them, examining their notes and making comments and suggestions for the next day.

'Among the one thousand and one interesting facts you may not know about me,' Charlie said as he got to his feet when Victoria came in, 'is that I was once a bit of a birder myself. A couple of these good people saw a Lammergeier today. Very lucky. They're close to extinction.'

Victoria checked for an instant.

No, she hadn't the slightest idea Charlie knew anything about birds. It was a strange and unnerving revelation. Her entire journey, the journey which had started in the Natural History Museum and eventually led her to where she was now, deep in the South African bush, had started with birds.

'Let's eat,' she said crisply.

Charlie took her arm to lead her through to the restaurant.

As he touched her, Victoria thought of pushing him away. She didn't want any physical contact with him. She hesitated. Then she decided against it. It was at least a gesture of courtesy, and whatever else he'd done, Charlie had always been courteous in his own maddening way.

They had dinner. As soon as they'd finished eating Victoria stood up.

'I'm tired,' she said. 'I'm going to bed. If you want company, go and rejoin your birding companions. What do we do tomorrow?'

Charlie frowned.

'I'll trawl for local knowledge. I'll figure out something. I'll let you know in the morning.'

Victoria went back to their bungalow.

She collected the notes she'd made in India, and took them across to Charlie's room. His door was unlocked. She laid them on his bedside table and returned to her own room. After a moment's thought she firmly locked her own door. She knew herself too well to trust herself if the bastard turned the handle and found he could come in.

It would never be like that again.

That part of it was over, all over. She had brought it to an end, and she'd decide how it would finally be wrapped up, tied with string, and sealed with wax. Charlie was history. Dishonest and despicable history. She was using him now, not he her.

Victoria undressed and got into bed.

As she lay back she wondered what he'd make of her notes, how he'd react to them, how he'd breathe life into them and flesh them out into his own imagined narrative. Charlie would try, she was sure of that. He had vast, protean energy, and the story had become a compulsion to him, far more compelling than any other story in the years she'd lived with him.

This one was different. This one was allowing him to flower as a writer.

It wasn't the same for her.

It was utterly different. Victoria's relationship with Charlie was over. Finished. Concluded, ended, liquidated, and buried. She tried to think of other terms of finality. She couldn't, but those were enough. What she was left with was a longing – a deep and heartfelt need to know the truth about Grandfather and the birds, about Eric Yeats and Sophia and Granny Lomax.

The American novelist William Faulkner, whose strange, convoluted books Victoria loved and which, ironically, Charlie had introduced her to, had once written, she remembered now, 'The past is all we've got.' She remembered too why the phrase had come back to her. She had quoted it to the gaunt Evans who, she was certain, had raided her apartment.

Her past was mysteriously spilling out all round her. She wanted to know what the mysteries were. She wanted to solve them. She wanted to know where she came from and then, maybe, who she was. She wanted to position herself, in the jargon phrase she rather enjoyed, to move forward into the rest of her life.

Infuriatingly, Charlie had re-emerged as the conduit who might take her there.

She went to sleep.

Sometime in the early hours of the morning she woke. Someone was trying to turn the door-handle. She lifted her head from the pillow. It could only be Charlie. She smiled and went back to sleep again.

In the morning she found another sheaf of papers pushed under the door.

38

Ruthven swung round in the saddle.

Sophia was a few yards behind him on the placid little grey named Buttercup, the turbaned groom a further few yards behind her.

'Jankarit, you wait for us here,' Ruthven said. 'I'm going to stretch Lancer out for a while and see if I can't ride some sense into him. Too damn full of oats and energy. The memsahib can catch up with me at her own pace. Buttercup won't follow, will she?'

Lancer was a handsome but nervous and excitable young stallion with a gleaming bay coat. He'd been bridling and side-stepping ever since they left the stables.

'No, sahib,' Jankarit answered. 'Buttercup safe as rocks.'

Ruthven glanced at Sophia.

'You heard the expert,' he said. 'I'll pull up and wait for you half a mile ahead. Take your time. I want a spin – I think I've got even more energy than Lancer.'

Ruthven reined the stallion in. He turned the horse three times in tight, controlled circles. Lancer whinnied and snorted and his eyes rolled. Then Ruthven loosened the reins and kicked gently at Lancer's ribs.

Within seconds they were in full gallop.

It was early morning and the great rolling sweep of the Raj Hotel's park was a mosaic of dusty tracks, spaces of carefully tended green turf, and copses of trees with wells of shadow beneath them. They bent in and out of the trees, racing from darkness into sunlight and then into darkness again.

Lancer was surefooted and Jankarit was training him for polo. He galloped faster and faster. Dust rose from the ground and spiralled away behind them. The only sounds were the fierce pounding of the horse's hooves and the pumping of its lungs. The rush of the morning breeze stung Ruthven's eyes and the constantly changing patterns of light flared off his face.

They came to an irrigation ditch and the stallion rose effortlessly into the

231

air, jumping it with feet to spare on either side. Then, even faster it seemed, they were galloping on again.

Ruthven felt an exhilaration, a delight, of an intensity he'd never known before. Part of it was the freshness of the morning, part the magnificent young animal beneath him, part the sure and confident control he had over the stallion. There was something else, something far more important.

Somewhere close behind him was Sophia.

He felt Lancer begin to slow, to labour slightly. The stallion hadn't yet grown into his full strength. At full gallop they'd done enough. Ruthven pulled him up and swung out of the saddle. He stood holding the bridle and patting the horse's neck. They were both flecked with sweat.

A few minutes later Sophia came up to them at a stately canter. She was riding side-saddle. She reined Buttercup in and dropped easily to the earth. Until three weeks ago she hadn't ridden since before the war in Africa, but Jankarit was a fine teacher and she was fearless, and she picked up the skill again quickly.

'From the way you set off,' she said, smiling, 'I didn't think you'd stop until you reached the Himalayas.'

Ruthven smiled back. 'Just practising, but we'll get there.'

He looked at her.

Sophia was wearing a long cotton skirt, a cotton jacket, and highly polished riding boots. The skirt and jacket were in faded shades of blue. Knotted casually round her shoulders against the morning chill was a cloak printed in a brilliant Madras pattern. The wind had lifted and tangled her hair, and her eyes were glowing.

She was, Ruthven thought, not just the most beautiful woman he'd ever seen, but the most beautiful who'd ever lived.

'Good morning, Helen's queen,' he said.

Sophia gave him a slight frown. 'Who's Helen?'

'She caused a little trouble at a place called Troy.'

'That one!' Sophia laughed. 'Don't try to flatter me, Jack Ruthven. It'll get you—'

She paused. 'Everywhere.'

Ruthven had learnt of her impending arrival almost by accident.

By now a full colonel, he'd decided to leave the army at the end of the year. Meanwhile, he was continuing with what he'd been doing since he was recalled from the trenches in 1917, ostensibly still training Gurkha soldiers, but devoting more and more of his time to Intelligence-gathering.

It meant shuttling backwards and forwards between Nepal and India, or more accurately between Kathmandu and Delhi. He'd been in Kathmandu for six months, he had a month's leave due to him, he'd decided to spend it at the Raj. The second evening after his arrival he came in from exercising the polo ponies with Jankarit, and walked up to the desk to collect his room keys.

The under-manager behind the desk was reading a telegram that had just arrived from London.

'Good news, Colonel, excellent news.' He beamed at Ruthven. 'We have first-class entertainment coming almost immediately your direction. Head office notifies at short notice they send us a most superb young singer, a Miss Sophia, for guests' delectation.'

He went on, smiling. 'I am utterly sure you will be most, most happy.'

Ruthven went up to his room, dumbfounded.

Sophia arrived five days later.

During those five days he'd been unable to think about anything else. It was almost seven years since he'd seen her, but for every day of those seven years she'd continued to obsess him, to haunt him. He knew a little of what had happened to her, her escape from Germany and the picking-up of her singing career. Eric's letters had told him that.

The rest was a mystery.

By the day of her arrival, Ruthven had decided to treat her appearance quite casually. He wouldn't even be in the hotel, he'd be out somewhere exercising the ponies with Jankarit. And then if they encountered each other that evening or later in the week, he might perhaps offer to buy her a drink and they'd talk inconsequentially about the past.

That was his plan, considered and sensible.

It foundered, it was wrecked, on the evening she was due to reach the Raj. He was indeed out exercising the ponies with Jankarit. At 4.00 p.m. he'd been constantly glancing at his watch, Ruthven abruptly told the groom he'd had enough for the day. They took the horses back. Ruthven went up to his room. He bathed and changed.

Then he went down to the lobby and waited.

He felt like a pathetic adolescent schoolboy, lovelorn and entrapped in coils of chemicals and longings, of desires and visions he was powerless to control. Ruthven cursed himself. Twice he got up and left, and twice helplessly he came back to continue his vigil.

Sophia arrived at 6.00. He glimpsed her silhouette through the glass-panelled doors as she climbed the steps. She walked into the lobby surrounded by the hotel servants carrying her luggage – and his heart turned over.

Ruthven knew he could have been nowhere on earth except where she was.

'Jack!'

She'd seen him as he stood up. She hesitated for a moment in surprise. Then she stepped forward and kissed him lightly on both cheeks.

'How strange, but what a delight! What on earth are you doing here?'

'On one level, taking time out from my soldierly duties,' he replied. 'On another, and much more important, waiting to welcome you.'

Sophia's professional engagement at the Raj didn't start until the following evening.

That night they dined together without any urgency about her being on stage, or the tiredness she felt after her performances. They talked. At the start it wasn't always easy. Seven years of separation spanned a vast gap in both their lives. Ruthven knew far more about Sophia, Yeats' letters had seen to that, than she did about him.

Yet gradually as they continued they began to communicate.

They began to laugh, to exchange not only news, the facts and figures of what had happened to them, but the ideas and perceptions and experiences that belonged to the time between Africa and now. Ruthven avoided Germany. That, he sensed, was still raw and painful. Sophia avoided his time in the trenches for similar, if paradoxically quite different reasons.

'And Eric,' Ruthven said, 'when did you last see him?'

'In London before I left. He's wonderful. He goes on looking after me. In fact he sacked my last agent, found me a new one, and arranged for me to come here.'

'Did he say you might find me?'

'Eric said it was possible.' She smiled. 'You know what he's like. Always arranging things, springing surprises. He's a conjuror – rabbits out of hats.'

Ruthven wondered.

Sophia was probably right. Eric was a conjuror, a magician who delighted in manipulation and sleight of hand. He always had been. He couldn't have known for sure that Ruthven would be at the Raj, but it was a reasonable guess. And from the point of view of Sophia's career, a booking at the hotel made complete sense.

'I ride every morning,' Ruthven said. 'Would you like to join me? It's best early before the sun's properly up, and that may be too early for you. But it's lovely out there in the park.'

'I don't mind how early it is, but I don't know how to ride.'

'Jankarit can teach you, so can I.'

'Then I'll be there.'

Sophia was waiting for him in the lobby even before he came downstairs at 7.00 the next morning.

Ruthven checked as he saw her.

His breath caught in his throat.

Seven years seemed an immensity of time but she was still only twenty-five. Not only beautiful, but of a beauty the intervening years had fleshed out, had made more magnificent, more mature and assured. Her face had kept its bloom, but its bones were stronger, her strange blue–green eyes just as enigmatic but keener. Her body was as slim and graceful as before, but somehow more rounded and even more supple.

He walked beside her down to the stables. Jankarit was waiting for them with Lancer and Buttercup saddled and bridled. The groom showed Sophia how to mount, and positioned her carefully with her legs balancing each other on the side-saddle and her skirt draped across them.

Jankarit led her away. He made her trot and then, running at the head of the little grey with the bridle in his hand, he showed her how to canter. Jankarit returned panting and smiling.

'The memsahib is natural for horses, sahib,' he said.

Sophia was laughing too. 'I think I'm going to like this, Jack.'

They set off with Jankarit's watchful eye on her.

That first morning they didn't go far. But with each successive day they ranged deeper and deeper into the park, and sometimes out on to the rolling plain that lay beyond.

After the first week Ruthven would often tell Jankarit to stay behind and wait for them.

The two of them, he and Sophia, would walk ahead side by side on horseback, or dismount and tether the animals. They'd stroll for a while or, if the morning was particularly hot, they'd sit in the shade of a cluster of trees. Occasionally they'd lie on their their backs, close to each other and acutely aware of the other's presence, but separated, Ruthven thought, by a distance he couldn't ever imagine being bridged.

Sophia was apart from him. It wasn't that she belonged to Eric. She belonged to no one. Perhaps no rare and strange woman ever did.

She was, as he'd impulsively christened her, Helen's queen.

And it didn't matter. He was happier during those days than he'd ever been in his life. The safari all those years ago had been, goodness knows, a momentous and unforgettable experience. It wasn't like this. There'd been tensions then. Not now.

Now there was peace.

He could see it in the dreaming look on Sophia's face. He felt it in himself, in the humming of the bees that thronged round them, in the darting monarch butterflies, their wings crimson, mahogany and gold, which boldly trod their faces as they rested, in the outpourings of bird-song. Even the horses shared it. Lancer sweated, but the sweat dried and his shaking flanks stilled. Buttercup aimiably cropped the grass.

At night, every night, they'd dine together and afterwards Ruthven would listen to her sing. Sophia performed for an hour. Her voice was just as he remembered it but somehow, like her body, fuller and more mature. It had kept all its freshness, but it had become more flexible and resonant. There was an understanding it hadn't had before, an undertone of acceptance, sadness, and strength.

As a professional engagement it was a triumph.

'Never have I seen the like of this, Colonel,' the under-manager remarked in awe to Ruthven after one performance towards the end of Sophia's stay. 'I mean, with permission, sir, look at them. They find themselves in the presence of radiance.'

The little Indian was right.

The audience were standing and cheering.

It was spring and the Raj was full, yet it wasn't only the resident guests who packed the immense dining-hall each night. Members of Delhi's European, Indian, and Anglo-Indian community were coming to the hotel – often from miles away, from their great villas and palaces on the city's outskirts – to hear her.

They arrived in their carriages or their huge wax-polished cars, their Rolls-Royces, Bugattis and Daimlers, they listened, then they retired to the bars. There they divided into two groups. The men, the European diplomats, the British colonial administrators, and the Indian princes, mingled and drank whisky. The women, most of them Indian and wearing elegant jewelled saris, sat and drank coffee and talked.

'The manager, Mr Mahatri, he is entirely pleased, Colonel,' the under-manager went on. 'For hotel business this is, oh, so very fine. We will be seeing Miss Sophia again, do not doubt me of that, I beg you.'

Sophia passed them on her way up to her room.

She always went to bed as soon as the show was over. Ruthven could see how much the performances took out of her. Her eyes were drowsy, her cheeks briefly hollowed, and her wrists trembled. Several times he'd begged her to give up the early morning ride and sleep in instead. She always adamantly refused.

'The sun, the light, the grass, those beautiful horses,' she answered. 'Jack, they're so much more refreshing and restorative than a wasted hour or two between my sheets. No, I shall ride with you.'

That night she smiled at them as she headed for the stairs.

'Miss Sophia, may I say bless you for your exquisite God-given talents?' the under-manager said. 'They are a complete and utter enrichment of our poor lives. I wish you sleep well, dear memsahib.'

'Thank you.'

Sophia gave another smile and vanished into the cavernous shadows of the staircase that led to the Raj's upper floors.

And then it was over. Or rather Ruthven thought it was over.

Sophia had been booked for a month.

The days of the first three weeks tumbled past, but they tumbled lazily and unhurriedly through the morning rides, the heat of the afternoon, the singing at night. There was tomorrow and it would be the same again, and after tomorrow there'd be another tomorrow – companionable and exhilarating, filled with delight and discovery, reaching out into other endless tomorrows.

In the last week the tomorrows narrowed down. They weren't infinite after all. They were measured, shrinking spaces of time before Sophia's departure. To Ruthven's astonishment they accelerated until they were moving with the speed of a cataract.

The cataract reached the lip of the gorge and spilled over. It was Sophia's last night. In the morning she and the days they'd shared would be gone, swept away in the cataract's fall.

Ruthven listened to her. She sang with an almost unbearable poignancy, with a splendour and sorrow in her voice he'd never heard.

When she finished, without waiting to speak to her – they rarely talked to each other after Sophia's performances apart from a short and quiet and to him, it had always seemed, tender goodnight – he went up to his room. He would say his goodbye in the morning. The evening was too highly charged with the memory of the day's ride and the echo of her voice in his mind.

Ruthven undressed and lay down on his bed with his arms crossed behind his head. He tried to sleep.

It was impossible. He gazed at the large open windows. As always, the sky outside was filled with stars. They were always bright, but tonight they seemed fiercer and brighter than ever, the constellations wheeling and turning in great sprays and catherine wheels of silver-white radiance against hanging panels of black velvet.

Sophia had been dressed in black velvet when she sang. The under-manager, with the wonderful eloquence of the Indians, had described the guests as being in the presence of radiance.

'Jack.'

Ruthven sat upright.

He didn't know what time it was. He didn't know if he'd been dozing. If he had, it took him barely a second to come out of sleep and register her at the open door.

There was a window on the far side of the corridor behind her with the moonlight streaming through it. He could see Sophia was wearing a sari. He couldn't tell what colour it was, but it was shot through with lines of gold. The soft misty cloth folded gracefully round her body as if she'd worn nothing but saris all her life.

She closed the door and the moonlight was cut off. Ruthven tracked her by the shimmer of the golden threads as she crossed the room's darkness, and walked silently to the window. He watched her as she stood silhouetted looking out onto the park below.

'This is where we take the horses and ride. Out there, I think I can just see it, is that lovely group of – what do they call the trees? – magnolia oaks, I believe, where we lay side by side and talked—'

She was speaking, Ruthven knew, as much to herself as to him.

'I'm going away, Jack. I don't want to, but Eric insisted. Here for a month, he said, then on to Rangoon. Back here again if it worked out, he said, and it has, but that won't be for months yet—'

Sophia shook her head.

'Oh dear, how strong he is, how he takes charge of one's life. Sometimes so fine, sometimes such a brute. I might have been wrecked without him, but I could be wrecked with him. Well, I'm going to make my own small act of defiance.'

She turned from the window and came over to the bed. She smiled and touched Ruthven on the forehead. She turned slowly in a circle and the sari fell away from her, falling in a small golden cloud on the floor.

Sophia was naked.

For an instant the starlight played over her body, the sloping curve of her shoulders, her breasts, the flat sheen of her stomach, the triangle of hair at her groin, her long sinuous legs.

'I want to be with you, Jack. Will you permit me?'

238

She didn't wait for an answer. She lifted the sheet and slipped in beside him.

Ruthven stiffened for an instant in shock.

Then he lost all sense of place and time, even of being. He turned and held her. He buried his face in her hair, sweet-smelling and tousled and tangled. He felt her eyelashes move against his skin like the beat of a bird's wing. He felt her heart beneath his chest and her nipples tightening and her legs suddenly part and the space between them open.

Afterwards he rocked and soared, and he knew she was rocking and soaring with him.

The rhythm between them, the ferocious physical bond between them, swiftened and grew closer until it was unbearable. He could hold it no longer. His back arced and he came to a climax, a wild impetuous climax, and the terrible, terrifying moment of discharge was unleashed. He called out, he never knew what he had shouted, but he fell away as it finished and enveloped her in his arms.

He lay there huddling over her, protecting her. The bed smelt of seaweed, and Sophia was soft and gentle beneath him. He licked her skin and it tasted of salt.

'My God,' Ruthven said several minutes later, his voice still blurred. 'What have I done?'

'You've made love to me, Jack.' He felt Sophia's lips move against his face as she smiled. 'It's just what I wanted.'

'But—'

He stopped. She answered his unspoken questions.

'No, we're not married. And, yes, I might become pregnant and have a child. And, no, none of it matters. Between the three of us we can handle everything. I'm the woman. In the end, all the decisions come down to me.'

'The three of us? You mean Eric as well?'

'I'm here because he sent me here. Wasn't it worth it?'

'Oh, Sophia!'

'Go to sleep, Jack Ruthven, and sleep well. Just think of my arms about you. I'll see you in the morning.'

Ruthven didn't see her in the morning.

Normally he woke with the first light. That day for some reason he slept until 9.00. By the time he was up and dressed, Sophia had left.

Ruthven spent the next two days riding out with Jankarit and exercising the polo ponies. Then it was time for him to head north again for Kathmandu and the Gurkha training camps.

As he settled his account before leaving, the Raj's under-manager said

239

happily, 'Excellent news, Colonel. We have managed with delight to book Miss Sophia for a further headline engagement. She will arrive, we trust, in September. What a true feast, sir, for her legion of admirers.'

39

'Liar!'

Victoria laid down the typewritten pages and glared at Charlie.

'You've no business doing that,' she added angrily. 'That's pure fantasy, over-heated titillation.'

'What is?'

'The stuff about Sophia seducing Jack.'

Charlie wrinkled his face.

'I doubt it. Maybe I might have read between the lines, taken a little artistic licence, but it's there all right in what you gave me.' His expression held a hint of mockery. 'Your Sophia was a liberated woman, an extraordinary woman. You modern girls don't know the half of it. You think you invented sex. They were at it like rabbits for generations before you were born.'

He paused. 'I know it's sensitive and I did try to consult you before I wrote it. You'd locked your door.'

'So you tried to come in?'

'Absolutely. It was a professional obligation. Also I was lonely – it does get lonely if one's writing in the early hours.'

Victoria flushed.

Of course she knew he'd tried to come in. It made her both angry at his impertinence and in a strange way flattered.

'How would Angela have felt about that?' she asked.

Charlie closed his eyes wearily. 'Angela's gone back to Magnus. It was a mistake, and I told you so. You know it damn well.'

'Who dumped who?'

'Please, Victoria, this is pointless and demeaning for both of us—'

'I asked you a question,' she snapped, cutting him off. 'You used at least to have a few social graces. A fairly ordinary one is giving an answer when you're asked something.'

He was silent for a moment.

'In which case, since you want to know, she left me. Naturally it was more complicated than that—'

'I doubt it,' Victoria interrupted him again with a hard, tight smile. 'It's the only convincing thing you've said. And it leaves Angela with just a vestige of good sense still clinging to her.'

'Victoria,' he raised his shoulders helplessly, 'what do you want me to say? That I missed the deadline, fluffed the copy? That actually – and it's true – I love you?'

'Actually – and it's true – you're a shit. And actually – also true – if you tried anything like that, it would just prove you're an even bigger fibber than I thought. Don't, Charlie, don't—'

She stabbed her finger at him.

'You haven't got much dignity left. Hang on to the little that remains. Any more porkies and you won't be just threadbare, you'll be naked to the wind. Remember that? One of your elegant phrases. You taught it to me.'

Victoria stopped.

She was panting and shaking with anger. In her rage she must have stepped towards him because she suddenly realised he was backing away before her.

Victoria stopped. She contemplated him in silence.

'What about Ruthven, my grandfather? An extraordinary man too?'

'Maybe, although not to his mother or his wife. No man ever is. We're all flawed. I feel sorry for him. Occasionally I almost feel sorry for myself.'

Victoria laughed coldly. 'My heart bleeds.'

'Look, Victoria.' There was anxiety, almost contrition in his voice. 'Whatever's happened, whatever I've done, whatever the muddle, how about a temporary ceasefire? I've got an offering, an olive branch, something else I've written.'

She looked at him suspiciously. 'What?'

'Nepal, or rather Kathmandu. It follows on, but,' he held up his hand, 'read it later. We're here. How many people get the chance to roam Umfolozi? Let's not waste it.'

Warily, grudgingly, Victoria agreed.

A day of peace in the rolling hills of the African bush, she thought, wouldn't do either of them any harm. It might even help heal some of the fearsome damage that had been done, to her at least, by the events of the last month.

Victoria ordered packed lunches from the lodge and they set out.

The day passed, as she'd hoped, tranquilly and quietly. They walked

242

the savannah, pushing through the waist-high winter grasses, dry and yellow-gold and scented with African dust. They ate in the midday heat under a thatched roof in a viewpoint above a lagoon.

They watched the antics of a family of bush-pigs with their tiny striped piglets, the wallowing wart-hogs, the stately grandeur of a nyala bull and its cow, a nervous pair of blue-sheened wildebeest, a quarrelsome bunch of baboons, and a set of mischievous vervet monkeys. The king of the mud-pool was undoubtedly the majestic rhino: prehistoric, double-horned, and small-eyed, he ambled slowly about his fiefdom, expecting every other creature to defer to his pleasure.

For the first time since she had embarked on her quest, Victoria felt at peace. The peace ended abruptly as the light began to fade.

'Miss Ruthven? Miss Victoria Ruthven?'

Victoria turned, startled.

The day had passed swiftly. Now the sun was dipping towards the horizon and the animals round the water-hole were preparing for the challenges of the night.

'Yes?'

There were two of them.

They'd come up silently behind the rough wooden table at which she and Charlie were sitting in the hide. Both wore uniform – not the khaki shorts and insignia-crusted bush shirts of the camp rangers, but the tailored grey of the state police.

'Can we have a word, miss? Nothing to worry about. Just a couple of questions to clear up a little misunderstanding.'

Charlie was already on his feet and pushing himself between Victoria and the two men.

'Not without me you don't.'

He fumbled in his pocket for his press accreditation, holding it up for inspection. The first officer, red-necked and with the heavy bulk of a Boer farmer, glanced at it briefly.

'That won't be necessary, sir. It's a private matter. A family matter. Miss Ruthven will be back with you in a minute.'

The clipped South African vowels were flat, emotionless.

Victoria said, 'Leave it, Charlie. Let me talk to them.'

Charlie glowered at the men. 'Stay away from open windows.'

The younger policeman smiled. 'Very witty, sir. Please tell your newspaper we now have double glazing.'

He turned back to Victoria. 'Can we talk at the car—'

He glanced at Charlie again. 'We've got a mike there, sir. Everything goes on tape. You can even hear the sound of breaking glass.'

He grinned again.

Charlie looked as if he was about to lurch towards him, but Victoria put a restraining hand on his arm. She followed the two policemen out of the hide. They looked, she thought wildly, like a rhino and a vervet monkey, the large, older one the rhino and his young, mischievous companion, the talkative one, the monkey.

The police jeep was parked 200 yards away on the access track that led to the hide. Its intercom radio was crackling. The senior of the two officers reached in and switched it off. The younger one pulled out a stool and set it on the ground.

'Take a seat, Miss Ruthven,' he said. 'This shouldn't take us more than a moment or two.'

Victoria sat down.

For an instant she regretted doing so. It placed her at a psychological disadvantage, looking up at the two men towering above her. Then both of them sat down on the jeep's running-board opposite her, and their eyes were level with hers. A small wave of relief ran over her. They were also, she sensed, not hostile but almost as puzzled as she was.

'Well now, Miss Ruthven,' it was the older man who spoke, 'we know you've been making inquiries about family history. Fine. No objection, no objection at all. Trouble is, family history reaches up and down. And when it reaches up, it reaches right down again – straight to simple folk like us. Right, Jan?'

The younger policeman nodded. 'Right, man.'

'We get instructions, miss,' the older policeman went on. 'Well, suggestions we call them now in the new South Africa. You'll know what I mean.'

Victoria frowned.

She didn't know what he meant. All she could think was that in some roundabout way she was being warned off. She asked him bluntly if it was so.

The senior policeman took off his hat and scratched his head thoughtfully. She was right. He wasn't only puzzled. He was out of his depth and almost embarrassed.

'Let's put it like this,' he said. 'Why don't you just enjoy our country? Visit our parks, cook yourself a brai, drink our good wine. Just have a good time with your boyfriend, and go home with happy memories.'

'Why?' she demanded. 'Have I done anything wrong?'

'I certainly hope not,' he chuckled. 'I'm sure your friend would stop you if you tried. He seems to know all about our open windows—'

He paused and his face hardened.

'Someone made, well, let's call it an unauthorised night-time visit to the museum at Rorke's Drift. Why the silly buggers at the top didn't let him have what he wanted anyway, I don't know. That's no concern of ours. But it was a burglary, we know who did it, and we could hold and deport both him and his companion—'

He stood up. The younger man got to his feet beside him.

'Just fatherly advice, miss, but worth remembering.' He raised his hat. 'Have a nice peaceful stay in our country.'

Victoria rose too. She began to walk away. Then on impulse she swung back.

'How did you know who I was, what I'm doing?'

He shrugged. 'South Africa's tribes and families, miss,' he said. 'Tribes and families, they know each other's business.'

The words were almost identical to the ones Franjie Viljoen had used when he explained how he'd found Mama N'duma. Victoria shivered. She walked on.

Charlie was anxiously waiting for her at the entrance to the hide.

'What happened?'

Victoria told him.

'It was a warning,' she finished. 'But about what I don't know and I don't think they did either. They'd just been told to move us on and preferably out. They weren't chiefs, just spear-carriers.'

Charlie frowned.

'Spear-carriers take orders from chiefs. Someone's been pulling strings.'

'Then why didn't they simply arrest us?'

'I imagine because they'd been told not to,' Charlie answered. 'They'd been sent to keep us out of trouble, not get us into it.'

'Who the hell could have sent them?' Victoria asked in exasperation.

'People think countries are big,' Charlie said. 'They're not, not at the top, they're all small, even China. Just a few people and a few interests press the buttons and pull the levers.'

'And Silverback's one of them here?'

'It could well be—'

Charlie stood gazing out over the bush.

The landscape was already coated with gold in the fast-fading evening light. Mist was rising from the streams that threaded the rolling hills, and the air was filled with the calls of birds homing to their roosts for the night.

'I'm not buying that story about the military refusing permission for us to look at Yeats' war record. I think we were set up.'

'But why?'

Victoria stared at him. She knew Charlie well enough to see that he was genuinely bewildered.

'Convenience. In case they want to get rid of us. This is modern South Africa. A responsible member of the Commonwealth. Not the high old days when someone like me lost his way to the toilet and accidentally fell through a sixth-floor window in the local police station. Things are different now, you put people on outward-bound planes. But the old ways die hard, and the thinking's the same.'

'And that's the message?'

Charlie lifted his shoulders.

'I can't think of any other. Loud and clear, I'd say, we're being told: Hands off, folks, stay away. That's my guess.'

Charlie's voice was as always confident and positive, but there was something tentative and puzzled behind the words he used.

For once he seemed vulnerable, almost frightened, as much out of his depth as the two policeman, for all the protective shield of their uniform and guns, had been. The three of them were lost, stumbling without a compass in an unfamiliar and hazardous landscape.

The policemen had gone. They were no concern of Victoria's anyway. Charlie, strangely, still was. As she studied his face and the uncertainty on it, she felt a sudden inexplicable rush of tenderness towards him. Against all her instincts, she took his arm.

'Let's go back to the lodge,' she said. 'I want to read about Sophia and Kathmandu.'

'It's very short and maybe a bit limp,' Charlie said.

Victoria laughed wickedly. 'I'm no stranger to things like that.'

To his credit Charlie had the grace to redden and then to laugh.

40

Copy from Charlie – The Silverback Story

'It's not true. I mean, surely you could be wrong, you could have made a mistake—'

Ruthven stopped. He knew he'd been stammering. He looked at Sophia, astounded.

'Oh, you are a dear, Jack.' Sophia laughed and touched his cheek gently. 'So sweet, so innocent, so naive. You must be the only person in the hotel who hasn't noticed.'

She tapped her rounded stomach.

'Where did you think it came from? That I'd been making a pig of myself on Shanghai fried noodles?'

Sophia paused. 'After all, I did warn you it was a possibility, didn't I?'

Ruthven shook his head. For several moments he said nothing.

It was the end of Sophia's second engagement at the Raj. Her performances, as far as Ruthven could gather, had been even more rapturously received than before, but from his point of view the whole occasion hadn't worked out as he'd planned.

Ruthven had hoped and longed to spend the whole month there with her. He'd got delayed in Nepal. He'd finally set off for the south only to be called back after two days' riding to deal with some emergency in camp. He'd at last left again, he'd ridden frantically, changing horses and barely stopping to sleep at night, and he'd eventually caught the Delhi train.

By the time he reached the hotel there were only five days of Sophia's visit left. They had been wonderful days. The pattern had been just as before. They'd ridden with Jankarit in the mornings, they'd walked and talked in the sun and shadow beneath the trees, Ruthven had listened entranced to Sophia singing at night.

She hadn't come to his room and although Ruthven ached to hold her in his arms again, in a way it was enough just to be in her company, to see her smile, to hear her laugh. Except the days had passed with terrible terrifying speed, and now the time was over.

And more than that, Ruthven hadn't even noticed what had happened to her. He felt such a fool, such an insensitive idiot, his cheeks kept flushing.

'What are you going to do?' he asked.

'Have my child, have your child.' Sophia smiled again. 'It's what women usually do.'

'But how, I mean where?' Ruthven knew he was starting to sound incoherent again. 'I should be with you. Only you finish tonight, and tomorrow I have to go back to Nepal.'

'That shouldn't necessarily separate us,' Sophia said quietly.

'What do you mean?'

'I could come with you.'

'Sophia,' he looked at her appalled, 'it's impossible. Nepal's in the mountains. It has no facilities. It doesn't admit European women. It's a closed country.'

'Nowhere on earth is a closed country to me, Jack,' she answered. 'And no facilities? You were telling me only yesterday about your excellent field hospital outside Kathmandu. And to get in? Truly, I don't think that will be very difficult. A sari, a head-shawl, a little walnut dye on the face. I'm just another of your servants—'

She stopped. She stared at him with an intensity in her eyes he'd never seen before.

'I'm carrying your son or your daughter, Jack Ruthven. Are you not going to be there when your child is born?'

Ruthven was already opening his mouth to protest. He was silent. He turned away.

It was utter madness, but it was possible.

The air of the Kathmandu valley was clear, fresh, and healthy. The little army hospital was primitive but Freddie Wilberforce, the medical corps doctor who ran it, was highly experienced and a qualified surgeon. He must have carried out endless deliveries. And Sophia was right. The border checks were almost non-existent, the country was too wild. With a little disguise she could easily pass for one of his servants.

There were two other factors.

He would indeed be with Sophia when their child was born. That and her presence at his side over the months ahead was dizzyingly irresistible. There was something far more overwhelming, more irresistible still. Sophia had obviously made up her mind. Ruthven doubted whether the Devil or God himself could divert her from a course of action she had decided on.

It was certainly beyond Ruthven's own powers.

He turned back to her. He managed a confused smile.

'I know you've got a sari,' he said. 'You'd better send someone out to buy some walnut dye.'

They were probably the happiest months in Ruthven's entire life.

Entering Nepal proved as easy as Sophia had prophesied, as easy as if Ruthven, an accredited officer, had been travelling with his servants on his own. No one questioned Sophia's presence as a member of his entourage. They reached camp and Freddie Wilberforce examined her.

'The lady says you may hear the verdict.'

Wilberforce emerged beaming from the consultation tent.

Ruthven followed him back in. Sophia, also smiling happily, was sitting on the raised bench that served as an operating table.

'Just about the healthiest mother-to-be I've ever had the good fortune to cast my eyes over,' Wilberforce said. 'I'll be watching her of course, but if we have any problems, then I'm a Dutchman — and the Wilberforces weren't born in Holland. Go and enjoy the mountain air, the pair of you.'

Sophia lowered herself to the floor. She gave Ruthven a light, quick kiss. Then, hand-in-hand, they walked outside.

Long afterwards Ruthven tried to recollect the time that followed.

In a way, the way of events and occasions, there was almost nothing to remember. There couldn't be. Little happened in the valley. He and Sophia had separate tents in the encampment, separate but close together. Ruthven spent every day training and instructing the young Gurkha recruits, sometimes leaving with them for week-long exercises.

Sophia spent most of her time reading — Ruthven, Wilberforce, and the three other officers there all had considerable collections of books. When she wasn't reading, she walked. She ranged out into the valley's meadows. She came to know the peasant farmers and their womenfolk, watching and often helping them as they went about the business of their lives.

Often again she simply sat above a stream. She let the drift of dragonflies, birds, and small water-mammals swirl round her, and thought and dreamed.

Then Ruthven would come back to find her absent and search until he found her. They'd walk back and eat quietly, companionably together.

So little, Ruthven reflected afterwards, and yet so much. A comfort, an ease, a familiarity between themselves and the landscape and its people. The stars shone at night. Water-buffalo lowed and bellowed. Rhododendrons, azaleas, primulas, and orchids flowered and faded. The great chain of the Himalayan mountains abided always above them, and Sophia swelled.

She didn't grow fat.

Her face, her arms, her legs remained as fine and elegant as they had ever been – although her skin, Ruthven noticed, shone as never before. Only her belly pushed out. When the birth came, it happened with extraordinary speed.

Ruthven woke in the early hours to hear her calling for him. He raced across the few yards between their tents. Sophia was heaving and sweating. He turned, ran across the encampment. and woke Freddie Wilberforce. Wilberforce tumbled out of his bed and ran with him back to Sophia.

'Out, old fellow,' Wilberforce said as soon as he'd glanced at her. 'This is in my bailiwick, not yours.'

Ruthven waited outside.

Occasional agonies of worry flooded over him – several times he heard Sophia cry out in pain and anguish – but he trusted Wilberforce, and he was right. The birth, if any birth can be, if any new human can be pushed out into the world without trauma and distress, was simple and straightforward.

'Right, come in and take a look.'

Wilberforce had stuck his head through the tent flap.

Ruthven noticed his hands were covered in blood, but he was smiling. Ruthven went inside. Sophia was lying spent and pale on the bed. She too was smiling, an exhausted shadow of a smile. In her arms was a swaddled little bundle.

'You've got a son, Jack,' she whispered. 'He's lovely and he's going to be called Harry, for England and St George.'

She closed her eyes and held the child to her.

'Strong as a young otter,' Wilberforce said. 'Come back here if you sire any more, Ruthven. Sometimes it's a real pleasure for us sawbones to go about our legitimate business. Much more fun than taking the scalpel to gangrene.'

He clipped Ruthven jovially on the shoulder, so hard that Ruthven almost toppled over.

Three weeks later Ruthven, Sophia, and the infant Harry left Kathmandu for Delhi.

Ruthven's tour of duty in Nepal was over and so was the term of his commission in the army. He would have to go back to London to tidy up the odds and ends, and formally notify the authorities that his service was ended. Then he would head for South Africa, where Sophia and Harry were already bound.

They spent a final night in India together at the Raj.

'Eric,' Ruthven said suddenly over dinner. 'We'll all soon be together again. What does he know about this?'

250

'I wrote that I was pregnant,' Sophia answered. 'I didn't say who the father was, but he'll guess of course.'

'Will he mind?'

'Jack, you know him far better than I do. You tell me.'

Ruthven thought for a long time. Finally he shrugged.

'I love him, but I don't know him.' He smiled. 'The pair of you, you're as complicated and enigmatic as each other. We'll see.'

He lifted his glass. 'Meanwhile, to Harry. We belong to each other, Harry belongs to all three of us.'

Sophia threw back her head. She laughed and drank to her son.

41

Victoria laid down the script.

There were tears in her eyes. So that was what had happened. That was the truth. And it was the truth.

She knew it as surely as if she had been there. She closed her eyes.

The elegant Madame Villedieu in Paris had been right to point out the striking physical resemblance between Victoria and the young woman of the Renoir painting. The likeness wasn't just physical – there was much else about Sophia that Victoria recognised in herself. There was the determination, the energy, the disregard for convention. There was recklessness and selfishness too, and a willingness to manipulate others.

Sophia had borne a child, but was never a mother. She had chosen a husband, but was never a wife.

Vain, self-seeking, wilful. There was no doubt that Sophia was all of those things. She was also, as Charlie pointed out, one hell of a woman.

Sophia. Blood of her blood. Tragic victim or conniving vixen?

And what of the woman she had always known as Granny Lomax?

All her life she'd believed that the sturdy young Scotswoman who gazed out from the photograph in her mother's bathroom was her grandmother. If Victoria had thought about her at all, it was only to wonder that her handsome, brilliant grandfather should have chosen to share his life with such a homely consort.

Two women, two men, a child. And she, Victoria, the last of the line, couldn't rest until she had unravelled the knots which bound them.

She glanced at her watch.

It was getting late. Charlie would be swapping stories in the bar, waiting for her to join him for the brai which had been promised for that evening. She bathed, dressed again with care, this time more casually in baggy linen trousers tightly belted over a well-cut shirt, and made her way to the main building to join him.

'Victoria, over here! Someone wants to meet you.'

Charlie's voice held a note of triumph.

Across the crowded room Victoria could see that his companion was a woman – from the neatly bobbed grey hair, she wasn't young. It was hard to assess her age from a distance, but her figure was trim and elegantly clad in a tailored jacket with a sweeping skirt which revealed small buttoned boots.

Victoria made her way through the tables towards them.

'Victoria Ruthven – Miss Henrietta Lomax. Your cousin, Victoria.'

'I guess you didn't even know you *had* a cousin, Victoria.'

The woman held out her hand.

Victoria shook it.

The woman's hand was bony, but dry and warm. At close quarters she was much older than she'd appeared across the room, certainly seventy and perhaps closer to eighty. There could be no doubt about the relationship with Granny Lomax. The shared likeness, the strong angular face and bold grey eyes, was so striking it was uncanny.

'No. I mean yes,' Victoria stammered. 'I mean, I did know there had to be Lomax relations somewhere. You do look very like Granny from her photographs.'

The old lady smiled. 'I know exactly what you mean. Physical resemblance is always a little unnerving, but sometimes it's all we have to go on. We'll have plenty of time for family gossip tomorrow when I sweep the pair of you off to my lair.'

Victoria's glance ranged in bewilderment between the two of them.

'It's all settled, isn't it, young man?' Miss Lomax added.

Charlie nodded. 'Your cousin is very persuasive, Victoria.'

'But how, why, I mean how did you find us—?'

Victoria found herself stammering again. She broke off.

'I've already told your friend. I don't think I need go through it again. He can explain it to you over your supper. I meanwhile am going to my bed. I will see you both in the morning—'

Miss Lomax stood up.

She placed a pair of gold-rimmed spectacles on her nose and gave Victoria a steady, appraising glance.

'Please don't think me rude, dear. It's just that I'm approaching senility and blind as a bat.' After a moment she nodded, apparently satisfied. 'Just as I thought. Appearances are so important. You're a beautiful girl, Victoria, and I imagine a clever one too. I think we'll get along fine.'

Her stick was hanging over the back of her chair. She picked it up and walked away.

Victoria gazed after her, astounded, until she disappeared. Then she rounded on Charlie.

'What the hell is all this?' she demanded.

'Let's do what she suggested. Go through and eat.'

They went out to the brai. Over dinner Charlie told her.

'I came down for a drink while you were reading,' Charlie said. 'One of the under-managers was waiting at the desk. He asked if I was with you, Victoria Ruthven. I said yes. I thought it might be something to do with the police again. But no. He said a Miss Lomax was waiting to see me in the bar. I went through and there she was.'

'But who is she?' Victoria asked.

'She'll tell you tomorrow, but I gather she's the niece of your Granny Lomax.'

'How on earth did she know I was here?'

'She was a bit elusive about that. She'll probably tell you, but it isn't hard to figure out from what she let on to me—'

Charlie paused. 'Your Granny Lomax left her a major holding in Silverback. Miss Henrietta must be one of the richest women in South Africa and that, blossom, means rich.'

'Where exactly are we going?' Victoria asked.

'Durban,' Miss Lomax answered. 'Or if you want to be really precise, a little way into the hills to the north. It's about four hours' drive.'

It was 9.00 a.m.

The two of them were sitting side by side in the back of Miss Lomax's air-conditioned Mercedes. Her chauffeur, a smiling black Tswana named Moffat, was at the wheel in front. Charlie, with precise instructions about how to get to their destination, was somewhere in the hired car behind.

Victoria hesitated. 'I hope you don't mind my asking, but why haven't I haven't been told of you before?'

Miss Lomax laughed.

'No doubt because your family decided not to. My dear papa

emigrated to Virginia after the clearances, although the rest of the family stayed behind in Scotland. It was my father's sister Margaret who married your grandfather.'

'I never really knew Granny,' Victoria said. 'She was somehow shadowy. Grandfather Jack didn't talk about her, nor did the great-aunts.'

The old lady laughed again.

'I can well imagine. Maggie was a servant-girl. She didn't have the breeding for a wife, except she became one. None of the Ruthvens ever really accepted the marriage. Still, I hope Jack's sisters are well, fearsome old trouts they must be these days, just as bad as me.'

'You *know* the great-aunts?'

'Of course, dear. My father had made a lot of money in the States. I came over to London to meet society and do the season. I was considered quite a catch.'

Miss Lomax's eyes shone at the memory, and she looked almost girlish.

'I was pretty too, and what they called in those days, dare I say it still, spirited.'

Victoria smiled at her, 'I can well believe it, Miss Lomax.'

'Thank you, my dear. Although please call me Henrietta, as I call you Victoria.'

'But you never married?'

A bark of laughter and an emphatic shake of the head left no doubt as to Miss Henrietta's feelings on matrimony.

'I took lovers, naturally. So much more rewarding than husbands. Where was the sense in marrying a man who would see it as his God-given right to allow me a handful of pocket-money, my own money, and absolutely no say in how the rest of it was spent? No. Not for me.'

'And then what happened?'

'My dear Aunt Maggie, your Granny Lomax, took me as her companion to the Cape for the winter. And I fell in love.'

'In love?'

'Yes. I mean really in love – not just some sentimental young girl's nonsense. Grown-up, full-blooded passion. Not with a man, but with a place. This place – the most beautiful place on earth. The land, the people, everything. Never regretted it. Not for an instant.'

Victoria nodded.

She too had felt the pull of Africa, felt at home under the wide skies, felt her spirits soar at a glimpse of distant violet hills and the endless expanse of clean ochre-coloured bush and sand that reached yearningly towards them.

'My goodness, are we here already?' Miss Lomax sat up and leaned forward. 'We are, I truly believe we are. Well, child, ready yourself to meet my one true lover.'

The Mercedes slowed to glide between two white pillars which marked the entrance to a wide avenue of limes leading between massed ranks of neatly pruned vines. Beyond, Victoria could see the snowy facade of an elegant mansion, tall and graceful with gleaming windows and a riot of wisteria over the porch. A perfectly manicured sweep of lawn flanked herbaceous borders filled with delphiniums and drifts of violet cranesbill.

'What do you think, my dear?'

Victoria swung round to look at her, her eyes gleaming. 'It's the most beautiful place I've ever seen.'

The old lady nodded.

'I pick my lovers well. Welcome to Stellenfeldt, the field of the stars in Afrikaans. We still have so much to talk about. But first we must eat – or Mama Mathilda will never speak to me again.'

Charlie arrived only ten minutes later. They had lunch – roast guineafowl stuffed with wild berries – in the rose garden, the scent of the flowers echoing the delicate perfume of the pale pink wine which accompanied the meal. After a bowl of tiny scarlet strawberries accompanied by thick golden cream from the estate's own herd, Miss Lomax folded up her napkin and leaned back in her chair.

'Now we have broken bread together, my dears, I think I owe you an apology.'

'An apology?' Victoria asked. 'For what?'

'For having you followed.' She paused, her face calm. 'Well, not exactly followed. Let's say I asked to be kept informed of your movements, which was why I knew where to find you.'

'Why did you need to do that?' Victoria asked again.

'My dear, you clearly have no notion what the name Ruthven means here. Our family's joint holdings account for a measurable percentage of the country's wealth. To be a Ruthven here is not unlike being a Rothschild in Israel. We were concerned you might impetuously get into trouble. Alerting the authorities to your presence seemed the simplest solution.'

'So that was why those two ham-fisted policemen "reasoned" with

Victoria?' Charlie shook his head. It was almost the first time he'd spoken.

'Yes—'

Miss Lomax's grey eyes were steady. 'I'm sorry if you found it offensive. It was meant only to be helpful. Unfortunately our policemen have an automatic reaction to journalists. Even in our brave new South Africa, old habits die hard.'

'Miss Lomax,' Charlie said, 'does this, like everything else, it seems, originate with Silverback?'

Miss Lomax took another sip of her wine. She settled herself back in her chair.

'I think I had better begin at the beginning. Of course it's not really the beginning, but it's my beginning and as far back as I can reliably take you. My Aunt Maggie, your Granny Lomax, Victoria, if that's how you still see her, although I think you know the truth now . . .

'She was a remarkable woman, Margaret Lomax. She had to do the best she could under difficult circumstances. Cape Town was busy then – very exciting. A stop-over on the way to India, the place where the wildest of the rich Europeans came to spend their winters. German counts, English earls, Russian dukes. Snobbish of course, but buccaneering too. New frontiers, new money, rough diamonds. It suited *me* fine – and there was motherly Aunt Maggie to scoop me up if things went really wrong. And Sophia, of course—'

She shook her head and smiled wistfully.

'I loved Sophia, although she wasn't much of what's now called a "role model" for a young girl. She was older than me, and married. She was still beautiful and wild, and she sang like an angel. But she was trouble – even I, young as I was, could see that. It was a strange life at Meerlust, which was where the four of them lived.'

'The four of them?' Victoria interjected.

'Five if you count young Harry. It must all have been terribly confusing for the child. But then, in those days not many lived what you might call normal lives. A lot of box-and-cox among the married set, divorces and remarriages all over the place. Even I knew the Yeats-Ruthven ménage was quite a scandal.'

'Whatever the arrangements,' Charlie said, 'not many of those relationships ended in a double murder.'

Miss Lomax looked at him sharply. She didn't answer.

'Meerlust,' Victoria prompted her. 'What was strange about that?'

'How can I explain Meerlust? An extraordinary place. Not as beautiful as Stellenfeldt, my field of the stars, but quite magnificent in its own way. A folly, like one of those eighteenth-century fantasies built by aristocrats so they could play at being milk-maids. Except that at Meerlust it wasn't a game – it was all real.'

The old lady fell silent for a moment, lost in thought.

'Looking back on it now, that was where all the troubles began – with the twin houses and the crazy double lives they led. Even I could see there'd be trouble, and I was far younger than any of them. Sophia used to ride over most days – it was an escape from what had become reality. And she loved being here, which is why we became such friends. But all this must be as confusing for you, Victoria, as it was for young Harry. There was no doubt Sophia led them all a dreadful dance.'

Again, the old lady came to a halt.

Victoria leaned forward. She took Miss Lomax's hand and urged her on.

'Please, Henrietta,' it was the first time Victoria had used her name, 'just for me, please tell me what happened, both the before and the after.'

Miss Lomax cleared her throat. She drank some more wine. Then she started to talk again.

Charlie, sleepy-eyed and apparently distant from what she was saying, sat listening as keenly as Victoria to every word. Victoria knew he was storing up the information to write again.

42

Copy from Charlie — The Silverback Story

'Miss Lomax?'

Ruthven took off his hat and stretched out his hand.

'Yes,' the young woman replied.

'I'm very happy to meet you, to welcome you to South Africa.'

Ruthven studied her for an instant.

He'd thought it would be difficult to find her in the throng of passengers streaming off the liner that had just docked at the Cape Town quay after completing the voyage from Southampton. In fact it could hardly have been easier.

Highland Scots girls looked exactly what they were, and they stood out in any crowd. No one who knew them could have confused them for anyone else. Miss Lomax, Maggie Lomax, was a classic example of a type Ruthven had known from his earliest childhood. She was about nineteen. She was tall, fine-figured with bold breasts and a narrow waist, dark curling hair and level slate-grey eyes.

She wasn't beautiful, her face was too angular for that, her hands too raw-boned and splayed, but she had an expression that combined an appealing youthful vulnerability with the Celtic confidence that finds itself at home anywhere.

Ruthven took to her instantly. She came from the glens. She was familiar, she was safe, she was home.

'You know my young sisters, I believe,' Ruthven said when they'd loaded her luggage into the car he'd hired.

'Aye,' she replied. 'Octavie and Maude, well, Miss Octavie and Miss Maude as I should call them now, we grew up together. Inseparable, we were, until they went south to school.'

Inseparable.

It was, it occurred to Ruthven, a long and unusual word for a Highland girl to use. Her accent, too, wasn't quite what he'd expected. It had the Highland burr, but it was also more delicate than he remembered in the voices of the servants at Glenmoray.

261

'And you stayed on in the north?'

'No, sir. I went to Edinburgh,' she answered. 'My father was head stalker to Lord Craigallen. Well paid, it was, and he was ambitious for me. For four years he put me into Merchistoun Girls. Then he fell on the tops and broke his hip, and he couldna work any more. His Lordship discharged him and I had to come back hame.'

That explained it, Ruthven thought.

The Scots' education was the best in the world, and best of all in the great Edinburgh academies. There was a long tradition of Highlanders sending their best and brightest to be taught there. Maggie Lomax had had four years of it. It explained her accent and her vocabulary.

'Miss Lomax,' he started, but she cut him off.

'Maggie, if you don't mind, Colonel. Nae one's ever called me anything else.'

Ruthven smiled. 'Of course. Maggie, my sisters will have told you about young Harry. I regard him as my son. I have taken out legal papers to adopt him. I want him well cared for, well raised, well loved. Will you do that?'

'I grew up with bairns, Colonel, my wee brothers and sisters. I can handle another.'

They rattled on over Cape Town's cobbled streets towards the hotel where Ruthven had taken rooms for the night. The following morning they drove to the house at Meerlust.

The empathy between Maggie and the child was so immediate, so direct and uncomplicated, Ruthven could hardly believe it.

They arrived late in the afternoon.

The first part of the journey was by car, the second when the crudely metalled road gave way to a rough dirt-track by horse and carriage. Harry was waiting eagerly for them at the top of the steps that led up to the house. By his side was his ayah, an old Malay Cape Coloured woman named Hope.

Harry raced down to greet them as the carriage pulled up.

At six he was a handsome, elfin little boy, a darting, leaping dolphin of a child, with an easy smile. He had Sophia's curling auburn hair, cut close in his case against his head, and Ruthven's grey eyes. But there was already something wayward and feckless about him.

He clutched Ruthven round the legs. He ran away and hid behind a pillar, peering out warily at Maggie. Then he returned to inspect her.

'Who's she?' Harry demanded.

'Maggie,' Ruthven answered. 'She's come here to keep you company.'

Harry scowled. 'I don't like her.'

Magie was quite unperturbed. 'You don't have to, my hen. But I think we'll find a road to rub along together.'

'I'm not a hen,' Harry shouted. 'I'm me!'

'Of course you are, hen. And I'm me too.'

Ruthven laughed. 'Harry, Maggie comes from home. Back there we call people hens when we like them.'

Harry stamped his foot. 'Hope calls me little ostrich. I like that. I like her. I don't like any of you. You're vultures!'

He glowered at them both. Then he ran away and disappeared. Maggie picked up her hand-baggage – the servants had taken the rest – and carried it into the house.

'Hens, ostriches, and vultures,' she said as she went through the door, 'they're all birds. We can live together.'

They were the last harsh words Ruthven heard pass between the two of them.

Within days Maggie had not only won Harry's trust, she'd become his closest friend. Hope, poor Hope, his guide and mentor until then, was discarded, relegated to the kitchen. Hope no longer had a role in his life.

From then on Maggie was both Harry's bible and his touchstone. It was invariably 'Maggie says this', or 'Maggie says that', or 'Dad, Maggie told me today ...'

Ruthven was delighted.

Maggie was everything he'd hoped and expected her to be, and he wrote and told his sisters so. Harry learned to read and write. His use of words improved out of all recognition. His accent changed from a rough blend of Afrikaans pronunciation and the sing-song vowels of the household blacks, to something close to the cadences of the Scottish Borders.

The years passed and Maggie's role became ever more important, not just in Harry's life but in his own.

Ruthven was often away. While he was absent she looked after and ran the house. When he was there and had to entertain guests, as Ruthven increasingly did, she gravitated naturally from housekeeper and organiser of the dinners to hostess at the table.

Ruthven remembered the first time she sat down to dine with him and his friends. He'd had to press her, pleading the numbers were uneven, but in the end it hadn't proved too hard to get her to agree. Afterwards he'd thanked her.

'I am grateful,' he said, 'I trust it wasn't a burden.'

'Eating's never a burden to a Scot,' she smiled in reply. 'Least of all for a Highlander. As you well know, Colonel, we can never be sat below the salt. The salt is set where we are.'

For a twenty-six-year-old young woman, which was all she was then, and a *stalker*'s daughter at that, it was, Ruthven reflected afterwards, an extraordinarily confident remark.

But then, as he'd gradually become aware, Maggie was not merely confident, she was sure of herself and fearless. Three more years passed. Ruthven became more and more dependent on her. She ran the house, she guided Harry's life, the now-adolescent boy adored her, to a large extent she guided his own life.

Ruthven decided to go away for two weeks – he could do so securely now with Maggie in charge behind him. Not on business, not to collect birds, for no reason except his own reasons – to be alone and think.

He went to the Drakensberg mountains in Natal.

He took no one with him, not even a bearer. He climbed and walked and slept out under the stars, just as he'd done as a child in Scotland and later as a soldier in Nepal. By day he watched the animals and wheeling birds of the uplands. By night he lit small fires and sat close to their flames. He let the silence and space invade him and nourish him.

Then he returned to Meerlust. He waited for two evenings after he got back. On the third evening when they'd finished supper and Harry had gone up to bed, he asked Maggie – by then she always dined with them – if she'd come through to his library.

'Maggie,' Ruthven said when they were both seated in front of the fire, 'there are a host of ways I could put this. Being a soldier, I'll choose the simplest. Will you marry me?'

He could have explained endlessly the reasons behind the question. With Maggie there was no need. She knew everything, or almost everything, and nothing he might have argued would have made any difference.

Maggie looked down at the flames. She touched her neck thoughtfully. Then she raised her head. Her eyes as always were steadfast.

'Yes, Colonel, I'll wed ye.'

Ruthven leaned smiling across the space between them and took her hand.

'You'll make me, as they say, a very happy man.'

Maggie held his hand but she didn't press it affectionately as he'd expected her to do.

'Ye and I know each other well,' she said. 'We should make a fair fist of it after all this time. Harry, well, mebbe it will suit the dear boy too. Better perhaps for him that I'm viewed as your wife rather than a bidey-in—'

She paused. Something, Ruthven knew, was troubling her. Maggie came out with it in her usual forthright fashion.

'Mr and Mrs Yeats,' she said. 'Mr Eric and Miss Sophia. I've never asked this before, but I think I'm entitled to ask it now. They come over here from across the river all the time. Harry hasn't got a mother. Is it Miss Sophia?'

'Yes,' Ruthven said quietly.

'And you're his father?'

Ruthven nodded.

'Very good,' she said. 'I don't need to know the whys and the wherefores. Only where I and the boy stand. I'll look after the two of ye as best I can—'

She hesitated. It was unusual for her to do so, Ruthven knew. She was always so direct and uncompromising. When she went on there was an uneasy edge of foreboding in her voice.

'I just hope the arrangement won't lead to trouble, Colonel.'

'Of course it won't,' Ruthven said, dismissing her worries, 'and if you're going to be my wife, can't you address me a little less formally?'

Maggie laughed. 'In due course, mebbe, and at the right moment. But leave that to me, Colonel.'

They were married at St Xavier's church in Cape Town.

Eric Yeats gave Maggie away.

Eric, Sophia, and Harry were the witnesses who signed the church register. Eric had arranged a small party at the Mount Nelson. They drank champagne after the ceremony, the few guests talked happily, then they drifted away. Ruthven and Maggie, at Eric's insistence, spent their first night as a married couple in separate bedrooms in the hotel.

'You'll be far too tired to want to be together,' he said. 'Save that and all the silly physical nonsense that goes with it for later. Just rest.'

Long afterwards Ruthven recognised that the mischievous, manipulative Eric had been as so often unerringly right.

The night of one's wedding wasn't the right time to sleep with one's new wife. The right moment came later, much later, when all the tension and uncertainty and drink of the day were behind one. In Ruthven's case it happened three days afterwards.

They spent two days at the Mount Nelson as Eric's guests. Then they returned to Meerlust. That night they got into the same bed for the first time.

Ruthven held Maggie in his arms for a while. Then he started to caress her and eventually he made love to her. He embarked on it as something of

265

a duty, as the proper and honourable way of putting a seal on the marriage. To his surprise, and although he'd had no experience of sex except with Sophia, Maggie was a keen and sinuously energetic lover.

He fell away from her when it was over, exhausted but curiously satisfied and happy.

'Maggie, that was lovely,' he said. 'I never thought that you—'

Ruthven stopped. He wasn't sure what he'd been going to say next, but it didn't matter.

Maggie interrupted him.

'That I didn't know about such things? Oh, Jack, how little ye know about Highland girls, and ye a Highlander yourself. Shame on ye, man!'

Maggie shook with laughter. She turned over and went to sleep.

In the morning they embarked on their married life together.

43

'I have a surprise for you, my dears.'

The sun was overhead and the morning was nearly gone.

Victoria and Charlie had risen late in their quarters in the guest wing at Stellenfeldt. It was clear that after her story-telling of the night before, Miss Lomax was tactfully leaving them to their own devices for the morning.

Breakfast – freshly squeezed orange juice, grapes as big as plums, cornmeal muffins and real American coffee – had been left ready for them on the vine-shaded verandah. While Victoria wandered round the estate, Charlie had been putting the finishing touches to the manuscript he'd assembled during the night.

Now their hostess had come to find them. Victoria stood up to greet her.

'A surprise?'

'A visitor. I think you'll find him interesting.'

'Another policeman?'

Victoria's question was only half joking. After yesterday's confession, nothing the old lady could do would have surprised her.

'Worse. I have found you a lawyer.'

Miss Lomax's grey eyes were bright. She was clearly pleased with herself.

'Why should we need a lawyer?'

'Sam Wade isn't just a lawyer. He's South Africa's foremost expert on company law. He probably knows more about the affairs of your family than they do themselves. He is also something of an amateur historian. I think you'll find him fascinating.'

She looked sternly at Victoria. Then she nodded in silent confirmation of what was clearly her own decision.

'I've decided to help you, child, and I never do things by halves. I intend, as your family might see it, to sleep with the enemy. I'm sorry to say it's partly out of spite – I never liked those two old witches, Jack's sisters, your great-aunts. They never approved of

Jack marrying Maggie. But also because Sophia would have wanted me to. I can see so much of her in you, my dear, it quite unnerves me. I loved her very much – and I can see no reason why you should be deprived of your birthright, whether or not it offends your family's notions of propriety.'

'Do you think that's the reason they're making it . . . difficult?'

'Partly, but not entirely. There's all sorts of skeletons in all sorts of cupboards. That's where Sam Wade comes in.'

'Why should he be willing to help me?'

'Because I asked him.'

Charlie opened his mouth, but Miss Lomax held up her hand to silence him.

'No, young man, I shall *not* explain why Sam is willing to do as I ask. You will simply have to accept he has good reason, the request is ethically correct, and he will not be presenting a bill.'

She smiled at Victoria. 'I am aware, my dear, that your family has already played the financial card. You may as well know I don't approve of it.'

'But I can't possibly accept—'

Victoria flushed with embarrassment.

'Of course you can. Sophia wouldn't have hesitated. I'm helping you because it is perfectly clear to me that no one else will. Whoever you inherited your spirit from, it certainly wasn't your dear mother. She was always a goose, never had a notion in her head worth tuppence, and your father is not here to protect you. It will give me pleasure to thwart those old harpies. Whatever game they're playing, it's not one with which I have any sympathy. Young women no less than young men are entitled to control of their own destiny.'

She tilted her head. They all heard the clatter of horse's hooves in the yard.

'This will be Sam. I'm going to leave you. You'll have plenty to talk about without my prompting.'

The young man who swung easily off the muscular roan cob didn't look like a lawyer on his way to visit a client. From the foaming withers of the horse and Wade's sweat-stained khaki shirt, it was clear that he had ridden hard.

Victoria studied him doubtfully.

He looked far too young to be as successful as Henrietta Lomax implied. He was certainly no more than in his early forties.

'You must be Miss Ruthven. Delighted to meet you. Sam Wade.'

He held out his hand, carefully wiping it first on a clean silk handkerchief he pulled from his breast-pocket.

'Please excuse the informality. It's just quicker to come over from Meerlust by the hill than by road, and my horse needed a workout.'

He gestured at his riding clothes, smiling at her. It was clear that Sam Wade was of the old colonial school of lawyer – formal and courteous. His voice too was perfectly modulated, with scarcely a trace of the South African accent. Winchester and Cambridge, Victoria guessed, smiling back.

'It's not often I get a chance to ride to Stellenfeldt,' the young man continued. 'But Miss Lomax insisted I come over immediately. She can be most persuasive, as I'm sure you've discovered. You're fortunate to have her on your side.'

'We are indeed,' Victoria replied.

Sam Wade turned to Charlie.

'And you must be Charles.' The hand came out again. 'I occasionally see what you write, I try to keep up with the British press, and must say I count myself an admirer.'

Charlie looked suitably flattered.

Sam Wade, Victoria thought, knew exactly which buttons to press – including hers, as now, when he turned back to look at her with undisguised admiration.

'Please forgive me, Miss Ruthven, but the likeness is quite extra-ordinary. There's a portrait of Sophia at Meerlust—'

He broke off and for an instant his face reddened.

'I *am* sorry. I shouldn't have said that, it was most indiscreet. It's only because I've known your family all my life—'

Victoria laughed. 'Don't apologise. You're not the first to point it out, and no doubt you won't be the last. But do tell me about your connection with the family.'

'Miss Lomax didn't explain? My father was your grandfather's lawyer. I simply inherited his responsibilities, at least as far as Meerlust is concerned. I have power of attorney, and so on. Basically I cope with any problems which arise. I come out for a day every few months, and today just happens to be one of those days. The place has been kept exactly as it was, as I'm sure you know.'

'I know nothing at all,' Victoria said. 'It may sound odd, but I imagine you're used to that if you know my family.'

Wade frowned. 'Surely, as the residual beneficiary, and the sole residual if my memory serves me, you must be aware of all these things?'

'I'm not. I don't even know what a residual is.'

'Well, that's simple. Basically, the last of the line, the final inheritor. I can take you through it all in detail, if you like. Miss Lomax says you're to have access to all the documents you want.'

'Miss Lomax?' Charlie asked. 'Why should she have to give permission for Victoria to look at her own family documents?'

'That's confidential,' was the answer, 'but I assure you it's the case. More important, the permission is there.'

'I assume we're talking about Silverback,' Charlie said.

'I'm sure you both know the Silverback Foundation is a private holding company.' Wade's voice was smooth. 'It's answerable only to its shareholders through its directors. I think you can draw your own conclusions from that.'

'It still doesn't really answer my question.'

'Then let me put it like this,' Wade said. 'The company was moved offshore in the late fifties, when it became clear it wouldn't be long for sanctions to be applied to the movement of capital. My father arranged it, and just in time too, if I may say so. Sharpeville followed soon afterwards. Silverback's declared holdings here are a matter of public record. Its accounts, its investment plans for the future, which can of course be made through nominees, and so on, are solely a matter for its managers, the offshore directors.'

'Meaning that no one has a blind clue what it's up to?'

Charlie was a journalist. He wanted facts and answers, not smoke-screens and evasions, and there was an edge of anger and frustration to his voice.

'I'm a lawyer, Charles, if I may call you that,' Wade said. 'Not a framer of financial legislation. The politicians decide and act. I merely interpret and guard my clients' interests.'

Charlie was about to say something else, to make an outburst, Victoria thought. She put a hand on his arm and restrained him.

'What are these documents,' she asked, 'the ones to which I *am* permitted access?'

'Archive material, I suppose, and rather fascinating—'

A combination of relief and what Victoria sensed was genuine interest made Wade's face animated.

'It's a hobby of mine, the early days. Extraordinary times, and little studied now as we "Africanise" our whole history. Not always pretty, I have to say. Business methods could be, to say the least, unusual – and a good many downright dishonest. Treaties signed with native chiefs who'd never seen a pen, lands bribed away with whisky and a handful of beads. The colonial period wasn't exactly politically correct. It's only because your family was so concerned with its privacy that the archives at Meerlust have been kept intact. The papers there, frankly, have never seen the light of day.'

'Archives?'

'A library full of them. The dealings of your grandfather, his principal business partner, Mr Eric Yeats, and various of their colleagues.'

'And that's what Miss Lomax says I can see?' Victoria asked.

Wade nodded.

'When?'

'If it suits you, I'd suggest now. If I ride back on my horse – give me a small head-start – and you take your car, we should arrive at more or less the same time. I'll steer you through the past as best I can.'

'Jesus wept!'

Charlie's words were perfectly apt, Victoris thought to herself as she gazed up at the dark bulk of Meerlust.

Jesus would indeed have wept, but probably not as loud and long as his mother. No woman could possibly have been happy in such a place.

Where Stellenfeldt had a feminine grace, with its curved pediments, perfectly proportioned rooms, its clear windows and rambling garden, Meerlust had a rough masculinity, almost a brutality about it.

The approach was down an avenue of oaks whose dense foliage met overhead. Beyond loomed the blood-red mass of the twin dwellings, their slate roofs crowned by a forest of tall chimneys shadowed by giant evergreens. Pillars of red granite supported narrow windows of dark stained glass – mahogany and indigo.

Two huge dwellings built of dark granite brooded on each side of a wide paved courtyard enclosed on one side by a high wall, on the other by a heavy iron gateway which could clearly be lowered or raised like a medieval portcullis. The courtyard was in deep shadow, partly because of the height of the buildings and the forest of tall chimneys, and partly because of the evergreens which crowded the walls.

Wade was standing at the top of a banistered staircase which rose to the first floor of one of the houses.

'Come along in – it's cooler inside.'

The interior was no less threatening than the exterior. The hall was panelled in smoke-blackened oak and the ceiling was high and ornately plastered. Heavy draperies obscured such light as there was. In the dimness, it seemed to Victoria that every surface was loaded with ancient weapons of war – muskets, assegais, ceremonial swords. Hunting trophies lined the walls.

Victoria shivered. Wade smiled at her.

'It is a little overpowering, I know. But you'll get used to it. I have.'

The lawyer led her towards a heavy door on the far side of the hall.

'There used to be two sets of archives, just as there were two sets of everything. After the accident—'

Wade hesitated, his eyes searching Victoria's face to see if his reference to the murders had distressed her. Satisfied they hadn't, he continued.

'Afterwards, your grandfather moved the Yeats belongings over here. Easier to keep an eye on, I imagine. Later they decided to shut the whole place up. There was another house in Cape Town, the one in London, and Bowley of course. Never came back, as far as I know. And here it's been ever since, just as it was on the day they left. There's a watchman – a bit like me, he took on his father's responsiblities. He knows we're here. He'll lock up after we've gone.'

Wade opened the door and held it back for Victoria and Charlie to pass through.

'It's all yours. Take as much time as you need.'

The library was panelled in the same dark oak as the hall, but lit by narrow windows of dark coloured glass which cast a pattern of aquamarine and crimson on the Persian carpets which covered the slate floor. There were glass cases of stuffed birds and pinned butterflies piled in every corner.

Instead of books, the walls were lined with ledgers – hundreds of them, all neatly named, dated, and stacked in their correct order. One entire side was occupied by the records of mining activities – yields, man-hours, machinery allotted to Potsmasburg Iron, Umgababa Zinc, Oranjemund Diamond, the great mining names which Victoria recognised from her dealings on the stock-market.

Charlie's nostrils flared and his eyes shone like a child's at a birthday party. He began to pull out boxes and pile them up on the gleaming mahogany table which ran the full length of the room.

Victoria decided to explore the other building on her own.

She crossed the courtyard, mounted the identical flight of steps which led to the mirror-house, and entered. The same gloomy hall, the same heavy ceiling with its plaster-work cornices, the same tall windows with stained glass letting in crimson light. And in the centre, the same double staircase rising to the upper floors.

Victoria hesitated.

She climbed upwards. If Sophia was here, if her presence was here, it would be in a bedroom – she must surely have made herself a feminine sanctuary in this masculine house. Victoria found it at once, at the top of the first flight. The room was chintz-draped, full of plaster cherubs and little garlands. An enchanting, delightful room, a room of warmth and happiness, a room made for pleasure and seduction, with mirrors and lights and a lace-draped bed, frivolous and pretty.

In this grim fortress it was Sophia's fragile and feathery nest.

Victoria retraced her steps, looking for the library.

The same oak panelling, but this time it was not ledgers which lined the walls, but thousands of cabinets with shallow drawers. The drawers slipped out easily as if on castors. Inside were layer after layer of bird-skins, just visible through the fine tissue paper which protected them. A faint odour of camphor and the oddly dusty scent of parchment rose from the drawers. The plumage on the skins was still brilliant, the tiny beaks and claws still perfect in their scaly green and ebony hardness.

She returned to the mirror-house on the other side of the courtyard. Charlie was standing jubilant in the room where Wade had left them.

'Nothing later than 1939, the date of the murders. But before that everything's here. All the early stuff – when Yeats was doing his deals and building his empire. What we've got is the root-system which nourished Silverback—'

Charlie lifted his head from the ledger he'd been studying and glanced at her.

'Yeats provided the genius – he was the financial wizard, the gambler with the foolproof system. If the boundaries of a mining area didn't quite fit, he moved them. If a river needed for a mining process was on an inconvenient course, he had it shifted. If a deal turned out to be duff, he simply rewrote it. God only knows how, but it's all here. He documented everything. He was a pirate – he took impossible risks and somehow made them pay off.'

Charlie paused thoughtfully.

'What's truly strange about Silverback, as far as I can tell, is it was never more than a shell, a fraud, a sham from the start. They didn't find diamonds on their great safari north. At best it was zircon, at worst quartz. It didn't matter. Yeats made them all believe, he made the investors believe. And in the end everyone won. He drew in the money, he invested it across the board, they all became rich—'

Charlie stared at her, shaking his head, bemused.

'And he didn't need to do anything. Because of his father he was immensely rich anyway. He didn't have to work. He didn't have to share his energy and entrepreneurial talents, and the wealth they generated, with your grandfather and Sophia. Why—?'

Charlie threw out his hands.

'Yeats put every penny he made back into their joint kitty. If honesty's the right word – it's probably not – it was the only honest thing he ever did. Silverback was really a forgery, a counterfeit banknote which is only valuable when it's exchanged for the real thing. He kept swapping the notes around, the banks and the investors never noticed, and then eventually they became good – they became real.'

'If you think Silverback was a forgery, take a look at this.'

Victoria had removed one of the bird-skins from the drawer in the second of the Meerlust mansions. Now she spread it out for Charlie's inspection, just as Rory Watson had done for her on Christmas Eve.

'See here? And here?' With a finger she traced the tiny stitches.

Charlie peered down. 'Where did you get this?'

'In Eric's house. There are hundreds of them, perhaps thousands. All beautiful and most of them, I'd guess, like this one.'

Victoria lifted her head.

'God knows, I'm no ornithologist. But I went to Roberts, the classic reference work on South African birds. This skin is labelled a jacana,

274

a lilytrotter. It should have chestnut and white feathers. So it does. It's also got a sheaf of crimson underwing plumage. No jacana's ever had that—'

'It's another of Yeats' forgeries.'

44

'Miss Ruthven? I'm Josh Meyer,' the man said. 'How can I help?'

He was stocky and broad-shouldered with dark waving hair, horn-rimmed glasses, and powerful splayed hands.

Victoria had found him by the simple means of asking the head-porter at the Mount Nelson Hotel for the name of the best taxidermist in Cape Town. For several generations the hotel had been used by trophy-hunters returning from expeditions to the interior, who wanted their skins and trophies mounted before they left for Europe.

It was still used by them, although they went there now for a few days' relaxation after the bush rather than to wait for the next sailing. Most of the expeditions today were photographic safaris, but there were still enough hunters to support a number of taxidermy businesses. The oldest and best-known of them, Victoria was told, was Meyer & Sons.

They'd been active since the end of the nineteenth century, and the present owner, Josh Meyer, was the fourth member of his family to head the firm. She'd telephoned and made an appointment to see him.

He stood in front of her in his white laboratory coat, friendly but slightly simian-like – the backs of his hands were thick with the same dark hair that covered his head – in a room that smelled of formaldehyde and was walled with glass cabinets.

'Would you please take a look at this?' Victoria said.

She opened the bag in which she'd stored the skin she'd taken from Meerlust, and placed it on the table.

'Sure.' He picked it up. 'May I ask why?'

'I'd sooner you looked at it first. Just tell me what you think.'

Meyer started to examine it.

'Well, it's a jacana, of course, but you'll know that. Old, I'd say, the plumage here's a bit faded, but a real nice, a real professional piece of work—'

He stopped.

He'd turned the skin upside-down and stretched out the wings. He peered down at their undersides and frowned. He carefully spread a few of the feathers and went on frowning. Then he glanced up at Victoria.

'What is this?' Meyer asked.

'I know nothing about birds,' Victoria answered. 'I was hoping you'd tell me.'

Meyer gave her a speculative look. Then he returned to the skin.

He teased the underwing feathers out further still. He reached for a magnifying glass and studied them. He uncurled the claws of the feet and ran his blacksmith's fingers with extraordinary delicacy up the sheaves of down that cloaked the legs. He pressed open the bird's mouth and held the magnifying glass over its tongue.

Meyer put the skin down.

'You're not kidding me?' he said. 'You really know nothing about this?'

'Nothing, I promise you. But I do want to know. That's why I'm here.'

Meyer gazed at her. He seemed to believe her. He nodded.

'Well, now—'

He pushed his glasses up on to his forehead and rubbed his face.

'I'd say this was a joke, an elaborate, complicated, and expensive joke – it costs for things like this. The basic skin's a a jacana's, a lilytrotter's. I'm no ornithologist, I just clean and stuff and mount. But jacanas I do know. They're among the prettiest of our African birds, and I get dozens of them brought in to be put up for display. What they don't have are these—'

Meyer showed her the underwings. On either side was the little tuft of scarlet feathers Victoria had spotted herself.

'Those come, I'd guess, from a carmine bee-eater. They've been patched in. Skilful, very skilful, the way they've been fitted. And the claws, feel—'

He took Victoria's hand and guided it up the bird's legs. Under the downy sleeves of feathers she could feel a thin rib of what seemed to be stitching.

'Now, as I say, I'm not an ornithologist, but I don't think the claws belong there either. There's no need to stitch them in. The legs dry out down to the talons. You just leave them. Those claws belong to another bird.'

Victoria withdrew her hand. She sat in silence for a moment.

'Is there anything else you can find out?'

'I can take the skin apart, I guess,' Meyer answered, 'do a real forensic on it. Look at the thread and the wiring and the techniques used. Trouble is, there'll be damage. A skin of this age, it's very fragile. It'll be hard to reassemble afterwards.'

'Doesn't matter.' Victoria shook her head almost violently. 'It's mine and I want to know about it.'

'Fine.' Meyer lowered his glasses back over his eyes and smiled. 'You've set me a real challenge. Never had one like it before. Come back, say, at the same time tomorrow and we'll see what I've uncovered.'

On the way back to the hotel Victoria thought it wasn't really her own bird-skin she'd given Meyer to destroy.

Technically, legally, she'd stolen it. Just as she'd stolen the papers from her great-aunts. Technically, legally. There was nothing technical or legal about her relationship with her grandfather. He was the one man in her life she had truly loved and admired – and that was simply that.

If he was a fraud and a forger, she'd find out and acknowledge it. If he wasn't, she'd find out and disprove it. Either way her life would never be the same again.

And either way, Victoria realised with astonishment, it wouldn't really matter. She would still love him.

'Well, you sure kept me up most of the night,' Meyer said when she returned next day.

Victoria started to apologise but, chuckling, he waved her apologies away.

'One of the most interesting things I've done,' he went on. 'I put animals together and build them up. This time I'm going the other way, breaking one down and taking it apart. Goddamn fascinating it was, if you'll forgive my French. Only problem is, like I warned you, there's nothing much left.'

On the table in front of him were small heaps of bones and feathers.

'I could try a reconstruction but, frankly, there's little point.'

Victoria shook her head. 'I said it didn't matter.'

'Right,' he said. 'We start, as we know, with a jacana. On to its wings, small grafts of carmine bee-eater secondaries. Grafted, too, are the below-knee-joint legs belonging, I reckon, to a red-footed falcon. You'd need a scientist to confirm that, but we get a lot of red-foots in here to mount and I'm fairly sure. Finally—'

Meyer lifted the bird's head.

'The tongue. Jacanas are insectivorous. Raptors feed on flesh. The tongue membrane surface is quite different, smooth for the first, rough and knobbly for the second. This is a raptor's tongue. The throat's been opened and a different tongue inserted. Again, it's been very skilfully done—'

He paused.

'Someone's taken a lilytrotter and converted it into a hawk. The technique's brilliant. It wouldn't pass today, but sixty or seventy years ago no one would have questioned it.'

Victoria stared at what he'd shown her. She raised her head.

'Who could have done that?'

'Really want to know?' He glanced at her quizzically. 'I think probably us, Meyer & Sons.'

He laughed. 'I'm Jewish, Miss Ruthven. You must know about us Jews – plenty of chutzpah, no shame, and always at the cutting edge of technology. I'd guess my grandfather did this. Apart from the technical expertise, I can tell you why. Look—'

He picked up a length of faded yellow silk thread, as fine as a filament from a spider's web. The warmth of his hand made the delicate gossamer spiral into a coil.

'I unpicked that from the inserted feathers. It sewed them to the skin. Now look at this.'

Meyer held up a wooden bobbin. It was bound round with the same fragile thread.

'I still use it for really difficult work,' he said, 'Kalahari robins and Khama larks and such, the specimens the scientists bring in. It's old stock, been here for maybe a hundred years, you can't get it any more but it's still the best. My grandfather laid it in. I'd guess it was his work and his thread. When this lot's gone, it's gone.'

Meyer spoke with the wistfulness and passion of an artist describing a pigment that was about to become unavailable to him for ever.

Victoria inspected the litter of feathers and bones again, pathetic little mounds of rubble they looked now.

'Why would anyone fabricate something as bizarre as that?'

Meyer spread out his hands and laughed.

'Lady, am I Solomon or what? Whoever it was, my grandfather or someone else, they were just doing what they were told.'

'But why?'

Meyer pushed his glasses back on to his forehead. He rubbed his face again.

'A joke, like I said, that's the obvious answer,' he replied. 'If not, then it's something different. It's deception, it's taunting, it's cruelty like vengeance is cruelty. Who am I to say?'

Victoria stood up.

She asked how much she owed him for the work he'd done in diessecting the skin. Meyer adamantly refused to be paid anything.

'Except,' he said as he showed her to the door, 'if you do find out how this came about, write and tell me. I'd like to know why my own grandfather, had he done so, instructed the feathers of a bee-eater and the talons and tongue of a hawk be grafted on to the skin of a jacana—'

He smiled and shook her hand. 'We Jews, we remember our families and we're incurably curious.'

Victoria walked back to the hotel.

She would tell Charlie what Meyer had told her, she knew that. She felt committed now to tell Charlie everything she learned. And she knew Charlie would write it out, he'd continue to construct his own narrative of what had happened from the bald and often fragmentary facts she gave him or he acquired for himself. The hidden, tantalising story had, she sensed, become almost as much of an obsession to him as it was to her.

For the first time, intrigued, Victoria wondered what he'd make of this, of the fact that Cape Town's best taxidermists had been employed well over half a century ago to doctor ornithological specimens.

45

Copy from Charlie – The Silverback Story

'What have we got?' Yeats called out. 'Anything interesting?'

He hurried towards Ruthven from the tents of their camp-site.

They were on the southern edge of the Kalahari desert, just inside across the protectorate's border with South Bechuanaland Africa. It was very early in the morning. The sun had only just lifted above the horizon, and the sky was still shining with the dawn bands of turquoise, crimson, and lemon-coloured light.

Within minutes the colours would fade.

The brutal summer heat and a dead dry whiteness, sterile and harsh, would spread out to fill the air and linger for hour after hour. The heat would press down as fiercely as the weight of the boulders on the plateau's stone floor, and the arid air would scorch everything. Then with the onset of evening, the rainbow of light would briefly return before darkness and the cold that came with it set in.

Ruthven loved the Kalahari evenings and the nights that followed for their invigorating chill.

For the cries of the returning sandgrouse and the calls of the pearl-spotted owls that haunted their camp, hawking for insects drawn to the lanterns and the fire. For the bronze and scarlet sunsets that flared above the horizon. For the cascades of stars, drifting into infinity beyond the Southern Cross, that followed them.

Most of all he loved this, the early morning.

The cool dawn wind, the scatter of frost on the sand, the spoor of the noctural animals which had wandered round or through the camp. Reading their tracks if one was skilful enough, and Ruthven was, was like flicking through the pages of a treasured anthology of poetry – everything was familiar and always there was something new.

There was a particular lioness whose prints he'd come to recognise. She'd been past in the night, this time with a couple of what he guessed were almost fully grown cubs. A honey-badger, a ratel, had nudged round the cooking pot, fearless of the flames, knocked it over, and scooped up what was left of their evening meal. A pair of jackals, silver-backed he thought, had traced a delicate and inquisitive circle round the camp.

Ruthven was fascinated by them all. Most of all he was fascinated by the desert's birds.

'Much as usual,' Ruthven said as Yeats reached him. 'Night-jars, late-roosting larks and robins, a hornbill which must have been blundering about and lost its way, a few weavers. I've let them all go apart from this little fellow.'

Cupped in his hand was a tiny bundle of quivering bones and feathers with angry black eyes on either side of a snapping beak.

Ruthven handed the bird to Yeats who examined it carefully.

They'd trapped all the birds, including this one, in a looped net strung out in an arc on poles above a watering-hole. The idea – as almost every idea did, Ruthven reflected somewhat ruefully – had come from Yeats.

Yeats had noticed that when birds came in to drink in the morning and evening, they came low and carelessly and close to the ground. They could be shot of course, but particularly with the smaller birds their carcasses would be mutilated. He decided to try to capture them in nets.

The first experiments were a failure.

He and Ruthven bought woven reed fish-nets from the Kalahari river bushmen and staked them out in tight flat planes. The birds collided with them, fell to the ground, and flew away. Gradually, testing the idea again and again, they modified the technique.

They paid the bushmen to make much finer, almost silken nets, and of double the width the bushmen used for fishing. They hung the nets in the same places and on the same poles, but now they drooped with great sagging bellies. It worked. The birds still collided with the mesh but now instead of bouncing away, they tumbled down into the cavernous pockets below and stayed there until they were released.

'It's a lark,' Yeats said. 'Insectivore bill, spread feet, desert colouring. We should take him – it's not one we've come across before.'

The bird was struggling and straining in Yeats' hand.

'Let the little bugger go,' Ruthven said. 'We'll find him again.'

Yeats looked at him curiously, enigmatically. He smiled.

He raised his hand and tossed the bird into the air. An instant later a cascade of song poured down over their heads as the terrified creature, trying to orientate itself by sound, beat its way upwards into the sky.

'Do you know what, Jack?'

Yeats was gazing up, following the path of the disappearing lark.

'You're far nicer than me. Decent and brave and fair-minded. I'm not. I'm a scoundrel and we, the scoundrels, are going to inherit the earth. We're also going to make fortunes for the chosen few like you as we do.'

'For Christ's sake, Eric, grow up!'

Ruthven walked away.

He went back to his tent.

He hated quarrelling with Eric, he loved the man as much as ever, but often these days it seemed impossible not to fall out with him, even over so small a matter as whether they should kill or release a bird. Eric had always been combative and teasing. Now, it felt to Ruthven, that was changing into something darker.

Eric still smiled, he still had his wonderful impish humour and laughter. But he was starting to become provocative, to goad and hurt. Yes, he backed down when he'd gone too far. He'd chuckle and joke and make peace. But a certain anger, a cunning and cruel anger, was never far below the surface.

And Ruthven knew why. He'd try to block it out of his mind, to escape it. He couldn't any more than either of them could escape her.

Sophia.

She and Eric lived across the shallow Meerlust valley from him and Maggie in a house that was almost identical to Ruthven's, although Yeats' was a little larger, a little grander. They saw each other every few days, often every day. The houses were only an hour's carriage drive apart. When the road was completed and they could use cars only minutes would separate them.

Young Harry flitted like a ghost, a troubled ghost, Ruthven sometimes thought, between them.

Harry loved Maggie. There was never any doubt about that. She was the rock in his life, firm, unchanging, the chart the boy used to navigate between tears and laughter, right and wrong. Maggie, his 'mother', was secure. Sophia, his godmother as Harry was taught to call her, wasn't at all secure.

Sophia was strange and dreamy.

She told Harry stories about London, Paris, and India. About singing – and sometimes she sang to him – and maharajahs and Chinese warlords in Shanghai and merchants who sent their ships round the world. She told him about liners and adventures and dolphins skimming the waves.

Harry was enraptured by it.

Meerlust sat in a tight little inland bowl of farmland and vineyards. Sophia gave the growing boy the universe and the stars that lay out of sight beyond. It was intoxicating – and dangerous.

The two women, as far as Ruthven could tell, had little difficulty with each other. Different as they were in background, they were warm and cordial to each other, they got on well, they had a child to share. And being women, being natural nurturers, Harry ranked at the top of their concerns. Each gave him the best she could.

The trouble was that Harry, like a silver-flanked Highland sea-loch mackerel, slipped through the nets of warmth and support they stretched out for him.

In spite of all they did, Harry swam sadly and mysteriously on his own.

At the time Ruthven didn't notice it. What he did notice, it came to him very slowly, were Eric's increasing outbursts of irritation and sometimes anger. Being Eric, sly and cunning Eric, they were masked at first with something else.

He'd blame Ruthven for choosing the wrong camp site, for shortcomings in their bearers and camp staff, for the route they'd taken. On the surface it was nothing more than good-humoured teasing, and the complaints always came with a laugh. Underneath, Ruthven gradually realised, there was something bleaker and fiercer.

Ruthven struggled in his mind to work out the cause.

It wasn't Maggie. Yeats had always treated her with good-humoured tolerance as an excellent servant. Sometimes he'd pretend to forget her name and refer to her as 'Agatha — or whatever your delightful wife's called'. It irritated Ruthven and he used to protest angrily, but it wasn't worth a major confrontation. Yeats would laugh and apologise, and they'd go on as before.

Nor was it Silverback.

Under Yeats' dynamic direction, the company grew and grew. Ruthven was occasionally useful as decoration, as ballast in negotiations with banks, as the expatriate Scottish grandee who was becoming famed as an explorer and naturalist and whose name looked impressive as the titular chairman, but he wasn't really necessary. Yeats could have done it all on his own.

No, it was neither Maggie nor their business activities. It could only be Sophia and the boy.

'I've just been counting,' Yeats said later that evening over supper by the fire. 'Know how many skins the boys have pegged out and dried?'

His eyes were sparkling and his ill-humour had gone.

Faced with his energy and enthusiasm, Ruthven's worries and uncertainties faded too.

'Almost two hundred.' Yeats laughed. 'We'll ship them off to Meyer's in the morning. Old Meyer will think it's a Passover blessing for weeks on end. I'll pop in every day to make sure he doesn't attend a bar-mitzvah until they're done—'

Another gale of laughter shook Yeats' increasingly corpulent body.

'In time to come we'll be famous, heart's companion. Or rather you will be. The collection's logged in your name. The British don't like upstarts and I'm much too modest to compete with a Ruthven—'

Yeats had been drinking heavily that night. He still was. He took another gulp of brandy.

'Let alone, of course, with a Sophia. But then she's rare, isn't she, a Helen among women? Let's toast the angel and her offspring.'

Ruthven raised his glass as Yeats emptied his tumbler.

He smiled uneasily.

46

They flew from Cape Town to Johannesburg, hired a car, and drove north-west to Mafeking.

'It's unique,' Charlie said at the wheel as they entered the city. 'Or more accurately the country it once governed was. The Bechuanaland Protectorate, Botswana as it is now, is just up the way. Botswana's as big as France. It was the only country in the world which for most of its existence had its capital city in a different country.'

Victoria frowned. 'What do you mean?'

'The two were always separate countries, but the British empire ran both. We decided it was simpler to administer Botswana from Mafeking. Then when the winds of change began to blow and we gave Botswana its independence, we had to create its own capital as a parting gift. We duly did, round Chief Gaborone's mud huts. But a lot of its records are still here.'

Victoria gazed out of the window.

Mafeking was like so many other South African towns she'd seen over the past ten days. Shanty townships on the outskirts, neat white villas in the European suburbs, a ring of modern buildings, and then at the centre the old colonial heart of the original settlement.

They checked in at their hotel, and set off again almost immediately to keep the appointment Charlie had made at the records department at police headquarters.

'Good morning, sir. Good morning, miss. Inspector Heinie van Groot. Now, let's see how we can help you folks.'

Van Groot was tall and heavily built with shrewd, sharp eyes in a granite-coloured slab of a face that like so many Afrikaaners' never seemed to have seen the sun.

A few years ago, Charlie had told Victoria, he probably wouldn't even have seen them. Foreign journalists then, particularly to the police, were regarded as poisonous, trouble-making scum. Since the end of apartheid, the new regime had insisted on an open-doors policy in government departments. South Africa was now part of the international community of civilised nations.

It meant that even the state police were expected to open their files – at least the ancient and harmless ones – for scrutiny. What van Groot really made of his new masters and their radically different approach was impossible to say.

His expression was inscrutable, but at least his manner was courteous.

'You are researching, I understand, the famous Yeats murders in 1939,' he went on. 'I have taken down our library files on the case.'

Van Groot tapped a thick bundle of documents, strung together with rusting clips between dusty and faded grey card covers, on the desk in front of him.

'They contain witness depositions, medical and forensic reports, corner's findings, everything we have. There is a small reading room down the passage. You are welcome to study them there for as long as you wish.'

Something in van Groot's voice suggested he thought it would be a pointless exercise.

'Have you read the files yourself, Inspector?' Charlie asked.

Van Groot gave a short dry chuckle.

'Man, everyone who takes on this job reads up the Yeats case,' he replied. 'Like I said, it's the most famous murder in southern Africa, better known down here even than Lord Erroll's killing in Kenya which happened a year or two later. Everyone would like to find an answer. It's too late, far too late. All in the past and everyone who might know is dead.'

'But did you form any views of your own?' Charlie insisted.

'You're pushing me, man.' Van Groot chuckled again. 'I'm not paid to have views. But sure, privately I have one or two ideas.'

'Would it be too much to ask what they are?'

The Inspector paused. He shrugged. 'How much do you know about the murder?'

'Little more than the outline,' Charlie answered. 'Yeats had set up camp at Maun on the edge of the Okavango delta. One night there was a disturbance, the sounds of shouting. The next morning he was found dead, so was his wife. They'd both been shot. One of the reports in our cuttings library, admittedly very old and far from reliable, says their bodies had been carried downriver, attacked by crocodiles, and then washed ashore.'

Van Groot nodded.

'That's about the long and short of it. Yeats had gone to Maun with a friend, the explorer Colonel Ruthven. They were business partners and keen on birds. They wanted to collect specimens. They'd both taken their wives with them. Ruthven got to Maun first and when Yeats arrived a week later he set up a separate camp.'

Van Groot pointed at the files.

'It's all in there in the depositions. Separate camps for friends may seem odd to outsiders, but not if you know the bush. They both had a lot of boys with them, trackers and cooks and so on. You get problems with hygiene and water and the rest. It was normal then, it still is.'

The South African rubbed his jaw.

'Both the camps were just outside Maun. Maun was different then, Christ, was it different. A real frontier border-post used by real hard guys, hunters and prospectors and traders. I doubt they'd ever seen rich men like Yeats and Ruthven before with their pretty ladies, their fancy tents, and their gangs of boys doing every damn thing. And, so help me God, did the Maun people drink! My dad told me the old hands said Riley's bar on a Saturday night was like Chicago.'

'You think one of them killed him?' Charlie said.

'I'm a policeman. I know money and drink accounted for most of the crimes while I was out on the streets here.'

'What about the disturbance and the shouting?'

'That's not difficult,' van Groot replied. 'Yeats and Ruthven went into Riley's for a beer that night. Then they went back to their camps. Someone they'd met followed Yeats and asked him for a loan maybe. Someone loaded with beer to the gills, or maybe just a thief. Hell, there'd have been a lot in Yeats' camp worth picking – fancy guns, money, his wife's jewellery. Yeats spotted him, they had a shouting-match, and Yeats ran him off. The man came back with his gun and that was it.'

Charlie was silent for a moment.

'Except nothing was taken from the camp,' he said.

'Killing two people sobers you up faster than a gallon of black coffee.' Van Groot chuckled. 'I've seen it on the streets, in the kaffir shabeens on Friday nights, time and time again. Black or white, it's the same, it changes everything. The man saw what he'd done. He came straight down to earth. He knew if he looted the tent, it was likely to be traced to him. He ran.'

'If the Yeatses were killed in camp,' Charlie went on, 'why were their bodies found downstream on the river bank?'

'You sober up, you start to think,' van Groot answered. 'This guy who's suddenly starting to see things more clearly, he knows he's still got a problem. He pulls them into the river for the crocs to mess them up. Their teeth, they'll put a little more distance between him and the bodies. Then he runs.'

'What about the boys with Yeats in the camp? They must have heard everything.'

Van Groot looked at him, smiling almost patronisingly.

'It was white man's business, man,' he said. 'They pulled their blankets over their heads and went back to sleep. White man's business isn't any concern of theirs. All they want is for their mealy-meal to be there in the morning.'

'Thank you, Inspector,' Charlie said. 'It sounds likely, but I'd still like to look at the files.'

'Be the guest of the Mafeking police department.' Van Groot waved his hand. He'd obviously been pleased to be consulted, to give his own version of what might have happened.

Charlie and Victoria set off down the passage with the files under their arms.

They spent the rest of the day reading through them, exchanging papers from time to time and only leaving the room to get coffee from the police canteen. At 4.30, his shift over, van Groot looked in to say goodbye, and an hour later they themselves left.

Back in the hotel bar, Charlie looked at Victoria over his beer.

'You've said almost nothing all day, sunshine,' he said. 'Any conclusions in the silence?'

Victoria revolved her own glass between her hands.

'We're not detectives.' Her voice was hesitant. 'But at least you're an investigative reporter. You're trained. I'm not, but one thing struck me. Four out of five of the depositions say a woman was shouting. Who was she? Sophia? Grandmother Lomax? Or someone entirely different – the wife of one of the African boys?'

Victoria lifted her shoulders in a puzzled gesture.

Charlie leaned forward and touched her wrist.

'You're wrong, angel. We're both detectives and better than van Groot. What he said was plausible, but it doesn't measure up. I figured the same as you. People heard a woman shouting and it wasn't an African. There weren't any wives with the boys, there never were in camps like that. It could only have been Sophia or your grandmother.'

Charlie finished his drink. 'We'll have something to eat. Then you can go to bed. While you're asleep, I'll try to pluck something out of the darkness.'

They had dinner and went up to their room.

Grudgingly Victoria had agreed that to stretch out the expenses, they'd share a room. After seven years of living together, it seemed absurd not to, although she'd insisted on twin beds. She undressed in the bathroom and came back in her pyjamas to find Charlie setting up his laptop word-processor.

'I doubt I'll find the answer tonight,' he said as he sat hunched over the machine. 'The resources of the South African police haven't produced it in almost fifty years. I think it lies in Maun. What I may be able to do is sketch out the context of the killings. I've got some ideas. I'll try.'

'You'll only be guessing, Charlie,' Victoria said as she climbed into bed.

'Life is a matter of guesses, blossom.' He began to tap the keys.

She turned away from the light and huddled down between the sheets.

Victoria felt almost more desolate and confused than after her encounter with Rory Watson in the Natural History Museum. She'd abandoned Charlie, or rather Charlie had abandoned her, and she'd set out to prove Grandfather's innocence of the charges of fraud and deceit Watson had levelled against him.

The truth about Ruthven had proved far more elusive and complicated than she'd ever imagined. Now, little more than a month later, in what she thought grimly was a wonderful irony, she was back sharing a room with Charlie. Not as his lover and companion, but as his subordinate and researcher on a story where their interests were totally at odds.

She wanted reconciliation. She wanted to understand and resolve the past. Charlie, because his work and career demanded it, was after drama, scandal, and exposure.

She closed her eyes helplessly.

She heard the light drumming of the keyboard as Charlie worked. Strangely, in spite of all the distress he'd caused her, the sound was familiar and comforting.

Victoria slept.

47

Copy from Charlie – The Silverback Story

'Jack, are you sure this is a good idea?' Sophia asked.

'No, I'm not,' Ruthven answered grimly. 'Far from sure, but it's the only thing I can think of worth trying.'

They were sitting in a space of dappled sunlight and shade beneath a clump of trees on a promontory known locally as Bushman's Balcony that ran out over the shallow Meerlust valley which separated the two houses.

They'd ridden out there and the two horses were cropping the grass a few yards away. They'd ridden together two or three times a week for the past few years. At the start they'd pretended their encounters were accidental. Ruthven wasn't sure whether Maggie or Eric had ever believed that. They certainly didn't now.

Ruthven and Sophia rode out to be together. Both the other two knew it.

What either of them made of it, Ruthven wasn't sure. Or, rather, in Maggie's case he was fairly sure. Maggie was crisp and pragmatic. She didn't ask questions to which she didn't want to know the answers. She'd come from a humble and damp stalker's cottage to find herself mistress of a handsome mansion in the African sun.

In her own practical way she loved Ruthven, he didn't doubt that, and she certainly loved Harry. Maggie knew Sophia was Harry's mother, she knew the attachment between Ruthven and Sophia was deep and complicated – probably unbreakable. But Maggie wasn't a woman for jealousies, resentments, or complications. She'd been taught to value wholesome oatmeal in bellies and a good peat fire against the cold.

If her husband, Colonel Jack, wanted to ride out with his fancy lady, let him. It didn't threaten her. Anyway, menfolk came back, they always did.

No, Ruthven thought, the problem wasn't her. It was Eric.

'How's he been?' he asked Sophia.

She considered.

'He drinks more and more,' she said. 'I don't know what he's like when he's away – and of course he's away so often – but when he's here a bottle of spirits goes every evening. It doesn't seem to do anything to him. Sometimes he's distant, sometimes close and funny and warm. But he's always watching me. And then, of course, he rides over to you.'

Ruthven nodded.

Yeats had taken to appearing at the house at almost any hour, from early in the morning to late at night. Sometimes Ruthven would wake to hear the clatter of Yeats' horse's hooves on the cobbles, and the deep-throated call of the Tswana night watchman as he greeted him.

Ruthven would pull on a dressing-gown and go downstairs.

'Jack, Jack,' Eric would exclaim, embracing him. 'I know it's fearfully late, old fellow, but I couldn't sleep and I knew you wouldn't mind.'

Ruthven would smile. 'Of course not. Let's have a brandy.'

They'd go into the large raftered living-room and Ruthven would pour him a drink. Then they'd talk. They talked about everything from the past to their bird collection to Silverback and the future of southern Africa. Always in the end the conversation would revert to Sophia.

'How's beloved Agatha?'

It was Yeats' invariable prelude to speaking about his wife.

Agatha was Yeats' code-name for Maggie, the last but still to Ruthven the most infuriating expression of Yeats' one-time homosexuality. Yeats only used it when he was drunk – and as Sophia said, it was often impossible to tell whether he was or not. It was meant to hurt and demean Maggie.

'Maggie,' Ruthven would answer quietly, 'is fine. And please, Eric, call her by her name.'

'Oh dear, oh dear, humour's out of fashion, is it, we're no longer wearing laughter this year, is that right? Thank God you told me. Think of the mistakes I might have made in company. I must remember—'

Yeats would scratch his head frantically as if trying to get something into his brain. Then he'd lean back and his expression would change. It became colder, harder, filled with anger and regret.

'So what about my own darling Sophia? You see her most days, don't you, Jack? How's she?'

Ruthven shrugged. 'I see her sometimes when I'm riding. She seems fine.'

'Fine, Jack, fine? That's a word for the weather, not for a woman.'

Yeats wanted to say more.

He began to struggle out of his chair and tried to stand. He couldn't make it. He fell back and stared at Ruthven. Then he passed out. Ruthven lifted him and carried him over to a sofa. He tucked a cushion behind

296

his head and draped a warm cloak, a jackal and genet-skin cross, over him.

Ruthven went outside and called for the night watchman.

'Take Bwana Eric's horse to the stables,' he said. 'The bwana stays here tonight.'

'Yes, sir.'

As Ruthven went up to bed he heard the clip-clop of hooves as the horse was led away. He climbed in and lay beside Maggie. Eventually he slept.

In the morning Yeats was gone before he woke.

'What do we do, Jack?'

Ruthven shook his head.

His mind had drifted away, drifted to all those nights and days when Yeats had imposed his increasingly destructive presence on them. He remained brilliant, the most brilliant man Ruthven had ever met.

The original Silverback diamond strike had dried up. It was only a tiny mine, the last outpost of the clay reef that reached from Kimberley into the mid-African highlands. But it had yielded enough to allow them to re-invest and diversify. Yeats handled the investments.

He had no formal training as an economist, a geologist, or anything else. He simply followed his nose. His judgement was flawless. He put Silverback's diamond money into railroad stock, into other mining ventures, into farms and vineyards, into real estate in the expanding towns.

As the company grew, he brought in other investors. Their capital allowed it to grow still further. And then typically, being Yeats, at the height of its success, he changed everything.

Yeats changed Silverback's structure. He sold his personal stake. He created the Silverback Foundation, and put the money into that. He became the Foundation's lifetime chairman. The Foundation effectively controlled Silverback – and he controlled the Foundation.

'What's love, Jack?' Sophia asked.

Ruthven glanced at her and smiled. 'For serious?'

'I'm always serious.'

He plucked a stem of grass and chewed it.

'Wanting someone you want to be with more than anything in the world to be happy, and not being with her. And then still wanting her to be happy with someone else – and doing your damnedest to see she is.'

'Her?'

'Yes,' he said flatly.

'Why did you get the five of us into this, Jack?'

Ruthven didn't answer. There was no answer he could give.

Everything had grown out of happenings, almost, he thought, out of fate. It had just fallen that way. Leaving Harry and Maggie aside, the cards the three of them had played to construct their lives were dealt long, long ago. He wasn't the only one in the game. Eric and Sophia were just as much equal players.

'I'm not happy,' she went on. 'You know that. I want to be with you.'

Ruthven closed his eyes despairingly.

'You've got Eric and I've got Maggie. Between us we have Harry. It may not be ideal, but that's what we decided years ago.'

'Years pass, Jack. Things change. Why are the horses here? Why do we ride more and more often together? Why does Eric drink so much? Why is Harry so troubled – and you know he's troubled?'

Ruthven shook his head. Again he had no answer.

'We made a mistake,' Sophia went on. 'One can mend mistakes. But one has to do so quickly. We've all got so little time.'

Ruthven stood up. Sophia rose too.

He looked at her. He'd seen Sophia in cycles. As a slender young girl at his birthday party in Cape Town before the war. As a maturing but still young woman in India after the war's end. Now as a truly mature woman approaching her forties.

She'd always had her head-turning beauty.

It was never quite as vivid and heart-stopping as it was today. She'd shed certain things from the past, qualities that didn't suit her. An occasional laziness, a petulance, a youthful arrogance. Now she stood before him as if she was naked, although in reality she was wearing a tailored riding-suit in green felt.

Her eyes, those extraordinary blue eyes flecked with gold, were steady and thoughtful. Her cascading auburn hair still had its turbulent sheen, but the face it enclosed was finer and more sculpted. Her body beneath the riding-suit was fuller but somehow more graceful and elegant than it had ever been, her wrists delicate and her legs seeming to stretch for ever until her boots enclosed her feet.

Ruthven had to turn away. If he'd gone on looking at her he'd have been lost, as so often in the past. He walked over to the horses.

'We'll go up to the delta,' he said. 'Maggie and I will go ahead. You and Eric can follow when he gets back from his trip. We'll make separate camps but for once all four of us can be together. Eric and I will look for our birds. Then at night we can gather and talk.'

Ruthven turned with the bridle in his hand and smiled. It was, he knew, a lame and unconvincing smile.

'We can make it work. For God's sake, Sophia, we must make it work.'

Sophia didn't return his smile.

'I'll come, Jack,' she said. 'I'll do my best. But I don't think it'll work. I think you're packing a powder-keg and putting a fuse into it. Tell Maggie not to bring any matches.'

'We should get back,' Ruthven said abruptly.

They rode down the hill and parted at the river crossing, the drift as the Afrikaaners called it. Ruthven splashed through the water and turned to look back on the far side.

Sophia had vanished.

48

Victoria and Charlie drove from Mafeking to Gaborone.

In Gaborone they boarded the daily internal flight to Maun, 500 miles to the north-west at the edge of the Kalahari desert and on the rim of the Okavango delta. Now Victoria sat gazing out of the plane's porthole window, just as she'd done on the flight to Kathmandu.

It was difficult to conceive of a greater contrast between two landscapes than the one she'd looked at then, the jagged and glittering peaks of the Himalayas veined with rainbows of light, and the one below her now.

The immense stone plateau of the Kalahari stretched away into the morning heat-haze on every side. It was grey–brown and utterly flat, mantled only by drifts of apparently dead scrub, runnels of sand and rock, and a few pans – salty-white depressions like the pock-marks on the moon's surface.

It was the most desolate and inhospitable place she had ever seen. It looked cruel, pitiless, and incapable of supporting any life apart from the occasional vulture that wheeled on the thermals beneath them.

'Hard to believe it's one of the richest environments on earth,' Charlie said, leaning across her. 'But it is. Where you get vultures, you get life. Look at those—'

He pointed at the network of spidery white paths threading the scrub.

'Game tracks. When a rains year comes, the whole desert blossoms like an alpine meadow. It used to support some of the biggest concentrations of wild animals in all Africa. They've dwindled to a fraction of what they were, but they're still there. They can ride out the drought years. When the rains come again, they bounce back. Or they did.'

'Why not now?' Victoria asked.

'Cattle,' Charlie answered. 'Black southern Africa's a cattle culture. We believe in pounds, dollars, and marks. They believe in cattle. Every year the herd gets bigger. The farmers tap into the underground water,

301

the cattle spread out and break down the top-soil. Then they have to move on, and the wild has to retreat.'

The plane began its descent into Maun.

'Not just the animals, but the birds too,' Charlie added. 'The desert and the delta used to have more bird species than the whole western Palaearctic, which means from Iceland to the Urals. That's why your grandfather and Eric Yeats came here. Now the birds are vanishing too . . .

'Anything you see flying,' Charlie finished grimly, 'look at it carefully. You'll see it, your children won't.'

The plane landed and bumped to a halt.

They got out. Charlie picked up their bags and they walked into the little airport building. The heat was dry and searing, the sunlight whiter and harsher than Victoria had ever known. Charlie walked over a four-wheel drive pick-up taxi truck.

'Riley's,' he said.

The Tswana driver nodded. As they set off, Victoria stared at the little settlement through eyes narrowed against the sun.

It was sprawling, jerry-built, ugly, and cloaked in constantly drifting curtains of grainy dust. There was also something robust and bold and vital about it. Black-skinned Herero women, clothed in ankle-length dresses made up in cascades of brilliantly coloured cotton they'd been taught to wear by German missionaries, walked gracefully between the ramshackle houses.

The few shops were thronged. Rugged bustling landcruisers hurtled down the pitted roads, swinging without signals between ten-foot wire-stockaded gates into the compounds of the bungalows belonging to white hunters. Everywhere there were shouted greetings, groups, black or white, gathered in discussion, echoing laughter.

And always, Victoria thought, on every side, the constant silent presence of the great delta and the even greater desert. Maun didn't own the Okavango or the Kalahari. They, delta and desert, owned the tiny frontier town that for all its energy was no more than a child's sandcastle erected on the immensity of the stone plateau.

It was here that four of the most important people in her past had come to be together – and two of them to die.

They reached Riley's. They got out and Charlie paid off the driver. The hotel was a low, rambling building, wood-framed and green-painted with a verandah running around the outside. Charlie rang the reception bell.

As they waited, he said, 'Riley was a trader. He came here in the early twenties. He started this, he started Riley's garage, he opened Riley's store. Now there are all manner of lodges and stores and a bank, but Maun is still really Riley's.'

They took a twin-bedded room.

Victoria had a shower and changed out of her sweat- and dust-stained clothes. She lay down and slept for a while as the late-afternoon heat faded. Then in the early evening she joined Charlie on the open verandah.

'What now?' she asked.

'An ice-cold beer for you,' he replied, 'and another one for me to add to the several I've had to drink to cool me down. And then we'll wait. I've staked out the fishing-lines up and down the river. We'll see what bites.'

The man joined them an hour later. He strolled on to the verandah and propped himself against the railing bar beside their table.

He was called Dannie Leroy.

He was a former white hunter. He was small and wiry, he had a cropped stubble of grey hair, and he was in his late seventies, although he might have been ten years younger. In Maun he could easily have been a shambling, rambling drunk. As it turned out he was shrewd and alert, and all he drank was carbonated water.

'Hullo, there, folks,' he said. 'They told me inside you were interested in our local famous scandal. Care to tell me why?'

'Yes—'

Charlie as always had been about to answer, but for once Victoria got there before him. She kicked him under the table to make sure he remained silent.

Leroy's manner was neutral, but his eyes were watchful and wary.

'I'm Victoria Ruthven, Colonel Ruthven's grand-daughter. And in case other people say that when they're not, this should answer it.'

Victoria took out her passport and pushed it across the table. Leroy glanced at the name and the photograph inside.

'Fine, I believe you.' He gave her a cautious smile. 'We still get bloody journos sniffing around. Come from every whichwhere. All they want to do is dig up shit – pardon my French – and plaster some of it over Maun. But you look like the genuine article.'

'I hope so.' Victoria gave her most winning smile back at him. 'How can I help?'

'What happened that night?'

'Funnily enough I was right here on the deck, right where we are now. It was a little bit later, but listen—'

He raised his hand.

Victoria listened. She could hear nothing at all except for the immense silence of the delta and the few sounds, the calls of frogs and roosting birds, that the extraordinary resonance carried from miles away.

Leroy chuckled.

'Don't hear nothing, do you?' he said. 'Except, on the other hand, you hear everything from right across the bush and the water. I heard it all. Came out with my beer, and I heard it. Two camps they'd made on either side of the Boteti. Everyone knew. Came in to eat here, bought supplies from the store, hired boys to go into the delta . . .'

Leroy sipped from his glass.

'That night, maybe 10.00 p.m. it was, there was shouts, screams, afterwards shots. Two or three shots first from a hand-gun. Then another shot. I listened. Good strong moon. Sounds came through clear, but too far away to see anything.'

He took another sip from his glass of water.

'In the morning, well, you must know. Mrs Yeats dead, I helped pull her ashore several hundred yards downstream then. Mr Yeats too. Same place except the crocs had got to him, God knows why they hadn't touched her but they hadn't. There was an inquest, the first ever in Maun. The coroner came from Mafeking. Decided Yeats had killed her in a drunken rage, and then turned his gun on himself. That was it.'

Victoria sat in silence.

'Was that it?'

'I'm just a hunter, miss. I only know about guns and game. I can't do people and crossword puzzles—'

Leroy stopped.

Old as he was, he was still strong and confident. Now, Victoria knew, he was uneasy. He looked at her speculatively. He got up from the rail. He wandered across the verandah and came back.

'I'll tell you what,' he said, 'if you'd like, I'll show you tomorrow where the whole damn thing happened.'

Leroy picked them up from Riley's at 8.00 a.m. in his battered Toyota Landcruiser.

He drove them out of Maun along a sandy track and eastwards to the bank of the Boteti river. He parked the truck and got out.

'This was Colonel Ruthven's camp.' He indicated a shelf above the river near where they'd stopped. 'Mr Yeats and his wife camped over there.'

He pointed across the water at a very similar platform on the other side of the broad, shallow, and slow-flowing stream.

'This was where they died?' Victoria said.

'We pulled the bodies ashore downstream, as I told you,' Leroy answered. 'But, yes, this is where it happened.'

Victoria looked at the river.

It was still early in the morning and the water was serene and beautiful.

Jacanas, lilytrotters, the living exemplars of the skin she'd taken from Meerlust, were patrolling the reeds. She heard a fish eagle give out its mewing call, and glimpsed a pair of frisking impala deer swirl and vanish into the grass beyond. A pied kingfisher dived and a battaleur eagle planed the thermals above.

It was one of the most beautiful sights she'd ever seen – and death had come here. Violent, murderous death to her grandmother and Eric Yeats.

She turned to the lean-boned little hunter.

'You know what happened,' Victoria said. 'What was it?'

Leroy rubbed his jaw. He looked at the same time sorrowful, puzzled, and stubborn.

'I know about guns,' he said. 'I heard them. First the pistol shots. Then the last shot. Not from a hand-gun. The last shot was high-velocity, it came from a rifle. Mr Yeats didn't kill himself. It was impossible. Someone else killed him.'

Victoria stared at him for a while.

What he'd said to her echoed almost word for word what Evans had told her in London, what Evans in his turn had been told by his father who'd investigated the killings. Yeats might have shot Sophia, but he hadn't committed suicide afterwards. Someone else had killed him.

She took Leroy's arm and they walked back to the Toyota.

'Thank you, Mr Leroy,' she said. 'It may be difficult, but I think you're helping me lay ghosts to rest.'

Charlie was trailing behind them. He'd got out his notebook and was furiously scrawling on the lined pages.

Victoria knew what it signalled.

Hunched over the little ironwood table in their bedroom at Riley's, he'd be writing again that night. Improvising, guessing, using his imagination to fill in the spaces between the lines of what they knew, he'd construct another pyramid of words slugged Charlie.

Whether what he wrote would be true, she would never know. No one would ever know. The only ones who knew the truth, Ruthven, Sophia, and Yeats, were all dead. All Charlie could do was try to divine a dark, murderous and long-lost past.

He might not get it right, but in the attempt he might at least provide some sort of understanding and reconciliation.

49

Copy from Charlie – The Silverback Story

Ruthven knew instantly, as soon as he saw Yeats, that the expedition was likely to end in trouble.

Ruthven and Maggie had arrived in Maun a week earlier.

They'd made camp a couple of miles outside the little frontier outpost close to the Boteti river. It was a fine site. There were mosquitoes and tsetse fly of course, but the water was clear, the ground on which they'd pitched the tents level and drained, and grass on every side for the horses.

The desert-hopping plane that brought in Yeats and Sophia arrived at dusk. By the time everything had been unloaded it was full darkness. They decided not to make camp that night, but stay at Riley's hotel and pitch their tents next day. Yeats rode over in the morning in advance of the ox-drawn waggon carrying his supplies.

It was barely 9.00 a.m. when Yeats swung himself down from the saddle, but he was already drunk.

Ruthven looked at him in shock as Yeats came forward with deliberately steady and careful steps. He hadn't seen Eric for a couple of months – Yeats had been away pursuing Silverback's interests in Angola – but the change in the man was devastating. His eyes were shadowed, his cheeks puffy and pale, his hands trembling.

'Jack, how wonderful!' As Yeats embraced him, Ruthven smelt the waves of brandy fumes on his breath. 'I must not be sentimental but it's like the old days, is it not? The two of us together and the wild surrounding us. Now—'

He stepped back, almost over-balancing, and glanced round.

'Where am I going to tell the boys to place us? The citadels of our dwelling must be linked, but with a decent private space between. Hasn't it always been so? How about over there?'

He pointed across the river where another shelf of sand lifted above the water.

'Why not here, Eric, side by side with us?' Ruthven said. 'You don't want to lug everything across.'

'Oh, but I do, Jack, I do. I fancy the idea of islands of life in the stream of life. We can look at each other and sing songs across the water. Anyway, it's shallow and the oxen can pull the waggon over in a trice.'

Ruthven tried to argue him out of it, but Yeats was adamant.

The waggon arrived, the oxen dragged it over, Yeats' camp was set up. A couple of hours later Sophia arrived too on horseback. By then Yeats, mercifully, had collapsed on to the truckle-bed his Tswana camp boys had erected for him and fallen asleep.

Sophia swung her leg over the horse and dropped to the ground.

'How is he?' she said bluntly.

'Not good,' Ruthven answered. 'In fact, worse than I've ever seen him. What's happened?'

Sophia shook her head despairingly. 'Where's Maggie?'

'She's resting too although for a quite different reason – the heat.'

'Can we talk?'

Ruthven nodded.

He led her to the river bank and they sat down. Chestnut-feathered lilytrotters, tiny and elegant little birds, patrolled the reeds in front of them, and occasionally a crocodile raised its menacing snout above the water's surface.

'What do they call it, Jack?' Sophia said. 'Going to hell in a hand-basket, isn't that the phrase? It's happening to him. He's tossed himself into a cataract, and it's carrying him away.'

'Why?'

'I just don't know.'

'Problems with Silverback?'

'I doubt it. From what he tells me everything's going better than ever.'

'Then problems with you?'

She turned and stared at him. 'Eric's never had any problems with me. You only have problems with people who matter. I don't matter. You do. If Eric has problems, and my God he does, then they're with you.'

Ruthven gazed down into the water.

'Will you be all right if I leave you here with Maggie?'

Sophia laughed. 'Of course. She's lovely, sturdy, and sensible and bright. You picked yourself a fine woman, Jack Ruthven.'

Ruthven glanced at her. He could think of many things to say, but he said none of them.

'I'll take him up into the delta,' he went on. 'We'll collect our birds and I'll try to sort it out.'

*   *   *

'Why, Jack, why did it all go so horribly, miserably wrong?'

Yeats was sitting with his arms clasped round his legs and his head resting on his knees.

The two of them, he and Ruthven, with a couple of Tswana camp-hands and two paddlers for their makoros, their dugout canoes, were alone together in the swamplands somewhere south of Chief's Island in the Okavango delta. They'd been there for ten days, travelling the waterways, changing their camp-site each day or so, living mainly off what they fished or shot.

And, of course, collecting birds.

Ruthven kept his checklist with him as Yeats always had done in the past too. This time Yeats had left his list behind. Their only record was going to be Ruthven's. They'd found several new species, new at least to them – malachite kingfishers, a vulture they didn't know, an owl which seemed to hunt the waters for fish.

They'd shot the birds, skinned them, dressed the skins with salt, and stored them in Rowland and Ward's 'famous, newly-improved storage containers – a boon for all hunters and naturalists'. Now they were making their way back to Maun.

'Come on, Eric,' Ruthven protested. 'It hasn't gone remotely wrong. We're having a marvellous time.'

'I don't mean this.' Yeats waved his hand. 'Of course we are. It's where you and I should be. No, I mean back at home—'

He reached for the glass at his feet.

Ruthven had hoped that in the delta Yeats would stop drinking. It was a forlorn hope. Yeats had insisted on bringing two cases of brandy with him. He'd already got through one and was well into the second.

'No, Jack, no. Why can't there just be the two of us? We could have such fun, do such good things.'

'Well,' Ruthven said patiently, 'we've got Sophia, Maggie, and Harry. We can't just ditch them. And anyway they're all a boon and a blessing. They don't inhibit us. They enrich our lives and still leave us free. For God's sake, man, look at where we are!'

'Maggie's a Scotch drab. Sophia's turned into a witch. Harry's a little wastrel, a lightweight, a paperweight, who's going to booze and gamble away anything he's given – and believe me, I know, Jack, I'm an expert on wastrels, I'm one myself.'

'For Christ's sake, Eric, go to bed!'

Ruthven stood up angrily and strode away.

He made several turns of the camp, walking in circles up and down the paths the hippo had made in the reeds on every side. Then he returned to

309

the fire. Yeats was still sitting there, his arms still propped on his knees. He looked lost and vulnerable and desolate.

Ruthven knelt beside him. With an uncontrollable surge of affection, he put his arms round Yeats' shoulders. He held him and felt Yeats trembling. Gradually the shudders faded.

'You push me to the limits, dear fellow,' Ruthven said.

'Lovers always do,' Yeats answered. 'I just wish we were the only lovers in the world.'

'Maybe it should have happened like that, but it didn't. We've got the others. We must look after them.'

'Biology and women.' Yeats shook his head. 'The serpent and the apple. The deity should have planned it better. I thought I could love her for you. I thought I could look after that magical voice and make it, make her, a bond to keep us together. I can't. She's started to hate me and I her.'

'Don't, Eric, don't,' Ruthven pleaded, holding him tighter.

'I'm going to bed, Colonel, my only true and beloved Colonel.'

Yeats tried to rise. He couldn't. Ruthven had to help him to his feet and half-carry him to his tent. He sat Yeats down on his bed.

'Get me a stiffener, would you, old fellow?' Yeats asked. 'It'll help me sleep.'

Ruthven looked at him.

Another drink was the last thing Yeats needed, but he knew it was impossible to argue with him. If Ruthven didn't get him the brandy, Yeats would simply blunder around in the dark until he found it. He might well fall into the fire while he was searching. Ruthven fetched the bottle and half-filled a glass.

'Bless you,' Yeats said.

'I'm going to bed. You're becoming a fearful trial, but I still love you, my old and true companion.'

He smiled and touched Yeats gently on the head.

In the man's muddled and drunken state it was all Ruthven could think of to say. The gesture had to be soft, too. Any more vigorous expression of affection and Yeats would have toppled over. Ruthven turned to leave.

'Jack, before you go, there's something—'

Ruthven turned and glanced back. Yeats wasn't looking at him. His glazed eyes were fixed on the shadows rippling across the sheet of canvas as the night breeze plucked at it.

'Remember our jape at Eton, the gorilla skull that got us into so much trouble and almost had me turfed out?'

Ruthven laughed. 'Of course.'

It had been the second schoolboy escapade that had got them both into trouble. The first – the pheasant-poaching adventure – had got Yeats expelled from their preparatory school.

At Eton they'd decided to make a palaeontological discovery. They'd bought the skull of a chimpanzee, glued sheep's teeth into its jaws, buried the skull, and then dug it up – claiming it proved gorillas once roamed the Windsor area.

As a story it even made the national newspapers, but the hoax was quickly exposed when the glue began to melt. Briefly the careers at Eton of both Ruthven and Yeats hung in the balance, but the headmaster decided to treat it as an adolescent prank and allowed them to continue their studies.

'We've always been in hot water, haven't we? I mean, right back to our prep at Downstill where they caught us canoodling, and they did me kick me from their portals.'

Yeats half-emptied the glass. He examined it. Then he drained it and filled it again.

'Jack, I'm a natural-born japester, quite incorrigible,' he went on with precise but leaden slowness. 'I've been up to my old tricks again over the past few years. Not against you. Against Sophia, maybe, but against life really, all it's done to me. If it comes out—'

Yeats managed to lift his head. His voice was suddenly slurred.

'Not against you, darling boy. Just because you both defeated me and I mind, mind terribly, and because I'm a mischief-maker that's what I've done.'

Yeats fell across the bed. For a few moments he sobbed, the tears streaming down his cheeks. Then he passed out.

Ruthven heaved him on to his side, unbuttoned his sleeping-bag, and draped it across him. He went back to his own tent and lay on his back for a while. Ruthven tried to work out what on earth Yeats could have meant. He had no idea. All he could think was that it was some drunken meandering fantasy.

He fell asleep. In the morning they returned to Maun.

Three nights later the disaster happened.

There was no particular reason, as far as Ruthven could tell, why it should have happened then.

They were back at their camps outside Maun.

Certainly Yeats was still drinking heavily, perhaps more heavily than before, but not noticeably so. He would ride across the river at mid-morning and sit outside their tent pouring himself glasses of brandy from the bottle he kept in his saddle-bag. Then he'd return in the evening, insisting Ruthven

311

ride with him into Maun in search of what he called lights, music, and dancing girls.

The journey took them barely half an hour.

They'd hitch the horses to the balcony rail and enter Riley's bar. Yeats would order a bottle – too tiresome, he said, to keep calling for glasses – and they'd stay there until midnight. Then they'd ride back. Yeats would have had seven or eight drinks for every one of Ruthven's, but he managed to keep himself upright in his saddle.

'Sleep well, Jack.' He'd sweep his hat off his head as they reached the river. 'Greetings to your harpie. Pray blessings on my vixen.'

He'd kick his horse viciously, plunge into the shallows, and splash through to his camp on the other side. The stars glittered in the spray as he made his maddened dash across.

When Ruthven lay down beside Maggie he'd often be trembling. Trembling at the terrible anger and resentment in the man he still loved more than anyone in the world.

He was still the finest companion Ruthven had ever had. Everyone in Riley's felt the same. The hunters, the traders, and prospectors were drawn to him like a magnet. They came into the bar simply to be with him. It wasn't just that he bought them drinks, although he did, cavalierly and recklessly, it was the stories he told them, the laughter he engendered, the teasing and joking and the fireworks of his antics.

He set Maun ablaze by his very presence and he knew it and delighted in it.

'Don't we have fun, my heart's companion?' he would say as they left.

They did have fun, wild, uproarious fun that Maun would never forget. And still, when Ruthven returned to his tent, he would shiver. Maggie held his hand until he became quiet. Then he'd fall asleep.

On the Tuesday night, the third night after their return from the delta, there was a sudden and rare rainstorm. Yeats crossed the river in the downpour and suggested that with nothing else to do, they might as well go into Maun much earlier than usual. They did, and they also returned much earlier than normal.

The sky had cleared by the time they got back and the night was filled with stars. A half-moon was lifting over the Boteti and owls were calling everywhere. Yeats wasn't as drunk as he often was, but he was still drunk and there was a strange savagery in his mood.

Usually he talked as they rode. That night he sat in silence on his horse, slumped and brooding. They reached Ruthven's camp and Ruthven dismounted. Ruthven lifted his hand to pat Yeats affectionately on the knee,

312

as he always did when they parted. Often Yeats would lean down and ruffle Ruthven's hair in return.

Not then.

Yeats whirled his horse away before Ruthven could touch him. He kicked the animal to the edge of the river. Then he paused briefly and looked back.

'By the living God, you will have cause never to forget me, Jack,' he shouted.

He rode into the stream.

Ruthven walked his own horse to the tethering-post. He took off the saddle and bridle, put on a head-harness, and tied the animal up for the night on a grazing rope. Carrying the saddle, he set off for his and Maggie's tent.

He desperately wanted to talk to Maggie. He wasn't sure why, except he felt a fearsome sense of worry, of foreboding, that with her calm practicality she might be able to ease. Ruthven had seen Yeats in every kind of mood from buoyant, exuberant happiness to black, almost theological despair. He'd never seen him as he'd done tonight.

Yeats might be riding his horse, but the Devil was riding the man.

Ruthven was lifting the tent flap when he heard the first scream. He froze. He didn't even have to think who'd screamed. It was a woman and her voice was the most familiar, the most beloved, he'd ever know.

Sophia.

Ruthven dropped the saddle. Before it even reached the ground he heard the first of the shots. Ruthven hurled the tent flap open. He glimpsed Maggie's startled face as she began to sit up in bed. She must have heard the scream too – and there were more coming now. Ruthven ignored her. He seized the rifle that he always kept beneath his own bed on safari, and threw himself back outside.

Ruthven raced along the bank and down to the river's edge.

The half-moon had risen. Together with the incandescence of the Kalahari stars the moon made the night air bright. Across the water someone was frantically splashing their way towards him. It was Sophia. She was wearing a white lace night-dress. Spray was cascading round her and she kept stumbling and reeling. All the time her screams rang out.

Behind her, pursuing her, was another figure, darker, shadowier, with the thick outline of a heavy pistol in his hand. Yeats.

Yeats tripped and fell. For a moment he disappeared beneath the surface. He rose like a dolphin and fired again. The water must have entered the pistol's breech. In a brief moment of silence Ruthven heard a dull click. Yeats spun the chamber, blew into it to clear the blockage, and raised the gun again.

Ruthven swung his rifle to his shoulder.

They both fired at the same instant.

Yeats was hurled back as if he'd been kicked in the chest. Sophia plunged forward. Ruthven tossed the rifle away and waded across to her. She was lying face down like some strange water-lily floating on the river's current. Her struggles to reach him and the movement of the stream had plucked up her night-dress and tangled it round her neck.

It had left her naked, naked and warm and beautiful, just as she'd been when she came to him that night in the Raj. And beyond her – Ruthven could just make out his floating body in the shadows of the shallows – was Yeats. Both of them, the two people he'd loved most in all the world, dead. Dead because of him.

Ruthven left them there.

He went back to the bank. He dropped to his knees. Vaguely he was aware of Maggie joining him and putting her arms round him. He barely noticed.

He watched the two bodies float away and he wept.

50

'Mum, it's me,' Victoria said wearily.

It was 12.00 noon. She'd flown through the night from Johannesburg to London. The flight had been delayed for four hours and she'd only just got in. Her eyes were sore, and she felt dehydrated and drained.

'Darling, where are you?' There was what Victoria thought was a genuine edge of concern to her mother's voice. 'I've left so many messages. Where have you been?'

Victoria glanced at her answering machine.

The little red light which flashed each time someone called was blinking incessantly. There must have been twenty or thirty messages for her. She hadn't even bothered to play them.

Charlie had dropped her off at her flat. She'd let herself in and telephoned her mother.

'I've been away. I've just got home,' Victoria replied. 'I'd like to see you.'

'Darling, I'm longing to see you. I've been so worried. Come round straight away.'

'No, Mum. I want to see you and the lawyer, Mr Carter, together. I'd also like the great-aunts to be there if that's possible.'

Her mother hesitated.

'Octavie and Maude are in London at the moment,' she said. 'They came down from Glenmoray yesterday for the sales. Why don't I try to round them up for tomorrow? I'll see if we can meet at Mr Carter's office. But, darling, I really do want to talk to you first.'

'I'd like to get it over with,' Victoria said. 'What about this evening at six? I'm sure Silverback's worth enough to Mr Carter for him to find a window in his diary. And I'd sooner it wasn't at his office. Why not your flat?'

There was another pause at the end of the line.

'Darling, you really are being very difficult.'

'Nothing like as difficult as I could be.'

315

'Oh, dear. Well, I'll try. I'll come back to you. Will you be there?'

'I'll be here. I may be asleep, but the machine will be on. Goodbye, Mum.'

Victoria put the telephone down before her mother could say anything else. She dialled the Natural History Museum.

'Dr Rory Watson, please,' she said.

He came on the line almost immediately.

'Rory, I've been away,' Victoria said. 'I've just got back. I'd like to see you about the Ruthven collection. How about this evening?'

'Yes, Victoria.' He sounded both nervous and eager. 'Can we have dinner? It's my late work night anyway. I can tell Sally I've been held up.'

'No, Rory,' she said firmly. 'Not dinner. Just a drink and a quick chat. I'll be in that pub across the Cromwell Road – what's it called? The Phoene, as far as I remember – at seven. See you then.'

Victoria put the telephone down on him just as she'd done on her mother.

She lifted the tape from the answering machine, slotted in a new one, and turned the ringing switch to silent. She'd play the messages left for her while she was away when she was ready. Meanwhile the new tape would record any new calls.

Victoria stripped off her clothes. She had a quick bath and crawled into bed. She was asleep within seconds.

'Darling!'

Her mother kissed her at the door of the flat. She stood back and looked at Victoria.

'You look wonderful, so brown and beautiful. You must have been in the sun. But you're exhausted, angel, too. I can see it. What on earth have you been up to?'

Victoria ignored the question. 'I'm a bit tired, Mum. I've been catching up. Another good sleep tonight and I'll be fine.'

Victoria had found the message from her mother on the answering machine when she woke a couple of hours earlier. It told her that Mr Carter and the two great-aunts would be at her mother's flat at 6.00. She followed her mother through into the sitting-room.

Octavie and Maude were sitting on either side of the fire just as they did at Glenmoray. Mr Carter was seated beside Octavie. His face was bland and uncommunicative. The two old ladies' expressions were at once nervous and aggressive, their features set in tight, grim, and somehow frightened lines.

Victoria glanced round the room. Everywhere, on every surface, there were photographs of Grandfather.

She'd always known they were there.

She'd never before realized quite how many there were, quite how much he dominated not only the room but all their lives. From his Victorian childhood to his old age as a benign white-haired patriarch, the fount of wisdom, trust funds, and safety, he seemed to have been watching over them, their custodian and guide, throughout their existence. He was there before them. He'd remain there after them.

Her mother sat down next to Maude. Victoria pulled up a chair facing the four of them. She had thought she'd be nervous. In a sense it was like facing a ring of interrogators, of accusers. In fact she found she wasn't nervous at all. She felt strong, almost serene.

'I've been away,' she said. 'I've been to India, Nepal, and Africa. I've learnt a great deal about Grandfather. I think I was entitled to. After all he is, well he was, my grandfather, the only one I ever knew. In fact, the only man in my family I ever knew.'

There was complete silence as she spoke.

'I've found out where our money comes from. I've learnt about Silverback, about all the deceptions and lies as grandfather and his friend, Eric Yeats, built it up, the false maps and the bribes. I've also discovered the good things about it, that it didn't do any real harm then and maybe now could be of real benefit.'

She paused. 'And I've learnt who my grandmother was.'

Both the great-aunts stiffened then.

Octavie drew in her breath with a strange hoarse, hissing sound. Maude shook her head as if she was trying to push something away. Victoria's mother sat quite still.

'She wasn't Granny, Granny Lomax as you sometimes call her,' Victoria went on. 'My grandmother was Sophia Yeats, godmother Sophia as you taught me to call her. She was my father's mother. I'm her grand-daughter.'

She stopped again. There was another silence.

'Miss Ruthven, Victoria,' Carter said, 'may I ask where you are leading towards?'

'Nowhere,' Victoria answered crisply. 'I've been told lies all my life. Now I've found out the truth. You probably think it matters, that there'll be complications and exposures, that I'll be angry or vengeful or do something to upset your apple-carts. Not a bit. It's just about people. People who may be dead but who I've come to know, that's all. I can live with that.'

Carter studied his hands. 'If I may say so without sounding patronising, you're a very mature young woman.'

Victoria shrugged.

'Darling,' her mother said, 'even if any of this were true, it would be deeply hurtful if it came out.'

'Not to me, Mum. But to you and the great-aunts, yes, I accept that. And because strangely enough I love all three of you, it won't come out.'

'Is there anything else?' Carter asked.

'Plenty,' Victoria replied. 'But just like the things that were kept from me, I'm going to keep them to myself. I don't think anyone here would want to know anyway.'

'Can I rephrase that? Is there anything we can do for you?'

Victoria smiled. 'Take the wheel-clamp off the fund Grandfather created for me. I need to pay my rent.'

Carter smiled back. 'I'm sure that won't be a problem.'

Victoria glanced at her watch. She was due to meet Rory Watson in ten minutes. She stood up and kissed the great-aunts in turn.

'I've got some books of yours, Great-aunt Octavie,' she said as she stooped over the old lady. 'I've read them. I don't need them any longer. I'll see they're returned to you.'

Her mother accompanied Victoria to the door.

'This has been much too short and much too fraught, but you've been very sensible, darling,' her mother said. 'I'm so happy the unpleasantness is all behind us. Come and have supper tomorrow. We'll go out and talk about something more interesting.'

'I'll let you know, Mum,' Victoria said noncommittally.

Rory Watson was waiting for her at a corner table.

Victoria went over to join him. She gave him a quick kiss on the cheek and sat down.

'How are you, Rory?' she asked brightly.

'Fine. It's wonderful to see you again, Victoria. Are you sure you can't stay on for dinner?'

Watson was just as nervous as he'd sounded on the telephone, and his face was haggard. This, Victoria knew, was going to be difficult.

Victoria shook her head. 'I can't, Rory. In fact,' she glanced at her watch, 'I can only stay for a few minutes.'

Watson looked dismayed. 'We've got so much to talk about.'

'What we've got to talk about,' she said, 'are the so-called Ruthven forgeries.'

He frowned. 'What do you mean? I thought we were going to talk about us.'

'Is the museum still going to publish its paper?'

'Of course. We've found even more doctored skins since you came in. We've put in a draft to *Nature*, and we're discussing its final form with the editor.'

Nature, Victoria had learnt from Charlie, was one of the best-known and most respected scientific journals in the world. Its stories were often picked up by the popular press and television, and republished everywhere.

Victoria sat in silence for a while.

'Rory,' she said eventually, 'I know many of those skins are forgeries, clever and malicious forgeries which have deceived people for years. The trouble is, they weren't made by Colonel Ruthven.'

Watson stared at her. 'I don't understand. They're all in the Ruthven collection. He gathered them and gave them to the museum.'

'As you know, my grandfather had a close friend and fellow-collector, a man called Yeats, who was also his business partner. My grandfather acquired most of the skins, Yeats had them mounted. In the end for some reason they fell out. If you look at the dates on the forgeries, I think you'll find they cover a five-year period in the late thirties. That was when they started quarrelling.'

Victoria gave him a very carefully edited version of what she knew, without any reference to the long relationship between Ruthven and Yeats, to Sophia, Silverback, or Yeats' murder.

'Yeats committed suicide in 1939. Check the dates again, but I doubt you'll find any forgeries after then.'

'Are you telling me Yeats set out to discredit Colonel Ruthven?'

'In a word, yes. I'll never be sure, but I think the taxidermy records prove it.'

She told him what she'd learnt from Meyer and the long-ago accounts of his family firm.

Watson hunched forward over the table.

'Even if you're right, I don't see what difference it makes. They're still forgeries.'

His voice was vague. It lacked any conviction. He was, Victoria thought, utterly confused.

'It makes a world of difference,' Victoria said crisply. 'You're a scientist, Rory. Isn't science about truth, not lies? If you say Ruthven made these forgeries, you and the museum and, indeed, *Nature* will be telling a lie.'

'I'll go back and tell the great and the good what you've said,' he replied. 'I'll suggest we look at it again. No promises, and it's only for you. It's bloody strange.'

'We're all strange, Rory. You and me, Ruthven and Yeats, the great and the good too.'

He glanced up. 'I wish you'd stay, Victoria.'

Victoria got to her feet. She ruffled his hair.

'I'll still be visiting the museum. We'll see each other again, but this part, our part's over. Bless you for listening, bless you for being a scientist, bless you for being a seeker after truth—'

She bent down and kissed him again.

'Give my love to Sally.'

Victoria turned and left.

She went back to her flat, lifted the telephone, and dialled Charlie. He was either out or working because the answering machine was on. She left a message.

'It's me, Charlie. Tomorrow, 4.30 p.m. in the bird galleries at the Natural History Museum. Let's wrap this one up.'

She laughed. Charlie would pick up the teasing echo of the phrase he used so often to excuse himself for being late.

She was still exhausted but before she went back to bed she played through the messages that had been left for her.

Most of them, as always, were routine, social calls from her friends. Two were different. The first was from the engaging and rogueish music-hall historian, Mr Gable.

'Good evening, delightful lady,' he said. 'You may not believe this, I scarcely do myself, but my amanuensis, the invaluable Kevin, has unearthed further cylinder recordings of Miss Sophia singing. He is transcribing them in what I think he calls "enhanced digital mode" for you to listen to. I will forward the results in due course. Kevin and I are still not in wholehearted and cordial agreement with Britain's telephonic empire over charges. If you can send a small further contribution to oil the troubled waters between us and the mandarins of communication, art and culture will bless you. As indeed do I.'

Victoria smiled.

She made a note to send him another cheque. The second message was from Jean-Luc Chagall in Paris.

'M'selle Ruthven, I visited Madame Villedieu today at her request,' his voice said. 'What she proposes may come as a shock, but I trust a pleasant shock. She has no children. She is making arrangements to distribute her considerable fortune and possessions. She has decided to bequeath the Renoir portrait of your grandmother Sophia to you. She feels it appropriate. She has asked me to handle the matèr. Perhaps you will telephone me to discuss it.'

Victoria blinked.

She stood quite still for a moment. Then she turned off the recording machine – the other messages could wait until morning – undressed, and lay down on her bed.

Granny Lomax, fond and kind and wise Granny Lomax, had left her a gold ring and her collection of reference books. They were, Victoria knew, Granny Lomax's most valued possessions. Sophia, her true grandmother, had left her nothing except, because of her strange and tangled life, what Victoria knew now would be a vast fortune. That and a few of her songs and her portrait by Renoir.

Far more important, Sophia had left Victoria herself, the tangle of impulses, directions, longings, and desires Sophia carried in her genes. Sophia had inherited them, and she'd passed them on to her granddaughter. Sophia had walked among, inspected, and in the end chosen bastards as the companions of her life and heart.

Victoria smiled.

She'd done the same. She knew where the decision originated and the reason for it. She felt at one with Sophia. Bastards, both of them knew, were more interesting.

Victoria turned over and went contentedly to sleep.

51

It was half-past four on a February afternoon.

Outside it was dark and cold and raining as it had been when Victoria walked into the museum on Christmas Eve. Inside even the same grey-haired attendant was on duty at the ticket desk.

'We close in twenty minutes, miss,' he said.

It was almost exactly what he'd said before. She smiled at him.

'I know. I'll have a quick look round anyway.'

As the man handed Victoria her ticket he peered at her. It was almost as if he recognised her too, but he wasn't sure enough to say anything.

'You'll hear the bell at ten to five.'

Victoria was conscious of him watching her as she walked away.

She went into the bird galleries. Charlie hadn't arrived yet and there was no one else there. She walked slowly along the lighted cabinets looking at the displays inside. There must be a chance, Victoria supposed, that Rory Watson might appear unexpectedly as he had two months ago. She didn't mind if he did. She could handle it now.

She could handle almost anything now.

Victoria turned a corner at the end of one of the aisles and strolled on. Several of the birds in the cabinets she wouldn't have recognised before – bee-eaters, rollers, eagles, pied crows – were now familiar to her. She'd seen them alive in the field. They looked quite different there, vibrant and bright against the sky as the sun caught them. She understood now why people like Eric Yeats and Jack Ruthven became fascinated by ornithology.

One day she might even take it up herself.

Victoria smiled.

Two months. It seemed infinitely longer. For once that absurd phrase, a phrase she'd always derided when she read it, could have been true: it might have been a lifetime. Even her face when she caught it in reflection in the glass looked older. It

323

was probably her imagination, but even that could have been so.

Certainly everything had changed.

She'd come into the galleries looking for sanctuary. She'd been temporarily in utter misery, but all the underlying certainties of her life, the certainties she'd taken for granted, her job, the income from her trust, her family – above all her family with its anchor in her grandfather – remained. Even at her lowest point that day, Victoria knew the misery would heal and the certainties would still be there.

She was wrong.

One by one they'd crumbled. Grandfather first. Then her job. Then, spitefully and inexplicably it appeared at the time, her family and her income. And swept along with it all as part of the same destruction, her own confidence, her belief in herself, her trust in anyone.

Victoria had set out on a search.

She'd thought it was a search to find out the truth about Ruthven and the birds. In a way it was. It was also, she'd come to realise, just as much a quest for herself, for her past and for her future. She'd been recklessly bold and defiant at the start. It had led her into mistakes like sleeping with Watson.

She didn't regret the mistakes. Perhaps they were inevitable, but they were mistakes all the same. Then she'd faltered. The boldness evaporated, and she found herself lonely, confused, and uncertain again. And then her confidence, a new and quite different sort of confidence, came back, and she'd carried on to the end.

Which, ironically, was the place where it had all started. With Charlie. Victoria smiled again. That too was different now, although he probably still didn't realise it.

'Victoria!'

It was Charlie's voice. She turned. He was hurrying towards her along the aisle.

'Sorry I'm late. Something I had to wrap up.'

'You're always late, Charlie. There's always something you've got to wrap up.'

'No, blossom, this was exceptional. I've written the whole thing out. I just needed to check some odds and ends—'

He paused and kissed her on the cheek.

'A good craftsman needs no false modesty,' he went on, 'but modestly, I'm good. It's the best thing I've ever done. Has the lot from the answer to a legendary unsolved murder to the roots of the

Silverback Foundation, and the role it could play in post-apartheid southern Africa. And it's more than a story. There's far too much material for that. It's a real book in the making—'

Charlie broke off. 'I'm sorry, I forgot about the family conference. How did that go?'

'Peace,' Victoria answered. 'A ceasefire rages along the Ruthven front.'

'I knew it would, I'm so glad. In which case, let me tell you more. I'm truly fired up about this one.'

Victoria looked at him. She was barely listening to him as he went on talking.

Charlie.

Big and strong, masculine and sophisticated, glamorous and in his own way brilliant, for seven years he'd dominated her life. He'd been more than a mentor and lover to her, he was an icon. She knew his faults, of course, his skilful boasting, his laziness and unpredictability, at the end his careless, almost callous unfaithfulness.

Charlie still made every other man she'd known seem timid and insipid.

He was a buccaneer, a romantic, at times virtually a visionary. Those seven years with anyone else would have spiralled down into dullness. With him they'd been constantly charged with laughter, they'd been exuberant and exhilarating. Like an awe-struck schoolgirl, Victoria had tolerated everything because of that.

She *had* been a schoolgirl. She wasn't one any longer. She wouldn't put up with it any more. Except he was still the same and none of the good things about him had changed and, worst of all, she still loved him.

'Charlie—'

She interrupted him in full flow as he was speaking about his plans for the book.

'Listen to me.' Victoria took a deep breath and steadied herself. 'There isn't a story, there isn't a book.'

Charlie gazed at her, astounded. He frowned.

'What the hell do you mean? Of course there is. You know, you helped make it. It's the chance of a lifetime. No writer gets a subject like this twice. What on earth are you going on about?'

'Just what you say, chances and choices . . .'

She turned and stared into one of the cabinets.

It contained a display of mounted robins from around the world,

325

several of them with the European robin's characteristic red breast. Her eyes fastened on one of them. She saw the label beneath it. It was a Kalahari robin which, she read, could imitate perfectly the songs of twenty other desert birds.

Victoria smiled.

It wasn't, she thought, a bad description of ambitious journalists who would juggle oranges, tell lies, thieve, manipulate, and invent, do almost anything to get their stories. They were at times, like Charlie, despicable. And yet without them the world would be an infinitely sadder, less interesting, and more dangerous place.

She'd been tense for a few moments until then. Now she was calm.

'The chance, Charlie, is to stay with me,' she said. 'The choice is between me and the story. Write the story and I'm gone. Spike the story and I'm here.'

Charlie shook his head, his dark hair, greying now at the temples, spilling round his face in confusion.

'Why?'

'Because it will hurt and damage people, vulnerable old people. Because it won't serve anything. Silverback will go on. The Foundation's not threatening anyone or any institution in Africa. Most of all because of me—'

Victoria rounded on him then, her face taut with anger and her eyes glistening with tears.

'My grandfather wasn't a forger, but he was probably a murderer, a murderer in passion and maybe in self-defence. I think Yeats would have crossed the river and killed him too. Fine! We both know that. Only, I don't want anyone else to know it. He had his secrets. I want to keep mine. Right?'

She was blazing at him, almost shouting at him. Charlie recoiled. Then the museum's closing bell cut through her words.

Charlie waited until the bell stopped ringing.

He was silent for several moments. Victoria was shaking. She saw he was trembling too. He looked round at the bird displays. He stilled himself. He glanced back at her. Slowly Charlie raised one hand with his index finger pointed upwards. He brought his other hand down across it, parting the fingers so the index finger speared through them.

Victoria knew exactly what he meant.

It was a gesture he'd made so often in the past when one of his

326

stories had been killed. Almost always it had been accompanied by anger and a scowl of frustration. Not now.

Charlie was smiling. He'd spiked the story, the book, everything. He'd do what she wanted – and he was happy.

'Why don't I take you out to dinner?' he asked.

'Why don't you take me out to dinner for the next fifty years?' Victoria answered. 'Although you'd better find some other good stories to pay for them. I rather fancy caviare.'

The grey-haired attendant at the ticket desk gave her a smile as they walked out of the museum and down the steps into the chill darkness of the Cromwell Road.